**A COLLECTION OF FOUR NOVELLAS**

# MURDER KNOWS NO SEASON

# CATHY ACE

FOUR TAILS PUBLISHING LTD.

# PRAISE FOR CATHY ACE'S WORK

## *The Cait Morgan Mysteries*

'Ace is, well, an ace when it comes to plot and description.'
**The Globe and Mail**
'In the finest tradition of Agatha Christie...Ace brings us the closed-room drama, with a dollop of romantic suspense and historical intrigue.' **Library Journal**
'...a sparkling, well-plotted and quite devious mystery in the cozy tradition, all pointing to Ace's growing finesse at telling an entertaining story.' **Hamilton Spectator**
'Cathy Ace is a fabulous writer. She has a great way with words. It is wonderful to read an intelligent woman's writing.' **MysteriesEtc**

## *The WISE Enquiries Agency Mysteries*

'...a gratifying contemporary series in the traditional British manner with hilarious repercussions (dead bodies notwithstanding). Cozy fans will anticipate learning more about these WISE ladies.'
**Library Journal, starred review**
'In my review of Cathy's first book, 'The Corpse with the Silver Tongue' I compared her style of writing to Agatha Christie. While this book features four protagonists, the style is still the same. I also loved the setting...I strongly recommend this book and all of Cathy Ace's books.'
**Lynn Farris, examiner.com**
'A brilliant addition to Classic Crime Fiction. The ladies...of the WISE Enquiries Agency will have you pacing the floor awaiting their next entanglement...A fresh and wonderful concept well executed.'
**Alan Bradley,**
**New York Times bestselling author of the Flavia de Luce mysteries**
'Cozy fans will enjoy their chitchat as much as their sleuthing.'
**Publishers' Weekly**
' ...a pleasant mélange with a garnish of death and danger.'
**Kirkus Reviews**

ISBN 978-1-7751754-4-5 (print book)
ISBN 978-1-7751754-6-9 (electronic book)

**Novellas in the collection 'Murder Knows No Season':**

*WINTER: The Corpse with Eight Faces – A Cait Morgan Mystery*
First edition copyright © 2008 Cathy Ace; second edition copyright © 2018 Cathy Ace
*SPRING: The Case of the Desperate Duchess – A WISE Enquiries Agency Mystery*
Copyright © 2018 Cathy Ace
*SUMMER: Out and About in a Boat – A standalone thriller*
First edition copyright © 2008 Cathy Ace; second edition copyright © 2018 Cathy Ace
*AUTUMN: The Fall – A DI Evan Glover Case*
First edition copyright © 2008 Cathy Ace; second edition copyright © 2018 Cathy Ace

# CONTENTS

**DEDICATION:**

For Ella, Evelyn, Edna, Trevor, Nolan and Oliver

# WINTER

## THE CORPSE WITH EIGHT FACES

### A Cait Morgan Mystery

So here I am, standing over a corpse, and wondering what to do next.

I teach criminal psychology, so of course I know what I *should* do; I should steel myself to examine the body. But I don't want to. Because that means she's really dead. And I don't want that to be the truth of it. So I'm just going to have to use my professional background, and not inconsiderable intelligence, to get my head around this entire situation by thinking through what brought me, Cait Morgan, to this point; because only then can I even begin to contemplate what might have brought *her* to this point.

Maybe if I'd known I was about to spend a weekend cooped up in a snowbound hunting lodge in the middle of British Columbia with a killer on the loose, I wouldn't have got onto the minibus that brought me here from the airport. But I didn't, so I did.

With hindsight, I suppose I should have seen this coming; I'd agreed to attend a birthday party for someone I hadn't seen since we'd left school thirty years earlier, and she'd also invited her three – yes three – ex-husbands, her just-fired literary agent, and her estranged mother. Add her current fiancé, whose temper turned out to have a fuse about a quarter of an inch long, and you get the picture.

But let's get back to the minibus . . . I'd just got off a flight from Vancouver to Kelowna; it only takes about an hour, so you're longer at the airport than in the air, which is pretty annoying. But it was better than having to fly all the way to the UK for the party, which was where it was originally supposed to be; back in the Land of My Fathers. Not that I ever had more than one dad, of course, but that's what we Welsh people call Wales. Back in the Land of my hostess's Fathers, too, if you catch my drift. You see, Meg Jones and I went to school together in Wales, where we grew up two streets apart – both apparently poor, but certainly happy.

While there's no denying that my position as Assistant Professor of Criminology at the University of Vancouver means I've certainly fulfilled my late-parents' hopes and dreams for me, it's equally unquestionable that Meg has far surpassed all possible expectations any of us from Manselton in Swansea might have had for her – she's one of the world's wealthiest authors, with a string of bestsellers to her name and a few movies too. You know her, I'm sure.

Yes, *that* Meg Jones, romantic novelist par excellence.

Anyway – the minibus.

Initially the Big Birthday Bash was going to be at the old house she'd bought in Wales, but the renovations weren't finished in time, so she'd rented an old hunting lodge outside Kelowna, BC, close to where she'd just bought herself a vineyard. Yes, I know most of us are happy with buying wine one bottle at a time, or maybe by the case at a push, but Meg never was one to stint – as evidenced by the three ex-husbands – so I guess she thought that buying a whole vineyard was the way to go. Given there aren't many choices of route to Kelowna, and the Coquihalla Highway is a slippery mess for most of December, all her guests were meeting at Kelowna Airport, so we could travel to 'McKewan's Lodge' together.

I was the last one getting onto the minibus; living by my mother's dictum that you should always go before you leave, I'd been going . . . and they'd almost left without me. Which, upon reflection, might not have been a bad thing – but I do agree that hindsight is always twenty-twenty.

As I stood at the top of the minibus steps, trying to spot a place to sit, I ran my psychologist's eyes over my fellow guests; Meg had told me who would be there in one of her emails, which had popped up in my 'inbox' from time to time over the last year or so. You see, we'd only recently got back in touch after pretty much thirty years of not having so much as spoken to each other on the phone.

To cut a long story short, I'd spotted Meg promoting the first movie to be based on one of her books on a late-night chat show. Having overcome my initial disbelief that it was, in fact, the girl who'd been my best friend at school, I emailed her via her website, and, eventually, she phoned me.

That first phone call was odd; she was apparently sitting in her mid-town condo overlooking the Manhattan skyline, while I was at the kitchen counter in my little house on Burnaby Mountain in British Columbia . . . but we could have been back at Llwyn-y-Bryn School, ducking out of gym class and sneaking a smoke behind the bike sheds.

It was great to hear her voice, to hear her news, and to discover she hadn't changed at all, really. She was the same old Meg, and I was the same old Cait – Best Friends Forever . . . and we'd been that when the phrase actually meant something. But, of course – as Best Friends do – we'd drifted apart as the years had passed; inseparable between the ages of five and eighteen and after that – well, we were certainly going in different directions. Like I said – long story, short.

Okay – that minibus . . .

I grunted general greetings as I pushed along the vehicle's little aisle, which was barely wide enough to cope with my hips and winter coat, but I persevered because I thought it would be fun to sit at the back and try to work out who everyone was as we drove to our final destination. Some people acknowledged me as I passed, but most were peering out of the steamy windows at the surrounding mountains, which were missing their summits; it was three-ish and the sky, while still holding some promise of maybe another hour of daylight, was thickening with blue-black clouds. Upon reflection, I should have seen them as metaphorical, but at the time I only saw them for what they were – storm clouds gathering, ready to dump a whole lot of snow on us.

Sitting at the rear of the bus I could see the backs of heads, and that was about it. From the sketchy explanations Meg had sent me I was pretty certain that the bald, liver-spotted head belonged to Joe Gray, Meg's New York-based ex-literary agent, and I assumed it was his wife, Martha, sitting next to him. He was apparently well into his seventies, and looked to be one of those types who'll retire when they die. Maybe. His features reminded me of a garden gnome, but without the whiskers or the bonhomie. And there was no red, pointy hat, of course. He wasn't the warm, fuzzy type, to be sure. At least, that's what Meg had said in an email to me when she told me she'd fired him, about a month earlier. I wondered why on earth she'd invited him.

His wife was swathed in real furs and, almost literally, dripping with diamonds; her small, chubby hands sparkled as she fiddled about with her hairdo, trying to ensure the headrest didn't mess it up at the back.

Across the aisle was a woman sitting alone; I was surprised that I didn't recognize her, because I was pretty sure it was Meg's mother, Jean Jones. Of course I'd known her when I was growing up, but I couldn't place the woman at all; I remembered Meg's mum as short and round with a red face and thick, dark hair. This woman might well have been short – it was difficult to tell given that she was seated – but she was extremely thin and had snow-white hair cut in a 'pixie' style. I'd noticed as I'd passed that her face was pinched into a look of disapproval, and that she had a sallow complexion to boot. Sour-faced would just about sum it up. And that wasn't how I remembered Meg's mum at all. Odd for me, given that I've got this famous 'photographic memory' thing.

Directly in front of me was a man I had no trouble recognizing; Luis Lopez, Meg's fiancé, and a world-famous TV cop – thanks to a highly-rated series where every conceivable type of crime committed in LA was solved by Luis, pretty much single-handedly, and with a 'suspend your disbelief' reason for him to have to remove his shirt in each episode. Like the rest of the world I was glued to the screen every week as Luis strutted his unquestionably well-worked-out, thirty-something-year-old stuff for all to see.

Now here I was, little Cait Morgan, sitting within a foot of the man many women would like to kidnap and make their love-slave. Truth be told, knowing he would be there had meant I'd made up my mind to definitely come; of course I wanted to see Meg again, but to see Luis Lopez in the flesh? Well, a girl would fly a lot further than an hour from home to do that. I could even smell his aftershave wafting back toward me; like him it was dark and exotic.

Alongside Luis was a tall, round, ruddy man with a thatch of unruly iron-gray hair, a checked three-piece suit, and a bow tie. Given that I work at a university, it didn't take much of a stretch for me to peg this man as Dan James, Meg's husband number three, a professor of English at Harvard, and the man Meg had walked out on before she'd set off on her now-famous epic journey across the USA. He was the one who'd told her she'd never hold down a job for more than a week because she was too dumb. Oh boy, must he be eating his words.

In case you haven't been keeping up with your supermarket magazines, that was how Meg came to write her first bestseller; the day after her fortieth birthday she walked out on husband number three – Dan – took herself off across the USA on a series of buses, and wrote as she travelled. Upon her eventual return to New York, she quite literally bumped into Martha Gray in the hat department at Macy's, they'd struck up a conversation, Martha introduced Meg to her agent husband who read Meg's manuscript, and the rest – as they always say – was history. Except, of course, that in this case is was *her*story, with Meg's first book – about a forty-year-old woman walking out on her husband, taking a bus trip across America and finding true love – becoming a bestseller for months, and then a mega-grossing movie.

I suspected that Meg didn't need to put pen to paper ever again, she'd probably made so much money from that one book; but she did keep putting pen to paper, and each book became yet another 'fastest-selling-ever' volume. A signed copy of a first edition of 'The New Meg Jones Book' could become serious collateral in certain circles.

So, if the fat, ruddy guy dressed like a professor was the professor – and husband number three – then the other guy with what appeared to be a wife must be Peter Webber, husband number one – with his now-wife, Sally. Once again, I felt a bit wrong-footed, because I thought I should have met Peter when we were all growing up in Manselton together; apparently he'd lived in the street behind Meg's, but she'd assured me I'd never known him, though we both suspected I must have known *of* him. In my defense, Peter was a popular name at the time. However, he looked so old that I struggled to imagine he was only my age; I mean, forty-eight isn't old, is it? No, the sandy-haired guy with the sandy-haired wife beside him definitely looked a lot older than me . . . at least, he looked a lot older than the person I see in the mirror in the morning when I'm not wearing my reading cheats.

Meg had told me in a recent email that the only reason she'd married husband number one, Peter, was so they'd have enough 'points' to be able to emigrate to Canada in the early 1980s. Of course I'd known at the time that about two weeks after we'd finished our A-level exams in the June she'd gone and got herself married, and had been out of the country before I'd even left for university in the October. Finding that out had floored all of us who knew the girl for whom hedonism was an art form, and the idea of being married was something she'd laughed at, almost as hard as she'd laughed at the idea of having children.

But, at the age of eighteen she was married and gone . . . and I'd left Swansea for university in Cardiff, where I met new people with whom I'd share stories over a few pints about the 'Deadly Duo', which was how Megan Jones and Caitlin Morgan – Meg and I – had been referred to since we'd met on our first day at school.

I was always sure Meg would make her own inimitable way in the world . . . and I'd been right. Straight out of school she'd married Peter, and they'd moved to Vancouver where he'd worked as a lighting technician in the booming movie industry of the day, which Meg and I had agreed in recent emails was ironic, given that was where I was living now. Then she'd moved to New York, as Peter followed various movie shoots, where she'd divorced him – I had no idea why – and had taken up with, then married, someone called Adrian, husband number two. He wasn't mentioned on her website as anything more than a name; 'Adrian, a musician'. I guessed he was the wrinkly guy sitting at the front of the bus.

Meg had never mentioned him in any of her emails to me, so I knew nothing about him. There was something vaguely familiar about his face, but I couldn't put my finger on it. Despite the darkening skies, he'd been wearing sunglasses when I got onto the bus, and had a deerstalker pulled down on his head. It takes some nerve to wear one of those things, so I suspected he was no shrinking violet. (We psychologists are good at spotting that sort of thing, you know.) He was thin, almost to the point of emaciation, gray-haired, and had long, tapering fingers . . . I'd noticed them right away. Why did he look slightly familiar? A photographic memory is all well and good – except when it lets you down.

Anyway, then Meg had gone on to divorce this 'Adrian' person, husband number two, after a few years, and married Dan James, husband number 3, who eventually took up a professorship at Harvard. He'd been offered the post thanks to the phenomenal success of some poems he'd written. I've recently read them, by way of research, and they are . . . well, I suspect 'puzzling' would be the kindest word, because he likes to use a lot of Greek quotations; not allusions, which I could probably cope with, but actual Greek. All very Ezra Pound-like. He was the husband Meg had left to take to the road, after which she met the Grays, acquired great fame and wealth for herself, and she'd just recently announced her engagement to the ravishing Luis Lopez, who'd played the lead in the movie they'd made of her first book.

Quite a life for a girl from the terraced streets of Manselton.

Our arrival at McKewan's Lodge was pretty chaotic; the huge, log-built edifice, named for the man who'd built it back in the 1930s, rather than for the family which now owned it, had a large covered porch, which proved useful because it took forever to get all our bags off the little bus. Finally over the threshold, and out of the swirling snowflakes, Luis offered to carry our bags to our rooms.

Meg, our hostess, was nowhere to be seen; I thought at the time she could have made a bit more of an effort to be there as we arrived, but it turned out she'd been tied up in the kitchen with the caterers, who were just finishing their preparations and keen to get away before the snow really settled in.

It took about half an hour, but eventually we'd all worked out which rooms we were in (at least Meg had possessed the foresight to pin names to doors) and we'd all pulled out of our cases whatever it was that needed pulling out of our cases. The lodge was pleasant enough; it was old, and there hadn't been many updates made during the previous seventy years or so, but it was spotlessly clean. I discovered later that the current owners used it as their summer home, and it did, indeed, feel truly homey, though it had clearly originally been built to accommodate guests, which was handy.

My room was small, but adequately and pleasantly furnished. It was somewhat unusual in that it had three doors: the one I'd entered through, from the upstairs landing-cum-balcony that ran around three sides of the house; one that opened onto my own little bathroom, which was very 'countrified' with bead-board, wainscoting, and a wonderful old claw-footed tub; the third door was locked – I discovered later that it led to another bathroom on the other side of my room. The house had been designed that way – bedroom, bathroom, bedroom, bathroom, with connecting doors throughout to allow for maximum flexibility of set-up. I thought how unusual that must have been in its day, but I liked the arrangement.

That said, I made sure the key in the door between my bathroom and the next bedroom along was turned and sitting in the lock in such a way that no one could mistakenly enter my bathroom from their bedroom. I squinted into the lock mechanism in the door between my bedroom and 'next door's' bathroom; I could see the key in the lock there too, which was good, because I didn't want anyone coming into my bedroom via their bathroom. I hoped the sound-proofing provided by all the doors was effective, because – well, you know . . . bathrooms and connecting doors can be tricky.

Having checked out my immediate surroundings, I decided I should make my way down to the Great Room, where we'd all agreed we'd meet as soon as we were sorted. Years of living in London means I naturally lock doors, so I made sure the key to my room was in the pocket of my comfy, stretchy, black cord pants, and I headed down the wide, fir-plank staircase that led to the entryway.

The Great Room was just that – huge and rather cavernous; it occupied one entire side of the lodge. It was cheerily, if predictably, decorated; the obligatory stuffed moose, elk and deer heads stared down at us, forlornly, from above a great stone fireplace – the unmistakable focal point of the room. There was even one of those antler chandeliers, so beloved of Canadiana interior decorators, which I suspected had been an original fixture. Around the roaring fire was a collection of comfy-looking armchairs and sofas, replete with plaid upholstery and Hudson's Bay blanket throws.

Meg ran down the wide staircase just after we'd all meandered in; a fantastic entrance, if ever there was one. We all stopped making the small-talk we'd been forcing, and turned to see the woman who'd invited us for her birthday weekend. She looked amazing – a closely-fitted amethyst sweater atop a pair of brown slacks doesn't sound like much, but it worked. Her dark, sleek hair was pulled back in a neat French twist; pearl earrings complemented her deep tan; she was perfectly made-up to look as though she was wearing no make-up at all, and was carrying what looked like a gin and tonic in her hand – classy and sassy at the same time.

I immediately felt frumpy, even more overweight than I really am (which is quite an amount anyway) and craved a G & T. I loved her and hated her, in equal measure. There she was; Meg – my Meg – all grown up and looking like a million dollars.

'My darlings!' she exclaimed to the room in general. 'Thank you all so much for coming to my little party. How wonderful to see you all.' Her accent was a strange mixture of Welsh inflection and Mid-Atlantic pronunciation.

There was a slight pause; I'm sure I wasn't the only one who was wondering who she'd greet first. It was like the school playground – who would be picked first, who'd be left till last?

'My darling,' called Luis, and he was on Meg in an instant, kissing her cheek and stroking her arm, as if to signify ownership. 'You are looking wonderful, as usual. But where have you been? You were not in your room, I looked.'

Luis's had a strange way of speaking that I'd never noticed when he was on TV; he didn't so much speak, as declaim. And he looked shorter, and more compact, than I'd thought he'd be; muscular, but quite petite. In fact, Meg was my height, about five-four, and he was just the same height as her. TV's a funny thing – they say it puts twenty pounds on you, and I reckon it must put a good ten inches on your height too.

Having been greeted, in the appropriate manner, by her fiancé, Meg turned her attention to me – yes, me.

'Cait – darling Cait . . . you haven't changed a bit,' she said, lying. Even I know I've gained at least fifty pounds since I was eighteen, and at forty-eight my skin tone isn't what it used to be, nor is my hair color

– which I staunchly refuse to amend with chemicals . . . but I silently blessed her mendacity and moved to enjoy the hug she was coming toward me to deliver. But, as she came closer, I could see something in her eyes I'd never seen in the old Meg – an iciness lurked there. I was surprised.

As a criminologist specializing in psychology and victimology, I have worked for years to train myself to notice, and understand the implications of, all those details about people most others miss; their body language, micro-expressions, the minutiae of their appearance, their interactions with people, and their surroundings – those unspoken signals that belie their words, and sometimes even their conscious actions. And, despite her glossy shell, I could tell that Meg Jones was an unhappy, bitter woman, with an anger burning her up. I wondered what it could be.

These thoughts took just a second, so I was able to respond to her welcome wholeheartedly; we hugged as though we were eight years old.

'Everyone – this is Cait, Caitlin Morgan, my Very Best Friend. We met as we were walked through the school gates by our mothers on our very first day at school . . . so she's someone who knows the real Meg Jones, and someone I'm sure you'll all grow to love and admire as much as I do. She's very clever, doesn't suffer fools at all, and is a wicked chess player . . . you have been warned.' People smiled politely. 'On top of that,' continued Meg, 'she's a criminology professor, which is going to be interesting . . . considering what all of you have lurking in your closets.'

Meg was smiling with her mouth, but her eyes were glinting with hate. It was a bizarre welcome, and it stunned everyone in the room. Puzzled looks were exchanged between people who'd met for the first time on the minibus. It was as though Meg had thrown down a challenge, and she was waiting to see who'd pick it up.

'Listen to you, talking about "closets"; what's wrong with calling them "wardrobes", like you always used to? Very American you've become.' It was Meg's mother, Jean. Her tone was biting, disdainful; as soon as she spoke I vividly remembered her from my childhood – she'd always been pleasant to me, but I'd heard her talking to Meg just like that when she was a little girl, when she'd thought I couldn't overhear.

'Hello, Mam,' said Meg heavily. I knew Meg and her mother hadn't been in touch much for the last thirty years, but, nevertheless Meg had invited her; now she sounded as though she wished she hadn't.

'Hello, Meg – no hug for your mother then?' Jean continued in her broad Welsh Valleys accent; I hadn't heard an accent like that since I'd left the UK.

'Of course,' replied Meg, flatly. Everything about her demeanor was screaming 'keep away from me', but Meg hugged her mother, briefly and weakly, then she turned and announced, 'This is my mother. She's come all the way from Wales, and I'm sure she's tired, hence her snappish comments, which are so unusual for her.' Meg was clearly mocking her mother. 'You too, Adrian, I bet you could do with an early night, given that trip all the way from Seville.'

'I'll be fine,' replied the mysteriously familiar 'Adrian', who now, without his hat or sunglasses, looked a bit like a much older version of a rock star I'd doted on years earlier; you're not really allowed to have crushes when you're over sixteen, so my adoration of Dax O'Malley had always, publicly, been based upon his musicianship, not his rakish good looks, wicked charm, and bad boy image.

'You always could just keep going, and going,' was Meg's bitter reply. 'Say hello to Adrian O'Malley, folks, husband number two. Though maybe you know him better by his stage name Dax, if you've heard of him at all, that is.'

The Grays were looking mystified, but my heart was beating a lot faster than it had been a moment earlier. It was Dax O'Malley. No wonder he'd looked familiar . . . but, good grief, the life of a rock star had taken its toll on him. I was trying to come to terms with the fact that Meg had been married to Dax O'Malley; why the hell hadn't she told me that? Had it been such a terrible experience that she couldn't talk about it, or even write an email about it?

People were nodding politely at my erstwhile heartthrob, who was standing right next to Luis Lopez, one of my current ones . . . and it was all getting to be a bit much for me. Why wasn't anyone offering me a drink? I could really do with one.

'And this is the great Professor Dan James, husband number three,' added Meg, still in bitter tones; she made his title sound like an insult as she hissed it at us and flung an arm toward the man in the checked suit. Dan James was tall, and wide, and seemed to dominate the room; even his smile was big, and his rosy cheeks were the sort that should have been above a Father Christmas beard . . . in fact, with the right costume he'd have made an excellent Santa, even his voice was perfect – a cross between the man in the famous red suit and the Jolly Green Giant.

'Good evening all,' he boomed loud and low. 'And thank you, dear Meg, for so graciously inviting me to this wonderful weekend of well-wishing in the wilderness.' He seemed pleased about the alliteration. I cringed. Oh dear, a bombast. How sad.

'Oh give it a rest, Dan. None of us are impressionable little students, sitting at your feet hoping for a pearl of wisdom to drop from those flaccid lips.' Meg certainly wasn't holding back – it didn't sound as though she liked anyone she'd invited.

'And husband number one, everyone; Peter *Webber*.' Meg nodded toward the sandy-haired man with the piercing blue eyes. The strange emphasis she'd placed on his surname puzzled me – it wasn't as though it was a particularly fancy name or anything. It was odd.

What was also odd was how biting Meg was being. Her emails had always been upbeat – well, they'd read as upbeat anyway; but that's the trouble with emails, of course, there's no inflection, no sense of tone.

'Hi folks, good to meet you all,' said Peter Webber in a quiet voice. Totally American accent, none of the Welsh sing-song left at all. But his eyes . . . I remembered Peter at that moment; he'd been weedy and small when we were young, but with the most electric eyes – which was ironic, considering he'd become an electrician. He used to hang around the shop at the top of our street, but Meg had been right, I'd never really known him – just seen him about. He'd gone to St Joseph's, the local catholic school. No wonder we hadn't mixed – my Mum and Dad thought Roman Catholics were almost diabolical. I'd never understood that. Still didn't.

'This is my wife, Sally,' he continued evenly. 'I'm sure Meg will find it in her somewhere to be nice to her at least – they've never met before, and Sally was hoping to meet the delightful person Meg seems to be during all her TV interviews.'

Wow, Peter had a spine. He might look pasty and nerdy, but at least he was standing up to Meg.

'But, of course, Peter,' cooed Meg, mocking him, 'I'm sure I'll be nice to Sally; Sally herself looks so . . . nice.'

Meg had insulted the woman before they'd even exchanged a word. I was beginning to feel uncomfortable; where the hell was the Meg I'd been corresponding with for the last year, let alone the girl she'd been 'back in the day'?

'I'm very pleased to meet you,' said Sally Webber hesitantly. I wondered for a moment if she was going to curtsey. But she didn't; she contented herself with a bob of her head, but I suspected that if she'd had a forelock, she'd have pulled it for the World Famous Meg Jones.

'The Grays – Joe and Martha,' said Meg, nodding toward the couple who were standing with their backs to the fireplace. 'Joe was my literary agent until recently, and Martha's just along for the ride, as usual.' Martha Gray opened her mouth as if to speak, but clamped it shut in disgust, pulling her husband closer with her fat little bejeweled hand.

'Uncalled for, Meg,' was all Joe Gray said, curtly.

He spoke for us all. Me included. I wasn't liking this Meg at all.

'And that's all folks,' quipped Meg, acidly. 'What a funny bunch we are; but, hey, thanks for coming. I guessed Joe would – he wants me back on his books, and Luis hasn't got much choice, have you, baby? You have to be seen spending time with your loving fiancé, don't you? But as for the rest of you? Well, I wonder why you all came. It's not as though any of you want to see me, is it? So what do you all think you can get out of me? Why did you all come? That's the million dollar question, right?'

I felt I had to speak. The tension was almost unbearable. This wasn't how it was supposed to be.

'Oh, come on now, Meg,' I said, as lightly as I could, 'I know I'm delighted to see you . . . you're looking great, and I'm so pleased at all the success you're having. And look, three ex-husbands and a fourth-to-be, and there's me with not even one. How lucky can a girl get?'

'Oh dear, sweet Cait – you might be bright but you sure can be dumb,' was Meg's rather cutting reply. 'If you had any idea what these three put me through . . . or what this one can be like –' she gesticulated with her glass toward her exes, then Luis – 'then you wouldn't call me "lucky" at all. Smarten up, Cait – life's short and then you die . . . all you can do is make the most of the ride, and mine's been bloody bumpy, to say the least.'

This didn't help the mood, and it seemed Luis Lopez was far from happy with the comments Meg had made about him. 'You should not speak like this. It is not polite. These people have been important in your life. And I have done nothing to deserve your unkind words.' He was declaiming again.

'You've "done nothing to deserve my unkind words", Luis?' was Meg's sharp, mocking retort. 'You've driven me to this stuff for a start.' She waved her glass, showering the hearth-rug with its contents.

Maybe that was it; Meg didn't look drunk, but maybe she was drinking so much, on a regular basis, that she was able to control her body, if not her words, or mood. I knew that was possible; I'd seen it before. Lived it. But that was all a long time ago, and far behind me; just believe me when I tell you that when you live with an alcoholic you can actually make yourself believe they've stopped drinking. You want it to be true, so you tell yourself it is true . . . until they snap, that is. Until they change before your eyes and their inner, booze-fueled demons come screaming out at you. But, yes, they can be very controlled, physically. Up to a point.

'Back on the sauce then, Meg?' It was Dax O'Malley. I told myself I had to think of him as 'Adrian'; he wasn't Dax anymore. His voice was gravelly, his accent no longer tied to his Boston roots, but floating somewhere in that international place that is the 'Rock Star Universe'. His infamously straight-laced Spanish wife, who had encouraged him to give up his excessive lifestyle, then touring, then recording, and to procreate something approaching an entire soccer team, ruled his life with a rod of iron – at least, that's what the newspapers said. I wondered if it were true, or whether he was just an average guy with an extraordinary drive, and bucket full of talent.

'You never were interested in the booze, were you, Adrian? You preferred other forms of mood management, right?' Meg was being cruel, and she knew it. 'Did Jocasta, or Jacintha . . . or whatever that womb on legs you married after me is called . . . did she get you off it all? All?'

'It's Jovita, as you well know, Meg. Don't be like this. You never used to be a bitch,' replied Adrian, almost plaintively. 'Where's all this coming from? Is it all just gin-talk?' He was echoing my own thoughts.

'Gin-talk? Oh no, Adrian. You'll all be delighted to know that I've been seeing a shrink – yeah, a shrink. Luis's idea, wasn't it, darling? When I bought that house in LA, he was the one who got me started with it. And I've stuck with it; three times a week for six months now. Very LA – very "American", Mum. Like closets.' She looked at her mother with a cruel smile on her lips. 'And do you know what the freshly-shrunk Meg knows that the un-shrunk Meg didn't?'

I knew I wasn't the only one in the room who wanted to know the answer to that one.

'I have a feeling you're going to tell us, whether we want to know or not,' boomed Dan James. 'How very theatrical this all is.'

'Ah, Dan – theatrics would be something you'd know all about; acting the part, that's all that matters to you, isn't it? You didn't think I was the right leading lady for you to have on your arm when you entered Harvard's hallowed halls, did you? So you were going to dump me. Eight years of my life, about to be flushed away. I knew it. So I jumped before you could push me. I escaped that humiliation, at least. But this isn't theatrics – this is me. The "me" you've all created. That's what Meg knows now; that she's been made into the person you see today, by the people you see today. Are you all proud? You should be. I'm wealthy beyond belief, I sell more books than any romance writer, ever, and every screenplay I choose to attach my name to out-grosses even those special effects masterpieces they're all so keen on these days. You Dan? You're a pathetic, washed-up pseudo-professor, who, if he didn't have tenure, would have been slung out on his ear years ago for fiddling with the sophomores and for not having written anything that's sold more than a hundred copies in over a decade.'

Meg was on a roll – we could all feel it, and, like me, everyone was wondering who would be next.

Sally Webber – of all people – came to our rescue.

'I wonder if there's any chance of a drink?' She spoke quietly; I wondered if she'd been taking anything in – then, noting her rather vacuous expression, it occurred to me that maybe she was just as dumb as a box of hair, and hadn't picked up on the tone of the exchanges. 'It was quite a journey from LA and I could do with something. A soda, maybe?'

Sally smiled sweetly, and her words seemed to have an amazing effect on Meg; her body lost its tension, and she relaxed. Meg nodded at Sally, and broke into a smile.

'I'm sorry, Sally – you're right, I should be a better hostess.' Meg's voice sounded warm and genuine. Bizarre. 'The caterers have set up a sort of bar in the kitchen – why don't we all go through and get ourselves something? There are some little snacks too – though you don't want to spoil your dinner; I'd planned on us eating in about an hour – the meal they've prepared will be ready by then.'

It was as though a switch had flicked in Meg's head somewhere; she was acting like a totally different person, with no carry-over of her previous vindictiveness at all.

Mine wasn't the only puzzled face in the room, then relief swept visibly through the little group; at least, it was visible to me in the way bodily tensions relaxed, eyebrows were lowered to their normal resting places, and pallid complexions colored up, while ruddy ones calmed down. Jean Jones even shook her thin little body as though she were a dog emerging from a chilly pond. We were all doing the same thing, mentally.

Meg walked ahead of us, leading the way to the kitchen across the entry hall, seemingly oblivious to the stress she'd caused since her Grand Entrance.

It was going to be tough to try to act as though nothing weird had happened, but it seemed the whole group had tacitly agreed to some sort of pact to do just that . . . and things went rather well, really, until what turned out to be the end of dinner, which was when I messed up in such a way that it might well have led to murder.

Upon reflection, I suppose I should admit that Meg might have had something when she said I'm very clever, but that I can be dumb; if ever I was to prove that to be the case, it was that evening. Though, in my own defense, I don't think it was really my fault – just my doing.

We'd all enjoyed our drinks and snacks, then we turned our attention to getting dinner served. We all pitched in, and soon we were sitting down at the vast oak dining table that was a part of the open-plan kitchen, which mirrored the Great Room. We tucked into a feast of roasted local duck with local vegetables, and a lot of wine – which was not just local, but from Meg's own vineyard. Admittedly the wine had been made before Meg owned the property, but that didn't stop us all complimenting her on each type we tried. And we tried more than a few. After a couple of hours of eating and drinking we were getting a bit raucous – all except Sally, who, it turned out, didn't touch alcohol; she claimed she was allergic to it. Right.

I should make it clear that we were getting loud in a nice, friendly way. I was sitting next to Meg – and it was the pleasant, old Meg who sat down at the table that night; we were raking over old times, laughing at past fashion faux-pas, past adventures, past boyfriends, past . . . everything. And that was the problem – we were talking about the past; I said to Meg that she'd had such an interesting life she should think about writing a book about it – an autobiography. And she replied that she sort of had already, but that she was keeping it a secret just for now.

And then came one of those moments in life that you'd give anything to change – to go back to, and make it un-happen. Let's call it an accident, or, if you're the type who believes in that sort of thing . . . which I don't . . . the intervention of Fate.

Everyone seemed to stop talking at the same time, and the only thing you could hear in the room was me whispering loudly to Meg, 'Really? You've written your autobiography? Am I in it?'

As I looked around the table it was quite clear that everyone was thinking exactly the same thing; were they in it? I can recall their faces quite clearly, and every one of them was horrified. I swear some of them had even stopped breathing.

'Oh Meg, what have you done?' Peter Webber sounded distraught.

Meg stared at me venomously – and all I could do was mouth my apologies to her.

The cat was not going back into the bag. No way.

The wine that, until then, had warmed the conversations around the table, now fueled heightened emotions in everyone. Myself included. As I studied Meg I could tell she'd made a decision. She stood. She swayed a little, and steadied herself.

All eyes were on her. Which Meg would she be? What would she say?

'I wanted it kept a secret for tonight – but now you know.' She spoke quietly. 'I was going to tell you tomorrow, on my birthday. Yes, I suppose you could say I have written my "autobiography". I've worked on it with my doctor . . . my shrink; it's been an incredibly cathartic process. I found out a lot about myself by doing it. And, yes, you're all in it. And, yes, I've told the truth. That was the whole point of it. And, yes, the reason I invited you all here this weekend was that I need to talk to you all, individually, about how you played a part in making me the person I am today. It's an important stage in my therapy. My doctor says it's critical to my future well-being, and I agree with him. There. Now you know.'

Meg wasn't being mean; more than anything she sounded resigned. And relieved. She drank down the glass of rich ruby wine that stood beside her empty plate. I noticed that Adrian did the same. As did Luis and Dan.

A tear trickled down Meg's cheek. She ignored it. 'I don't expect any of you to understand,' she said, 'but I needed to do it. I have to face up to my past, to be able to face my future.' Meg's voice wavered. It sounded to me as though she were reciting some sort of mantra.

'And you don't give a damn who you hurt in the process, do you, Meg?' Adrian pushed back his chair and rose to his feet. There was a fire in his eyes. Was it anger – or terror?

'Hurt? You lot?' Meg's voice was suddenly charged with fury, strong and loud. 'Oh yes – I could hurt all of you if I wanted to. I know all your dirty little secrets, don't I? Every one of you has a stain on your conscience – there's quite literally a skeleton in each of your closets.' She glanced pointedly at her mother. 'But that's not what this is all about. Believe it or not, I didn't ask you all here to point out that you've got away with something that could have ruined your life. You, Sally – I know nothing about you . . . though I suspect that's because there's little to know. Picked a new wife who wouldn't ask too many questions, eh, Peter? Clever boy. But the rest of you?' She stared at her empty glass. 'No, I can't do this now. Sod the lot of you. You'll all have to stew on it overnight – I'm off to bed.'

Meg threw down the napkin she'd been clutching and twisting, and stomped out of the room, her head down, tears streaming down her face. She made for the stairs.

The room was silent. Then Sally Webber spoke. 'I suppose we'd better sort out around here before we go to bed. I'm pretty good at filling dishwashers.'

Every face, including that of her husband, turned toward her in amazement. Once again she seemed to be completely oblivious to the implications of what had just happened.

We were all in shock, but we rallied, and dealt with the mundane task of clearing away what had, to be fair, been a very good dinner. As I carried plates and cleared glasses I couldn't help but wonder what Meg had meant about skeletons in closets.

I knew I had none; except I had to admit the media frenzy that had enveloped me after I'd found my ex-boyfriend, Angus, dead on my bathroom floor all those years earlier, might have made someone think otherwise. But that was all behind me. I'd left that in the UK; I was a Canadian now, and had been for years.  Besides, the authorities had completely exonerated me – publicly, no less, due to the huge interest the tabloids had taken in the case of the initially inexplicable death of the alcoholic, violent boyfriend of a criminologist.

It all came flooding back as I gathered up the stemware – the photographers following me everywhere, the tutorials I hadn't dared attend, the lectures I hadn't cared to deliver . . . the way my life had been raked over, and embellished with all sorts of wicked untruths. It had been a nightmare – a nightmare I hoped was over. But maybe that sort of thing never really goes away. Why would Meg think that anything she could say or do regarding that part of my life could hurt me more than I'd already been hurt by it?

It was clear I wasn't the only one going through the process of self-examination; everyone was in their own little world as we filled the dishwasher, hand-washed and wiped the stemware, and finally made our way to our rooms – where at least we could all be alone with our thoughts, and not have to put on a brave face for the rest of the group.

Eventually I snuggled down under the patchwork comforter on my bed. It had been an emotional day, and I thought I'd never sleep. But I did. Until I received what was, to say the least, a rude awakening.


'Cait. Cait. Wake up. It's Meg – I'm sure she's dead. She won't answer her door – to her own mother.'

It was Jean Jones, knocking at my door and screaming for me. I stumbled out of bed, discovered my bedside lamp wasn't working, stubbed my feet into slippers in the half-light, and pulled a robe around myself. The air was chilly. As I opened the door the first thing I noticed was that Jean's lipstick matched her dressing gown exactly.

Burnt orange – not a good color choice with that sallow skin, I thought. True, it was an odd thing to notice, but, there you go, I did.

It was about the only thought I managed before I realized I had a truly horrific hangover, and chided myself that I really should have drunk more water before going to bed the night before.

I also realized that upright wasn't a good position for me, and, as Jean dragged me mercilessly toward Meg's bedroom door I thought my head was going to drop off; mind you, if it had dropped off that wouldn't necessarily have been a bad thing because it would have taken my hangover with it. But, as it was, I was stuck with the headache, the quickening waves of nausea, and the noise caused by Jean thumping on Meg's door ricocheting around inside my skull.

When Jean stopped hammering, my head stopped banging too; I was grateful for the relief, but she'd proven her point. Meg didn't respond. I reasoned that, if Meg felt anything like I did, she was probably hiding under the blankets hoping her mother would leave her alone; I knew I was.

'See!' was all Jean could manage as she flung her arm toward the locked door. She was wild-eyed and sounded vindicated. I felt resigned to the fact I'd actually have to do something, then Luis's head and bronzed, bare torso appeared along the corridor.

'What is it, this noise?' he asked.

I pulled my robe around my sadly unsupported bosom, and surreptitiously checked the corners of my eyes for yukky bits.

'Meg won't answer her door. It's locked, and Jean is worried about her. Can you check your connecting doors to see if she's awake?'

I'd summoned all my powers of control to make my mouth and furry tongue form that one sentence, and I was spent. It did occur to me to wonder why Luis had his own room, as opposed to sharing one with Meg, but I couldn't cope with everything that was going on all at once, so decided to shelve that particular issue until later – when we knew why Meg wasn't opening her door.

As Luis disappeared into his room with a grunt, I tried hard to make spit, but my mouth was as dry as the Valley of the Kings in August – where I've been, and I can tell you it's exceptionally dry. As Luis re-appeared wearing slippers and a robe, he was shaking his head – something I seriously doubted I'd ever be able to do again, given my sorry state.

'The door, it is locked,' he declaimed with astonishment.

Jean pounced. 'See!' she screamed, sounding doubly vindicated this time. I winced. Jean was very close, and very loud.

Unsurprisingly, given Jean's performance, heads were popping out of doors all around the landing.

'What's going on?' asked Peter, seeming to speak on behalf of everyone. Sally was peering out from behind him in their doorway, like a field mouse hiding behind a wheatsheaf.

I tried to clear my throat to speak, but Luis's voice boomed around the huge space of the atrium and landing, 'It is Meg. She is locked in her room. She will not answer her mother. Her mother is worried.'

I felt like adding something along the lines of *'la plume de ma tante est dans ma valise,'* as Luis's stilted phrases took me back to years of pointless, parrot-like repetition in French language classes. Luis's explanation created little by way of a reaction from anyone, except Jean, who took the ensuing five seconds of puzzled silence as her cue to let rip. Loudly.

'Meg's dead – I know it, I can feel it in my bones. I'm her mother and I know something's wrong. Why won't anybody listen?'

As though we had a choice.

A murmur of disbelief rippled around the emerging group, and my overwhelming feeling of unreality was compounded as Luis proclaimed, 'I will break down the door.'

Before anyone could protest, he had bounced off the sturdily built cedar-plank door in question with a loud, 'Ooff'. I was pretty sure bruising would soon set in beneath the perfect tan, but I suspected a rather more enduring hit had been taken by the ego of the man who was known worldwide for flinging himself through carefully constructed stunt-doors on a weekly basis.

No one knew what to say – here was melodrama mixed with embarrassment. To top it all, my stomach was beginning to churn; if I'd drunk a lot the night before, I was pretty sure Meg had drunk more.

What if she'd fallen? What if she'd thrown up and . . . a gag reaction set in as I stupidly thought of vomit, and I had to work hard to control myself. While I was grappling with a stomach full of stale red wine and supporting myself against the wall, people began to stumble toward Meg's room.

Soon everyone was gathered outside her door, trying to calm her mother. No one seemed to know what to do next, so, being the control freak I am, I spoke up.

'If we're all sure she's really fine, but want to make sure, the only way to do it is to get into her room. But let's not go wrecking a borrowed house unless we have to. Has anyone got a key for her room? Are there spare keys for any of these rooms?'

There were shrugged shoulders all around and a sad-faced Luis said, 'We were told to be careful with the keys to the rooms, they are the only ones. Originals. Meg has a master key, but I think maybe it is in her room.'

It seemed there was no other option but to break open the door, after all.

'Okay then,' I croaked resignedly. 'Now, if all you . . . boys –' I chose the word carefully so as to avoid any possible insults – 'just run at the side of the door where the lock is – not the side where the hinges are – I'm sure it'll open. After all,' I added in deference to my hostess's fiancé, 'Luis must have weakened it already.'

Luis smiled his warm smile in gratitude as the men gathered to rush at the door.

It worked, and the door flew open with a loud crack.

Luis fell into the room and Peter flopped on top of him; Adrian grabbed the doorframe to prevent his angular body from joining the huddle. I cast my eyes across the room toward Meg's bed. She was lying on her side looking peaceful, but ashen.

Jean made a move, but I grabbed at her. 'No,' I exclaimed, every hair on my neck quite literally standing on end. I knew at that moment that Meg was dead and, as my criminology professor's mind went to work, I noticed that her body was lying in an unnatural manner; it didn't look as though she'd died in her sleep.

Instinctively, I knew something was wrong with the scene, but – in the shock of the moment – I just couldn't grasp what it was. My 'photographic' memory has helped me tremendously during my professional, academic, and even personal life – but that was one unwanted picture I knew would haunt me forever. The detail was burned into my mind's eye. It would never go away.

Sometimes I really hate my so-called gift.

'She's my daughter, she needs me,' screamed Jean as she thrust me aside, and with two bounds was across the room, sitting on the bed, and pulling Meg's limp body into her arms. She clutched Meg's corpse to her chest and screamed for her daughter to wake up. She shook Meg, wailing and crying into her daughter's tousled, long, dark hair. It was phenomenally dramatic; Jean looked – and sounded – like some tragic Greek heroine.

Everything seemed to be happening at double speed and in slow motion at the same time; people with still-groggy voices crowded at the door; cries of shock and disbelief were on everyone's lips; Jean was screaming; the inside of my head was banging. Someone had to do something.

'Listen up,' I called above the hubbub. Everyone fell silent and looked at me as though . . . well, I don't know what they expected, and I didn't know what I was going to say, but I just sort of took charge.

'Everyone move back from the door – yes, you too Luis.' Meg's fiancé was still flat on his stomach taking in the whole scene from floor level.

'But Meg . . . is she . . .?' Luis's unasked question hung in the air. He looked pitifully desolate as he peered up toward me.

'I told you. I told you she was dead,' screamed Jean as she held her daughter's body tightly to her breast. 'You wouldn't listen. You didn't believe me. But I knew. I'm her mam. I'm her mam.' She sobbed and moaned, all the time rocking and swaying. Then she turned toward our weird little group at the door and, without provocation of any kind, snarled viciously at us, 'You won't take her away from me. I'm not leaving her alone.'

Her eyes flashed with hatred, then, quite suddenly, it seemed as though all the passion disappeared from them and she looked at Meg as if for the first time. Jean took in the sight of all of us huddled and heaped in the doorway, tears welling in her eyes, and said softly, 'Oh my God – Meg's dead. She's really dead. What will I do now?'

I have to admit that my heart went out to Jean; in a split second she'd been transformed from a tigress to a lamb. She let Meg's upper body fall, completely ignoring it as it tumbled from her grip, and she walked toward me repeating the question, 'What will I do now?' over and over, wet-faced and hopeless; a lost soul in a frail body that had just aged ten years in two short minutes.

'Come with me, dear, I'll get you a brandy,' came an unexpected voice – it was Martha Gray, pushing her husband to one side. She enveloped Jean within a wing of a pink chiffon negligee.

'Someone call 911,' I barked. Luis made a dash from the floor toward his room. It seemed my powers of speech had returned, and my hangover was a thing of the past; I continued to be the only one with any sort of plan of action, so I went for it.

'We need to get out of here and shut the door until the police come.' I sounded as though I knew what to do, but I hadn't been involved in a sudden death like this since I'd had my formal training in crime scene management years earlier, when a real body had turned up at the 'fake' crime scene. This was an even bigger shock than that: I hadn't gone to school with that body; I hadn't played at being Emma Peel in the school yard with that body; I hadn't been quaffing wine and swapping old memories a few hours ago with that body. Getting out and leaving everything as untouched as possible, Jean's intervention aside, was all we could do.

'You can't leave her hanging out of bed like that.' It was Adrian; he spoke with surprising authority.

We all looked at how Meg's body was balanced on the edge of the bed, where she had fallen from her mother's arms. It was a precarious position.

I hesitated. All my training told me to not touch anything, but this was Meg – she could fall. Of course, I immediately told myself she couldn't get hurt . . . but then reasoned with myself that if she fell off the bed, then that would be as much of a disturbance of the scene as if she were lifted back onto it. I knew in my heart that, for some inexplicable reason, we'd all feel better if Meg was placed 'safely' back on the bed.

'Okay, I'll lift her up,' I almost whispered. I turned to the others, 'But only me – you all stay there.'

I tiptoed across the room until I reached Meg. Oh Meg. Dear Meg. I tried to control my emotions.

Reaching under her shoulder I gathered up her right arm and lolling head. She was cold, but not icy. She was certainly still mobile, though I could tell that rigor mortis was setting in. She was surprisingly light. I shifted her as little as I needed until she wasn't likely to fall.

There. She was safe.

Not a body, but an old friend.

I had to fight to hold back the tears. I had to be professional.

As I re-joined the group at the door I wiped my damp hands on my robe.

'Well done,' said Adrian, in a soft voice, and we closed the door as well as we could, given that it was badly splintered.

There was nothing we could do but await the arrival of the police.

'The power, it is out, and the telephone it will not work – it is dead.' Luis's voice echoed around the dim landing. The word 'dead' hit us all like a hammer. Only Luis seemed to not notice. 'Does anyone have a cellphone? I did not charge mine last night,' he added.

As he said it I kicked myself that I hadn't been sufficiently well organized to recharge mine before I had gone down to dinner.

'I'll get mine,' barked Joe Gray.

Now there's a man who'll never be without his mobile communication devices, I thought, as the dealmaker returned to his room as fast as his twig-like legs would carry him. And thank goodness for it today, was my next thought.

Joe reappeared at the top of the stairs and passed me the sleek device with his liver-spotted hand.

'You do it,' he ordered.

I suspected Joe never asked for anything, rather he got what he wanted by instructing people to simply do his bidding.

Obligingly I took the phone, checked the signal – which was weak – and moved around the staircase until I found a spot where the signal was stronger.

'You guys all go and get dressed and so forth, then maybe someone could get some coffee on the go? Maybe rustle up something for breakfast? There's nothing we can do until the police get here,' I shouted from my perch at the top of the stairs, and the little group straggled past me, into their various rooms.

I was alone by the time the operator finally answered. I briefly explained the situation, gave my name and our location, then, after a few moments, I found I was speaking to what sounded like a twelve-year-old girl, who informed me she was the shift supervisor and that she was sorry, but no emergency response could be offered at the present time.

I almost exploded. 'About ten minutes ago we discovered the body of Miss Meg Jones, noted author, in her bed. She has no pulse and is cold to the touch. We need first responders, now.' I was pretty proud of myself – I felt I had acquitted myself very professionally.

'Anyone there with medical, paramedic, or police experience?' She sounded like the bossy type.

I let my mind skip through the group and was sure of my answer.

'No. At least, not that I'm aware of. I'm a professor of criminal psychology, but I don't have the expertise we need here. We need professionals. Now, please.' I suspected I sounded abrupt.

'Well there's the problem, you see. We can't send anyone for probably the next twenty-four hours.'

I was non-plussed. 'What do you mean?'

'Have you seen the weather, Professor Morgan?'

'Well, it's terrible, that's true,' I replied grudgingly as I peered through the tall windows ahead of me and saw snow swirling furiously, 'but surely you can get out to us – we're not that far off the main road. We're just about an hour outside downtown Kelowna for goodness' sake. This is an emergency after all.'

'I happen to know the property, professor, and I'm afraid that's the issue; not only can we not get to the lodge, but the whole of that valley is cut off. It has been since about three this morning. Heaviest dump of snow in the history of recorded weather fell last night, almost two meters in some areas. And it's drifted. All the local crews are out trying to open roads right now, and our emergency response vehicles are dealing with a multiple vehicle incident on the section of the highway near the airport. Also, until these winds die down, we wouldn't be able to get a chopper to you.'

'So what do you suggest we do?' I knew I was using my most sarcastic tone, and I could even hear my Welsh accent getting stronger; apparently it does when I'm angry.

She replied calmly, 'Keep everyone away from the body. Keep the room locked. Try not to disturb anything in as wide a circle around the room in question as possible, and keep the room cool. We'll get there as soon as we can.'

I pulled myself together. 'Have you any idea how long that might be?'

'Difficult to say at the moment, professor. The weather forecast isn't good, I'm afraid. Says we're in for high winds and snow for at least the next twenty-four hours, which is why we can't promise anything. It's pretty bad.'

To be fair, she sounded genuinely sorry and her voice had lost some of its gruffness. I began to realize that we could, probably, be a lot worse off than we were. The house wasn't terribly cold, so I assumed we still had heat, and I'd noticed gas rings in the kitchen last night, so we could eat. And Meg wasn't going anywhere.

Poor Meg; if I could keep her room cold enough there wouldn't be a problem with the body for quite a while. We just had to hope they would get through sooner rather than later. I had lost my sarcasm and ire by the time I responded.

'I understand, Ms . . .?'

'Supervisor McCarthy,' she replied.

'Okay, Supervisor McCarthy, I'll make sure we keep the scene as it is.'

'You called it a "scene", professor. That makes me think you suspect foul play. Is that the case? I really should alert the RCMP if you think there's something amiss, even if they can't get there immediately.' She sounded genuinely concerned.

That question.

I half-closed my eyes; if I can get to the point where everything blurs I can recall the thing I want to visualize much better. In my mind's eye I saw Meg lying on her side in bed, I saw the flowers on the bedside table, the bedclothes. What was it about Meg, before Jean had gathered her into her arms, that wasn't right? That didn't mesh with what I'd felt when I'd moved her? If I wasn't clear in my own mind, what should I say to this girl?

Then she added the questions that changed everything.

'If you're thinking foul play, any idea of who, or how, or when?'

Upon hearing those words, I knew immediately what had been nagging at me; rigor and lividity progress at roughly the same rate, after death, so if Meg had died lying on her side, as we had found her, there would have been a lividity stain on her face where it lay on her pillow – but there had been none.

She hadn't died lying on her side in her bed – she'd died in a different position, maybe even in a different place, and had been moved after death. I sat down on the stairs. Hard. Truly speechless.

Meg had been moved after death.

That meant that, even if she'd found the prospect of facing everyone the next day too daunting after her performance at dinner and had killed herself, someone had still moved her body.

Who would do that? And why?

Or had someone killed Meg? Murdered her? Shut her up before she could reveal their 'dirty little secret'?

That would make more sense. Horrible, frightening sense.

But if that was the case, then reason dictated that her murderer was downstairs, making breakfast; no one could have got into McEwan's

Lodge, and safely away again, if we'd been snowed in since the early hours. It had to be one of us.

'Professor Morgan – are you okay?' the young voice sounded worried.

I gathered my thoughts, and was immediately on my guard.

'I'm here – sorry, you cut out for a moment there.' I had to think fast. 'We'll make sure we keep Meg's body safe,' I replied, avoiding her questions. 'Thank you, Supervisor McCarthy, for your concerns – I'm sure you must be very busy. But, please send someone, anyone, as soon as you can?'

'Will do. I'll pass on the message it's urgent, and maybe you could at least create a photographic record of the scene of death?'

I'd planned to use my phone to take happy snaps of an old friend at her birthday party, not to keep a record of her corpse.

'Yes, you're right. I'll do that,' I said. I was resigned to some pretty unpleasant duties.

We said our goodbyes, then I was alone in the dim morning light.

I made my way down to join the others in the kitchen-diner, and became the center of attention.

I looked at the group before me with different eyes; what was I seeing there? Fear? Hope? Anxiety? All those emotions, and more, were evident – but the question was, which one of them had Meg's murder on their conscience?

'So?' Luis's question hung in the air. I swallowed hard and prepared to put on the best act of my life.

'They can't come right now, and they can't say when they can get here – the snow's a couple of meters deep in places, and they're working on opening up the roads. There's nothing any of us can do for poor Meg.' I tried to sound comforting. 'They've asked us to keep her body cool, and off limits. They'll be here as soon as they can.'

Sadness and resignation bubbled throughout the group.

'So it's a waiting game?' asked Peter Webber, knowing the answer.

'Sounds like it,' replied Joe Gray.

I knew there were things I had to do, alone, so I made a suggestion. 'I have to pop upstairs to dress, but how about that breakfast? And maybe someone could light a fire? And what about the power? Maybe Peter could work on that?'

A general murmuring ensued, as people agreed to undertake certain tasks.

I was relieved, and got back to my room – fast. I knew what I had to do; pull on some clothes, then sneak across the landing and take photographs of my dead friend. However, more than anything, I wanted to sit and cry, but I didn't have the time. Before I could mourn Meg, I had to work out if she'd killed herself, and – if not – then try to work out who might have killed her. It might not be easy, because – if Meg had been telling the truth the day before – it sounded as though everyone at the lodge might have had a motive.

And so I stood over my old friend's corpse, and steeled myself to do what I had to do.

The first thing I had to do was decide how best to use the remaining battery charge in my phone. I toyed with the idea of calling Bud Anderson; he'd been using my skills, on a contract basis, for a few months because he felt a victim profiler was a useful additional tool for him in his role heading up the Integrated Homicide Investigation Team in Vancouver, and the surrounding Lower Mainland. However, I was still getting to know him as a person, and didn't want to jeopardize how he might think of my professional abilities when I was this closely connected to a murder case. I needed that extra income, and the work I'd been doing for him was fascinating – plus, it was a wonderful way for me to be able to test my theories on real cases.

On the other hand, the photographs of the crime scene were a necessity, something the cops might rely upon – when they finally arrived. So I decided against a probably uninformative phone call that might raise questions about my ability to self-direct, and opted to use my phone as a camera instead.

I began with photographs of everything in Meg's room, which seemed to be exactly the same as my own; except for the pattern on the comforter, the fixtures and fittings were essentially the same, as was their location. I couldn't find a suicide note – not so much as a scrap of paper.

I reckoned that, since she'd been moved in any case, there was no reason to not examine her body for any signs of what might have killed her. Meg was wearing a dark-brown silk-satin nightgown; it was good enough for a red carpet appearance. The first thing I discovered was that she'd died sitting up, leaning back, with her legs straight out in front of her – the indications of the lividity were clear; her lower back, buttocks, the back of her legs and her heels were all purplish.

Maybe she'd been sitting up in bed, leaning against a pillow? That was the sort of position she'd have been in, and for at least a couple of hours after death. I thought about using a meat thermometer to get her body temperature, and thus allow a calculation of her time of death, but, even if I could have come up with a good reason for hunting about for such a thing in the kitchen, the thought of having to push it through her skin and into her liver was just too much for me. Meg had gone to her room around ten p.m., and we'd found her at about eight a.m. That would have to do. I'm a criminologist, not a forensic scientist – I'm not good with that sort of stuff at all. In theory, it's fine. But in reality? Yuk.

There were no bottles of pills, no potions or powders lying about, and still no sign of a suicide note. I couldn't see any obvious weapons, nor a mark on her body; not a pinprick, nor signs of her having ingested anything corrosive. The lack of petechial hemorrhaging in her eyes suggested she hadn't died from asphyxiation.

I hadn't been as thorough as a medical examiner, but I thought I was doing pretty well, given the circumstances. The only odd thing was that Meg's hair was a mess – a real mess; it had been sleek the previous night, now it was tangled and matted. And, in parts, damp.

I checked the bathroom; like the bedroom, it was pretty much the same as mine, but Meg had added her own extensive collection of high-end toiletries and cosmetics. Again, there didn't seem to be anything out of the ordinary – not if you were a multi-millionaire, in any case.

The bath was dry, as was the bath mat. All her towels, including the hand towels, were dry. I wondered about that. She'd clearly removed her make-up before retiring – and it looked as though she'd brushed her teeth and applied some frighteningly expensive night cream. So, a normal preparation for a night's sleep . . . then what?

There was nothing to signify an intention to kill herself; nothing knocked over in a possible struggle; nothing at all to suggest how she might have died. Zero.

I realized time was passing, and that my absence downstairs might arouse suspicion – especially in whomever had done this to poor Meg – so I took one last look around the bathroom and bedroom, allowed myself to bid a final farewell to my old friend, and left Meg alone, pulling the door closed behind me.

I tiptoed back to my room, pretty sure no one had seen me, then decided I really did need some sustenance, and took myself off downstairs. As I walked into the kitchen so did Peter – but it was clear he'd ventured out into the snowy wasteland beyond the front door; he looked pinched and chilled, though his cheeks were glowing.

'Any luck?' asked Adrian, who was pouring coffee.

Peter shook his head. 'Something happened to make the panel blow several fuses all at once, and there's been some arcing and a burn-out.

I've fixed it alright, but it seems the power isn't reaching the house from the power lines – I guess there must be a ton of them down in this weather. It looks like the auto-switch for the generator worked, but that, too, has blown. I won't be able to repair that main generator. However, I found an ancillary generator in the shed; it's powerful enough to service the pump from the well, but that's it. So, no power for anything else, but we'll have water, at least.'

I butted in, 'But, I used the loo this morning – it flushed just fine.' I sounded surprised, because I was.

'Mine too,' added Adrian.

It seemed the tragedy had removed some of the usual 'embarrassment' factors that accompany normal life.

'This property is on a well system – bound to be this far out, I guess. Every toilet tank would have one flush in it,' said Peter, 'but without me hooking up the back-up generator to the well-pump, that would have been it. I just hope the little one doesn't give out. May I suggest those of you who can, fill your bath with water while we have it – then at least we can resort to buckets to flush, if the need arises.'

'Thank goodness we've got an electrician on the premises,' I commented, suspecting we could hold out for a while with no light or heat, but that no water would have made life a complete misery. 'Any idea what might have blown the main panel?'

'No,' replied Peter, 'but, frankly, we're lucky the whole place didn't burn down; it doesn't look like they know what a building code is in this place. No GFCIs, old wiring, and I swear both the generators are held together with duct tape.'

Never very technically minded, I had to ask, 'What's a GFCI?'

'One of those special outlets you get where it'll trip before you get a shock. A mini-breaker. You know, they have the little reset buttons on them?' replied Peter, gratefully taking a mug of coffee from Adrian.

I understood what he meant. 'Got it.'

'Hey,' said Adrian, sounding upbeat, 'it could be worse – we've got water, thanks to Peter here, there's no shortage of logs out back for the Great Room, and there's gas for cooking – so we won't starve or freeze. I guess we can wear all our clothes to bed if we need to; those little fan heaters won't be much use without any power.' Adrian poured another coffee from the glass cafetière, and passed it to me.

'I haven't got a fan heater in my room,' I said, wondering why not – not that it would be of any use now, as Adrian had pointed out.

'There isn't one in our room, either,' said Peter.

'Maybe it's just me,' observed Adrian.

'Are you guys bringing that coffee? Today would be great.' Joe Gray sounded annoyed; I suspected he always sounded that way.

'Sorry, we kept Adrian talking,' replied Peter.

'Hey, Joe, Peter's managed to sort out enough power so we have water – isn't that great?' Adrian sounded delighted.

Joe Gray looked underwhelmed, and shuffled back toward the Great Room, where his wife had clearly been a member of the fire-building party.

He shouted across the entry hall. 'Martha – the water's back on. Go for it, baby.' He cackled.

'Oh Joe – don't talk like that. It's embarrassing.' Martha Gray blushed, then she took herself off upstairs as fast as she could go, given her girth and age.

I wandered into the Great Room with Adrian and Peter. A series of 'Atta Boy' calls rang out for Peter, whose efforts were much appreciated by everyone, Joe Gray aside. Then everyone swooped down on the coffee. Luckily, the topics of flushing toilets and the advantages of a gas hob were front and center, so no one asked me where I'd been or what I'd been doing.

Despite the good news about the water, the mood soon became glum; we were all trying too hard to avoid the one subject that was bound to be consuming our thoughts – Meg's death.

Jean Jones wasn't talking to anyone; she sat alone in an armchair, nursing a brandy bowl, and staring, red-eyed, into the dancing fire.

Peter nodded his head toward Jean and whispered, 'Taking it badly, poor thing. Anything we can do for her, d'you think?'

I gave it some thought. 'I don't think so, Peter; even though they were estranged, she's still lost a daughter. It's going to be tough for her.'

'Do you think she's sick in any case?' he continued. 'Her color's not that good, is it?'

I looked at Jean once more; this was the first time I'd seen her in proper daylight, and Peter was right, her color wasn't good. She was slightly jaundiced, but maybe that was her natural skin tone; Meg had always tanned well . . . maybe she'd inherited that sallow, easy-tanning gene from her mother.

'You're right, but she has just had one hell of a shock, Peter. Let's give her some peace and quiet for now.'

'There's no need to whisper about me. I am in the room, you know,' called Jean in our direction.

I was amazed she'd been able to hear us – we'd been whispering really quietly.

'Sorry, Jean,' replied Peter, 'we were just wondering if there was anything we could do for you, that's all.'

'Well, you can't bring her back, so no. Bloody stupid question, really, Peter Webster. Typical of you, that is.'

Poor woman – she couldn't even get his name right.

'Sorry, Jean,' said Peter again, then he went to join his wife, who was calling to him from a sofa that offered a view across the undulating white valley, and the white hillside beyond.

Jean Jones shouted across the room to me, in a voice that everyone could hear, 'So, Cait, are you going to work out who killed Meg, then?'

Martha Gray had just reentered the room, so we were all present for Jean's little bombshell. You could hear the intakes of breath, waiting for my answer.

I decided to go on the offensive. 'Yes, Jean – I think I should. Or maybe we can all work it out together.' I had to bear in mind the fact the killer wouldn't want me to uncover their identity, and I didn't want to go putting myself in danger. 'Let's face it . . . we're all thinking the same thing, aren't we? That someone here, in this room, killed Meg. And, after yesterday, we're all wondering what it was she knew about us that might have meant someone decided to stop her from "telling all" in her autobiography.'

'Exactly,' shouted Sally Webber. 'I said that to Peter this morning. There's been nothing but funny goings-on since we got here, and I don't like it.'

'Funny goings-on' was the most inappropriate euphemism for murder I could imagine. But it was coming from Sally, after all.

'How did she die, Cait?' asked Sally, outright. All eyes were on me.

'It's not clear,' I replied, honestly enough. 'But she didn't kill herself, I can be pretty sure of that.'

'Why?' Sally again.

'No note, no obvious signs of a way by which she could have done it . . . and her body was moved after her death. Did anyone here do that?' I thought it best to be direct.

Heads were shaken all around the room.

'If she'd killed herself, or died peacefully in her sleep, why would someone move her afterwards? And why would they keep it a secret?' I asked.

'It could have been natural causes,' suggested Dan James in his booming voice from beside the fireplace. 'You know, just died and keeled over, in bed.'

'Like I said – there are clear signs on her body that tell me she was moved after her death; a couple of hours after her death, actually. She died sitting up. We found her lying down. And, no, she couldn't have fallen that way, just due to gravity. So we're back to the same questions – why would someone move her, and not now admit to that?'

More head shaking all around.

'So, not suicide, and not natural causes. That only leaves one option,' I said.

'It makes no sense—' began Adrian O'Malley.

Joe Gray interrupted. 'Oh, come off it, Adrian – that's just dumb. It makes perfect sense that someone might want to kill Meg; I don't know what she thought she had on me, because I can't think of a thing, and – other than my wife and Luis – I don't know the rest of you from Adam, so who knows, it could have been any one of you who wanted her dead.'

'You don't know what Meg had on you? Now, isn't that interesting, Joe.' It was Dan James again. He looked like a cat licking cream. 'I think I might have an idea what it was. I'm surprised you don't.'

'Oh, and you're totally without blame, are you?' snapped Martha Gray at the ruddy English professor, rushing to her husband's defense. 'Meg and I had long, intimate chats about you, Dan James, so you be careful what you say about my Joe and my Meg. There's such a thing as libel, you know.'

'It would be slander, actually, Martha, but thanks anyway.' Joe Gray's comments were calm, for him. They seemed designed to quieten his wife, rather than praise her.

'Listen to that one, will you,' piped up Jean Jones, who was now sitting on the edge of her seat. 'Thought you were like a mother to her, didn't you, Martha? Well, you weren't her mother, I was her mother. Not anyone's mother, are you? Know what I mean, Martha? Meg and I might not have talked much over the years, but when we did talk, you can be sure she told me about your "long chats". All about them. Maybe you were the one who didn't want their secrets coming out. But there, I'll say no more on the subject.'

I wondered who'd accuse who next.

'That's enough, Jean; your temper and your anger is upsetting Sally.' Peter Webber's voice was quiet, yet strangely commanding. 'Can't we all just be quiet, and wait?'

'You should know all about keeping quiet, you're good at that – right?' Adrian O'Malley surprised me with that one. His eyes were narrow, and he seemed nervous, but he pushed on nonetheless. 'Meg told me about you. Does the wife know, I wonder?' He left that comment hanging in the air.

Luis Lopez had been sitting quietly on the floor beside the fire while all the barbs had been slung around above his head.

Then he joined in, declaiming, as usual; I found it very irritating. 'But Peter is a good man. I cannot believe you would speak against him, Adrian. If anyone has kept something from his wife, and the world, it is you. I am famous, like you once were. I have people who throw themselves at me; I know what this is like. But you, you have a real skeleton in your closet – like Meg said. I do not think you will have told anyone about this skeleton.'

'Ha!' exclaimed Joe Gray. 'All this talk of closets and stuff is getting boring. Come with me to make more coffee, Luis.'

The mood was broken, but I'd made some real progress; in less than ten minutes I'd gleaned that whatever it was Meg knew about the people in that room, she'd clearly shared the knowledge about each person with someone else. I didn't think anyone would be lining up to share their own dark secret with me, but they might tell me what they knew about another person. It was worth a shot. Now all I had to do was get each person alone, and use any devices possible to get them to come clean about what they knew about someone else.


I decided to begin with Joe Gray. He was heading for the kitchen, and Luis hadn't moved, despite Joe's encouragement, so I volunteered to help with the coffee, and hotfooted it after the brusque little man. It sounded as though he knew something about Luis Lopez, or was I imagining it? I had to find out.

'I'll give you a hand with the coffee; I'll be glad to get out of that atmosphere for a while.' I'd decided to play 'pathetic' for Joe; I couldn't imagine he'd fold for a strong woman, but he might have to put a dumb one straight. 'It's all a bit much for me, Joe. I mean, I know I'm a criminology professor and all that, but I don't deal with actual crimes, you see, just the textbook stuff.'

I was lying, but he had no way of knowing about my contract work with the I-HIT squad, and Bud Anderson.

'I guess that's what all you academics are like – no idea about real life.' He sounded bitter.

'Luis doesn't seem to be taking Meg's death as badly as Jean is, does he? I mean, he seems to be taking it rather well, wouldn't you say?' I thought I'd cut straight to the chase.

'Luis? He was pretty good for Meg's profile for a while. They were only too happy to have her on all those chat shows and use the photos of the two of them together. Good for business, was Luis. All those women watching him strip off every week, then reading her books and imagining him as the love interest? Yes, he had his uses.' Dismissive. Bitter. I wondered why.

'So, with Meg's profile being so high, I bet you were sorry to lose her as a client.'

Joe Gray put down the coffee pot and stared at me with his beady black eyes. He sneered. 'What the hell would you know about it? I've put the last four years of my life into building that woman's career, then she threw it all in my face. All because of him. That *bubkis*.'

'Why "*bubkis*", Joe? It means less than nothing, doesn't it?' I was playing dumb, and it seemed to be working.

'Yeah – Luis is certainly less than nothing; he's a nothing pretending to be a something. Something he's not.'

'How do you mean?' I felt I was getting close.

Joe Gray laughed; it wasn't a pleasant laugh. 'You got it that the doors between them were locked this morning?'

I nodded. I'd wondered about that.

'Well, she wasn't missing out on anything by locking them.'

'You mean, they didn't sleep together? Ever?'

'No point. Meg wasn't his type.'

'But they're engaged.' I tried to sound puzzled.

'Engaged? Yeah – that was good for her last book. And I'm sure they could have kept it going for a while. You know he's been "engaged" twice before? But never married. None of them'll go that far. They'll go along with it for a while, then they realize how dumb they'll look when the truth comes out. And out it'll come, you can be sure of that. Some day. There's an actual movement that "outs" stars, and it was my job to make sure no one outed him while he was with Meg. She'd told me she was going to break off the engagement, but not before that little snake got her into all that psychobabble stuff. I was the one who introduced them, so I guess I only have myself to blame. Brought it all on my own head.'

So, Luis Lopez was gay. I reasoned it was probably something he wouldn't want made public; while being gay might not be the problem in Hollywood it had once been, he probably wouldn't get the roles he wanted if the truth came out. A gay man playing a straight romantic lead, or a gay man playing an action cop, is not something that's seen every day. He was on the gravy train right now – the world finding out about his true sexual orientation might dislodge him. Luis struck me as a man who liked fame; he wasn't known for ducking the paparazzi.

'So, do you think Luis might have killed Meg to keep his secret safe?'

'If I knew that then I'd be the professor,' smirked Joe. 'You're the one with all those brain cells Meg told us about. You work it out. All I'll say is that he might be earning a lot right now – but he spends it fast, too. It costs a lot to keep his men-friends quiet. But not all of them want money. There was one who just couldn't take the pressure – killed himself, about five years ago, when Luis was "engaged" to that starlet who's in all those action movies these days – you know, the one who can't seem to keep her clothes on?' I nodded, I knew who he meant.

'So Luis really does have a skeleton. In his closet.' The edit button that's supposed to control the links between my brain and my mouth seemed to have stopped working for a moment.

Joe Gray's eyes sparkled wickedly. 'Yeah – you could put it like that,' then he smiled in a different way – warmly – at his wife who'd come to see if she could help us in the kitchen.

'The cavalry – good; I'm gonna get back to the fire, I'm cold. I'm sure you two women can manage.' Joe waved as he headed back toward the Great Room.

'What can I do?' asked Martha Gray. She seemed relieved to have escaped the rest of the group.

'Not much – we just have to wait for the water to boil so we can fill the cafetière again,' I said gently. 'It was such a shame that Jean was so upset that she had a go at you, Martha, but I'm sure she'll feel a bit better soon. But hey, you were a good wife to come to Joe's rescue when Dan James started to say nasty things about him.'

Martha rolled her eyes. 'Professor Dan James is not a nice man, Cait, and that's the truth. Meg told me all about him. The things he used to get up to with those girls at his university? I found it hard to believe, I have to be honest.' I wondered just how sheltered a life Martha Gray had really lived – not that sheltered, I reckoned.

She drew closer to me – I felt a confidential conversation coming on, which was just what I wanted.

'I've never told anyone this,' she began, promisingly, 'but when I first met Meg she was still in a real state about Dan James, and she'd left him four years earlier. She never told me much about the other men in her life, but Dan had stripped her of her dignity, and that's the truth. She told me he once as good as killed a man, you know.'

I didn't know, but I wanted to find out.

'No!' I whispered, conspiratorially. I wanted Martha to feel as though we were two girls, having a gossip; it seemed she liked gossip.

'Yes,' she replied, clearly believing that I couldn't believe it. 'Not as in killing him outright, of course –' she sounded a little disappointed about that – 'but what he did to him definitely led to his death. It seems the young man had written some poetry that Dan criticized quite cruelly in class. It pushed the boy over the edge, and he dropped out of school. He'd worshipped Dan, apparently, and he just couldn't cope with his ridicule. The poor boy ended up living on the streets, eventually took to drugs and died, penniless and alone. And all because of how Dan James had treated him. It was as good as murder; Meg said so, and she worried terribly about the poor boy in question. She tracked him down, on the streets, and tried to make Dan go to him, before he died, to apologize; but Dan said that he had to speak the truth, and that the boy's poems were rubbish. Of course, no one at Dan's university knew anything about it; they thought the boy just couldn't cope with the workload and just dropped out, like they do. But Meg knew, and she never forgave Dan. She said that his pride would be his downfall.'

'Do you think he might have killed Meg to stop her from telling the story to anyone else?' I tried to not sound excited.

Martha Gray thought for a moment then spoke thoughtfully, 'The proud are often not brave. And I think whoever killed Meg must have been brave, or foolhardy. You say you don't know how she was killed, so I'm assuming you've discounted a lot of the obvious methods. So what's left? I think if you can work out how she was killed, you'll understand who would have been capable of doing it. And who would have wanted to do it enough that they risked it.'

Martha Gray beamed at me with a knowing smile. 'But I'm sure you know all that, dear – you're a bright girl. Now, let's get this coffee in to those people; we're both thinking that one of them must be a murderer, but they all need some coffee.'

As we worked together to get the coffee and all the accompanying necessaries from the kitchen to the Great Room I began to amend my first impressions of Martha Gray; I'd had her pegged as a vain and grasping woman, and Meg had characterized her as 'being along for the ride', but now I suspected she was, in fact, an astute woman, hiding her intelligence under a facade of fuss and fripperies. She'd been clever enough to give me a reason why someone other than she or her husband might have wanted Meg dead, as well as implying she herself had nothing to do with it; it wasn't just the coffee and extra croissants that were going to be food for thought as we rejoined the group that morning, because I couldn't help wondering what Martha's own secret might be.

The atmosphere amongst the group was strained, and it seemed everyone was trying to avoid making eye contact with everyone else; some were sitting, some standing, but no one, other than Peter and Sally Webber, were in close proximity to another person. I began to wonder if the Webbers were, in fact, joined at the hip, and could see I'd have problems trying to get each one alone. But then I reasoned that Sally had never known Meg, so it was highly unlikely she had anything to do with Meg's death . . . unless she'd acted to protect her husband. The psychology was right – she treated him almost as a part of herself; if Peter was a part of her, she might act on his behalf to protect herself. It was worth considering. No, I couldn't discount her as a suspect, after all.

'Have we any more sugar, do you know, Cait? Or butter?' Adrian was the only one in the room with a smile on his face.

'I could look,' I replied, trying to be helpful, but still feeling a tug in the pit of my stomach as my old heart-throb used my name.

'I'll come with you,' he replied, and the two of us headed to the kitchen. I was pretty certain that any extra butter would be in the fridge, so I looked there first, while he started opening cupboard doors, hunting down the sugar.

'So how's the investigation going, Cait?' he asked conversationally, his head inside a cupboard, his voice sounding even more husky than it had the day before. I wondered if he smoked; I hadn't seen him light up, as the house was strictly non-smoking, but maybe he'd ducked out for one when I hadn't been in his company. I knew I couldn't face the idea of venturing out into the snow for a quick puff, and was glad I packed my nicotine gum, which was soothing my addiction at that very moment.

I decided to play along with the 'casual conversation' thing. 'It's moving along, I guess.'

'I bet the Grays couldn't wait to tell you everything Meg had told them about others here; they seem the type.'

I decided to go for it. 'I have the impression Meg shared what she knew about each person here with at least one other person; that could mean someone else is in danger.'

Adrian looked thoughtful, then said, 'I get your point. If the killer is determined to keep their secret, it could be dangerous for whoever it is who knows what the killer's secret is – other than Meg.' His voice was low, but I caught every syllable,

'Exactly,' I replied.

'And it could become dangerous for you too, if the killer knows you've been told their secret. So why are you risking it, Cait? Why not just wait until the cops come, and let them sort it out?'

He deserved a truthful answer.

'There are nine of us here, Adrian. I know I didn't do it—'

'And neither did I,' he interrupted with a smile. 'But then, I would say that, wouldn't I?' His eyes twinkled wickedly.

I smiled at him, delighted to be sharing such an intimate moment with the man I'd idolized for so many years. 'Yes, you would,' I agreed. 'So let's assume there are seven suspects left. If only one of those is guilty of murder, do you think it's fair that six other people should have to tell their secrets to the cops, to protect themselves against suspicion? Don't you think it would be better if we could get this sorted before the police arrive? Then everyone except the murderer will be able to decide about making their secret known.'

Adrian nodded. 'You've got a point. But I don't have any secrets; when you're as famous as I was, you don't have anything in your life that the press hasn't raked over a dozen times. Everyone who cares to check me out online can find out about my bad habits and my dirty little not-so-secrets. My life's been an open book, whether I've wanted it that way or not.'

'But not recently,' I noted. 'You've been out of the spotlight for years now – maybe Meg knew something from your more recent past?'

'I don't see how she could have done; first of all, there's nothing to know, and secondly, she'd been out of my life since before I ever hit the spotlight. Sure, we kept in touch for a while after our divorce; it was a tough time for both of us, and, although we realized we couldn't live together anymore, we weren't totally done with each other when we split. We even got together occasionally for a night here, an afternoon there. I met her for coffee, once, after she'd taken up with that Dan guy. Can't see what she saw in him myself, but she seemed to like spending afternoons with him in their little Greenwich Village apartment writing poems to each other. And she said he looked after her, and taught her a lot about cultural stuff. You know – art, the opera, classical music. Don't get me wrong – I love all that stuff, but I saw nothing of that Meg. The Meg I was married to was one of the most hell-bent party girls I'd ever known. Great fun. Always the center of attention. We had some good times . . . and some not-so-good times, too. Maybe she was ready for some namby-pamby poet. But he doesn't seem the type; I can't picture him picnicking in Central Park, reading Greek to Meg . . . which was what she told me they did.'

I could picture Dan doing that; I could also picture Dan the bombast treating Meg as some sort of project. It must have massaged his ego to always be with someone who knew less than him. But Meg was quick to learn – I knew that from our school days – and I had a feeling it wouldn't have taken her long to catch up with Dan, whose 'knowledge' was, I suspected, voluminous rather than insightful.

I watched Adrian bend and stretch, opening cupboard after cupboard. 'So do you know someone else's secret?' I decided it was best to just flat out ask.

He turned and smiled. His green eyes sparkled. 'Maybe,' he said, enigmatically. I was hooked. Of course. I tried not to appear coquettish as I leaned nonchalantly against one of the big, old, oak counters.

'What do you mean, Mr O'Malley?'

*Don't flirt – don't flirt – married with lots of kids . . . not for you*, flitted through my head.

He said nothing.

'Meg never told you anything specific about anyone?' I had to press him; Adrian was clearly having a conversation with his conscience. I tried to help him along. 'Anything I can find out might help. After all, we know what's happened, and that it must be one of us who did it . . . so . . .' I let the thought float across the kitchen toward him.

'Peter Webber seems like a real nice guy – wouldn't you say?' he began. I nodded. He continued, 'Meg loved him a great deal, you know. She'd never have divorced him, except that he gave her no choice. She'd lived what she told me was a perfect life with Peter; they worked hard, saved their money, bought a little house, and he was doing real well in the movies – moving up whatever the ranks are for lighting people. Then there was a car accident; he hit a little girl crossing the road, and drove off. He went to work on a movie being shot in New

York, then stayed on for another movie, then another. Meg moved to New York to be with him, but she couldn't re-make the life they'd had; the dead kid was like a ghost between them, she said. They drifted apart, then got divorced, and Meg ended up alone. She was pretty much in free fall when I met her. She was working at a bar on Staten Island called Piffin's, where I played; we matched each other's wildness, and we clicked. Simple as that. No money, odd hours, but some great parties.'

'So that's Peter's secret, eh?' I asked.

'Yeah. Pretty crappy. He was telling me last night that he and his wife do a lot of work with young kids through their church; I guess we all compensate in our own ways – all try to make our peace somehow. Maybe we even over-compensate.'

I wondered how Peter's standing in the community would change if he was found out to be a hit-and-run driver. Might he have killed Meg to keep his secret? What if Sally knew? What if she *didn't*?

'But you have no dark secrets, Adrian – is that right?'

Once again, the globally famous eyes twinkled at me – and just at me.

'That's right, Professor Cait Morgan . . . not a one.'

He produced a pack of sugar and filled the sugar bowl.

'Better get back to the others, so you can try to squeeze a secret or two out of someone else, right?' He grinned, wickedly, and I nodded. 'I bet Dan James could tell you a thing or two; if he was Meg's cultural mentor, she probably spilled her heart out to him. She was a mess when we split – we both were. She'd have been looking for someone to trust . . . maybe he was the one.'

As we wandered back toward the Great Room Dan James came rushing toward us, a huge coffee stain across his shirt-front.

'Look at this mess,' he exclaimed. 'It'll never come out.'

'Have you burned yourself?' It was my first instinct.

'No, I'm fine – it wasn't that hot. You and Martha took so long to bring the coffee to us it was only lukewarm.' Dan clearly couldn't resist the temptation to criticize the efforts of another person; I could easily imagine him brow-beating a young student who adored him with a string of scathing criticisms of his writing efforts. I could cast him in that role easily enough . . . but as a killer?

'Was it black coffee?' I asked.

'Yes.' Dan James looked puzzled.

'That's good,' I said. He didn't look as though it were.

'What do you mean?' he snapped.

'If you get the shirt off right away and bring it to me in the kitchen, I can get the stain out for you. That's a cotton shirt, right?'

He nodded.

'Right then – so, quick as you can, get the shirt down to me here – I'll get a kettle boiling.'

Dan didn't seem used to being told what to do, so he trotted off upstairs quite meekly. He returned to me in the kitchen within about five minutes, holding the stained shirt, and wearing another – exactly the same.

'We'll need a large bowl and this water, when it's boiled,' I announced as he offered me the soiled shirt. 'Can you hunt about for the biggest mixing bowl in the place, please?' I thought it best to be polite, and meek, with this man . . . if I wanted him to tell me anything, that was.

Dan James was tall, so peering into the tops of cupboards was a much easier task for him than it had been for Adrian. I was beginning to wonder if I'd ever get out of the kitchen, but then told myself that at least this way I was able to get people away from the group.

The image of a lioness looking for stragglers at the back of a herd of wildebeest popped into my head; Dan James didn't look much like a straggling wildebeest . . . but that was how I had to think of him.

'It's terribly sad about Meg, isn't it, Dan? I'm sure you must be very upset?' He didn't look upset – well, okay he did, but it seemed to be more about his shirt than about Meg. He was distracted when he answered.

'What? Oh yes, a tragedy, a tragedy. A great loss to the world of popular fiction.' He was huffing and puffing.

'Not the literary community?' I suspected that would rile him.

'Oh no.' He looked surprised – horrified, even. 'I don't think Meg would have envisaged herself as a member of our community. She wasn't a literary writer – just a genre novelist.' He obviously made a huge distinction between the two. 'Meg wasn't well versed in literature; she'd read the basics as a child and had a pretty good schooling, I suppose, but she wasn't up to date at all. I taught her everything she knew, such as she had the capacity to retain my education . . . but you have to have the background to be able to use knowledge. My faculty prides itself on being able to spot and nurture raw talent – but, given that I teach at Harvard, we only attract those with the right backgrounds in the first place. Not that it works out well for every faculty, of course. Where is it you teach again?'

'The University of Vancouver.'

'Nice little place?'

I nodded, biting my tongue, and biding my time . . . we were still waiting for the kettle to boil on the gas hob.

'Don't know it myself,' he added, in a tone that spoke volumes about him, rather than my university.

'We manage,' was all I could muster, without embarking upon a pointless diatribe; I needed to find out what it was he knew about our fellow guests, not leap to the defense of my certainly imperfect, but nonetheless wonderful, place of work.

'So do you think Joe did a good job for Meg as her agent?' I asked. Dan had exclaimed earlier that he thought he might know what Meg had on Joe, so I thought I'd chance my arm.

'Joe? Joe Gray? I suppose he did. They sold a lot of books together, and I suspect he did some very good deals for her when it came to the movies. He's the type, after all.'

'What do you mean – "the type"?' I couldn't let that one pass.

'Oh you know – one of those hard-nosed, hard-hearted agent types who live for the deal and can't see the wood for the trees. His partner was almost the exact opposite; he had a real eye for good work, not just some sort of popular pulp that would rake in the dollars by catering to the lowest common denominator in society.'

I was intrigued – this was the first I'd heard about Joe Gray having a partner. 'I didn't know Joe had a partner,' I said.

'But of course he did,' replied Dan James patronizingly, panting as he crouched to look into one of the lower cupboards. 'Weiss & Gray – W & G – that's the name of the agency. But Julius Weiss has been gone for a long time now. I think that's what Meg meant about Joe when she said we all had a secret. A disgruntled writer came into the agency's offices one day – they'd turned down his manuscript – and he shot Julius Weiss in the head, then he took himself off and jumped off the Brooklyn Bridge. Joe was at some convention or book fair, or something, certainly he was out of New York at the time . . . and after Julius's death he kept the agency name, but continued the business alone. He never took on another partner. The strange thing about it was that Joe was the one who'd declined the manuscript; Julius didn't even know about its existence. The accepted version within literary circles was that it was Joe who was the murderous writer's target, not Julius; the guy shot the wrong man . . . though no one ever knew if he'd known that or not. The writer left the rejected manuscript on the desk beside Julius's dead body – covered in blood apparently – and do you know what Joe did?'

I couldn't imagine, but I was looking forward to finding out. I shook my head, which I knew was all the encouragement Dan James would need.

'Joe published the book he'd originally declined under the name of an imprint he invented, surrounded it with a lurid promotional campaign, and made a fortune off it. He quite literally made money out of his partner's death. That's the sort of man he is. And I know this to be the absolute truth because I happened to have looked into the imprint in question, when casting about for a publisher for my own work. Joe kept his involvement with the publication of the book a secret; I don't think that sort of action would go down very well amongst his fellow agents, do you?'

I didn't comment.

'And this all happened, when?' I asked, trying to work out how Meg might have known about it.

'It was when I was still in my infancy as a writer – so, about twenty-five years ago. And Joe has never looked back since.'

'And Meg would have found out about this because . . .'

'Oh, I told her about it, of course. When I found out who she'd hired as her agent I felt I had to warn her. You can't be too careful when you're dealing with that type.'

We were back to 'types' again; I thought about what Adrian had said earlier, and I decided to try another approach. Dan was, by now, stretching his stained shirt across the top of the giant mixing bowl he'd found, while I prepared to pour boiling water over it. He was, therefore, unable to 'escape'.

'Do you know anything more about Joe Gray? Or his wife?' I began to pour the water across the stain. Dan answered me through the steam.

'He just sort of appeared, apparently, with a pile of money, and bought his way into Julius Weiss's business; Julius was the one who started it, back in the sixties. Joe came along in the early seventies and they worked together after that. I don't know what he'd done before joining forces with Julius. Julius was highly respected; Joe has always been the sharp one. A lot of newer writers avoided W & G after Julius's day; they wanted someone who could help them make great work, not just shift volume. And volume is what Joe is known for.'

Dan's insights were interesting. And the stain on his shirt was gradually disappearing too, which was a bonus . . . for him. As we stood there, heads together over a steaming bowl I could sense Dan had more to say. It didn't seem within his character to be backwards in coming forward, and forward he came – at full tilt.

'And his wife – Martha? That's another thing. There was a rumor going about that she and the partner were . . . you know . . .' He winked at me.

I got the picture, and mouthed, 'Ah', knowingly.

He carried on, gossiping with glee; he was really enjoying himself – I could imagine him at faculty cocktail parties, full of high-balls and spite. 'There was some talk at the time of Julius's death that Joe was having Martha watched – you know, by a private detective . . . all very cloak and dagger. And the word on the literary street is that Joe found out what they were up to, and that he and Julius were going to break up the business. Then Julius was shot, and all the business stayed with Joe. Quite handy for him, I'd say; I'm not sure how many of their writers would have made the choice to move with Joe. But Julius's death meant they didn't have a decision to make.'

I wondered how far Dan would go with this train of thought – or gossip. 'So was the word on the literary street that Joe had a hand in Julius's death?' I pressed.

Dan James peered around the room as though he were afraid of being overheard, then he drew close to me and stage-whispered, 'I wouldn't put it past him. It seems very convenient that he was out of town when it happened, and that it looked as though he was the intended victim; that's such a good way to put people off the scent, don't you think?'

I knew that sort of plan had been tried before, sometimes to great effect, but I was still working on whether Joe's attention to detail for deal-making might have been put to use when it came to the attention to detail needed to set up the murder of his partner – and get away with it.

'Martha had a complete breakdown after Julius's death too – which just added fuel to the fire,' Dan continued. 'Went away to one of those euphemistic "Rest Homes", they said. For about seven months.' Dan James emphasized the time frame and raised his eyebrows in a very unpleasant manner. I felt like I needed a wash after talking to this guy. Yuk.

'What are you two doing here? Your shirt – it is clean?' It was Luis, carrying a tray of empty coffee mugs and pots. I'd obviously missed any chance I might have had of snapping up a second croissant.

I held up the shirt so we could all inspect it. The stain was, essentially, gone – but the shirt needed to be soaked or laundered . . .

and without any power, it was likely to be the former rather than the latter. Dan took the dripping shirt from me and wrung it dry over the kitchen sink.

'I think I'll soak this in my bathroom,' he announced. 'I don't want anything else being spilled on it. Thank you for your help, Cait – quite wonderful.' He dried his hands and scurried out of the kitchen toward the staircase.

'You did not want more coffee?' asked Luis, beginning to run hot water from the kettle into the sink – there being no point in loading up the dishwasher when we had no power.

'No, I'm fine with just the one cup, thanks,' I lied. Usually I like to mainline caffeine until lunchtime, then buzz nicely through the afternoon, coming down just in time for a restorative Bombay and tonic in the evening. But I'd have to manage on just the one mug . . . I had more important things to do.

'How about you wash, and I'll wipe?' I suggested. It seemed like a good way to get some time alone with Luis.

'That is an excellent idea. Jean and Martha have offered to prepare lunch when I have cleared these things away. I think that Martha is trying to keep Jean busy. Jean is not in good shape.' Luis's formal English was charming.

'How are you coping, Luis?' I sounded concerned. I was concerned. Was he a cold-blooded killer who'd just dispatched his pseudo-fiancé in an attempt to prevent her from not kissing and telling? Or was he truly sorry to see someone he cared for – in a professional, if platonic, way – gone?

'I am very sad. Meg was a special person. Very understanding.' He smiled a half-smile and I shot back a look of commiseration. 'Very understanding' was quite an understatement in my book. 'I do not know what I will do without her. We must make some plans to remember her properly; her fans would want that.'

Luis had touched upon something that hadn't occurred to me; there'd likely be some sort of outpouring of public grief for Meg's death. I'd been thinking of her in relationship to just the people at the lodge, and as my old school-friend. But Meg Jones had become so much more than that; I had visions of Luis accompanying a lily-draped casket through some grand Hollywood-style funeral. I suspected he'd play the part of the grieving fiancé with aplomb; it might even turn out to be just the thing to allow him to be able to stop visibly dating women for some time . . . he could portray 'devastated by the loss of my one true love' for years, if he played it well. I wondered if that thought might have pressed him to murder?

'Who would take charge of such a thing?' I wondered aloud.

'I will oversee it all, but I have asked Joe to handle the details; Meg and I were engaged – she and her mother were not close. It would be wrong for her mother to do it. It is my place. Joe knows the people to contact. Joe will do a very good job.'

'Joe introduced you to Meg, didn't he?' I asked, sounding quite innocent.

'But yes. He knew we would be good for each other.' Luis was being both truthful, and misleading, I noted.

'Do you know who will run all of Meg's business dealings now that she's gone? Would that be Joe?'

Luis shook his head. 'Meg has a good business manager. He will work it all out. He was against Meg firing Joe. I think Joe will once again represent Meg's work now.'

Maybe that was another reason for Joe to get rid of Meg? Without her around he'd be put back in charge of her work, and start making a percentage on all the sales that were about to be made posthumously. I was surprised he wasn't already on the phone ordering extra print runs of Meg's books . . . then I realized I'd been in the kitchen for so long he could probably have done all that already, and I'd be none the wiser.

'Have you formally asked Joe to take the reins again?' I was now truly curious.

'Joe has already broken the sad news to Meg's business manager, and he is the one who has asked Joe to "take the reins" again. I have only asked him to make the funeral arrangements.'

'There'll have to be an autopsy, you know, Luis. There's no way of knowing when they'll release her body. Then you'll have to get it from Canada to wherever you'll be having the service.' I didn't want to sound like a know-it-all, but in this case I did, in fact, know it all.

'We have discussed this already – while you were out of the room. Joe, Jean, and I have all agreed that Meg's memorial service will be in New York; she spent many years there. It is a more literary place. She has been living in LA just a short time. People will fly to New York for the service, I am sure. She will be cremated here, in Canada. We will transport the ashes only. Her mother will stay with the Grays until it is all over.'

It seemed I'd missed quite a lot. But, then, I'd learned a lot too. And I wondered what I might still learn from Luis. He might have been Meg's 'fiancé', but I was beginning to wonder how close their relationship had been; were they just social acquaintances with a fake public facade, or had they been real friends?

'You've lost your best friend, I'm sure.' I was acting innocent again, and, by now, I was wiping mugs and stacking them on the big draining board to air-dry.

Luis stopped washing and looked me straight in the eye. 'She was a true friend, you are right. I will miss our talks . . . our closeness. I will miss her warmth.' I guessed he was speaking figuratively, not literally.

'You don't have any suspicions about who might have done it, do you?' I whispered.

'I can only think it is Adrian,' he spat out, hatefully. 'He is a man with blood on his hands already, Meg told me. And I could see last night that he was afraid Meg might tell about the dead woman and the dead baby in his past. He was frightened. I saw that.'

'What dead woman? What dead baby?' I was shocked. Adrian O'Malley had a dark secret after all.

Luis spoke quietly – for him. 'The dead woman? A girl, very young, a teenager, found dead after one of his concerts, in his dressing room. He was taking many drugs, said he didn't know what had happened. He was very famous then, very rich. He made her disappear.'

What on earth did Luis mean? His slightly stilted use of English could obscure, as well as charm.

'How do you mean – "he made her disappear"?' I asked.

'I do not know, Meg did not tell me everything. What I know is that the police never knew about this girl being in Adrian's dressing room. Adrian told Meg this, that is how she knew. When they were married she was his inspiration. His famous song "The Muse You Are" was about Meg. He wrote that when she left him. It was his first big hit. She left him because of the dead baby.'

'Dead baby?'

'Yes, stillborn. His drugs, she said. Then she could not have babies any more. He killed their baby.'

Wow. When Adrian had made that comment about Peter being an example of people over-compensating to make amends for their past, he could have been talking about himself; his drug use had somehow managed to cause the death of the unborn baby that he and Meg were expecting . . . and then he'd gone on to have seven children with his current wife. Everyone knew Jovita O'Malley was her generation's equivalent of Yoko Ono – always portrayed as robbing the music world of a unique talent by stealing Dax O'Malley away for herself, but what if

Jovita didn't know about the stillborn child that he and Meg had lost? What if it came out that Dax/Adrian had no recollection of how a teen had met her death in his dressing room? Could keeping those two facts a secret have driven 'my life's an open book' Adrian to kill his ex-wife?

I didn't want to believe it. I couldn't believe it; for all his bad-boy image at the height of his popularity, Adrian seemed to be a genuine person . . . his body language spoke of openness and acceptance of others. Could he have killed Meg? I knew, only too well from my experiences, that anyone is capable of murder . . . given the right motive, and an opportunity. Could these deaths in Adrian's past be the motive he needed?

By now Luis and I had cleared all the dirty dishes, and I wanted to be sure there was nothing else he might be able to tell me before our chance to be alone disappeared.

'I'm very sorry for your loss, Luis. But I don't think that Adrian's the type to have killed Meg.'

'Type? What do you know about his type? Rich, famous people do not live like other people. They have their own rules.'

As I hung up the tea towel to dry, I realized that everyone I'd managed to get alone so far had presented me with at least one good reason for another guest wanting to kill Meg, and to stop her autobiography from ruining their life. The only people I didn't have anything on were Jean and Sally, and that Sally's reasons – if she had them – would be the same as her husband's. So there was only Jean left.

No one seemed to have heard anything bad about Jean. I told myself it was unusual for a parent to kill their own child – very unusual – so the chances that Jean had killed Meg were slim, but I felt I had to push on and get a proper understanding of the situation. I wondered who had the dirt on Meg's grieving mother?


I finally managed to get back to the Great Room. It was warm, and the fire was dancing merrily in the hearth. The mood in the room seemed to be more relaxed than when I had left it . . . which was about two hours earlier. I needed a sit down, and, for some reason, I fancied a Bombay and tonic; the dimness of the room, the firelight, the way people were just hanging about almost languidly – it made me feel quite 'festive'.

'How's the sleuthing going?' It was Adrian, at my elbow, with a warm smile on his face.

I couldn't have looked happy, because at that moment I wasn't feeling happy and making no effort to conceal the fact.

'You've had your nose to the grindstone out in that kitchen, Cait, so how about a drink?'

I know my face lit up; I'm easily pleased.

'I could kill for a Bombay and tonic,' I said. There was another one of those silences as I spoke – it seems I can actually create them to order. I couldn't take back my ridiculously inappropriate words, so I just added, 'Sorry – you know what I mean,' and hoped everyone did.

Frankly, given what I'd discovered to date about the nature of the people in the room with me, I was beginning to care less and less what they thought of me; none of them had any right to judge anyone, about anything.

'Oh, poor Cait,' said Adrian. 'Stay there – I'll get you one. Heavy on the gin?' I nodded eagerly.

'Anyone else?' called Adrian to the room.

'I wouldn't mind a glass of sherry,' replied Dan James, somewhat predictably. 'It's not as though any of us will be driving today, what?' Honestly, the way he tried to make himself sound English, when all he did was teach it, was laughable.

'I'll have another brandy,' said Jean Jones. Sally Webber looked horrified, and Jean noticed her stares. 'There's no use looking at me like that, young woman,' she chided Sally, 'I want a medicinal brandy, and I'll have one, thank you very much.' That seemed to be an end to the matter.

'You're right Jean, brandy is indeed medicinal,' agreed Martha Gray. 'Maybe a small one for me too, please Adrian?'

'So – a Bombay and tonic, two brandies and a sherry. Anyone else?' Adrian hovered.

'How do we know you did not poison Meg? You might poison us all.' Luis Lopez's voice rang out across the room from the book-corner where he was all but hidden.

There was what could only be called an 'awkward' silence; for once, I wasn't saying anything when it happened, which made a pleasant change. I wondered how many people were thinking that what Luis had said might be true.

'That's great, coming from you,' snapped Adrian. 'Here I am, trying to be helpful and lighten things up a bit – and all you and him can do –' he gesticulated toward Joe Gray – 'is put your heads together in corners and phone everyone in the world who can help you cash in on Meg's death. Besides – if Meg had been poisoned, and if there was any reason for it to have been me who did it, then Detective Cait wouldn't have been first to ask me to get her a drink, would she?'

All eyes now looked at me. I felt myself getting hot.

'Don't blush, Cait. We all know what you're up to,' continued Adrian. 'You've been pumping us for what we know about our fellow guests. You've just about covered all the ground now, right Cait? I've been keeping an eye on you; you've had everyone on their own out in that kitchen . . . except Jean and Peter, and Sally, of course. I'm sure you'll get around to them soon. Don't think you've got to hide it from the rest of us; we all know what you're up to. But you'd better be careful, Cait – if the killer thinks you know their secret, you could be next.'

Why on earth did he insist upon being so melodramatic? I wasn't in any danger. We were all sitting in one room, together; what could possibly happen? Things only happen when groups split up . . . when two people decide to go to the cellar, or the attic, for no apparent reason . . . that's when things 'happen'. And I wasn't planning on leaving the group at all. Then I realized that, at some point, I'd have to go to bed, and then I would be alone . . . and I didn't like that idea, so I stopped thinking about it.

'Maybe Luis is right – but maybe all I'll do is poison your drink, Cait.' Adrian was being wicked.

'But there's a flaw in your plan, Adrian,' I said. I had everyone's attention again . . . the group looked like the spectators at a tennis match, their heads bobbing this way and that.

'Go on then – what?' Adrian asked, his eyes twinkling. Deliciously.

'You might get rid of me because you think I know your secret,' I said thoughtfully, 'but you wouldn't know who'd told me . . . so there'd still be someone else, in this room, who'd know. But you wouldn't know which one to kill, along with me, to make sure that your secret died with us.'

'Okay then,' rebutted Adrian, quick as a flash, 'like Luis said, I'd just kill you all. I'd poison all the drinks. How's that?'

'Don't you think it would look a bit suspicious if the police arrived to find you the only survivor of a mass poisoning?' asked Martha Gray.

'I guess,' acknowledged Adrian. 'Okay – I'll let you all live . . . and I'll face up to whatever it is that someone knows about me . . . though, frankly, it can't be much of a secret.'

'You should not be too sure,' called Luis from his comfy armchair – then he slapped his hand over his mouth.

'Oh dear – I think someone's just given himself away,' said Adrian.

All eyes turned toward Luis; he looked terrified. Luckily he wasn't sitting directly beneath any of the stuffed animal heads, because the similarities might have been too humorous.

Luis rallied. 'I do not know what you mean.'

'Oh, I think you do, Luis.' Adrian's voice had changed; it had lost its levity. 'Meg told you something about me, didn't she? Something that maybe only she and I knew about? Did she tell you about the baby we lost? Was that it? The world-famous "breeder", Dax O'Malley, with a stillborn baby in his past? Yeah, that might be a secret, but that's because it was the way Meg wanted it. Only two or three people even knew she was pregnant. And the bigger part of the so called "secret" is probably that Meg blamed me for the baby's death. It's what broke us apart. Our relationship couldn't cope with the loss; that, and the fact Meg would never be able to conceive again. She said I was to blame because I was using; I told her that drinking like a fish and smoking like a train while she was carrying our child was like signing its death warrant. She never forgave me. I worked real hard to forgive her.'

It looked as though Adrian wasn't going to mention the young girl found dead in his dressing room. Interesting.

There was a series of little gasps around the room.

'That's so sad,' exclaimed Sally Webber.

'She never told me she'd ever been pregnant,' said Jean Jones, sounding angry.

'Me neither,' said Martha Gray, sounding equally miffed.

'Well, you're not her mother, no matter how much you act like you are,' said Jean Jones tartly. 'You're not part of our family; and if me saying I'll come and stay with you two in New York until the memorial service is giving you any ideas in that department, then I'll stay in a hotel instead.'

Martha Gray's expression told me she knew she'd been put in her place, and that she didn't like where that place was.

Jean Jones looked livid. 'Mother your own kid,' she snapped at Martha. 'Oh, no, I forgot . . . you can't, can you? Because you gave it away. Well boo-hoo for you. Your bed, lie in it.'

Martha and Joe Gray's faces both drained.

So the Grays had once had a baby? Meg must have told her mother about that during one of their very few mother/daughter chats.

'I'd always heard there was a child.' It was Dan James, speaking excitedly from his prime position leaning against the fireplace. 'One hears so much on the literary grapevine, of course,' he swaggered, 'but a good deal of it is complete tosh. So, Martha – was it Joe's, or was it

Julius's? I mean – everyone knows your "breakdown" happened right after Julius had been killed; he took a bullet meant for you, didn't he Joe? I wonder what else of yours he took. So, do tell, Martha – who was the father? I have to know.'

With Martha and Joe still reeling from Jean's comments, I wondered how they'd react to Dan's. There were many puzzled faces around me, most people not knowing who 'Julius' was, but I suspected they were working hard to put two and two together.

'I won't stand for this sort of talk.' said Joe. His voice had lifted half an octave.

'Oh Joe, what's to become of us?' cried Martha Gray. She was beginning to unravel. I've seen it before, and once it starts, sometimes it just won't stop. 'Has everyone always gossiped about this? I thought we'd been so discreet. Joe, I can't go on, I can't . . . it's all too much for me, help me. Tears were streaming down Martha's face.

'Now look what you've done – you unfeeling bastard!' Joe Gray was incandescent. 'Think you're so goddam clever, don't you, Dan? You swan around as though you're some sort of literary genius, eh? Well you're not. Meg told me about all those poems you wrote . . . together. The ones you published without giving her any credit. She told me what you said to her when she asked you why her name wasn't attached to them; telling her she was just an unschooled barmaid, that she had no place having her name on them alongside yours was just about the worst thing you could have done to her, Dan. If she hadn't waited tables and worked in bars, you'd never have been able to sit around in Greenwich Village on your fat backside all day, playing about with the words she'd written and shoving the odd bit of Greek in there to tart it all up . . . just so it would pass some phony 'literary litmus test'. You're a fake, Dan James, and if they find out about it at Harvard I don't care how watertight that tenure contract is, I bet they could break it, and you'd be out. Fraud is fraud, that's that.'

I was annoyed that my powers of persuasion hadn't wheedled this little nugget out of Joe when I'd had him on his own. I wondered if anyone else had held anything back; I was beginning to suspect they might have done.

Now it was Dan's turn to glow with anger; it suited him better than it suited Joe – Dan had the right coloring and shape for it. There was a very real possibility he might explode . . . he was so close to it already, with his shirt buttons straining.

'Look to your wife, man,' replied Dan James, trying to deflect the barbs thrown at him, 'can't you see she's distressed?'

'Distressed?' replied Martha Gray, obviously feeling she was now capable of sticking up for herself. 'I'm not half as distressed as I will be if this all comes out at synagogue. Oh Joe, you've got to stop them from telling anyone.'

Having spoken her piece, Martha Gray dissolved into tears again. Her husband looked at her sympathetically, but didn't move to comfort her physically, which I found interesting.

'Dan – and all the rest of you lot – listen up.' Joe's tone had changed; he was about to try to take control, I could see it in every move he made, in every glint of his eyes. 'There's a deal to be done here, people. If our secret is out, and if it's the only one – or one of only a few – then someone . . . anyone . . . here could hold that over us, forever. I say that everyone here should share their secrets with the whole group. That way, no one person has the upper hand. Right now some of us are exposed, some aren't. Let's level the playing field. Right Adrian? Right Dan? And what about you, Luis? You know what I know about you; I don't want to hold that over your head. Are you in?'

I couldn't fault Joe Gray's logic, nor could I fault him for, inadvertently, assuring my own safety; if everyone knew everybody else's secrets, then there'd be no point in the murderer targeting me. And I felt better knowing that.

'I'm in,' I said, as brightly as one cup of coffee, no gin and tonic, and a growing suspicion that anyone in the room might have killed Meg would allow me to be.

My inner being called Save Yourself, and she's usually worth listening to.

'My secret . . .' I continued, immediately drawing everyone's attention, 'is that I didn't, and I emphasize *did not*, kill my ex-boyfriend, Angus, who I found dead on my bathroom floor one morning some years ago, in Cambridge, England. I emphasize that I didn't kill him because the photographs of me being led to a police car which were splattered across the morning newspapers, and the Internet ever since, have led quite a number of people to quote the old adage "no smoke without fire" to my face, despite the fact I was completely exonerated. Of course the police hauled me in – why wouldn't they? As a professor of criminology I am only too well aware that most murders are committed by a spouse or partner, ex-spouse, family member or someone close to the victim. And only Angus and I were on the premises when he died. Of course they arrested me. But they let me go. They actually proved I couldn't have done it.'

I gave my comments a moment to sink in.

Suspicious glances flitted around the room.

I added, 'So there – my "secret", here in Canada, not back in the UK where everyone seems to know about it, is that I was once held on suspicion of murder. But, no, I didn't kill Meg. To be honest, I have no idea how Meg was killed. I can't think how anyone did it. Whoever killed Meg was very clever.' As I spoke my last sentence I tried to make sure I cast my eyes over everyone in the room; would anyone give themselves away by looking smug?

'I have something to say about how Meg might have died,' interrupted Peter Webber. All eyes turned from me to him. 'I've been thinking about the power panel, and I reckon somebody did something that involved the electricity last night, and that's why we blew a bunch of fuses all at once. It might not have been anything to do with Meg . . . but, just like you've been trying to find out our secrets, Cait, so I've been asking everyone about their power usage last night after dinner. People all did the usual stuff, in fact everyone did just about the same stuff as each other. The only possible overload condition was when both Adrian and Jean had their in-room fan heaters turned on at the same time. Those things drink power.'

'We haven't got a heater in our room.' Sally Webber sounded a bit annoyed.

'No, dear, I know,' replied Peter to his wife, patiently. 'I think that Adrian and Jean have them in their rooms because they both have a room that only has an aspect to the north, like Meg's did. Everyone else's room has at least one aspect to the west or east. The rooms with north-facing windows would probably be colder than all the other rooms, and that's likely why those rooms have the extra heater. But –' he returned his attention to the room in general – 'as I said, it seems that we were all able to use as much power as we liked throughout the evening. From what I can gather it seems Martha was the last one to use the power last night, and to find that it was still working just fine. Unless you used anything and it worked after four a.m., Cait?' I shook my head – I'd been sound asleep by then. 'Okay, that's final then – when Martha used her curling tongs at four a.m. they worked, so that's all I know.'

I was somewhat puzzled by why Martha would need to be using a curling iron at that time of the night, but I was more interested in the fact that – if electricity had somehow been involved in Meg's murder – then Peter Webber had just narrowed her time of death to between four and six a.m.; Meg's body wouldn't have been in the state of rigor and lividity it had been in when I'd examined it if she'd died after six, and now it looked as though it might have happened after four. His inquiries had been most helpful.

'So there you are then,' continued Peter Webber, 'no one's told me about any weird power-usage that could have caused what I saw at the panel, so I have to assume someone's lying. A simple power outage doesn't cause a panel to arc like that.'

'Who knew we had two sleuths in our midst? Way to go, Peter.' It was Adrian. He began what I suspected was a sarcastic round of applause. No one joined in.

'Well, that's not the secret Meg told me about you,' sniped Jean Jones, looking right at me. I could feel my eyebrows rise. Both of them. I thought we'd successfully got past my being the center of attention.

'What do you mean, Jean?' asked Adrian. Maybe he was sleuth number three.

'Cait said that her secret was about that boyfriend of hers being found dead. I knew all about that, of course. The talk of Swansea it was, when it happened. But that's not what Meg told me about you. She told me you cheated at school. All the time. She said it wasn't fair, but that you always got away with it.'

I was flummoxed . . . which is not something I get the chance to be very often – who does? Frankly, who wants to be?

'I don't know what you mean, Jean – nor what Meg meant. I never, ever cheated – at school or anywhere else for that matter; not in my whole life. Never.' I was trying to make sure I was being clear. I also knew I sounded hurt. Because I was.

'You used that photographic memory of yours – but you never told anyone you had it. That's cheating.' Jean's harsh tones were now benefitting from a liberal dose of venom. But at least now I knew what she meant.

'Yes, I do have a photographic memory,' I admitted. 'Not that such a thing actually exists, but I won't go into the technicalities right now . . . suffice to say I have an unusual ability to recall things I have experienced in great detail, at will. When I was in school I didn't even know I had the ability; I honestly thought everyone was just like me, and genuinely didn't understand why people couldn't remember things the way I did. When Meg and I studied together I would recite whole chunks from lessons we'd had weeks earlier; she told me I was weird more times than I care to remember. It was Meg herself who brought me a book from the library about memory that helped me understand how I was different, and how to begin to train my gift. By the time we hit the Lower Sixth I was quite good at it, and I used it to help both Meg and myself to get through our A levels. But that's not cheating – that's just me. I can't *not* remember things. To be honest, sometimes it's a curse; imagine walking around with all the experiences you've ever had right there in living color, playing on your internal movie screen. In fact, Meg's initial research on my behalf was to find out how to help me forget, not remember. Believe me – a person doesn't want to remember everything.'

It was clear the people in the room thought that my 'revelations' weren't terribly interesting; Dan, whose greedy face had lit up when I'd said I'd share my secrets, looked especially disappointed.

'Well, it sounds exactly like cheating to me,' concluded Jean, acerbically.

Frankly, I didn't give even one hoot, let alone two, how Jean felt – but it did hurt that Meg had mentioned my 'gift' to her mother in such a way. Despite her closeness to me at school, and her seeming to understand about my memory, had Meg really thought that my using it was 'cheating'? Was that why she'd been trying to help me to forget? Meg had always been good at all the creative things at school, like writing essays, and poems, and doing art; I'd been good at all the 'remembering' things. Being gifted creatively and using it to create isn't cheating – why should me using my memory be characterized that way? I was still stewing on this when I realized Adrian was speaking again.

'Well, thanks for those insights Cait, and Jean, but how about you, Peter? How about you stop your electrical sleuthing for a moment and do something really useful? Confess about your past problems? I'll tell you right now Meg confided in me about you – so if you don't tell them all, then I will . . .' Adrian's twinkling eyes were more malevolent than I'd seen them before. 'Or doesn't even the little woman know?' he added, pointedly.

'Peter?' Sally Webber choked back tears, and held her husband's arm close to her little body.

'I'm sorry, Sally.' Peter Webber held his wife close, hugging her. He was looking deep into her eyes as he spoke. It was quite touching. 'I hate to say it, but Joe's right. It's a good idea if we all tell everything. Then no one's on their own; none of us will tell, because we'll all have something to lose. I might as well do it. I believe Adrian when he says he'll tell them if I don't . . . and I'd prefer them to hear the real story.'

Peter turned his attention from his wife to the group. He cleared his throat, as if for a public speaking engagement. 'Before I tell you what I did, I want you all to know I'm not proud of what happened, and I've tried hard to make up for it ever since. But there's no question it was wrong. However, I have confessed it directly to my Lord, and know I am saved – so it doesn't matter what you think of me. But it does matter that no one finds out, because there are circumstances under which I could be deported from the US to Canada, and possibly put in jail for a long time.'

'But we're in Canada now,' snapped Jean. 'Will they put you in jail just because you came here for this weekend? Why would you come if they would?'

Fair questions.

'Because, Jean, the Canadian authorities aren't looking for me. They don't know, or care, who I am. They never found out who hit a little girl crossing the road one night in Chilliwack, BC, so they don't know it was me. I'd only had one beer after I'd left the set that day, but I panicked, and drove off. I wanted to give myself up – but Meg wouldn't let me. We were trying to get pregnant, and she didn't want to lose me. So I didn't go to the cops. Instead, I sat and watched the parents cry their faces raw on TV. I noted how the story moved from the newspaper's front page, to its inside pages, and then I saw how it disappeared from the news altogether. But the guilt never left me. Yes, this is the first time I've come to Canada since I left in the 1980s, but I don't think it'll be a problem. You see, even if they knew it was me who'd done it, they'd be looking for Peter Webster born January 9th, not Peter Webber born September 1st; I managed to fiddle around with a few bits of paperwork so I got my Green Card as a slightly different person than I was in Canada, and I became a US citizen as that "new" person. I've been "Webber" for so long now that "Webster" doesn't usually bring a response from me at all . . . though it was tough to start with. Not as tough as it must have been for those parents, losing their little girl, of course. My Lord has forgiven me, but for my entire life I must make amends. That, I believe, is the only secret I have. And now you all know. My fate on this earth lies with the people in this room; I'll be in my Lord's arms after that, and I will face His judgement then.'

Peter Webber had spoken eloquently; I couldn't have been the only one in the room knowing his secret was something none of us would have wanted to bear. But one of the things that struck me most about Peter's story was that – once again – Meg was the person who'd insisted the matter shouldn't be revealed at the time. Interesting.

'I love you Peter,' said Sally Webber, looking at her husband with eyes that glowed. 'We are all sinners. The Lord forgives us all. He sent his only Son to save us. I am proud of you, my darling.' She kissed her husband on the cheek. Peter smiled at her, and she at him.

I thought I might throw up.

'Good for you, Peter,' called Adrian across the room. 'Your version varies a little from the one Meg told me – but then I'm guessing that'll be the case for all of us. Maybe it's good that we all get a chance to put our own stories out there; Meg had a talent for making it seem like nothing was ever her fault, didn't she? So . . . who's next?'

I admired the way Adrian was managing the situation – though I did rather wish he'd remember his offer to bring me a drink.

'What about you, Dan? An outsider might think that the Grays have got it in for you; Joe's accused you of fraud and Martha was hinting at something else this morning. What about it, Dan? Are you man enough to confess?'

Dan James seemed to be shrinking as I looked at him. The bombast was deflating, to be replaced by a person with a much smaller ego. The phrase 'taken down a peg or two' wriggled into my conscious mind, and stayed there.

'I can understand why Meg thought she had a hand in creating my best-known works,' began Dan, 'and she did . . . in a way. She was an intuitive writer, but she was no poet. We'd sit and talk about themes I wanted to explore and she'd tell me her thoughts, and jot down little notes about a topic; it was like a parlor game for us. But she didn't construct the works – she didn't even understand most of the layers beneath their surface. They weren't her work – they were mine. But I never told her she was an unschooled barmaid, Joe. I would never have said that. I loved Meg. She'd been on her own for a couple of years since you guys had split up.' Dan nodded toward Adrian. 'She didn't mention a child to me. The first I heard about that was today – which is an odd discovery to make about one's ex-wife . . . about whom one thought one knew everything. I thought we'd never conceived because we were being careful; we'd both agreed that children weren't for us. She was fun, she inspired me, she helped me in so many ways, and I hadn't grown to despise her – not when my poems were published. That came later.' Dan James was a good speaker. Maybe his lectures would be more interesting than I'd originally suspected; he was holding our attention, and his body language spoke of earnestness . . . seemingly unforced. Or maybe he was just a wonderful actor.

He continued, 'You were right, Joe, we didn't have much money, and Meg held down whatever job she could, for as long as they'd keep her on. But that was the problem, you see? She went through job after job after job; got fired from them all. Something would go wrong with every place; she'd mess up the cash register once too often, too many customers would complain that she'd brought them the wrong meal, or she'd turn up at one in the afternoon for a shift that should have started at ten in the morning, and argue about it when the roster was right there on the wall. There was always something. So, yes, Joe, she did get through a lot of jobs, and she did work the worst shifts . . . because she was never anywhere long enough to develop the sort of seniority that allows you to choose better hours.' It seemed the process of recollection was painful for Dan James.

'I worked too,' he added plaintively. 'I wrote articles for PR agencies; pieces of fluff for filthy lucre . . . not under my own name, of course. I didn't want the literati to think I'd ever prostituted my talents, but I had no choice. Then I managed to get my poems published, and everything changed. I was the toast of the town – and when "the town" is New York – well, one might as well be the toast of the world. I was overwhelmed by the response. Truly overwhelmed. My work seemed to offer just what everyone who mattered wanted, at the very moment they realized they wanted it; it changed my life. It changed our lives. But Meg just couldn't cope. She didn't like the people I was invited to mix with; she felt she didn't fit in. She still worked because, although the book was well received, it was never going to make me any real money. So, often, I would be out "swanning about" as an outsider might see it, while Meg was pulling the late shift at a bar or a diner somewhere. The offer from Harvard was a lifeline; it offered a good, steady income. They wanted me so badly I was able to negotiate an excellent tenure deal, and there was accommodation thrown in. Meg loved the idea . . .'

'Hmm,' grunted Martha Gray. She looked as though she didn't believe Dan, and he noticed right away.

'I tell you, Martha, she did. She knew she wouldn't have to do any dreadful jobs anymore, said she wanted the life we were being offered in a beautiful setting, and that she was looking forward to being a supportive housewife. When we moved there she bought recipe book after recipe book; she threw herself into the life of the campus – for about six months. Then it was as though a light went out in her. I never knew what happened, though I had my suspicions. I swear I hadn't done anything to hurt her, or harm her in any way. She just changed. I couldn't reach her any more. It seemed as though, overnight, she turned into a complete shrew. There's no other word for it; nothing I did, or could do, was right – anything I said was deemed a criticism. I was either hanging around the house too much, or never home. I couldn't win. I didn't know why, and I didn't have the courage to face her with my suspicions. Then, just a few weeks before Christmas, she wasn't there anymore. Not a note, not a word; I came home from a lecture and she was gone. Some of her clothes were gone – things that made me, and our friends, believe she'd planned to go. Our friends said she'd probably come back one day – just walk right in as though nothing had happened. And I hoped she would . . . for months. Then I got served with divorce papers by a lawyer from Boston; and that was that. No goodbye – nothing. She got back in touch when she rolled into New York four years later and hooked up with you, Martha. But for all those years, when she was on her famous "road trip", I didn't hear a word from her – only from her lawyers.'

'Well, that's all very sad, Dan,' said Martha, 'but what about that poor boy who killed himself because of what you said about his work? What about that? That's a bit more of a juicy secret, don't you think? How would they take to that in your precious Ivy League?'

'I don't know what you mean, Martha,' replied Dan, sounding genuinely puzzled. 'There was no one who killed himself because of my critiques. What rubbish was Meg feeding you, exactly?'

I, too, was beginning to wonder about the extent to which Meg had seen the world through a somewhat distorted lens.

'Don't be coy, Dan,' mocked Martha Gray. 'A boy – whose name I either never knew, or cannot remember – was a student of yours; he looked up to you, worshipped you, in fact. You ripped through his creative efforts, and he dropped out; he ended up living on the streets and eventually died of a drug overdose. Maybe that turned Meg against you. That's what Meg told me. That was the secret she told me about you – that your heartless actions led to the death of a promising young man, who was cut down by depression because you undermined him completely.' Martha had spoken with searing emotion; she, too, knew how to hold a room.

Eyes turned from Martha to Dan; we all wanted an answer, and he seemed willing to supply one. It surprised most of the people in the room.

'I think you're talking about an upperclassman called Robert. It must be him. When I said that I didn't know why Meg changed, but that I had my suspicions – well, I suspected Robert was the reason she changed, but not in the way you mean it, Martha. I had good cause to suspect Meg was having an affair with Robert; it wasn't Meg who made me believe it, but Robert himself. He wasn't a pleasant young man. In fact, he was quite wicked . . . and not in a playful way. It was a part of my responsibility, of course, to review, critique and grade work submitted by my students as part of our creative writing workshops; Robert would include something in each of his submissions hinting that I was being cuckolded, or that he was familiar with my bedroom, or with intimate parts of Meg's anatomy. He toyed with me throughout the entire course. But he didn't "drop out" because of me, Martha; he'd been encouraged by the resident dean to seek counselling about his drinking and drug use. He was well known to the Cambridge police, and there were a number of complaints made against him at his hall of residence. No one was surprised when he didn't complete the course; I got the impression he'd dumped Meg before he'd left. But she tried to track him down; I found out about that because she used a private investigator and paid him with our credit card. She lied about why she'd hired him, but I guessed. I understand that Robert did, indeed, succumb to his hedonistic ways. Though it had nothing to do with me.'

There was a stillness in the room; the stillness that comes from no one knowing quite what to say next. So I thought I'd better speak up; sometimes, I think the sound of silence is highly over-rated.

'Every one of us is explaining our "dirty little secret" so reasonably, aren't we?' I knew I sounded sarcastic – I meant to. 'So who's next to portray themselves as having been hard done by by Meg?'

From his corner vantage point, Luis Lopez stood and declaimed to the room, 'I am a homosexual. It is nobody's business. I am more than my sexuality. But Meg, she helped me to keep this a secret so that I can continue to work as I do. Joe knew this. He introduced us. Meg and I had a very good relationship. I did not kill her.' Then he sat down again, as though he expected everyone to clamp their gaping mouths shut, and carry on as though nothing had happened.

'You're one of those gay boys?' shouted Jean Jones across the room with obvious surprise and disgust.

'I am a homosexual,' was Luis's blunt response.

'So what was Meg up to, saying she was going to marry you?' Jean was shouting. 'What good is a man like you, to a woman?'

'Meg and I were good friends. We cared for each other. We both gained from our engagement; she was more popular because she was associated with me.'

'Meg as the beard? The Phyllis Gates of her day?' mused Dan James.

'This was our business, nobody else's.' Luis was angry; he was ready to declaim us all to death. 'I will not stand for this,' he screamed, standing. 'My sexuality is only a secret because people are too small-minded to accept me in a wide range of roles in spite of it. It is their problem I have to work around. Not mine.'

'So why not tell us the whole truth, then, Luis?' said Joe Gray. 'Tell us about the guy on Sunset.'

All heads turned to watch Luis's reaction – and it wasn't good. He pushed over a little table beside his seat. A lamp clattered to the floor, the glass shade and bulb smashing. Luis's naturally deep voice rose in pitch as he spat words toward Joe Gray. 'You will not talk about my life this way. We have an agreement. You are as bad as Meg said. You are a schemer.'

'And your temper is as bad as Meg told me it was; maybe you're the one who lost it and killed her,' responded Joe Gray angrily. 'She said you were like a child – unable to cope when you couldn't get exactly what you wanted. Did it all get too much for you, Luis? Was Meg going to "out" you, so you killed her? Or were you afraid she'd share what she knew about the guy on Sunset?'

Luis shoved the broken lamp across the floor with his foot and howled like a coyote. Then he collapsed into his chair, and buried his face in his hands.

Finally looking up at us all, he spoke quietly, 'I had broken off a relationship with a certain person. It could not develop in the way he wanted. He was hurt by me, I know this. But I did not mean for him to take his own life. I did not believe he would do it. But he did. And it made me very sad. But this was not of my making. I did not kill Meg – because of this, or anything else.' Luis sounded quietly certain about that. We all let it sink in, with me reminding myself the man made his living as an actor.

There was a catch in his voice when he added, 'People can die around you when you are famous, and it can make life very difficult. This is true for you as well, Adrian. Meg told me about a young girl who died in your dressing room – did she kill herself because she wanted you, but could not have you?'

Now all heads swiveled back toward Adrian.

He shook his head. 'Oh man – so Meg told you about that? Wow – I thought that was long gone. Man, we had some wild times backstage in those days; I usually didn't know what day it was, what city I was in . . . or even the lyrics to songs I'd written myself, sometimes. I told Meg about one of our security guys finding a girl in our dressing room one night when we were playing in . . . somewhere – Ohio I think; none of us even saw her. They found her when we were on stage – no one knew who she was, or how she'd got in there. She was dead; OD'd by the look of it. Man that was bad . . .'

As I was listening to Adrian I thought how glad I was that it only seemed to be now, as he recollected his time on the road, that he used the word 'man' as he spoke; it was incredibly annoying, and quite sad really – a person in their sixties should have developed a sufficiently broad vocabulary to allow for a range of exclamatory remarks.

'So this girl's death, it was nothing to do with you?' asked Luis, his voice dripping with sarcastic disbelief.

'No, it wasn't. Honest,' said Adrian, bluntly. 'I never even saw her. Just heard about it.'

Everyone in the room seemed to be completely emotionally drained, myself included.

'If you're still getting that drink, Adrian, I think I might have a fizzy water, please,' said Sally.

Good grief, the woman was unbelievable.

It was as though we'd all been slapped in the face. I took stock; there we were, a strange group of people, huddling around a shrinking fire on a day that was growing dim beyond the windows. And the snow? Still falling.

Though the fire was burning down, I felt hot, and claustrophobic. But my mind had been piecing together everything that had been said, and I needed to do something . . . and to do it with Peter Webber; I needed time alone with him.

'Let's all take five minutes,' I suggested. 'But listen, before anyone leaves this room, there's something I must say.'

Once again I was the center of attention. Whoop-de-doo!

'You know I've been "snooping", and I believe it's a good thing we've all decided to come clean about our secrets. We all know one of us here killed Meg. And I believe we all want to know who that was—'

'Well, I certainly do,' interrupted Martha Gray, 'because I'm not going anywhere on my own until it's sorted out. Joe – you do not leave my side, you hear?'

'Surely the only one who doesn't want the killer to be found out is the actual killer?' said Sally Webber; I suspected it was the most cogent thing I'd heard her say all day.

'That's exactly my point,' I added, keen to get on. 'If you all agree, I'd like to look around everyone's room. I want you all to feel secure in the knowledge I'm not planting evidence, or whatever, which is why I'm going to suggest that someone accompanies me. Peter – would you do the honors? If everyone agrees, that is. But I'm sure everyone will, because only the murderer wouldn't want me poking about, right?'

I thought I'd made my point quite well. Everyone nodded; some cautiously, some with maybe a little too much enthusiasm. 'Thanks,' I said, quickly, and Peter and I collected room keys. 'We'll be as quick as we can – please all wait here until we've finished.' I didn't want anyone removing what might be incriminating evidence.

'Drinks anyone?' I could hear Adrian asking as I walked up the stairs. There was a G & T somewhere in my future, but not for the next little while, it seemed. My tummy rumbled, and I made a mental promise to myself that I wouldn't miss what was going to be a very late lunch indeed.

While Peter stood at the door, I ducked into Meg's room first. I didn't look at her body – I needed her cellphone from beside her bed. I picked it up and left the room, then checked the battery reading – it was in good shape; I'd only need to use it for one call, but it was a call I needed to make when I was alone, so it could wait.

I didn't know exactly what I was looking for, but I diligently worked my way through the two large double rooms being used by the Webbers and the Grays, then Dan's room, then Luis's – both of which were very much the same as my own. No one had brought much with them; we'd only been due to stay for two nights, and even Martha Gray had only packed a large overnight bag.

Peter and I chatted as I riffled drawers and closets, and pored over toiletry collections. Before too long he told me when he and Meg had reconnected, upon her buying a home in LA, they'd never actually met up. Rather, as with me, she'd kept in touch by email. Peter also made it clear that he and Meg hadn't kept in touch after their split, and that, therefore, everyone downstairs was a complete stranger to him, and Sally, of course.

Next, we went to Jean's room; it was at the back of the lodge, its windows facing north, as Peter had noted earlier. The room was almost totally dark, and I kicked myself that I hadn't suggested a search of rooms earlier in the day – the last of the light outside had all but gone. We clicked on the two flashlights we'd brought with us. How on earth did they find anything in those TV shows when all they have is a flashlight, I'll never know; believe me, if I could have turned on the lights, I would have done. However, without power, all I could do was stumble about in the gloom, variously illuminating disconnected pools of flooring, or pieces of furniture that seemed to leap out at me from dark corners. The room's layout was similar to my own, but different enough to cause a few stubbed toes and a little swearing.

In between my un-deleted expletives, I managed, 'But that's not quite true, is it, Peter? You do know some people downstairs.'

Peter leaped to his defense. 'No, you're wrong,' he said from the darkness that was the door to the landing. 'We really don't.'

'You know Jean,' I reminded him.

'Oh, Jean,' he replied, dismissively. 'I couldn't say that I know her. Or even knew her. She was Meg's mum, and that was it. I never spent any time at Meg's house when we were young, and, when we got together, got married, and then left the country . . . well, that was it; Meg never kept in touch with her mother at all. I haven't seen her since back then.'

'But I bet Meg talked about her a lot?' I pressed, as I poked around in the bathroom.

'Well, you're right there, I guess,' replied Peter, sounding thoughtful. 'Meg didn't have a good word to say about her, though. She just wanted to get away from her. We got married about a month after her father died. Do you remember Meg's dad?'

As I stood in Jean Jones's bathroom, peering into a hamper full of wet towels, I saw her dead husband as clearly as if he'd been standing in front of me; he'd been a short, round man, with heavy eyebrows and a broad, toothy smile. Whenever I'd seen him at Meg's house he'd always been wearing the same outfit; a long-sleeved undershirt and wide brown braces, which held his trousers so high they were almost under his armpits. He'd been a happy man; always a quip or a funny story, and – as often as not – some silly little trick that involved a ha'penny. All that had been when I was quite young, of course. As I'd become a teenager he'd become more distant, had become thinner – his waistline, and his hair – until finally, I recalled, he'd been a pretty bad-tempered man with a local reputation for rolling home from the pub at all hours.

'Yes, I remember him,' I replied.

'I think it was his death that made Meg want to leave Wales. She blamed Jean for it.' Even in the dim room, I could tell Peter was uncomfortable with the topic – his voice gave him away. 'What she told me was that her parents had a row one night . . . which seemed to be the norm for them, but this was a really bad one . . . and the next morning Meg found her father dead at the bottom of the stairs. Apparently Jean had insisted he had to sleep on the sofa, and he'd fallen while making his way down from their bedroom. His neck was broken. Meg was devastated. In fact, thinking back, it changed her in many ways; when we were together we were happy . . . but she always used to make me promise that if she ever said or did anything that reminded me of her mother I was to tell her, because she didn't want to become anything like her. I think Meg really was afraid she'd grow up to be like Jean.'

'That's not so odd,' I said as I finally rejoined Peter at the door, 'I mean, Jean's not exactly the warm, fuzzy type, is she? Who would want to be like her?'

'True,' replied Peter, still thoughtful.

I nipped into my own room, pretending a need for the loo, made a call on Meg's cellphone, then rejoined Peter. As I made my way toward the top of the stairs, Peter called to me, 'What about Adrian's room? Don't forget that one.'

'Oops, I almost did,' I lied. I pushed open the door and did my thing again with the flashlight. It was odd, but I didn't get any sort of frisson from looking into drawers that contained Dax/Adrian's underwear and socks; I'd thought there might have been, but there was nothing. Nothing except the mounting excitement I was beginning to feel as the case clicked into place in my head. By the time I closed the door to Adrian's room, and Peter and I had rejoined the group, I was pretty sure in my mind about who had killed Meg, and why. Now all I had to do was decide what to do about it.


When you look into the face of someone you know has killed, and who is lying about it, you can see their lie in so many ways. And when I walked back into the Great Room, I knew I was right; Meg's murderer was giving away their identity so obviously . . . why hadn't I seen it before?

I told myself not to be so tough on myself; I'd needed to work out the method and check everyone's room before I could possibly have been sure, whatever my suspicions. And even then, it was still hard to believe. But, there it was – body language, affect, tone of voice, micro-expressions, interactions, relationship to physical surroundings . . . everything was screaming: 'I did it', followed closely by: 'I don't care if you know it.'

Which was almost as interesting.

I had to remind myself that I was working with a theory . . . I didn't know for certain that the person I believed had killed Meg had actually done it. But I could see no alternative.

I wished there was someone there with whom I felt enough of a trusting connection to discuss my theory; someone whose opinion I would value. But there wasn't. True, I liked a couple of my co-suspects, but as for the decision I had to make? No, I had to decide alone, then follow through – and live with the consequences.

The group had, apparently, moved as one to the kitchen when Peter and I had gone upstairs, but it seemed they'd realized that cooking by gas with only the aid of candles might sound all well and good, but that it can get messy in a hurry, so by the time we returned to the Great Room there was a meal of cold cuts, bread, salad, and a giant cheesecake on offer.

As we all served ourselves, the light of the re-built fire flickering, the candles that had been lit lending a warm glow to the room, I could sense that everyone was feeling worn out by the tensions of the day. My watch told me it was five p.m.; it felt much later. I was achingly hungry, so told myself my decision about exactly what I should do, or say, should wait until after I'd eaten. But all the food tasted bland; I knew my body needed me to eat, but my palate wasn't up to it. Even the Bombay and tonic, that had been so tortuously long in coming, didn't refresh me.

I was beyond the comfort of gin – it was a tragedy.

By the time we'd all had our fill of savories, I knew that a difficult moment was approaching. I looked at the cheesecake that was, presumably, to have been Meg's birthday cake. I knew I wasn't alone in wondering about whether eating it was something we should, or shouldn't, do.

'I'll cut the cake,' said Jean Jones, determinedly, 'but I'd like to say a word or two first.'

A low murmur spread through the group. No one objected to Jean's suggestion.

She stood in front of the blazing fire, holding a cake knife. She created a dramatic silhouette; the long, serrated blade looked especially large in this tiny woman's hand, and it glowed with the reflection of the flames that burned behind her. The victim's grieving mother spoke loudly, her reedy, wavering voice just about cutting through the roar and crackle of the logs that sparked and shifted in the hearth.

'Meg wasn't a nice girl, and it sounds like she didn't grow up to be a nice woman . . .' It wasn't what people had expected from the mother of the deceased, that much was obvious. 'She made people miserable – that's what you've all been saying all day, isn't it? She made all you lot miserable anyway, and before you lot, she made me miserable too. Never applied herself as a girl, and she seems to have come by all her new-found wealth and fame almost by chance. I bet anyone who spent four years just swanning about on buses, and doing the odd job here or there, could write a book. I bet I could, anyway. No sense of responsibility, that girl. And not many morals either, by the sound of it.'

I could tell by my fellow guests' faces they were all wondering what might come next.

'But she's gone, now,' continued Jean, still in harsh tones, 'and they say you shouldn't speak ill of the dead. So I won't. But I haven't got anything nice to say about her . . . so let's eat the cake.'

And with that, she walked to the little table where the cheesecake had been placed, and sliced into it. She cut piece after piece. Sally sprang to her side, passing plates and forks to everyone around the room.

'Junior's,' said Joe to Martha, who smiled and ate greedily.

There were no other words spoken; what little conversation had bubbled through the savory course, was now over. Maybe, people were taking time to explore their own thoughts about Meg, as they ate the birthday cake she'd never share.

Personally, I was still grappling with what to do next, and trying not to choke on the cheesecake as I swallowed. It had a good texture, but I couldn't taste a thing. I knew Joe's comment to Martha meant the cake had come all the way from the famous Junior's in New York, and I wished I could have enjoyed it more . . . but I couldn't. Such a waste of a good cheesecake.

Eventually we'd all finished and, once again, there was a general movement toward the kitchen – everyone carrying something. Because it was so dark we all agreed the washing up could wait . . . which left us all with the dreadful feeling that we just didn't know what to do next; it wasn't as though someone could suggest board games, or charades, or anything like that.

We all wandered aimlessly back toward the Great Room, like a tide ebbing and flowing across the entry hall. Everything seemed unreal: we were all tired out, but it was far too early to retire to our rooms; we all wanted the day to be over, but knew we probably wouldn't sleep; none of us wanted to be there, but there was nowhere else to go.

Limbo doesn't sound unappealing, until you're stuck in it.

As we each tried to settle in our own way, Adrian – who was sitting between me and the fire – said, 'So – whodunit, Cait? Do you know yet?

Or do we all have to lock our doors tonight and pray the murderer is fine with killing just Meg?'

I knew this was my moment.

Should I lie and say I didn't know? Or should I tell the truth and explain what I believed had happened? Did I have the guts to go through with it? And, if I did . . . what would happen afterwards?

That was my main concern.

Would we all agree to lock the culprit away for the night and wait for the police? Would we all stay huddled in the Great Room and take it in turns to 'watch' the killer, thereby ensuring our safety? It all seemed ridiculously melodramatic . . . but that was the aspect of the thing that had held most of my attention.

The Aftermath.

I made my decision.

'Yes, I'm pretty sure I know who did it, how they did it, and why they did it,' I said flatly.

There was certainly no 'Ta-Daa!' about my statement, but the effect was pretty much what it would have been if I'd swung naked from the antler chandelier above our heads: shock, horror, and fear.

A quiet chorus of 'Who?', 'Why?' and 'How?' rippled through the room. Suddenly the air was charged with anticipation. Any doubt I might have had about the identity of the killer would have evaporated when I saw their reaction; they stared into the fire saying nothing at all.

'Are you going to tell us?' pressed Adrian.

'Yes . . . I'll tell you what I think happened . . . but then we'll all have some very big decisions to make. You'll understand what I mean when I've finished. This is complicated . . .' I sorted out my thoughts, and began to tell a story. I had to begin the right way; that would be important.


'The motive for Meg's murder was love. You have to understand that, to be able to understand anything else.'

Of course I had everyone's attention, but what impacted me was the reaction of one person in the room to my opening words. I was right, the motive had been love. And the removal of that love from the killer by Meg.

I knew I'd be talking for a while, so sipped my Bombay and tonic; it cooled my throat. 'It was love of a strange and warped kind; a love that depended upon ownership. A love that didn't place Meg at the center of the murderer's world . . . but which allowed the murderer to blame Meg for not loving them in the way they thought they should have been loved. As we look at each face around this room I think we can all agree that description could apply to quite a few people here. Peter, Adrian, Dan – Meg dumped you all; she didn't love you the "right" way. Martha – she didn't love you like a mother, but, Jean, she didn't love you like a mother either. Joe – she dumped you too, and I think your engagement was on the line Luis, right?' I didn't expect anyone to react to my rhetorical questions . . . but you never can tell, so I paused for a moment or two before continuing.

Nothing. Move on.

'You each drew me a different picture of Meg – Sally, you didn't know her, so, in total, you gave me seven different Megs to choose from . . . and I added my own Meg, of course. The Meg I knew was fun, wild, a bit of a daredevil, and had a brilliant creative mind – but it flitted about, never resting anywhere for long; she found it hard to buckle down and study, she didn't like to be with people who criticized her, or who couldn't keep up with her, and you were right when you said she never took the blame for anything, Adrian . . . she didn't, not during her school years and not, according to all of you, at any time after that either. Each of you met a Meg who was an increasingly damaged person; she dealt with the damage in her own way . . . which seems to have mainly consisted of ignoring it. But you can't ignore damage forever . . . it'll get to you in the end.'

The faces in the firelight were all looking anxious, and thoughtful. I knew they were digesting what I was saying, and, so far, no one seemed to want to disagree with me. I pushed on. I was trying to get them to understand.

'When Meg took off on her four-year bus journey, writing her blockbuster novel, she did so as a woman who'd had to face some tough times; she'd removed herself from everything she'd ever known, and left it behind for a new reality – alone. She'd known an idyllic life that was shattered by a tragic death with Peter; she delivered a stillborn child, and lost any chance to ever bear any more with Adrian; she lived through a psychologically challenging time way outside any comfort zone she'd ever known with Dan, and she'd had a disastrous affair with a young addict, who dumped her, and probably made her feel foolish, and used. Now – you might say that she'd brought much of this damage upon herself . . . and you'd be right. But what's interesting about we human beings is not that we cannot cope with what life throws at us, because we can; what's truly interesting is how we cope.

And Meg coped by running away. She ran away from Wales, then away from Peter, from Adrian, and from Dan. She was running away from you, Joe, and you too, Luis. She's always run away; that was Meg's way of coping. Which led me to think that maybe Meg had decided she'd run away one more time . . . and that she had, in fact, killed herself.'

I knew this statement would draw gasps, and it did. Gasps of disbelief, and gasps of relief . . . it was about fifty-fifty. Which, again, was interesting.

I waited for people to re-settle themselves. It didn't take long – they wanted to know . . .

'It was quite clear to me that Meg's body had been moved after her death. She died sitting up with her legs extended in front of her, and stayed that way for a couple of hours after death. Then she was laid in her bed curled on her side, the way we found her this morning. Luis, did Meg run a bath when she went to bed last night? Her bathroom connected your rooms – possibly you would have heard the water running.'

'She did not. It was odd. She bathed every night before bed. She . . . she told me this. She did not like showers, but she liked to feel clean sheets on clean skin. She had clean sheets put onto her bed every day. But I did not hear water before I went to sleep last night. If she took her bath last night it must have been very late, I think.' To be fair, Luis did appear to be thinking as he answered.

'It was very late, Luis,' I said, 'it must have been not long before four a.m. I'm surprised you didn't hear her.'

'I sleep very heavily,' replied Luis, a little defensively.

'How do you know Meg took a bath at four a.m.?' It was Adrian. He sounded genuinely interested.

'Because that's the only way it all works out; Sherlock Holmes famously said something along the lines of: when you've got rid of all the ideas that don't or can't work, then what you're left with is the only explanation, however odd it might seem. And that happened here. Peter helped a lot . . . thanks, Peter.' Peter half-smiled; he clearly wasn't sure that helping me was a good thing. I decided to keep plugging away.

'Martha said that the power was still working at four a.m.; that means Meg wasn't killed until after that time, because it was her murder that blew the fuse panel. That was Peter's helpful suggestion.'

Faces turned toward Peter; they were the faces of people trying to work things out for themselves. They were the faces of people who were failing to do so.

'Meg was killed by electrocution, in her bath,' I announced, there were gasps. 'Peter told us about the blown fuses; I knew Meg's hair had been wet when I held her. I knew there could only be one explanation, but I don't know much about exactly how electricity works; I know it can pass through the human body without leaving much of a mark, but I also know that the "Hollywood" way of just dumping a hairdryer, or a space heater into a bathtub won't kill anyone . . . because the circuit will trip to "off" before any damage is done. But Peter explained that this house isn't fitted with those newer outlets . . . which means that whoever did this to Meg either knew all about how electricity works, and knew that tossing an electrical appliance into the tub would kill Meg because those safety outlets weren't going to kick in . . . or they knew nothing about it at all, and just threw something into the bathtub believing it would do the trick.'

Again I waited for a few seconds, allowing people to think through what I was saying. 'Then there's the question of premeditation. Did the culprit plan to kill Meg – and to kill her this specific way – or was it the act of a moment of anger, with an electrical appliance to hand? I noticed there was no hairdryer in Meg's bathroom. Now, to be fair, there wasn't one in mine when I arrived either. Knowing we were to be staying at a lodge, as a guest, rather than a hotel, I brought my own; we women with long hair need to be able to dry it, or sit around for hours with it wet. Meg had long hair, and she was hardly the type to not have all necessary comforts with her, so I had to assume she'd brought a hairdryer with her too. But, as I said, there wasn't one in her bathroom. Would she really have gone to bed, or back to bed, with wet hair? No. I think what happened was that Meg had thrown herself into bed in a bad mood after leaving us last night, found she couldn't get to sleep, so decided to take a bath to calm herself. She died in her bath, sitting up, with her legs extended. I believe she would have locked her room when she left us all – if you recall she was in a conflicted state of mind – so I think she opened her door to her killer, and felt comfortable enough with them to take a bath in their presence.'

Glances were exchanged around the room. Everyone was trying to think who would be eliminated by this assumption.

'She might allow an ex-husband to see her that way, a current fiancé, a mother, a confidante, Martha . . . but probably not an ex-agent, Joe, or someone she hardly knew, Sally.' The field was narrowing, but not by much.

'So,' I continued, 'an appliance was dropped into the bath; possibly Meg's own hairdryer, which is missing. Meg suffered a fatal electric shock, the fuse panel blew, and the power went out. What happened then? Well, I can tell you that the murderer calmly put their hand into the bathwater with Meg's dead body still in it, and pulled out the plug; her body didn't show any signs of the puckering that would signify she'd been lying in water for hours, but it did show cooling, and that suggested she'd lain exposed to the air. Then, around six a.m. this morning, the murderer went back to Meg's room, lifted her from the bath, dried her off and put her onto her bed, on her side. Lividity had set in when she was in the bath, but rigor had set a little when she lay on the bed. The hardwood floors in her room didn't allow for there to be any visible drag marks, and Meg's body, as I discovered when I lifted her myself, was remarkably light. I reckon anyone here could have done it – getting her out of the bath would have been the toughest part, but the position of the claw-foot tubs in these bathrooms would have allowed for someone to hook their arms under Meg's armpits from behind, and pull. It would have been difficult, and wet, work despite the bath having been empty for a couple of hours, but the killer managed it. They also dried off the bath, and replaced all Meg's wet towels with dry ones. Which, by the way, was a mistake.'

Once again, there were suspicious looks flying around in the firelight. I was almost finished.

'The killer would then have put Meg's nightdress on her, tucked her in, and would have presented themselves as a member of the group that discovered her body, carefully concealing their guilt.'

'Peter wasn't up and about in the night – I'd have known about it,' called Sally Webber from her seat against the black window.

'And I know Sally wasn't. Not that it could have been her anyway,' added Peter, trailing off into silence.

'And Joe snores like a train – I wake when he stops; I'm afraid he'll stop breathing, so I know he didn't do it,' interrupted Martha Gray.

'You were awake at four a.m.,' broke in Luis. 'Perhaps you are the killer.'

'Be sensible, man,' said Joe Gray, 'why would Martha say she was up and about at the time of the murder if she was the murderer? Not even Martha's that dumb.'

'Thank you, dear,' said Martha Gray, then realized what her husband had said, and tutted.

'Couples might give each other an alibi, but everyone else? No.' I said, pointedly.

I knew I'd have to come clean soon. Not even I could cope with this level of tension for much longer. I forged ahead. 'You all know each other's secrets now – so you all have as much of a chance as I do of working out who had a good enough reason to kill Meg . . . though , of course, there's no such thing as a good enough reason to take a person's life. What I can tell you, as a professional, is that it takes more than a reason to kill someone. And it takes more than an opportunity – whether that opportunity is created, or naturally occurring. What it also needs is the ability of the killer to believe, deep within them, that they are truly more important than the victim; that their needs and desires outweigh those of anyone else. Sometimes a death is caused by a fleeting outburst – a fit of rage, a lashing out; in those instances the loss of perspective, the loss of judgement, the aspect of putting oneself before all else, is temporary – and it usually dissipates quickly, leaving guilt in its place. The killer may or may not make an effort to cover up the results of their fatal outburst, or their connection to it, but the feeling of terrible remorse, of a psychological burden they will carry for evermore, poses a real threat to their sanity, and their ability to live anything approaching a normal life thereafter. Was this such a killing? Is the murderer now feeling that burden? Or does the murderer still feel they were right to do what they did? That they were justified in removing Meg's ability to maybe expose them and their secrets?'

I couldn't wait any longer. It had to be done. I was sad. I was tired.

'So who here felt Meg should be wiped out, and with her any chance of their secrets coming out? Who felt so much more important than Meg? Was it about ownership? Was it, as I said, about love? And who here could kill? Has anyone here ever killed before? Peter – your hit and run; Adrian - an unexplained dead body; Dan – your wife's lover's work, ridiculed; Joe – your wife's lover dead; Luis – a suicidal ex. So many deaths. So much guilt. And what about you, Jean? What about your husband? I remember Mr Jones . . . I never did know his name; Meg called him Daddy. How did he die? Did he fall . . . or was he pushed? Why was Meg so keen to get away from you after his death? Why was she so frightened that she might become like you? Peter – it's time for the truth . . . you were lying to me, weren't you? Meg told you she saw something the night her father died, didn't she?'

Peter shook his head, then said, quietly, 'No . . . I wasn't lying. I just didn't tell you everything she told me. You see, Meg didn't see Jean push her father, she was hiding under her sheets because she was sick of the rows. She heard her do it. Apparently Jean screamed a whole bunch of obscenities, then Meg heard pushing and shoving. Meg believed her mother literally kicked her father down the stairs. That's why Meg had to get out.'

'Yes, it makes sense, to me,' I replied. 'That was the first time Meg ran away; that's where the pattern began. We psychologists like to find out when, where, and why, a coping mechanism is first utilized, you see. So –' we all turned and looked at Jean – 'what was it, Jean? A fit of temper and a hairdryer that was close to hand . . . or was it a planned action, using the little fan heater from your room? By the way, I know the answer, so just tell the truth, Jean.'

Jean Jones smiled a very unpleasant smile. 'Oh, you're so clever, aren't you, Caitlin Morgan? But just be careful girl; it's all well and good throwing accusations around, but there's no proof, is there? Not about Meg, nor about Hywel . . . that was Meg's father's name, by the way – Hywel. So you can say what you like. Sticks and stones, girl. I'm not saying anything more, and that's that. The police would never believe that a mother would kill her own daughter – nor her own husband. And you've got nothing; no fingerprints, no marks, no nothing.'

'How do you know, Jean?' Asked Adrian, sharply.

'Well, if everything was wiped down, like Cait said, then it stands to reason, doesn't it?' she gloated.

'I found the hairdryer in your room, Jean,' I said, flatly. 'Your hair is cut extremely short – not the sort of style that calls for a dryer that must have cost several hundred dollars, and has a North American plug on it; why would you own one like that anyway, given that you live in Wales? And what about the hamper of wet towels in your room, Jean? Why so many? You'd have needed to have bathed half a dozen times today to use all those towels. And when we found Meg's body we all looked like unmade beds; you were very well put together . . . burnt orange lipstick – before eight a.m.? Matched to your dressing gown, no less. Lots of attention to the wrong sort of detail there, Jean. And your constant referral to Meg as some sort of possession? What of that? You gave birth to her, but she'd stopped being your daughter a long time ago – why did you keep reminding us you were her mother?'

'Nothing on me – like I said, nothing,' repeated Jean Jones loudly.

Everyone in the room was clearly thinking through what I'd been saying, and it seemed to make sense to them too. I could tell Jean was keen to say something. I wondered if she'd stick to her very sensible plan to keep quiet.

She crowed, 'So how did I know Meg was even having a bath at four a.m., then, clever clogs?'

'Maybe you got up to use the loo and heard the water running—'

Jean cut across me, 'I wasn't next door to her, was I? She had that pretend-fiancé of hers one side, and bloody Martha Gray the other. I wouldn't have heard through all those rooms, would I?'

'—or maybe you were just going to try to talk to her about your secret; just a mother and daughter chat. She was about to take a bath, but let you in . . . you tell me, Jean . . .' I continued calmly.

'I'm not telling you nothing, 'cos you know nothing,' said Jean, vindicated.

'You're the only one here who's actually killed before, Jean – killed when they meant to,' said Peter Webber, holding his wife close to him. 'Whatever you say – and whatever Meg didn't say – I always thought she believed you killed her father.'

'Yes, none of us here have ever killed that way before,' said Adrian. 'I bet that makes a big difference, right, Cait?'

'Oh, yes, ask little Miss Smarty Pants, why don't you?' mocked Jean.

'It can do, Adrian,' I replied. I knew I'd sound like a know-it-all, so I just set about answering him. 'If you've come to terms with having taken one life, research suggests a person might find it easier to plan to, and to take, another. The mechanisms for diminishing, managing and coping with remorse are already in place, you see, and can be used to help justify future plans. Also, the unknown – the 'impossibility' of taking a human life – is no longer an issue for the killer . . . they know they've done it before, so they know they can do it again. Isn't that true, Jean? Once you've crossed a threshold, it's easier to return and cross it once again?'

'Rubbish – it's all rubbish. Don't pretend that any of you liked her . . . you must have all hated her. Look what she did to you all. She was a bad lot, was Meg. Just like her father; all fun and laughter when there were other people around, but when you were on your own with her? Not much fun then, was she? Yes, I can tell by your faces you all know exactly what I mean.'

'And where do you think she got that from, Jean?' It was Peter again. His eyes glittered in the firelight, but he still spoke softly. 'She got it from you. *You*. When Meg told us last night that we were the ones who'd made her what she was, she was right; we all chipped in our own little bit of hell for her. But Cait makes a good point; we all inherited a damaged Meg from you. I know these psychologist-types always say it starts with the mother – that you've got to go back to the womb and all that . . . but I think Cait's got it right. You killed Meg to stop her from writing about you and her father. She told me how horrible you were to her when she was growing up; how you would hit her, and undermine her every way you could. I thought she was exaggerating. Oh Jean, how could you? Your own daughter.'

Jean's fighting spirit was at its height. I could tell there was no way she'd confess, but wanted to push her just one more time.

I spoke again. 'You know what's ironic about all this, Jean? About what you did to Meg, and about what we've all been through here today? I called Meg's shrink this evening; the number was, predictably, programmed into her cellphone. I wanted to ask him about the "autobiography" they'd been working on together, and guess what he told me?'

I knew everyone wanted to hear this one.

'He said that what Meg had been doing was a part of her therapy, that she'd been working through past issues and writing them down, and that she'd invited us all here so she could apologize to us for how *she'd* treated *us*. She wasn't working on an autobiographical book, she'd just put together some notes for their sessions, and realized how she'd wronged us all. He knew exactly what she wanted to say to each of us – because he and Meg had discussed what she planned to say here this weekend; today, in fact, on her birthday.'

'And – what was she going to tell us?' asked Peter.

I replied, 'She wanted to apologize to you, Peter, for not letting you give yourself up after the hit-and-run. Adrian – she knew it wasn't your fault your baby had died, and she was sorry the death had poisoned her against you so much that she spread untrue stories about you and that unknown teen. Dan – she realized she hadn't supported you in the one way that mattered – with your work – and she wanted to come clean about the affair with your student Robert, the collapse of which, and his death, was why she left you. Luis – she was breaking up with you, but it was because she truly liked you, and wanted you to be happier than you could be by covering up your sexuality with her. Joe – she wanted to thank you for all you'd done and apologize for firing you and not trusting you. Martha – she'd broken your trust by telling your secret to her mother – she had to open up about that. To me, apparently she wanted to apologize for taking my boyfriend off me when we were sixteen . . . a boy who meant nothing to me six months after she stole him from me. And you, Jean? She wanted to apologize to you for not having been there to support you . . . as you've been battling cancer recently. She knew you wouldn't be able to travel for much longer, and was planning to take you around the world with her on one last Big Trip.'

I allowed time for all of this to filter through to the individuals, and the group.

We were a group now, an entity; we'd always have this weekend to bind us together. Nothing would be the same, for any of us, ever again. We all knew that.

No one spoke. We were all thinking about ourselves . . . and Meg.

Then Jean's harsh voice cut across our thoughts like a knife. 'Thinking about Meg, are you? Thinking about your futures? A year. That's about it for me. So I haven't got long to go, and I'll be with her. It was funny when you said she was killed for love, because she was . . . for the lack of love she gave me. If she was going to tell everyone about me and her father, then she didn't deserve the love of a good mother.'

'A good mother? A *good* mother?' Adrian had exploded; he was on his feet. 'What would you know about that? You killed your daughter because she didn't love you enough? Love has to be earned, it's not a right. You gave her life, then you poisoned it for her. You might be sick, Jean, but don't expect that to sway my opinion of you. You're a cold-hearted witch.'

'So will we tell the police about Jean when they get here?'

Needless to say, it was Sally Webber speaking.

Adrian was still boiling. 'Of course we will, Sally. She killed Meg, you stupid woman. What do you expect us to do? Draw straws and get someone else to confess to it just so that Jean can live her last year outside a cell? No way.'

'I don't know what we should do, but I know we should talk about it.' Joe Gray could smell a negotiation, and he was going for it. 'I mean, would anyone know that Meg was murdered? From an autopsy? Could we ask for there not to be an autopsy? Would there be bound to be an inquiry? Could we say we just found her dead . . . and forget all the rest of it? The memory of her for her fans would be much happier that way. I mean, it's not like she was a crime writer; if a crime writer died like this it could be great publicity. But a romance novelist? It kinda messes with the image – a murderous mom and all. It might be a kindness to Meg to not involve her mother.'

'You are right,' agreed Luis from his dark corner. 'It would be better for Meg's memory if she had just died. I will lie for Meg if this is what we agree. She lied for me. It is the least I can do.'

'That's outrageous,' boomed Dan James, who had something to say, at last. 'This woman has murdered an innocent person. Whatever any of us might think of Meg, she was, essentially, an innocent. And Jean killed her – because of pride, and to no effect in any case . . . because

Meg wasn't going to publish. Jean, you're a stupid, ignorant woman who put two and two together and got six. You killed your husband, and you killed your daughter; why should we let you get away with that?'

It seemed that at least two of Meg's ex-husbands agreed on something; they were both baying for Jean's blood. I wondered about Peter; would he prove to be the voice of reason? Whose side would he take?

'What about you, Peter? What do you think?' Martha Gray's question startled her husband. He looked at her accusingly.

Peter Webber looked at his wife, and then around the room. Again, as was his habit, he spoke quietly. 'At a time like this, I always ask myself "What would Jesus do?".'

Mouths fell open.

He continued. 'But, on this occasion specifically, I think it's better if we ask "What would Meg do?" She knew about all of us; it seems she had worked pretty hard to understand her own flaws. And what was she going to do? Forgive us all. She was going to take her mother on a wonderful trip, not throw her to the mob. I think, for once, we should take our lead from a mortal, rather than the divine . . . though I think they are both the same on this occasion. I think we should forgive Jean, and each of us should agree to tell one more lie . . . a lie that will protect Jean, but that will also protect Meg's memory from some pretty awful revelations. After all, who knows what might come out in a court of law if there's an investigation into what happened here this weekend.'

For all his talk about Jesus, I wondered to what extent Peter Webber was saving himself. Call me cynical, call me anything you like, but that's what I wondered.

Of course, everyone else got to thinking about what Peter had just said; I don't think it had occurred to anyone until then. I could feel the mood in the room change. And I didn't like it.

'Peter's got a point. It might well be what Meg would have wanted,' murmured Adrian.

'I suppose one could look at it that way,' rumbled Dan James from his fireside spot.

'Martha?' snapped Joe Gray.

'I think it would have been what Meg wanted,' she replied quietly.

'And I agree with my husband,' piped up Sally Webber.

So, once again, all eyes turned toward me.

See what I mean about 'Aftermath'? There always is one . . . and it always stinks.


I looked at the faces surrounding me. Already these people were my co-conspirators, and I could tell they wanted me to play along with their request that we should all lie about Meg's death.

Peter's comments had illuminated for everyone what I'd known all along; if Meg's death was portrayed as anything but natural or accidental, there'd be an investigation to seek to uncover exactly what I had uncovered – who might have wanted her dead, and why. And that wouldn't be good for the people sitting here in the firelight with me. Not good for their families, or their futures.

But good for justice. And good for poor Meg.

I have dedicated my career to those who've been wronged; if I didn't believe those who'd wronged them should be held to their responsibilities, why would I do that? Now I was being asked to do something that was utterly contrary to all my natural instincts. And I didn't like it. Not one bit.

If I agreed with everyone else, I'd be safe; otherwise, maybe I'd be the next one waking up dead. If I agreed, we'd all come up with a version of the discovery of Meg that could be seen as presenting a natural death; she could easily have died sitting up in bed. But I wondered about the forensics involved; I am at least sufficiently self-aware to know I have gaps in my knowledge-base.

I decided to play the situation out. For the moment.

'We could stick to the whole story about how we found her in bed,' I said. 'None of us will have to act that . . . all we'll have to do is tell the truth, which is always for the best. But there might be internal indications of electrocution that I know nothing about. So we'll have to say that someone originally found her dead in her bath – that her hairdryer must have fallen in by accident, and that she was pulled out of the bath, dressed, and put into bed all for decency's sake. If we decide to do this, I believe Jean should be the one who confesses that she did all that; it would be psychologically believable, and – since Jean did do it – she could truthfully answer any and all questions pertaining to the process. We all know that Jean's a good enough actress to carry it off; and she wouldn't want to bring any of us into it, because she's the one with everything to lose.'

Heads nodded around the room. It seemed like my plan was going to be accepted.

'But there is something else I need to know, before I could consider agreeing with such a plan,' I added. 'I need to ask Joe and Luis something; what happens to the income from Meg's as yet unpublished manuscripts, her future book sales, any movie income – all that? Do either of you know about plans for her estate?'

Joe and Luis exchanged glances.

'As far as we know,' said Joe, 'she didn't have any plans in place to circumvent everything going to her next of kin . . . her mother. We both believe she had no Will – her business manager mentioned it to her often, but Meg didn't deal well with "tomorrow".'

I suspected Joe was right.

I spoke again. 'So, Jean, for the rest of your short life, you'll be an incredibly wealthy woman. Who knows, you might even be able to buy yourself a cure for your cancer . . .' People shifted in their chairs; I wanted them to be uncomfortable, wanted them to understand the impact of what they were doing. 'But I guess that's unlikely. However, if everything of Meg's goes to you, who gets it all when you die? Have you any relatives?'

Jean shook her head. 'No relatives. My Will leaves everything to Meg.' She pushed out her chin defiantly. The irony was lost on none of us.

'Well, here's what you're going to do now, Jean; you're going to set up a charity that will get every cent after your death. It'll bear Meg's name and it'll support . . . what do we think is appropriate folks? Sex, drug and alcohol abuse counselling? Stillbirth grief counselling? Support and education in literature for young people? A creative writing program for teenagers . . . what?'

There was a general murmuring in the room.

'They're all good ideas, Cait,' said Peter, uncomfortably, 'but I have another suggestion; I know of a large number of very good charities that already exist. Many of them could do with a little help. Couldn't we band together and set up a foundation. We could help out lots of programs.'

This idea drew a louder rumbling of approval.

'How about you and Sally work with Jean, Joe and Luis, to make that happen then, Peter? And anyone else who wants to join in.' I said. I was hating myself a little less as I spoke. 'This could be something positive to come from Meg's untimely death that's greater than even she could have imagined.'

'Oh, Peter, you're so clever. Cait's so clever. Can we spend the rest of our lives giving away money to people who need it? Oh, what wonderful work. The Lord's work. How kind of Jean to do that with all of Meg's money.' Once again Sally had managed to stun me.

'So we're all agreed?' I asked, knowing that everyone was. 'Joe, Luis – did either of you mention any suspicious circumstances surrounding Meg's death to anyone you spoke to?'

Both Joe and Luis shook their heads.

I was pretty much on my last legs by now; I wanted my bed. But I still had a few things to say. 'I didn't mention anything specific to the emergency services' dispatcher, and, if I was hesitant about my feelings at the time, I can explain that by saying I was mystified that the body appeared to have been moved after death. So there we have it – Jean will not be accused of killing her husband and her daughter; we will all lie to protect her, and ourselves. Jean will accept her inheritance, graciously, and the four – well, five if we include Martha – of you will work with Jean to ensure the equitable distribution of Meg's current and future wealth. I'm sure that knowing your commercial efforts and deal-making will have a charitable outcome will redouble your efforts, Joe . . . maybe to the extent that you even have to drop your other clients and just work for the Meg Jones Foundation. None of us will ever speak about the things we have heard and done here this weekend, because we've all got too much to lose.'

I looked across the room at the killer. 'So, Jean, you're safe. Everyone's safe. All we have to do now is work on our consciences so that we don't have sleepless nights about this. And all you have to do, Jean, is come to terms with the fact that you killed your daughter for no reason – no reason at all. You put yourself before Meg; you believed that what people might have thought about you, even after your imminent death, was more important than your daughter's life. Maybe you'll manage to forgive yourself for that before the cancer gets you – but I never will.'

I stood – there wasn't much more to be done. 'I'm going to my room now. I'm exhausted. Maybe when we get up in the morning we can all see this in a different light. But I, for one, know I want to get away from here, and all of you, as soon as I can. As soon as the police have interviewed us all . . . which they will do . . . I'm off. Minibus or not – I'm out of here. Goodnight.'

I pulled myself up the stairs, crying with tiredness and . . . what was it?

The turmoil in my conscience.

I was struggling coming to terms with the fact that I'm naturally a 'retribution' person, rather than a 'greater good' one. I knew the decision – the pact – made downstairs was for the greater good, but had justice truly been served?

I knew I wouldn't sleep much that night; justice is such a huge concept that, when you start to think about it, it's difficult to stop.

It's so complex.

Should it be 'an eye for an eye'?

Or is it about forgiveness, and trying to create the best possible outcomes from tragedy and loss?

# SPRING

## THE CASE OF THE DESPERATE DUCHESS

### A WISE Enquiries Agency Mystery

Carol Hill pushed open the door to the WISE Enquiries Agency's office and knew immediately that it must have been Annie Parker who had closed up the night before. Annie always imagined no one would guess she'd been leaning out of the office window sneaking a sly smoke, but Carol's nose was hyper-sensitive to the merest hint of nicotine; as her doctor kept reminding her, you couldn't be too careful when you were trying to get pregnant.

Carol flung open all the windows, allowing the cool March air to waft in and carry the offensive odors away with it, then filled the kettle, ready to meet the demands of a nine a.m. meeting of all four partners in what had become their surely-doomed business venture.

Carol had prepared the financial statements necessary to prove to her three colleagues that they had very little time left before they had to make some Big Decisions about whether they were going to continue with their current undertaking. When they'd set up their private investigations practice three months earlier they'd all felt buoyant, invincible even. Brought together by a perplexing series of deaths, Carol Hill, Christine Wilson-Smythe, Mavis MacDonald and Annie Parker had formed themselves into the WISE Enquiries Agency; they'd decided it was a suitable name because their respective birthplaces were Wales, Ireland, Scotland, and England.

They all knew they'd never have been able to afford their office just off Sloane Square if not for the fact it was being donated free of charge by Christine's father – so that wasn't the root of their problem. No, the real issue was that they just weren't attracting enough business to sustain their needs for some sort of income for themselves. In fact, they'd only had three paying cases, each of which they'd managed to bring to a successful conclusion, but none of which had feathered their rather pathetic little financial nest. This was D-Day, as Carol had named it – Decision Day; what were their plans going to be for their immediate collective, and individual, futures?

Steeling herself for what she knew would be a difficult conversation, Carol also rehearsed how she'd give Annie what for about smoking in the office – when she finally arrived; Annie was usually a little late.

Carol wasn't surprised when Mavis bustled in fifteen minutes ahead of the meeting; Mavis's nursing and military background allowed her to plan any journey with precision. Indeed, Mavis was capable of organizing just about anything with an admirable exactitude, and was a wonderful business partner to have if a case even tangentially connected to the world of medicine; it seemed that, throughout her varied career, Mavis had established an enviable network of connections covering what appeared to be the entire British medical system, and beyond.

Annie hurled herself through the door at about three minutes past nine – complaining bitterly about the unreliability of the buses, and bemoaning her already sweaty state. As Annie wiped her face with a moist towelette, Carol told her exactly what she thought of her smoking sneaky cigarettes when she was at work.

Carol was pleased Annie didn't answer back with her usual cheek, but suspected she was thinking it anyway. She loved Annie almost like a sister, and their friendship of many years was something she held dear, but she knew her friend's shortcomings better than most, and didn't feel she should have to put up with them. So she said so. Directly.

Carol was feeling especially wretched, and wasn't looking forward to being the person who'd have to act tough when it came to finances – but she had to do it, because she and her husband David had agreed that, while they could pretty much get by on just his income alone, they'd been expecting Carol's new line of work to at least provide some additional money for the savings pot they were trying to fill to be able to buy a bigger flat, ready for whenever they managed to get pregnant.

The three women waited impatiently for Christine's arrival, with coffee and tea, but no biscuits; Carol felt they couldn't run to biscuits. Conversation was strained, especially following Carol's telling-off of Annie, with no one wanting to start The Big Discussion without all four partners being present.

By a quarter past nine Annie Parker had had enough. 'This is annoying,' she exclaimed, giving voice to the emotion filling the room.

'I know it's 'er dad's money keeping us 'ere, but why can't Chrissy ever be on time for anything?'

Carol almost smiled; Annie's broad cockney accent always seemed to shine most when she was annoyed, or whispering, or in danger.

Mavis MacDonald's rolling Scottish brogue didn't need an excuse – it was front and center whenever she opened her mouth. 'Ach, I know, dear,' she replied soothingly, 'but she's one of those girls for whom the world has always waited – so what can we expect?'

'True,' agreed Carol, resignedly.

'If either of us two other girls were this late for a meeting you'd be banging on about it for ages. Why do you let her get away with it?' Annie sounded more than a little irritated.

Carol knew she had a point, and decided to try to calm the situation. 'I love it when you call us "girls".'

'Well, you know what I mean,' sulked Annie.

It was true that none of the women had been 'girls' for some time; Mavis had recently retired from her post as Matron at the Battersea Barracks and was in her early sixties, Carol was past thirty – hence the panic about pregnancy, and Annie was absolutely not enjoying the hot flashes she was suffering in her early fifties. If you stretched the term 'girl' it could possibly be allowed for Christine who, still in her late twenties, was the youngest of the quartet of enquirers.

The telephone rang. It startled Carol, but she regained her composure and picked up the receiver. 'Good morning, the WISE Enquiries Agency, how may I help?'

Annie whispered loudly to Mavis, 'Listen to that posh accent she uses when she answers the phone. Hardly know she was Welsh when she talks like that, would you?' Carol saw her wink at Mavis, then roll her eyes, adding, 'I bet that's Chrissy with some pathetic excuse for being late.'

Carol did her best to focus on what Christine was saying on the phone. She listened intently, then replied, 'We're on our way,' before she hung up.

'So? That was the Honourable Miss Hoity-Toit, was it?'

Carol knew very well that Annie loved to make fun of Christine's high birth, but deep down felt respect for the daughter of a viscount, who had only recently packed in a highly successful career as a Lloyd's broker, played the piano, bridge and field hockey very well, could speak five languages fluently, and was on more charity committees than you could shake the proverbial stick at. And she was attractive.

And Mensa clever. None of which dented Annie's avowed duty to make sure Christine was kept 'in her place'.

Carol searched for words.

'Come on, Car, what's up?' Annie laughed.

Carol looked directly at Annie through narrowed eyes and, very uncharacteristically, let go with both barrels. 'I'm not a bloody "car", Annie, I am a person. I am Carol. Don't use that name for me, you know I hate it.'

Mavis's eyebrows silently told Carol she didn't care for her tone.

Carol chose to ignore Mavis, for once. 'You're both coming with me,' she said, standing and shoving all her communication devices into her large shoulder bag. 'Christine's in a mess – her cousin needs our help – urgently. Her Aunt Agatha wants us to come over to her house. I said we were on our way.'

Annie and Mavis exchanged knowing looks.

'Time of the month, Carol?' enquired Annie, sarcastically.

That was it; Carol burst into tears, she just couldn't help herself. 'Yes it is, and I'm feeling so wretched I'm sure I'm not pregnant. Again. But there's no need to be so cruel about it.'

Annie held her face, looking truly horrified, then stood and hugged Carol.

'Sorry, doll,' she said quietly. 'I never thought that . . . well, that's me all over innit? Silly old mare, me. Just ignore me, Car. And wipe them eyes while I nip outside and find us a cab; I'm assuming we can afford a cab between us? Where are we going anyway?'

'Wraysbury Square,' replied Carol as she sniffed into a paper hanky. 'Lord Wraysbury's house itself, in fact – you know, the big white one they always show on documentaries about the landed gentry. Turns out that Christine's father's sister – her aunt – is Lady Agatha Wraysbury. Who knew? When they say money goes to money they mean it, don't they? In London landowning there's Grosvenor, then Cadogan, then Wraysbury – they have to be worth billions.'

Mavis observed, 'Unusual for you to comment on social status in such acidic terms, Carol.'

Carol sighed, 'You're right. Sorry. Having been raised on a sheep farm in Carmarthen, then working in the City and meeting all sorts of idiots with fancy backgrounds, titles don't bother me usually, as you know. If you grow up on a farm you've seen enough of life to know that animals and humans are basically all the same, so why worry about what your title is, or isn't? But today – I'm just a bit off, Mavis. Sorry.'

Having walked to Sloane Square to find a cab, all three 'girls' finally stood at the door of the largest mansion on Wraysbury Square. It didn't have a number, it just said 'Magna' above the door.

'Why's it called that?' asked Annie.

Carol wasn't sure if Annie really cared what the answer was, but could tell at least Mavis was impressed that she happened to know all about it. 'It's a reference to the fact that Lord Wraysbury's estate, near Windsor, includes the little island where the Magna Carta was signed in 1215; apparently it was only ever signed by King John thanks to the noted intervention of Lord Wraysbury's ancestors, many of whom have continued to shape British, and by extrapolation much of the rest of the world's, legal systems.'

Carol chose to ignore Annie's eye-roll, and focused instead on Mavis's remark of, 'Highly informative, Carol. Thank you.'

The door was opened by a surprisingly handsome, strapping, young man of no more than twenty-five years, and no less than six feet and four inches; a delightful combination, as far as Carol was concerned. She immediately pegged him as being of great use to any rugby team.

'We're here at the request of Christine Wilson-Smythe,' announced Mavis briskly, the power of speech seeming, momentarily, to have left both Carol and Annie.

'Come in, won't you.' The smiling young man's strong Irish accent made it sound like an invitation to dance. 'I'll let Her Grace know you've arrived. Would you wait here in the library, please? I shall return presently.'

As he waved them into a vaulted room stuffed to the rafters with what Carol could see were law books, Annie blew out her cheeks in appreciation of their greeter's visible attributes, behind his back. Carol allowed herself a coy smile.

'Down, girls,' admonished Mavis with a twinkle, ever the matron used to overseeing young nurses when it came to Annie and Carol.

The strapping young man, sadly, didn't return at all – instead it was Christine who rushed breathlessly into the grand room. 'Thanks ever so for coming,' she gushed. 'I don't know what I'd do without you – Aunt Agatha's in such a state I've had to sit her down with a brandy. It's Jacintha, you see. Her daughter. My cousin. Jacintha's distraught because a young girl who works for her has gone missing, and she's sure something terrible has happened to her. Jacintha and Agatha don't want to involve the police – yet. They and Uncle Richard – Lord Wraysbury – have agreed to let us try to find the missing girl. The girl is a favorite of Jacintha's and some cash has gone missing too, but Jacintha is convinced this girl wouldn't have stolen it.'

Christine finally drew a breath, then added, 'We'll help, won't we? Aunt Aggie said money's no object, and I know WISE is desperate for a case that pays well, and she really is incredibly rich. I've agreed four thousand a day plus expenses, and a ten grand bonus when we find the girl. Will that do?'

Three astonished faces stared at Christine.

'Gordon Bennett! Good job, Chrissy,' said Annie, who was the first to react.

Carol was stunned. 'That would take the pressure off,' she admitted.

Mavis spoke thoughtfully, 'I think that's a fair fee,' she responded coolly, 'but we won't do anything illegal, Christine, and if it becomes clear a criminal act is involved, we'll immediately report it to the police, as we must.' She was being firm.

'But of course,' replied Christine sweetly. 'I didn't mean to imply any sort of impropriety – just that if we can find her assistant before we need to call in the police, Jacintha thinks it would be best for the girl's reputation.'

'Well, so long as we're clear on that one, Miss Wilson-Smythe,' replied Mavis formally.

'Oh, come off it, Mavis, it's me, Christine – don't Wilson-Smythe me, please. Anyway, it was Aunt Aggie who wanted a fee agreed before she'd even let me get in touch with you; she's very business-like you know. In fact, she might even give you a run for your money, Mavis.'

Mavis's eyebrows suggested she thought this hardly likely. She turned to Annie and Carol, purposefully hooking her short, neat, grey hair behind her ears as she did so; all three of her colleagues knew her mannerisms well enough to realize this signified she meant business.

Serious business.

Mavis spoke gravely. 'Well, what do you say, girls? It's a great deal more than anyone else has ever paid us, and if we find her quickly we could have the bonus money in the bank by the end of the week – then there'd be no worries for another few months, I'd say.'

Annie managed a: 'Du-uh, go for it,' and Carol vigorously nodded her agreement.

'Right then,' said Mavis. She turned militarily on her heel to face Christine once more. 'I'm assuming you're for it?' Christine nodded. 'Of course, we'll need to get all the facts as they are known,' continued Mavis, 'and we'll need real insight and information to be able to do our best, you know that, Christine – can you make sure the family understands that, and co-operates?'

'Of course,' gushed Christine. 'I told Aunt Aggie all that this morning, before I phoned you. By the way – we can have that nasty meeting about money some other time, can't we? Much better to be making it, than talking about it, eh?'

Christine was surprisingly light-hearted in her manner as she led her three colleagues upstairs to the morning room to meet her aunt. Carol wondered what the woman whose husband owned a ridiculous amount of land in London, and beyond, would be like. She hoped she'd be nice, and not stuck-up; Carol didn't like people who were stuck-up.

Mavis could tell – by the looks on their faces – that Lady Agatha Wraysbury wasn't what Annie or Carol had expected. As Matron of Battersea Barracks she'd met many family members of the retired soldiers in her charge, quite a number of whom had been titled, so she was less surprised than her colleagues by the sight that met them as they entered the morning room.

A woman around her mid-fifties, red-haired, freckled, compact and hard-bodied, sat curled in a large armchair upholstered in a jovial floral print, sipping amber liquid from a huge crystal brandy bowl. She wore faded jeans topped by a white shirt with a stripe that exactly matched her new-penny hair. Her feet were bare.

As she rose to greet her guests, it was clear she was just about five feet tall; she stood nose-to-nose with Mavis, but Annie towered a foot above her. Tea, coffee and home-made biscuits were already spread on a silver tray on a table beside her, and the duchess allowed Christine to take the lead in the conversation while she served refreshments.

'Now stop me if I get any of this wrong, Aunt Aggie.' Lady Agatha Wraysbury nodded as Christine began, 'Jacintha phoned you at seven a.m. because her assistant, Poppy Brown, had failed to arrive at Jacintha's florist shop with the stock she was supposed to have gone to the New Covent Garden Market to purchase this morning. Jacintha knows Poppy left the shop at about three p.m. yesterday afternoon, but she never arrived at the shop at four a.m. this morning to collect the van. The van's still there, but there's no sign of Poppy. Jacintha has already been to Poppy's flat, and there's no sign of her there either. And she couldn't see the cash in an obvious place when she used the key Poppy leaves at the shop for emergencies to go in to check if Poppy was at home. Correct?'

Lady Agatha nodded and replied in a pleasantly deep, rounded voice, 'Correct, dear. Jacintha has tried Poppy's mobile phone, but it's going to voicemail. Repeatedly.' She looked across the tea tray at Carol, Mavis and Annie. 'I'll admit, ladies, I have had misgivings about Poppy; true, her arms bear an inordinate number of tattoos . . . but this fact is not the root of my concerns. No, it's her choice in men-friends which has given me pause; Jacintha has told me some worrying tales about Poppy's proclivity for preferring to consort with men of a certain sort. And I have some grave worries that her choices might have led to . . . well, this. My husband and I have agreed we'll support Jacintha's decision to not call in the police at this time, but both he and I are terribly worried – because our daughter is terribly worried. Our call to you is our attempt at a compromise.'

Mavis could tell Annie was all but squirming with questions; she glared at her colleague, hoping she'd keep quiet for a moment longer.

Christine continued, 'Jacintha trusts Poppy, you see, and feels she wouldn't have done anything like run off with cash. Poppy is the only person trusted by Jacintha to purchase flowers from the market. Jacintha believes she's reliable, and totally trustworthy, Aunt Aggie.'

'You told me I had to be truthful when I spoke to your colleagues, Christine, and that's all I'm being. Truthful.' Lady Agatha's tone remained calm.

'And that's most helpful, Your Grace,' said Mavis, hoping to cut Annie off before she leaped in. It didn't work.

Annie cleared her throat. 'Any chance we could talk to Jacintha herself?' Mavis thought it was a sensible request.

Christine nodded. 'She can't leave the shop. It's Mothering Sunday in two days – so this is one of her busiest times of the year. She's overwhelmed. But I can get her on my phone and ask her whatever we want. She offered.'

Christine made the call, and put Jacintha on speakerphone. The process took about fifteen minutes, then the women allowed Jacintha to return to her duties.

Mavis referred to her notes. 'So, to summarize,' she announced, gaining everyone's attention, 'Poppy's been with Jacintha for more than two years; she began there to gain work experience, then became a trainee, and now is her trusted assistant. Poppy is habitually responsible for taking sums of cash home with her overnight, then collecting the company van from the garage beside the shop in Holbein Mews to arrive at the New Covent Garden Market to purchase flowers soon after it opens at four a.m. She's usually back at the shop, with the stock all suitably stored before seven a.m., at which time Jacintha comes down from her apartment upstairs, and they begin to create the floral arrangements either for the shop, of for deliveries to be made that day.'

Mavis paused and looked up. Everyone nodded.

She continued, 'Poppy left the shop at the end of her day yesterday, around three p.m., and told Jacintha she was meeting someone for a drink that evening. She didn't specify who. She was going home to change, and drop off the funds she'd need for the next morning. Jacintha hasn't been in contact with Poppy at all since then, with the exception of having received a "selfie" from Poppy, which the girl sent last evening around seven thirty p.m., saying she was having a lovely time. It shows Poppy and an unknown male. This morning there's been no sign of Poppy; the company van hasn't moved since yesterday, and Jacintha has discovered that Poppy did not go to the flower market this morning. She ascertained this fact by speaking to a couple of the people she knows there who were, indeed, surprised to not see Poppy there today – of all days – it being one of their busiest of the year, due to the fact most florists see an increase in business of around five hundred percent for Mothering Sunday floral purchases.'

Another check, more nodding heads.

'Poppy had a sum of ten thousand pounds when she left the shop yesterday, in cash. This is not the largest sum she's ever been trusted with. There have been no problems before. Jacintha is absolutely convinced Poppy is trustworthy.'

'She kept saying "Poppy's a good girl", didn't she?' said Annie. 'Your Grace says Poppy might have a bit of a weakness for men-friends who aren't all that pleasant.' Mavis could tell Annie was hunting for all the right words. 'Jacintha doesn't know who Poppy was meeting for a drink. Could that be something, do we think?'

'I know you'll think I'm a mother blind to her daughter's imperfections,' said Lady Wraysbury, 'but I don't believe I am. It's not easy growing up with money and a title in a society that's obsessed by both. It's so easy to get side-tracked, or just coast along for years without doing anything useful at all. I've seen it a dozen times in the children of my friends. But, from a young age, Jacintha knew what she wanted to do, and took a great deal of time learning how to do it, and become good at it. She has some wonderful contracts, and her floral designs have won awards. JWF is the shop at which most of London's better people choose to purchase the flowers they want to give to loved ones. She's doing well for herself, and I'm terribly proud of her.

But she's never been the best at judging people, and she's always had a weakness for "strays". I'm hoping this girl Poppy hasn't taken her in.'

Mavis understood what Lady Agatha meant. 'I have two boys myself,' she said, 'and I love them, true enough, but I could run off a list as long as my arm of the things they're no good at. However, that doesn't mean I can't be surprised by them, sometimes.'

'Jacintha thinks something bad has happened to Poppy,' said Christine. 'I say we give Poppy the benefit of the doubt for a while, and do what we can before getting the police involved; once they know about that cash, Poppy's reputation is in jeopardy. Maybe she's lying hurt somewhere, doesn't know who she is for some reason, or can't speak . . .' Her voice trailed off. 'We should check the hospitals and so forth straight away.'

'Could Jacintha send you the "selfie" she received, Christine, and you forward it to us all?' asked Carol. 'I'll dig up contact info for all the hospitals. I'll get myself back to the office to do it, because I'll have access to more and better equipment there. Why don't I get going with that?'

Everyone agreed, and Mavis said as Carol rose, 'I think we should all take a taxi back to the office. Christine – would you prefer to come with us, or stay here with your aunt?'

Lady Wraysbury answered. 'You go, Christine. I'm worried about Jacintha, of course, but more about how she's going to manage on such a busy day when she doesn't have anyone to help her, than about the money; it's a large amount, certainly, but we can help her with that. What I cannot do is find her an experienced florist at short notice, nor – apparently – a way to replace the stock she needed for today. I believe she's begging all she can get from her contacts at the market, and they're helping her out by delivering what they have left that she can use. Poor girl; if I had any ability in the flower-arranging department myself I'd lend a hand, but I have . . . oh my dear me! Why did I not think of that?' Lady Agatha shooed the women of the WISE Enquiries Agency out, saying, 'I have a girl who comes in to do the flowers for us here twice a week. I'll phone her immediately. Maybe she can lend a hand. You do what you can, and I shall do what I am able. Please keep me informed.'

Mavis left having developed a liking for the duchess, and also having been pleased to hear the woman's natural Irish brogue creep through the cracks in her clipped English accent just before they left, when she'd been at her most natural, and excited. A bit like Christine, really. The family connection was clear to see.

Lady Agatha called, 'Tell Riordan to hail a cab for you, I'm phoning my girl.'

Mavis nodded.


Poppy Brown peeled open her heavy eyelids, and sneezed. Everything around her was dark. She couldn't move; her hands were tied behind her back, and her ankles were bound. She was lying down, curled up in the fetal position. She tried to extend her body, but her feet and head hit walls. Wriggling around didn't help; there were four walls very close about her. She tried to sit upright, but there wasn't enough room. The words 'Little Ease' drifted into her consciousness from a history lesson somewhere in her past.

Gathering her thoughts and limbs about herself she managed, finally, to bring her feet through her arms so that her hands were in front of her body; she silently, and wryly, acknowledged that her years of gymnastics at school were paying off in the most unlikely manner. It was too dark for her to see the hands she held up in front of her eyes, and the cords binding her wrists were so tight she could barely feel her fingertips. She wriggled her fingers, trying to bring some life back to them, and did the same with her toes. Poppy had no idea where she was, or why she was there.

Finally able to rub her itchy nose, Poppy felt around her wrist-bonds with her tongue. She could make out narrow, flat leather cords that had been wound around and around her wrists and tied with many knots, in several places. She started to pick at a knot with her teeth, tasting the bitterness of the wet leather.

A slight movement of the air brushed her cheek. She turned her face toward the direction of the faint breeze and sniffed. Someone was frying bacon, somewhere not too far off. The smell set off her saliva glands, which ached as they watered. Poppy realized she was hungry.

She wondered when she'd last eaten . . . then what day it was, what time it was, and how long she'd been there . . . wherever 'there' was.

And she wondered why whoever had put her in this place hadn't bothered to do anything to prevent her from shouting out. Her instincts told her not to take advantage of this seeming oversight, but to try to get her hands free, or at least to try to get her eyes to focus on something – anything – to allow her some sense of place.

She was feeling totally disorientated, and, truth be told, more than a little frightened.

What the hell was going on?

As she nibbled at the leather on her wrists, she thought back to the last thing she could remember; it had been Thursday evening, and she'd met her brother Rob at The Hereford Bull on Gloucester Road for a drink and an early meal. He was up from Brighton for a long weekend with his girlfriend Helen, who lived along the road from the pub. Then . . . nothing.

What had happened to bring her to this place?

And where was Rob?

'Turn the gas down – you'll burn it,' shouted Gary to Natasha.

'Shut your bleedin' face, or cook it yourself,' Natasha screamed back.

'I ain't eating no sandwiches with no burned bacon in 'em,' shouted Gary toward the kitchen.

'All the more for me then,' came the reply over the loud sizzling.

Gary Gilchrist thought about his girlfriend's response, and decided to take action. He hoisted himself out of his armchair. As he peered into the grimy kitchen he saw Natasha Moon slathering margarine onto slices of thick, white bread. She looked up at him, defiantly, through clouds of greasy blue smoke, and poked out her tongue.

'Tash. You're bleedin' burnin' it, you silly cow. Turn the gas down,' shouted Gary, but the singer on the radio wailed ever louder as Natasha pushed hard on the volume button, and Gary's protests were drowned out. He walked away, grumbling to himself.

If it wasn't for the fact she was pretty accommodating between the sheets, Tash would have been out long ago, but she served her purpose, he supposed. However, he wondered if she had it in her to stick with him and keep her mouth shut, with what he had planned. She might be a good old party gal, but she'd already kicked up a fuss about trying to feed the girl he'd locked in the coal cellar. Tash knew too much for him to let her out of his sight now, he knew that. Maybe when he'd picked up the ransom money Tash would have to have a little 'accident'; after all, he'd be able to afford a much better class of bird when he was a millionaire.

He'd dropped off the ransom note last night. If they followed the instructions they'd be ringing soon. Gary looked at the clock on the mantelpiece – almost ten thirty. He'd better turn the girl's phone back on again. Not long now, he thought, and he snapped open a can of beer. It fizzed onto his hand. As he licked it dry, he noticed there was blood under his thumbnail.

Stupid bugger, fighting like that, he thought. Why hadn't the big feller just gone quietly? Obviously he should have put more of the stuff in his beer, but how was he to know he'd have the constitution of an ox? If only he'd passed out, like her downstairs, he wouldn't have had to knock him out the second time, and cut him. And when he'd cut him, he'd bled like a stuck pig. It was all over the inside of the van; he'd probably never get it off. Not that it mattered, of course, 'cos after he'd picked up the three million quid they were going to give him, he'd never need to go near no van ever again.

As he thought about the money, he wondered if he should have asked for more. The girl's father had more money than he knew what to do with, so of course he'd pay up. There hadn't been anything on the telly, so he was pretty sure he'd have kept the coppers out of it, like Gary had told him to in the note.

Yes, by this time tomorrow he'd be three million quid better off, and set for life. He'd be able to get out of this dump and travel the world in fine style. All he had to do was pick up the money and he'd be on Easy Street. He stabbed at the remote control, changing channels blindly, then spotted something that caught his eye.

'Tash, come here!'

'Bleedin' 'ell, Gary, do you want these sarnies or what? I can't be doin' two things at once, can I? What's up now?'

'Look at this on the telly. Showing off her flower shop, ain't they? Not 'cos she's gorn, but 'cos it's Mothers' Day coming up. See? Her shop, and a load more of 'em. Waste of money, flowers, right?'

'Yeah, right,' replied Tash. Gary wondered why she sounded so dreamy when she said it. Silly mare.

Gary and Natasha stood in front of the television laughing and eating their bacon sandwiches. Then the tiny silver mobile phone Gary had set upon the mantelpiece sprang to life.

'That'll be His Knobship, I reckon,' said Gary with a cocky wink, 'so turn the telly down and let's do it.'

Natasha adjusted the volume and giggled a little.

Gary pushed the button on the phone and said, 'Hello,' in the deepest, roughest voice he could manage.

'I say – who's that?' The voice was posh, a woman.

'None of your business.' Gary was purposely brusque.

'To whom am I speaking?' The voice was high, clipped, very precise.

Gary kept his cool. 'That's for me to know,' he replied, cockily.

'And for me to find out, I suppose?'

The woman was playing with him. Snotty cow. But he'd have the last laugh.

'I want three million, like the note to His Knobship said, or she's dead.' Gary made sure he sounded business-like.

'Note? What note?' the woman sounded puzzled. She was playing for time. He wouldn't let her get away with it.

'Don't mess with me – you wouldn't 'ave rung if it weren't for the note. Three million like it said, where it said, when it said.'

'But I've lost the note,' came the woman's plaintive cry.

Gary knew she was messing with him, and pushed the button to end the conversation. 'Tit,' he shouted at the phone.

'What did they say – what?' screamed Natasha, her eyes wide and wild.

'Maybe they've got someone who's not the police trying to trace the call, that's what. Some posh bird was talkin' rubbish. Ramblin' on, sayin' she'd lost the note.'

'How can they have lost the note?' squealed Natasha. 'You stapled it to that bloke's ear before you dumped 'im out the van, for Chrissakes.'

'Exactly,' replied Gary. 'You can't exactly loose nothin' stapled to a person's ear like that, can yer?'

'Yeah,' replied Natasha emphatically, then added an equally forceful, 'Nah.'

They both jumped when the telephone rang again.

'What?' shouted Gary when he answered.

'I'm sorry, I shouldn't have upset you,' said the woman's voice.

That was more like it. At least she knew who was in charge.

'I just wanted to clarify your instructions.' She sounded frightened.

'Look,' shouted Gary, just about holding onto the edge of his temper, 'like I said in the note, put three million quid in unmarked notes into a sports bag in the bin by the third bench along from the statue of the Frog Prince in Battersea Park. There are only three benches along there and each one has a bin by it – put it in the end bin by the end bench. Noon tomorrow. That's it.'

He turned off the telephone altogether and nodded emphatically at Natasha. 'And then all we've got to do is pick up the money and get out of here. You won't mind helpin' me with that little job, will yer, Tash?'

Natasha looked doubtful. 'I'm not sure about that, Gary. I mean, they might have police everywhere.'

'You don't think I'm that stupid, do yer? That bin by that bench is surrounded by trees – they won't see us till we've gone, and then it'll be too late. All you've got to do is dress up in them old overalls, act like you're emptying the bin, bring the bag to the van, and we'll be off.'

They shared a brown sauce-flavored kiss.

As his hands explored Tash's body, Gary's mind wandered back through the conversation with the Posh Bitch.

Lost the note? What did they take him for? An idiot? They'd pay up alright – and nothing on the news meant they hadn't called in the police. Now all he had to do was wait, collect the money and ride off into the sunset. He'd put Tash in the firing line, 'cos, essentially, she was disposable. But he'd hang onto her, while she had her uses.


On the way to the office, all four women received a copy of the selfie Poppy Brown had taken in a pub the previous night from Jacintha.

The quartet studied it as the taxi made slow headway through the gathering traffic.

'I know that place.' Christine was gleeful. She pointed to the background she'd enlarged. 'Those posters on the wall, for old films; they're at The Hereford Bull.'

Annie was impressed, and allowed herself to sound it when she commented, 'Good girl – it pays to know your pubs. Just what I'm always saying.'

'Are you sure?' Carol was squinting, and sounded dubious.

Christine was. 'Jacintha said Poppy was meeting someone at a pub on the Gloucester Road, and The Hereford Bull is there. Great pub food – menu on a blackboard. Nice brickwork. I know it well, and I've sat under those posters. I'm absolutely certain that's where this photo was taken.'

It was agreed among the group that someone should visit the pub, to try to discover the identity of the unknown man. As soon as Christine volunteered, Annie added she'd join her – on the basis that you never knew what might come up, and that she always enjoyed a trip to a pub, even if it was on business. So the pair left Carol and Mavis to return to the office, while they took up positions on the roadside, hoping to be able to get a taxi quickly.

Annie swore liberally at the traffic as the cab she and Christine had eventually managed to hail battled its way along Park Lane, then became embedded among others of its ilk on Gloucester Place.

Meanwhile, Christine continued in her fruitless attempts to reach Poppy on her telephone. Eventually Annie could tell she'd made a breakthrough, but couldn't make any sense of Christine's side of the conversation.

'That was quite extraordinary,' said Christine to Annie as she stared at the device in her hand. 'Some chap just answered Poppy's phone and as good as threatened to kill Poppy if I didn't follow instructions in some ransom note he thinks he's delivered.'

Annie was taken aback. 'What ransom note? Your cousin never said anything about a ransom note, nor did your aunt.'

'Indeed they didn't – and I'm sure at least one of them would have mentioned such a thing. But the man said he'd sent it to "His Knobship" which is very odd, because I know Jacintha's father would have mentioned something like a ransom note to Aunt Agatha, and she to us.'

Annie was worried, and puzzled. The cab driver, who appeared to have overheard some key words of their conversation, peered into his rear-view mirror with a look of concern.

'Did you hang up?' asked Annie.

'No, he hung up on me,' replied Christine.

Annie gave the situation some thought. 'I think you should phone him back, Chrissy, and find out what he thinks he put in his so-called ransom note.'

Christine paused for a moment, then agreed. She redialed Poppy's number. Annie waited with baited breath, trying to read the notes Christine was scribbling on the pad balanced on her knee. When the expression on Christine's face told Annie the call had ended, Christine pushed the redial button again.

'He's turned the phone off completely. It's going to voicemail again. There was something in the man's voice I didn't like; I think he was trying to sound sort of gruff and rough, but – underneath it all – I think he really was serious.'

Annie didn't like the sound of it; Chrissy was pretty good at judging stuff like that.

'Bum,' remarked Annie, succinctly. 'What does he want? Exactly? Did he say?'

The cab driver slowed long before he needed to at a set of amber lights; Annie was in no doubt he was straining to hear what they were saying, so ensured the privacy window was shut, and hoped it worked.

Christine whispered, 'Three million in unmarked notes, here . . .' She pointed at her pad, where Annie could just about read her scribbles. 'Then we have to do this . . .' Christine pointed to the notes again.

Annie understood why Chrissy didn't want the cab driver to know what was going on, and was aghast. 'You think they've kidnapped Poppy?' She'd never been good at whispering, but did her best. However, she wasn't quiet enough for her exclamation to have escaped the practiced ear of the cabbie; it seemed the privacy window didn't work too well after all.

'If some bloke wants three mill in notes, he'd better have a great big bag for it, and be a weight lifter, or have it in hundred-pound notes; and nobody takes them these days, not even us cabbies. Too many fakes around,' he said.

'Oi, we're having a private conversation back here,' snapped Annie.

'Sort of conversation you should be having with a copper, if you ask me,' retorted the cabbie.

'Look, mate,' responded Annie, her hackles up, 'number one, we're not asking you, and number two, we're private detectives and quite capable of sorting this for ourselves, ta very much, so keep your bleedin' nose where it should be – in other words, pointin' straight ahead and out of our business.'

She pushed the so-called privacy glass shut again with a bump, and could tell from the back of his head that the cabbie was silently responding to her outburst. She was glad that at least he was finally moving toward their destination.

'He might be right you know, Chrissy,' she conceded. 'I mean, we haven't really dealt with anything like this before, have we?' Annie kept imagining her mother having kittens about her getting mixed up with a kidnapping plot; Eustelle and Rodney Parker had migrated to the East End of London from St Lucia in the 1950s so their future children could have better career options than were available on their beloved, but poor, island. Annie was one-hundred-percent sure her mother wouldn't think of this bit of the reality of her life as a private investigator as representing that dream; Eustelle had told her exactly what she'd thought of her new job when she'd outlined the plans for the agency, and those plans hadn't involved anything as potentially dangerous as a kidnapping.

'Okay,' Annie continued, 'judging by the traffic, we've got about ten minutes before we get to The Hereford Bull. First things first – do you think this is just some chancer who's found Poppy's phone and is playing with us?'

'I think he's really got her,' Christine replied, sounding grim, 'and I think he might hurt her, too. There was something in his voice.'

Annie could tell the telephone conversations had really shaken Christine. 'Right then,' she said decisively, 'you call your Auntie Ag and find out if her husband got a ransom note for Poppy that he's forgotten to mention. I'll phone Car and pass on all this info; they need to know about this back at the office – agreed?'

Christine nodded.

Annie could tell her colleague was worried, and she couldn't help but wonder if more resources and experience than the WISE Enquiries Agency possessed were needed. Maybe she should try to persuade Chrissy to talk her cousin into calling in the police after all. It sounded as though Poppy was in real trouble.

As Annie phoned the office to bring their colleagues up to speed, Christine called her aunt. Annie was finished more quickly than Christine, so she sat quietly, cursing the traffic, and watching her colleague contorting her face as she spoke. It seemed it had taken some time for the duchess to make it to the telephone herself.

'Aunt Aggie?' Christine opened. 'Would it be alright with you if I allowed Annie to listen in? Good. Wait a mo.'

Christine handed Annie one of her pair of ear buds; Annie didn't care for the idea of putting an already-used ear bud into her own ear, but she could tell it was the only way she'd be able to listen without the cabbie overhearing the entire conversation. She shoved it in, and hoped the Hon. Christine Wilson-Smythe didn't have anything nasty lurking in her shell-likes.

Lady Wraysbury was speaking.

'No, no one has brought a note of any sort to the house, darling, I would have mentioned that. And I know Dickie would have mentioned anything of the sort he might have received at the House of Lords, or at his office in the City – he's been telephoning constantly to find out how this matter is progressing. And either, or both, of us would most certainly have mentioned a ransom note to you.'

Annie could tell that Lady Agatha was moving about as she spoke; she heard a door being closed somewhere in Magna on Wraysbury Square.

Lady Agatha now spoke more clearly. 'There, I'm alone now. Christine, what's happened? What have you found out?' Her voice had raised an octave.

Christine grimaced at Annie, then set about bringing her aunt up to date.

When she'd finished, her aunt was speechless for a moment, then with a trembling voice said, 'This sounds dreadful. I'll talk to Jacintha about contacting the police. I'm sure they'd be discreet. Of course, one doesn't like to ask for favors, but one might in a pinch.'

Annie was pretty sure that, if the Wraysburys asked, they'd get the odd favor from the Old Bill, and maybe even a few unbidden ones.

Christine wrapped up with, 'I'll call you back when we have more. We're going to the pub where we know Poppy met someone last evening. The aim is to find out who she met, and take it from there.'

Lady Agatha replied, 'Good luck, Christine dear, and do take care of yourselves. Sure my sister would never forgive me for getting you into any sort of trouble. Have me guts for garters, so she would.' Then she was gone.

Annie couldn't help but smile. 'Your auntie's got quite the brogue when she lets the posh bit drop.'

'To be sure we all have it beneath our elocution-lesson-enhanced English,' replied Christine with a wicked grin. 'To be fair, the area where my mother's family, and I, were raised – just on the border in the north of Ireland – doesn't bless one with the most attractive of accents, so it's a good job the English public school system ironed it out for all of us.'

'We're nearly there,' observed Annie. 'Do you think your uncle will get hold of the police, whatever Jacintha might say?'

Christine sounded resigned. 'I believe so, yes. I expect Uncle Richard will want to do that. He's terribly proper. Has to be, really. So I suggest we find out as much as possible at this pub, then at least we'll have done all we can. Did the other two have any news?'

'Mave's begun phoning all the hospitals – working outward from the center of London. Thank goodness her nursing career has taught her all the unofficial routes you can take to find out who's come through Emergency Admitting. She'll stick at it for as long as it takes. Nothing so far. Carol's sorted all the admin stuff for the case and she's sourcing contact info for Mave, as well as scanning news reports that might mention . . . anything helpful. And we're there,' she concluded, as the grumbling cabbie announced they owed him twenty-four pounds and eighty pence.

Annie shoved thirty pounds into his hand. 'Thanks for keeping your nose out of our business,' she smiled.

He looked at the notes and rolled his eyes. 'You need the coppers. Kidnapping's no lark. That's what I thinks,' he said, then he pulled away, performed a neat U-turn, and headed off into the traffic again.

The doors of The Hereford Bull were still locked.

Annie felt cross. 'They won't be open for another twenty minutes. I'll knock,' she said, and did so. Loudly.

The man with a bucket in his hand who opened the door immediately announced, 'Not open until eleven. Come back then.'

He moved to shut the door again, but Annie was too quick for him. 'Nice to know having such huge plates is useful, sometimes,' she quipped as she wedged her foot to prevent the door from being closed.

'You're much more useful than that, Annie,' said Christine quietly, which made Annie feel good.

'Ta, but hold your horses with the love-fest, and let's get this pub's landlord – or manager, more like – in front of us so we can show him that photo and find out if he remembers Poppy.' She lowered her voice, 'And I need to pop to the loo at some point soon, too. Bladder the size of a pea, me . . . if you know what I mean.' She grinned at Christine, hoping she'd get the joke, but she didn't seem to.

Instead, Christine pushed the door open again, elbowed her way past the man with the bucket and began screaming, 'I need to see the landlord, or manager, or whomever is in charge!'

Bossy *and* grammatically correct, thought Annie. 'You go for it, Chrissy,' she said aloud, and she joined in – proper grammar and all.

'What the bleedin' 'ell's goin' on down 'ere?' shouted a rumpled-looking man as he descended the stairs.

Christine decided it was best to be formal. 'I am The Honorable Christine Wilson-Smythe. This is my colleague Annie Parker. We have enquiries to make about a friend of ours who was here at your establishment last evening.' Christine pushed her phone in front of the man's bleary eyes. 'Do you remember this girl, or the man with whom she is sitting?'

Christine assessed the man was clean, and dressed ready for his work-day. She didn't believe she'd roused him from his bed, so felt less sympathy for him than if she and Annie had arrived hours earlier.

The man's face was lined, his eyes slightly pink. 'I'll need me specs,' he said, and scampered toward the stairs.

Christine had no reason to doubt he was speaking the truth, but felt somewhat unsettled by the glance he threw toward the pair of them as he climbed the creaking staircase. 'Leno, keep an eye on 'em,' he said to the cleaner as he disappeared.

The cleaner looked at the women with suspicion, and shuffled past them toward the bar. 'I'm nearly finished,' he said gruffly. 'Have to put the chairs down now. Don't you two move.' He rattled his bucket in their general direction, then began to lift chairs down from the tops of tables.

The rumpled man reappeared, and wiped a grubby pair of spectacles with the sleeve of his shirt. As he placed them onto his nose, Christine could see he was still eyeing her with suspicion. He peered at the screen, and enlarged the picture.

'Can't say I recognize either of 'em,' he replied. A bit cagily, though Christine. He handed the phone back to her, 'But then I wouldn't, necessarily, unless they was regulars. Gets busy in here, thank God.'

'Are you the manager?' asked Annie.

'Landlord. A proper landlord, me. John Thelwell.'

'Any chance I can use your loo, John?' replied Annie. 'Sorry, I wouldn't ask normally – you know, before you're open – but I'm desperate.'

The landlord appeared to take pity on Annie. 'Toilets all done, Leno?' he shouted. The cleaner nodded. 'They're over there,' said John, jerking his thumb toward a sign beside a door.

Annie scuttled off.

Christine handed the phone back to the man. 'Please take another look. The girl's not where she should be today. Her employer is worried about her. We'd like to get some reassurance she's just taking an unexpected sick day, and not in some sort of danger.'

The landlord rolled his eyes. 'If her boss is worried about her she must be one hell of an employee. Half a dozen of my casuals could go missing and I'm not sure I'd be any the wiser; come and go as they please do some of them. Especially the bloody Aussies. Off to find greener grass at the drop of a hat, that lot.'

Christine had to decide how much to tell the man; too much and she'd possibly cause problems no one needed, too little and he might not make as much of an effort to be helpful as he could.

'She's a bit more than an employee, truth be told,' she said, in her best conspiratorial tones. 'She and her boss have become friends; she's a wonderful second-in-command for her boss's business, and her boss has sort of taken her under her wing. This girl works at a florist; JWF.'

John Thelwell's eyebrows lifted. 'JWF? That's not a florist, that's *the* florist, innit? Ain't they the ones what do the flowers when anyone in the Royal family's in hospital?' Christine nodded.

John peered at her over his specs. 'And you're an honorable, eh?' Christine nodded again. 'Ah,' said John; it was a syllable which carried a wealth of meaning.

'Any chance of a G & T?' Annie gasped as she returned to the bar.

Christine allowed her surprise to show. 'You want a drink? At this time of day?'

Annie grinned. 'Has the Pope got a balcony?'

Christine tutted.

'And if it's a yes,' continued Annie, 'my friend here will not only be paying, but she'll also be having the same.' Having spoken, Annie collapsed onto a nearby chair, and undid the buttons and belt on her well-worn mackintosh.

'I really don't think we have time,' said Christine.

'I could give you a soft drink,' said the landlord hesitantly, 'but I wouldn't want to be selling nothing, outside hours.'

'Ta. How about a large T without any G? I'll imagine the G,' replied Annie.

He moved behind the bar, and Christine followed him. 'If you could just take another look at this photo. Please . . .'

'Not from the newspapers, are you?' John asked of Annie as he prepared her drink.

'Nah. Private eyes, that's what we are.'

John Thelwell looked astonished.

Christine wasn't sure Annie was handling things the best way.

'You two?' He sounded as surprised as he looked. 'Well, I s'pose it explains why the two of you's together. Not a likely duo, are you? Indian tonic, love? Or we've got Mediterranean, Sicilian lemon, elderflower, aromatic, or cucumber. Gawd knows there's enough of 'em these days.'

'Just ordinary Indian, ta. Can't stand all those fancy ones, me.' The landlord rolled his eyes in what Christine took to be silent agreement. 'And yeah, I keep this one in her place, when I need to,' quipped Annie.

Christine thought it best to laugh; she'd deduced that Annie was trying to build an 'us against them' alliance with the landlord. It might work.

'Nothing for you?' asked John of Christine.

She shook her head. 'No, thanks.'

'So you didn't recognize our girl, then, eh?' asked Annie, accepting the glass of tonic water from the man.

He reached out his hand for the phone. 'Lemme see that again,' he said. He replaced his spectacles and Christine believed him to be truly concentrating. 'Don't suppose you know if she drinks a Summer Cup gin with cucumber tonic, do ya? We had a girl in last night drinking that, sayin' she was sick of the winter weather. She looked a bit like this. And this bloke? Thinkin' about it, I 'ave seen him before.'

Christine felt her tummy clench with excitement. 'Do you know his name?'

'Lives local, I think. At least, he comes in with his girlfriend sometimes. Not big drinkers. Nice enough chap. Big bear, name of Rob. Not with his girlfriend last night, but this one. Didn't get a girlfriend vibe from her though. Small girl, right?' Christine nodded. 'Spotted a bit of ink on her wrists. Right?' Christine nodded again. 'Yeah, I reckon it's them. Rob Brown, I think. Girlfriend lives over in Cranley Mansions, just down the road. I know that 'cos the first time he came here his girlfriend had just moved in there and the lift was broken; right old time they had getting all her stuff up the stairs. Summer it was. Last year. Bleedin' hot. Sissy she is. Not Sissy Spacek . . . but summat like that. No, wait, it's . . . Sissy Siddons. No, that's not it.'

Christine wondered how long this might take.

'Got it. It's Helen Hunter. That's it. Always get her mixed up with Sissy Spacek. But she's really Helen Hunt, ain't she? Anyway, this one's Helen Hunter.' John smiled. 'Funny old thing, the brain, innit? What we remember, when we wants.'

'You're a prince, John, you know that?' said Annie. 'Don't s'pose you know what number she lives in, do you?'

John chuckled. 'You're havin' a laugh, ain't you? I reckon I've done pretty good with what I've given you. You're a private detective so you should be able to manage the rest on your own, if you're worth your salt.'

Annie laughed – Christine was enjoying watching her colleague work. 'You're right. Ta, John – and thanks for the drink. Chrissy, give the man a tenner. We'll take it from here. Most helpful, ain't he, Chrissy, doll?'

Christine took her cue, and handed over the money. 'You most certainly are, Mr Thelwell. Thanks ever so much. Our client will be most grateful.'

'Tell 'er she can send me some flowers,' he quipped, as Christine allowed herself to be dragged out of the pub by Annie.

'You phone Carol as we walk,' said Christine, 'see if she can locate a Helen Hunter in Cranley Mansions. I'll get in touch with Jacintha; I'll see if any of this means anything to her.'

Both women talked as they walked. The pavements were busy, but they didn't bump into too many people. Both finishing their phone calls at roughly the same time, Annie spoke first.

'She's in flat thirty-four. What did Jacintha say?'

'Robert Brown is Poppy's brother. He lives in Brighton, but spends most weekends here in London with his girlfriend. Poppy and he occasionally meet for a drink. She didn't mention it was him she was going to meet last night, but Jacintha said it wouldn't surprise her. Given that Poppy gets up so early she's only able to meet people in the early evening.'

Christine wondered why Annie was grabbing her arm. 'What is it?'

'Coppers. Look. Coming out of Cranley Mansions. Uniform, two of them, one woman, marked car.'

'I wonder what that's all about,' said Christine. 'I certainly don't think we want to be talking to them quite yet. Let's find number thirty-four.'

Christine looked at the numbers above the arched entryway that surrounded and protected the large glazed doors before them. 'If this entrance is for forty-five to seventy, then I suspect the other door will take us to one to forty-four. So we need the entrance the police were coming out of.'

The women shared a look of dread and set off along the car-lined street.

Entering the second set of doors they could tell that flat number thirty-four would be on the third floor. A rickety-looking metal-cage lift was on the right-hand side of the entrance. Christine pushed the button. The lift clanked to a stop and she hauled open the gate. Their ascent seemed to be at a pace slightly faster than immobile, and they crawled up, passed on the way by a young man carrying three bags of shopping, who bounded up the wide marble stairs two at a time – making better speed than them. Finally they shuddered to a halt, and emerged, gratefully, from the cage. Annie pointed along the corridor in front of them.

'There,' she nodded.

Christine pushed the doorbell, which bong-ed inside the flat. A slim young woman wearing a giant fluffy bathrobe, and rubbing her wet, long brown hair with a towel, pulled open the door and shouted, 'What now? I'm getting ready as fast as I can.'

Upon seeing Christine and Annie in the hallway she looked surprised and confused. 'I'm sorry – I thought you were the police again. Who are you? Now's not a good time.'

'I'm sorry to bother you,' muttered Christine, now dreading what she might discover. 'We're looking for Rob Brown. Is he at home?'

'Is he at home? No, he's not. The silly bugger's lying in St Martha's with his head split open and his ear nearly torn off, that's where he is. And I want to get to see him as quick as I can. Why do you want him?'

Both Annie and Christine felt the impact of this news. It wasn't good. Not good at all.

'What happened to him?' asked Annie, sharply.

The girl's eyes narrowed.

'What's it to you?' She looked from Annie to Christine, filling the doorway with her body.

Christine was also carefully considering the girl herself, and the situation. Must be the girlfriend: possibly in the shower when the police arrived; just been told her boyfriend's been hurt; declined a lift to the hospital; trying to get out of the flat to see him. Christine decided to take the direct route.

'I'm Christine, this is Annie.' She handed the girl a business card. 'Are you Helen Hunter?' The girl nodded, and her eyes narrowed even further. 'I'm terribly sorry about your boyfriend; we're trying to track down his sister, Poppy. We can't locate her, so it's important that we talk to Rob. He might be able to help us. But, in the meantime, it would be useful to know how he was hurt.'

Helen looked to be giving Christine's request some thought as she carried on rubbing at her hair. Then she lay the towel across her arm and nodded. She stepped back from the door and waved Christine and Annie inside.

'Well, it can't hurt, I suppose. The police just told me that Rob was found on the pavement, on a street in Belgravia last night, covered in blood. They think he'd been thrown from a moving vehicle. Something had been stapled to his ear. Stapled! I don't know what they meant exactly, but it sounds brutal. Anyway, he's got a possibly-fractured skull and he's lost a lot of blood. He'd been drugged too.'

Tears welled in her eyes. It was clear to Christine that repeating the news she'd just received had, for Helen, made it all real for her.

Reaching out a hand to find a chair, Helen cried, 'Oh my God – poor Rob. I mean he's a big bugger and all that, but he wouldn't hurt a fly. Why would anyone pick on him?' She buried her face in the towel.

'You need a cuppa,' prescribed Annie. The girl looked dazed.

'Maybe I do . . .' her voice was dreamy, 'but I want to get to my Rob.'

Annie and Christine looked at each other, and a tacit agreement was made.

'Right-o then, I'll make you a cup of tea while you get ready to get out of here, and you can tell us all about Rob, and Poppy – if you know anything about her – alright?' As she spoke, Annie aimed for the kitchen.

The girl put up no resistance and was clearly happy to be mothered, just a little.

'I'll just get myself dressed, then,' said Helen, and closed the bathroom door behind her.

Christine shouted, 'I'll give a friend of ours a ring and ask her if she can get us any inside info on Rob at St Martha's. She's good at that sort of thing.'

'Ta,' yelled Helen from the bathroom.

Annie called from the kitchen, 'You get yourself sorted, Helen, and I'll get a nice cuppa going – hot and sweet. Then we'll get you into a taxi and you'll be with Rob before you know it. Alright?'

'Thanks,' called the voice from the bathroom.

'Mavis will get right on it,' announced Christine to Annie. 'She knows a ward sister at St Martha's who was once one of her "girls", so we might get something. And Carol's going to investigate any and all odd goings-on in the Belgravia area last night. But what do you think? If Rob was with Poppy, and Rob ended up being dumped out of a car somewhere in Belgravia ... what does it mean for Poppy?'

'Gawd knows,' was Annie's honest reply. 'I haven't got a clue, but maybe Helen here'll know more than she thinks. Look, the tea's steeping, let me have a word with her while she's getting dressed?' Christine nodded her agreement.

The noise of the hairdryer inside the bathroom had stopped, and a slightly more alert Helen dashed from the bathroom to the bedroom in her underwear. 'I'll be five minutes,' she shouted to the two strangers in her living room.

'Alright, doll,' called back Annie, approaching the closed bedroom door as she did so. She shouted through the door. 'Did you see Rob before he went out yesterday at all, Helen?'

'Yes,' a muffled voice called over the slamming of doors and drawers. 'He was off to The Hereford Bull to meet Poppy, then he was due to meet up with some rugby friends afterwards. I didn't expect him to be home until late, if at all. He said he might be out all night; he often is when he's with his rugger bugger mates. Which is why I didn't miss him. Though, he usually phones to say when he'll be home. Oh God,' Christine could hear her crying. 'I should have known something was wrong ...'

'Now, now,' called Annie, as comfortingly as was possible, given she was shouting through a door, 'it wasn't your fault. If he'd said he'd be out all night then you couldn't be expected to know anything was wrong.'

'You're blaming yourself for nothing Helen,' added Christine.

Helen appeared at the bedroom door wearing an oversized England rugby shirt and jeans. Her face was wet with tears. She hooked her long hair behind her ears and gulped down a sob.

'I love him, you know? But I don't tell him enough. He's a lovely man; big, and cuddly, and fun. What if he doesn't make it?' The question hung in the air, to be joined by the trilling of Christine's mobile phone.

'It's the office,' she announced. 'Maybe there's some news from Mavis.'

Christine listened carefully and took notes, while Annie watched over Helen as she sipped at her tea, still crying.

'Listen,' Christine announced, having disconnected her call, 'Mavis tells me she's spoken to one of the nurses who's tending to Rob, and he's going to be just fine.'

A look of hope lit up Helen's face. 'Really?' Her expression showed she hardly dared believe the good news.

'Really,' comforted Christine. 'The damage to his ear is superficial – though, you're right, he did lose quite a lot of blood because of a neck injury. He has a minor skull fracture, but the nurse has seen much worse get fully mended. And there's no brain damage of any kind, though they're still testing him for a concussion.' Christine beamed at Helen.

Helen looked horrified. 'I never even thought of brain damage,' she cried. 'Oh, my poor Rob.' She started to sob again.

Annie comforted the girl and pushed her tea toward her once more. 'Come on, drink up, it'll do you good. And now you know he'll be alright, it won't be such a bad journey to the hospital.'

Helen took the tea, shakily, and sipped, then gulped, nodding.

'Anything else?' asked Annie of Christine, warily.

'Not that would interest Helen,' replied Christine. 'How about we find her a cab and let her get on her way?' she suggested, and nodded toward the front door indicating that they, too, should be on their way.

'Good idea,' responded Annie jovially. Before she took the mug from Helen's hands, she asked, 'Did Rob send you any texts or anything telling you what his plans might have been with Poppy last night, at all?'

Helen looked uncertain. 'I don't think so, but I was out with the girls last night; I get Friday and Saturday off, but work Sundays, see? Let me check my phone. I wasn't really awake when the police came.'

She scrabbled around in her handbag and pulled out her phone. 'Oh look, he sent me that photo you just showed me. And then a text: "Poppy a bit off color. Taking her home. Found someone to give us a lift." It was timed at eight twenty-two p.m. Does that help? Do you know where Poppy lives? Is she there?'

'We do, and she's not,' was Christine's concerned reply. 'Any other texts? He didn't say who was giving them a lift, did he?'

Helen shook her head, then finished her tea.

'Best we make a move,' said Christine.

Annie took the empty mug from Helen and asked, 'Got all your bits and pieces?' She made no excuses for the lack of ceremony with which she was hurrying along the young woman.

'Do you think I should stop and buy some pajamas for Rob on the way?' Helen asked as they began to rush down the stairs.

'I'm sure they'll have put him in something suitable there; why don't you just go and see him and ask him what he needs, eh?' Christine could see that Annie's mothering had stopped, but she managed to keep the concern in her voice. 'Look, there's a cab now.'

Annie jumped out into the path of a taxi, which screeched to a halt just feet in front of her. She dragged Helen toward the passenger door, pushed her inside and shouted, 'St Martha's Accident and Emergency – fast.' She slammed the door on the still-confused Helen. 'Give Rob our love,' she shouted at the disappearing cab, then she grabbed Christine by the arm and shouted, 'So?'

'Okay, don't yank at me,' replied Christine testily. 'We need to get ourselves back to The Hereford Bull – fast.' She pulled Annie's hand off her arm and led the way.

'Yes, I worked that one out. We have to find out if anyone saw Rob and Poppy leave with someone – though you'd think John the landlord would have mentioned it if he'd seen it,' replied Annie, striding out with her long legs. 'What other news did Mave get?' she asked breathlessly as they hurried along the narrow pavement.

'Mavis's nurse contact overheard more than I wanted Helen to know,' replied Christine. 'Apparently it was Rob Brown's overdeveloped neck muscles that saved his life; his assailant sliced at his throat and missed his carotid by millimeters, otherwise he'd have bled to death before they got to him. But, as it is, he'll be fine, in time. Mavis's contact also overheard the statement Rob Brown gave to the police; he said he met Poppy at the pub, as planned, but that Poppy was taken ill there. Some bloke they'd never met before offered to drive them to Poppy's flat in his van. Rob helped him get Poppy into the back of a white transit van. Then the bloke must have hit Rob over the head. The next thing Rob knew he was lying on the road, surrounded by paramedics and police.'

'Oh, bugger,' remarked Annie. 'That sounds serious.'

'And that's not all,' continued Christine, 'this nurse gathered from the police conversations going on outside Rob Brown's room that they couldn't see a number plate on any of the CCTV pictures of the van, and that they weren't having much luck tracing its whereabouts because, after dumping him on the road, it had driven into the underground car park on Park Lane and didn't seem to have come out again – but they can't find it in there.'

Christine and Annie were both worried.

'So we're going to the pub to try to find out who the man with the van is, right?' asked Annie, knowing the answer.

'Yes,' replied Christine, 'but I'm assuming that the police will have been there before us, given Rob's statement to them, so I'm not sure what we can find out that they haven't already discovered.'

'But we can try,' added Annie helpfully.

'Yes, we can try,' replied Christine as they rushed toward their quarry.


When Annie strode through the doors of The Hereford Bull for the second time that day, her eyes immediately locked onto John the landlord, who was standing behind the bar looking pink around the gills.

'You two again?' he said. 'What a morning this has turned out to be. Only just got rid of the Old Bill, ain't I? All to do with that Rob and Poppy Brown, like you two were on about. What's occurring? They wouldn't tell me nothing.'

Annie turned to Christine and said, 'He's all mine.' Then she leaned across the pumps and whispered as menacingly as she could, 'Someone accompanied Poppy and Rob Brown when they left here last evening. We need to know who that was.'

John didn't seem even slightly intimidated, which disappointed Annie. 'Like I've just been saying to the coppers, I didn't see them leave here with no one. I didn't see them leave here at all. I can't be keeping an eye on everyone's comings and goings all night.'

Annie admitted to herself he had a point. 'What about that young lad we saw arriving here for his shift this morning. Did he see anything?'

'Coppers asked him too, and he didn't.'

Annie rallied, 'He can't have been the only person working here for you last night. Can we speak to the other members of staff who were here then?'

John sighed. 'Like I've already said to the p'lice, the two others who were on last night ain't here now.' He looked at his watch. 'One of them was due to start five minutes ago, at noon, but he strolls in whenever he fancies, don't he?'

'Phone numbers?' pressed Annie.

John hesitated for the first time. 'Well, I gave them to the rozzers, but I'm not sure about giving them to you two. You're not official, are you?'

'Lady Jacintha Wraysbury, Poppy Brown's employer, is our client. We are, most definitely, official,' said Christine.

Annie rolled her eyes in an attempt to get Christine to back off. She felt she could get something out of John by playing the 'fellow Londoner' card.

A red-haired boy, who appeared to Annie to be aged about twelve, sauntered behind the bar. 'Hello, John, what do you want me to start with?' he asked.

John shook his head. 'Bloody Millennials,' he said to Annie then, to the youth, 'Simon, nice of you to grace us with your presence. You missed all the action; Plod wants to talk to you about a bloke you might have seen here last night. Helped a bloke and a girl out of here when she felt bad.'

The fresh-faced youth wrinkled his forehead, then said, 'Yeah. I saw them. I know the bloke you mean – Gary. Gary Gilchrist. Plumber. Comes in sometimes when he's got a job in the area. Why do they want to talk to me about him?'

The young man seemed genuinely curious.

'Never mind why,' snapped John, 'just give them a ring. I put the number on the side there. But don't forget who pays your wages around here; I need three barrels changing and we're low on tonics and bitter lemons, so sort that out. And I need them tables cleared and cleaned in the corner. So get that lot sorted, then you can phone them.' He rolled his eyes towards Annie. 'These young ones – want it all on a plate, eh?'

Annie nodded sympathetically. She couldn't lose this chance. Looking at the young barman she said aloud, 'Oh come on, he's just a lad, he probably doesn't know anything useful about Gilchrist anyway.'

Annie hoped the young man fancied showing off a bit. She was pleased to be proved right.

He replied swiftly, and with vigor, 'Well maybe I do, see? I know he lives in one of those big old houses out on St Peter's Terrace, just the other side of the Cromwell Road. He got really pissed – sorry, I mean drunk –' he nodded apologetically at Christine – 'in here one night and I couldn't shut him up. That's when he told me his name, and all about the house his mother left him when she'd died.' He lowered his voice. 'He kept shoving some pretty disgusting photos of his girlfriend at me; she clearly didn't mind showing her all to the camera, but then she'd have to be a bit of a slapper to go for him. If you'll pardon my French. He's a nasty bit of work, if you ask me. I can't imagine him helping out someone for nothing. Might do it if there was a few quid in it for him, I suppose.'

'Ta, doll,' said Annie, her insides squirming with excitement. 'Maybe he's a keeper, after all, John,' she quipped, then she grabbed Christine and said, 'We're off.' She dragged her colleague out of the door. 'If we're quick we might just get in ahead of the police.'

Christine was swift to react. 'Where are we going?' she asked, as Annie leaped into the oncoming traffic to stop a cab.

'St Peter's Terrace,' she shouted at the cabbie, answering Christine's question at the same time.

Once they were sitting, Annie pulled out her phone and called the office. Her voice was excited, Christine was agog.

Carol answered the phone; she used her best telephone voice.

'Car, it's Annie – we need an address for a Gary Gilchrist, St Peter's Terrace, not far from Gloucester Road tube station, north side of the Cromwell Road. He might be listed as a plumber, or if just the house is listed it might be with a different first name or initial because the house used to be his mother's.'

'Got it. Hang on. I need both hands . . .' replied Carol.

'Said the actress to the bishop,' quipped Annie to Christine, who flashed her colleague a weak smile.

'Number eighteen,' said Carol clearly, 'and who's Gary Gilchrist, when he's at home?'

'Pop me onto speaker phone and I'll fill you in as we go,' replied Annie. Mavis and Carol asked all the questions Annie expected, then Mavis asked an extra one, which worried her.

'Ach – well done so far, girls, but what are you going to do when you get there?' She sounded concerned. 'Do you not think it might be wiser to let the police take it from here, since they are now clearly involved.'

Annie's enthusiasm drained.

'Mavis?' mouthed Christine.

Annie nodded. 'Mave wants to know what we'll do when we get there.'

'Tell her not to tell anyone where we're going – if anyone asks – and that we'll keep in touch,' said Christine. Annie did as she was told, and ended the call.

'So – do we have a plan?' asked Annie, knowing the answer.

'What do you think?' replied Christine.

'Knock at the door and play it by ear?' suggested Annie.

'Unless you've got a better idea,' was Christine's glum response.

'Well, we've got about another ten minutes before we get there – maybe we can come up with something,' mused Annie.

'Hmm,' was all Christine could manage.

'Come on, girl,' urged Annie, 'put that Mensa brain to work; we need every little grey cell working for us. I know you can do it.'

Christine didn't look convinced.


Poppy was getting sick of the taste of leather. She'd managed to nibble through one knot, but had then realized that was a stupid idea; she'd be much better off trying to nibble through the flat strands that bound her wrists.

The smell of bacon had long since gone, but now her stomach was aching, she was so hungry; she'd already passed the point where relieving herself while fully dressed and curled up in a black, brick box was something to worry about, but the results were less than pleasant.

Poppy still had no recollection of how she'd ended up wherever she was, but, with every passing moment, she was becoming more angry, more frustrated, and more determined to get out. She had worked out that her eye teeth were the best to nibble with, but her gums and jaw were starting to ache with the effort. Then – finally – a cord snapped, and she was able to begin to unwind the leather loops; there was no point pulling at them because they only got tighter.

A few minutes later Poppy's hands were free. She rubbed her wrists, trying to get the circulation going. She patted her body to check for her mobile phone – of course, it had gone – so she felt around her surroundings. Initially, she discovered nothing new. She was in a brick box – brick walls and a brick floor, but now she used her freed hands to reach above her, where she felt something different – a wooden door. It moved; creaked. She didn't want to make a noise, so decided to try to free her ankles before feeling about any more.

This was more difficult than she'd hoped. She could feel the same leather ties on her ankles as she'd bitten through on her wrists, and even found several knots, but she had no idea how to release these bonds; she certainly couldn't chew through them.

If she couldn't free her feet, what about trying to open the lid of the 'box' and find out what was outside? It seemed to be her only option. She wasn't sure if she'd be able to move as slowly and smoothly as she wanted, but got herself onto her haunches and worked out that only one edge of the lid would move. As she lifted it a little, no discernable light came into her tiny world. In fact, nothing happened at all. She risked pushing it a little more, and then more. She had to raise it quite a bit to be able to peer through the gap, where she saw . . . nothing, just more blackness.

Encouraged that at least there was no one outside the box waiting to hurt her, Poppy pushed the lid as far open as it would go and slowly, and very painfully, straightened up to a standing position. Everything hurt. It was excruciating. She didn't know how long she'd been curled up, but it was long enough to allow her muscles to forget what it was to support her weight. She rubbed her legs, her arms, and her face. Even her hair ached. But at least she was out – well, in a manner of speaking.

'Rob, are you there?' she ventured. There was no response. Somehow, she'd known she was alone.

Poppy tried to make out what was around her. True, everything was still dark, but this darkness was less intense and she could gradually make out shadowy outlines of various types of junk, piled to the roof of what was, she assumed, some sort of basement or cellar. There were no windows, but, directly above her head, she could make out some little dots of light. They were arranged in a circle. Poppy puzzled over what it could be.

Then she got it.

Poppy was familiar with the iron coal-cellar covers that dotted some London streets; they'd allowed coal deliveries to be made from the roadside directly into the cellars below. They had one at the shop, which was the ground floor of an old mews house. She must have been shut in the coal-hole in a cellar, and there, out of reach above her head, and surely opening onto the street, was the metal cover. Not big enough for her to fit through, she knew that, but big enough so she could at least alert someone passing by to her predicament.

Now, if only she could get there; she judged the basement to be about ten feet high, so it would beyond her reach, unless she could get out of the coal-hole then find something to stand on.

Her spirits buoyed by this discovery, she decided to hunt about – carefully and quietly – for something that might have a sharp enough edge to cut leather, so she could release her feet. She placed her hands carefully on the edges of the coal-hole, and pulled up her legs. Swinging them out of the box was a painful job. She took a couple of moments to get her balance. She suspected the only way she'd get across the floor, other than hopping – which might be dangerous, was to kneel down and use her hands to pull herself about, which she did.

The floor was filthy and there were sharp little things that stuck into her palms, but she propelled herself toward a smallish pile of junk and tried to make out what was there. The faint light from above showed her what had been cutting into her palms – there was a broken window frame with some smashed glass in it. She couldn't believe her luck; all she had to do was get hold of a piece of the glass and she could use it as a cutting tool. She pulled her no-doubt filthy sweater over her head and wrapped it around her hands for protection.


Gary Gilchrist rolled onto his stomach and stubbed out his cigarette in the remnants of the bacon sandwich he'd discarded on the bedside table. He looked across at Tash as she lay on her back, blowing smoke rings toward the ceiling. He could do worse. But not much.

Natasha Moon stubbed out her own cigarette and looked over at her boyfriend. 'Gary . . .?' She sounded dreamy, and twisted her hair coquettishly. 'Tell me about how you got them again – you were so clever . . .'

Gary sighed. Ah well, string her along and let her bathe in his glory a bit longer. She really was a stupid, gullible, little tart.

'Like I said,' he began, sounding important, 'I'd stopped off to pick up some stuff from Bloko in Notting Hill. Just the usual – a bit of weed, a few tabs and so forth – and he asked me to take some roofies to a contact of his in a pub up by the Westway. I had a bit of time, so I stopped for a pint at a pub just across the Cromwell Road – you know, one of them posh ones – for a pint. Well, I'm in there, mindin' me own business like, when the two of them come in. The big one's sort of looking after the girl, and she's using all these names of flowers –

which means the Royal family; I seen that in the paper one day – it's some sort of code for the secret police what looks after 'em. She's got this bag with the name of that posh florist shop on it, and I gets closer, and he's telling her how well she's doing, and how well the shop's doing, and she's all "Yeah, we're the best, alright" and I thought "I know who you are, you snotty little bitch". They done that piece on her shop in that Sunday magazine, didn't they? About how much her old man's worth, right? And how she only gets all these fancy customers because of Daddy's money. So I 'ad the idea right there and then. I managed to drop a couple of the roofies into their drinks, and they carries on chatting like, till the girl starts to feel the effects.'

Natasha giggled, 'Did she go all floppy?'

Gary grinned. 'Yeah, sorta. So I goes over and offers them a lift to her place, all friendly like. The big one, the bodyguard, is feelin' it a bit too, but he helps me get the kid into the van, but then he won't play dead, so I thump him with an old bit of metal pipe I keeps in the van just in case, and down he goes too. I shut the doors and brought 'em back 'ere. Luckily, with the stuff I gave him, the bodyguard won't remember he helped me carry the girl downstairs. If he's alive, that is. And no one knows me at that pub. Only been there a few times before; one night I got a bit the worse for wear there, but nothing to make me stick out, like. And the rest you knows.'

'Why did you make me write the note?' Natasha sounded hurt.

''Cos you've got nicer writin' than me, pet, that's why.' He thought she'd buy it.

'Oh, really?' was her only response. 'And tell me again why you want me to pick up the money?'

'Because you'll look more natural in that cleaner's outfit in the park. And no one's going to see you anyway, so you'll be fine, don't worry about it.' She was beginning to get on Gary's nerves.

'I still think we should have fed her, Gary. I mean, she's got to be used to eating well, what with living in palaces and all.'

Gary snapped. He pushed down on Natasha's arm, heavily.

'Look, Tash – I'll say what we will and will not do. And she can miss a few meals. Christ, Tash, she's a duchess, you're not gonna make friends with her, are you? You're just some old slag from nowhere, and she's friggin' Lady Jacintha friggin' Wraysbury. We don't want her seeing us, anyway, do we?'

'But she's seen you already, Gary. And the big bloke did. Do you really think you killed him when you pushed him out of the van? Or will he have talked to the police already?'

Gary gave Natasha's arm a painful squeeze before he leaped out of bed and pulled on his underpants.

'Shut up, you silly cow. They don't know me, and they won't be able to finger me. If the bodyguard wasn't dead when they found him, then I've lost me touch. I knows just where to cut 'em to make 'em bleed, see, and there's been nuthin' on the news, so, no, I don't think he's talking to the Old Bill. I think he's dead. And I think His Knobship will pay up and they'll keep it all hush, hush. They're good at that, them lot with titles. Besides, when we get away with the money we can look like whoever we want.'

Gary Gilchrist headed for the bathroom, and some peace and quiet. He might have to shut her up sooner than he'd thought; she was starting to drive him bonkers. Same as all women, his mother included. She'd nagged at him for years and years, until he'd had enough. Still, she wasn't saying much now, was she? Not chattering away at him anymore, now she was under them bricks in the cellar.

He wondered how the Little Lady would feel if she knew she was locked up just feet away from the bones of a stupid old bitch who'd nagged her loving son just once too often. He smiled as he looked at himself in the bathroom mirror. Women – can't live with 'em . . . but you can kill 'em, and shut 'em up, he thought wryly.


Natasha lay on the bed, still worried, but now in a different way; what did Gary mean about cutting that bloke? And how would he know how to do it, anyway?

She'd always felt quite safe with Gary – yeah, he was a bit rough, and he'd given her a few slaps in the months they'd been together. But only when she'd deserved it, like he'd said. Which seemed to be more and more these days.

But, surely, he couldn't really be anything like they said he was at the Slug on the Cromwell Road; surely he couldn't be a 'psycho'. He could be quite thoughtful at times, quite nice. Of course, that was usually when he wanted something.

Natasha slapped her own hand when she realized she was nibbling at her nails; she'd almost managed to stop that. Gary said only babies bit their nails. She'd get up and make a cup of tea for them both – strong, like Gary liked it . . .

Annie and Christine jumped out of the cab at the end of St Peter's Terrace, and wandered along until they could see number eighteen. It was an unkempt house in a row of up-and-coming counterparts. With the standard Georgian three stories up, one storey down, these houses were obviously being bought up and renovated. But not the Gilchrist house; it was clear that whoever lived there cared nothing for the potential of the home, and owned neither a paintbrush nor a window chamois.

'So?' asked Annie, pointedly. 'Come on, Chrissy – you're the brainy one. We need something to get us in the door – something that'll give us a good reason to go through the house. I mean, we're assuming Poppy is there, right? I mean, actually inside the house?' Christine nodded. 'So what can we do that'll get us past a kidnapper with a kidnappee on the premises? How can we make him let us in? Come on, Chrissy – suggestions, please.'

'Hmm,' replied Christine. She looked thoughtful. 'We could be from the council; that might get us in and give us a chance to look around. A complaint about rats? Something like that?'

'I don't think he's the sort who'd welcome a visit from the council,' replied Annie glumly, 'and I don't think we look like rat-catchers, either. Besides, the last thing I want to do is go hunting around an old house that looks like it's probably really got more than its fair share of vermin.'

Christine bit her lip – which Annie knew was a sign she was deep in thought.

'I've got it,' exclaimed Christine. 'We could be estate agents with a client who wants to pay him lots of money for the house.'

Annie thought about it for a moment. 'Good one, Chrissy – it might work.' She sounded enthusiastic. 'Clearly he's a greedy bugger; we could play on that. But shouldn't we have a card or something with an estate agent's name on it?'

'You're right,' agreed Christine. 'We just passed an estate agents' office around the corner. Come on, let's go in, pick up some details and get a couple of cards for good measure; it doesn't matter what they say, so long as they're women's names, then we can come back and be them.'

'Good thinking, Batman.' Annie slapped her colleague on the back.

'Thanks, Dobbin,' replied Christine, her spirits high.

'That's "Robin" to you,' retorted Annie.

They each had a smile on their face as they rushed toward the estate agents' office that Christine had spotted.

Poppy had managed to free her feet. She'd taken off her shoes, rubbed her toes back to some semblance of life, and had re-tied her laces. She was as ready as she would ever be to attempt to get out of the cellar.

But, before she even contemplated trying to somehow get up to the tempting plate in the ceiling above her, she decided to try to find an easier way out – the door to the basement. She knew the staff in a house like this would have needed direct access to the coal to be able to carry it through the house to the fireplaces on each floor; so the question was: where was the door from the cellar to the basement?

Poppy seemed to be completely hemmed in by piles of junk that loomed up at her in the darkness, but logic told her she had got in there somehow, so there must be a path out – somewhere.

She was still quite wobbly, and moved slowly, trying to push her feet forward without knocking into anything. She held out her hands in front of herself, to help keep her balance.

Her feet found the edge of a pile of junk, then she edged along in a different direction and found another, then another. She couldn't determine angles, but she took her bearings from the little holes in the plate above; the plate was in the pavement, with the coal-hole part of the cellar extending out beyond the apron of the house, beneath the pavement. If this house followed the same general pattern as the shop, the door to the basement would be directly opposite the hole to the street – but that way seemed blocked.

Poppy stopped for a moment. She was feeling dizzy; no food, no water that she was aware of, no real circulation in her extremities and all this darkness had her dazed and confused. She felt so frustrated with her inability to master her surroundings she thought she might cry. She could sense tears welling, and felt very small and alone. Quite hopeless.

Why was she here?

Where was here?

What had happened to Rob?

Poppy felt that if only she could remember *something*, she'd be better able to come to terms with her predicament, but, other than having a drink with Rob at The Hereford Bull, her memory was a fuzzy, infuriating blank.

She sat down, hard, held her head in her hands, and wept. Silently. She didn't want anyone to hear her. All she wanted was to be safe; to be at home in the glorious daylight, with her brother.

In the silence, something caught Poppy's ear. It sounded like a front-door bell – the old-fashioned type that rings out loud. Maybe help was coming.

'Don't answer it Tash,' shouted Gary roughly as Natasha moved toward the front door.

'Why not?' she asked, surprised.

'Don't be so bloody stupid. Think, woman,' he spat back at her. 'I'm not expecting no one, and you certainly ain't, so it can't be anyone we wants to see. Besides, think about down there.' He nodded in the direction of the back stairs that led down to the basement and cellar.

'Oh, yeah,' replied Natasha. 'But it might be someone we want to see,' she added feebly. 'Who is it?' she called through the door, before Gary could stop her.

A woman's voice replied. It was muffled by the heavy door, but sounded friendly enough.

'My name's Annabel Dixon. I'm from Freed & Henry, the estate agents around the corner. I wondered if I could speak with the owner.'

Natasha turned to Gary and raised her eyebrows in query. Gary pulled her roughly from the door and stood close to it himself.

'I'm the owner,' he shouted. 'What d'yer want?'

'Well, I think this might be easier if you would open the door, sir,' came the reply.

Gary thought about it, then opened the front door a crack.

They certainly weren't coppers; two women. One was a bit of a mess – tall, black, gangly and sweaty, the other one was young and slim, not a bad pair on her, nice enough face – not that *that* was essential. She looked posh; pearls and a fancy haircut, you could always tell. They each held out a business card. Gary took them both and read them.

Estate Agents. The posh one was Annabel Dixon – that suited her that did, and the older black one was Susan Potter. She didn't look like a Susan Potter to him.

'So?' he asked gruffly.

Annie answered in character as Susan, who was currently sitting at her desk at Freed & Henry, eating a Pot Noodle, not five minutes from Gary Gilchrist's front door. Annie used her best posh accent. 'Might one enquire if you are the homeowner, sir?'

Gary smiled wryly. 'Yes I am, and there's no need to "sir" me, ta very much. Where you from, darlin'? East End?'

Annie looked at her feet coyly, then at Christine. 'Sorry, Annabel,' she said brightly to Christine, in her broadest accent, 'the cat's well an' truly out o' the bag.'

Then, to Gary, she smiled a cheeky grin and said, 'No pullin' the wool over your eyes, eh doll? Got a good ear on you. Mile End Road. Know it?'

'A bit,' conceded Gary guardedly.

'Look,' said Annie, lowering her voice and glancing about her furtively, 'me name's not really Susan Potter – I'm Annie, Annie Parker.'

Christine wasn't acting when she looked at Annie in horror.

'Anyway,' continued Annie, 'they've just taken me on at the estate agents round the corner, and this is my boss, Miss Dixon. They thought they'd give me a fancy name for all the fancy clients they're gettin' these days, but I can tell a real Londoner when I meet one, so here I am, plain, old Annie Parker from Mile End, and, my Gawd, have I got a sniff for you.'

Annie was laying it on thick, and Christine could see a glint in the man's eyes. She knew Annie was good, but this was brilliant. She decided to play along in her role as Miss Annabel Dixon – boss.

'Miss Potter, I mean Miss Parker,' she interrupted. 'This is not the way we do things at Freed & Henry – and I think we've put this gentleman to enough trouble already. He's clearly not interested in what we have to say.' She let the words hang in the air as she made to pull Annie away from the door. Christine hoped she hadn't gone too far.

'Oh, come on, Annabel. Sorry, Miss Dixon,' retorted Annie, 'I can tell you're not used to dealing with people who have something that someone else wants – but don't know it yet. Let me tell 'im at least, before you kick me out on my ear, that is.'

'Tell me what,' interrupted an impatient Gary.

'See,' said Annie triumphantly, 'I knew he'd know he was onto a good thing.'

'Look, will you two sort this out back at the office and just tell me what the 'ell you're on about – you darlin', spit it out,' shouted Gary at Annie.

Annie 'capitulated'. Drawing even closer to Gary Gilchrist, Annie repeated her act of looking around, as if to make sure she wasn't being overheard, then whispered in her best non-whisper, 'We've got a bit of posh tottie who's interested in buying your house. She's got more money than sense, and thinks she's spotted the "next big thing" in this part of the world. We could be talking a mill or more.' Annie finished with a conspiratorial wink, and all but poked out her tongue at Christine/Annabel.

Gary took in this statement for a few seconds then countered with, 'How do you know she's serious?'

Annie was ready for his question. 'Well Mr . . . ?' she paused, waiting for Gary to fill in the blank.

'Gilchrist.'

'Well, Mr Gilchrist – what a nice name – the lady in question is so serious that she's asked us to get particulars of the house – numbers of rooms, layout, dimensions, that sort of thing. You see, she's an interior designer and her husband is an architect – so they reckon they can do the whole place up on the cheap, by keeping it in the family so to speak, and make a killing on the resale. Now I know she's got lots of dosh, 'cos I know where she lives now, and let me just say this—'

'Miss Parker – remember our promise to retain client anonymity,' interrupted Christine, right on cue.

'Of course, Miss Dixon,' replied Annie, brusquely, 'all I was going to say was that she lives in a very expensive house and she's just sold another one in Italy – so she'd be a cash buyer for anything under a million two, which might interest sir.'

'It interests sir very much,' replied Gary, feeling his mouth moisten at the thought of over a million for a quick, painless sale. 'But I can't have anyone runnin' around the place today . . . it's not . . . very tidy,' he spluttered, not being as quick on his toes as the ladies of the WISE Enquiries Agency.

Christine's phone rang and she looked at Annie, indicating she should carry on with the conversation as she excused herself to take the call. It was Carol.

'Can you talk?' asked Carol, sensibly.

'We're with the gentleman now,' was Christine's reply – she pointed at the phone and mouthed 'the office' at Gary.

'Right then, so just listen,' added Carol.

'I understand,' was Christine's safe reply.

'Your Aunt Agatha just phoned me – the police have been there, at Wraysbury Square. Don't worry, I haven't told anyone where you are, or what you're doing – especially that, because I don't know anyway. They've told her what Rob Brown told them about Poppy passing out in the pub last evening, and both Lady and Lord Wraysbury are now fully involved in the police search for Poppy. They are gravely concerned. The ransom note was apparently stapled to Rob's ear, and was addressed to "Jacintha's Father". The police are puzzled as to how Poppy was identified as working for Jacintha. And they don't seem to have the Gilchrist name yet – obviously that boy you told me about at the pub hasn't phoned them yet, or else the information hasn't got through to the right person, or they'd be there at Gilchrist's house already, I should have thought.'

'Oh my God!' exclaimed Christine loudly – she couldn't help herself – she'd just put two and two together. She needed to be able to talk to Carol without Gary overhearing her. She looked at Annie and Gary as if in a fit of embarrassment.

'Just hold on a moment, Carol, would you dear – I have to talk to Mr Gilchrist for a moment.' She continued, 'Excuse me for exclaiming aloud like that, Mr Gilchrist, not very ladylike, I'm sure you'll agree.' Christine, too, could lay it on with a trowel when she wanted. 'But it's our client, you see. Well, our potential client; she's phoned the office to say she's found an alternative property – and it's something that's already represented by someone else. I'll just have to have a detailed word with Carol back in the office to brief her on what to say to the client. Maybe you can help Mr Gilchrist understand why it's even more important now that we do this quickly, Annie?' Christine prayed Annie would pick up on her meaning.

Annie did, and went to work. Clearly Gary relented, because Annie called over her shoulder as she crossed the threshold to number eighteen St Peter's Terrace, 'Follow me in when you can, Miss Dixon.'

Could Christine hear panic in Annie's voice? Surely not, she thought. But whatever Annie was trying to tell her, she had to talk to Carol. She kept her eyes trained on the half-open front door as she spoke rapidly.

'Look, Carol darling, I've got to be quick, speakerphone please?'

'Mavis isn't here,' answered Carol. 'As soon as you two said you were planning on going into the house she grabbed the first aid kit and ran out to get a cab over to St Peter's Terrace. She thought you might need her there.'

'Good thinking,' said Christine. 'Now listen – Annie's in already; she's good, but I need to be there too. And I think I've just worked out this whole stupid mess; this idiot Gilchrist doesn't know he's got Poppy Brown, assistant florist, hidden away somewhere – he thinks he's got my cousin, Lady Jacintha Wraysbury, herself.'

'Why on earth would he think that?' asked Carol, blankly. 'Poppy doesn't look anything like Jacintha. Well, I suppose they're both small-framed, dark-haired, young women. Maybe Poppy talks like Jacintha, I don't know. Maybe Poppy was passing herself off as her boss . . .' Carol seemed non-plussed, then added, 'Maybe Poppy looks enough like your cousin for some mean-spirited, opportunistic idiot to think she's the real thing. And obviously this Gary Gilchrist is just such a person. That's why he dumped poor Rob on the street where he did – in Belgravia, just along the road from Wraysbury Square. Mind you – what's really worrying is that he's got away with this much. I most definitely think we should tell the police what's going on,' she added firmly.

Christine was torn. 'If the police show up mob-handed while Annie and I are inside – and she's inside already remember – it won't matter if Poppy's there or not; we'll be the ones in danger. And if Poppy is there,' added Christine desperately, 'maybe Annie and I can get her out without it all turning into some sort of hostage nightmare with rapid response teams and goodness knows what else involved.'

There was a silence in the office at the end of the phone.

'Here's what I suggest,' said Carol, in her best 'organizing' voice, 'I'll telephone the police in ten minutes and tell them what's happening at the Gilchrist house, what our opinions are about the Gilchrist man himself, and why we believe he's done what he's done so far. During that ten minutes you get yourself and Annie out of the Gilchrist house – with some sort of opinion about whether you think Poppy's on the premises or not. The police can be on the spot five minutes after that, I should think, and by then we'll all have a good idea of who's where. Agreed?'

Christine agreed, still not sure they were taking the right course of action – her instincts were to charge in and save Poppy herself.

As Christine walked up the steps toward Gary Gilchrist's front door, Carol put her watch on the desk in front of her, willing ten minutes to pass without anything bad happening – to anyone. She wondered what she could do to make the time pass faster.

At that very moment, Poppy Brown's fingers found a metal latch on a wooden door that she was immediately sure would lead her out of the cellar. She clicked it, gently. She cracked the door open and heard a woman's voice call out, not far away.

'Mr Gilchrist – it's Annabel Dixon here – the front door's still open. I'm coming in now. Are you all upstairs?'

Poppy didn't know anyone called Annabel Dixon, but the voice made her feel safe, and gave her the courage to open the door further.

And then everything went horribly pear-shaped.


As Christine walked through the front door of number eighteen, St Peter's Terrace, she looked up the staircase ahead of her and saw Annie beginning to descend.

'You've got a lovely place 'ere,' Annie was saying in a chatty voice, smiling around at Gary Gilchrist who was just behind her. Hearing Christine enter below Annie called down to her.

'Oh, Miss Dixon – I think this is just what our lady is after – all the right rooms in all the right places, but Mr Gilchrist says we can't see the *basement* or the *cellar* –' Annie placed particular emphasis on the words – 'because they're full of junk. I said we could estimate their sizes and maybe come back another day to measure them up.'

Standing just inside the front door, Christine was quick to catch on. 'Ah, so there's a basement and a cellar,' she repeated, and transferred her gaze from Annie at the top of the stairs toward the door straight ahead of her, that she guessed led to the back of the house. The door was open, and she was taken aback to see a filthy, bloodied head, followed by a filthy, bloodied torso, creeping slowly up the back staircase toward her.

Christine couldn't help herself. 'Poppy?' she cried.

'Yes,' Poppy shouted back weakly, sounding frightened.

Christine knew the girl must be confused. 'You're safe now, Poppy. Just come toward me and I can get you out of here. Your brother Rob is fine. He'll be pleased to see you.'

Gary Gilchrist looked horrified. He pulled a Stanley knife out of his pocket and pushed out the small but deadly blade to its fullest extent. Annie was on the stair below him. He had her head in a vice-like grip in the blink of an eye. He held the triangular blade to her throat.

Annie stopped squirming and gripped the banister the instant she felt the blade touch the skin of her throat.

Gilchrist's voice was rough, angry and cold. 'Don't move,' he shouted into Annie's ear. She wasn't moving a muscle. 'And you – you stay where you are, or I'll cut this one,' he shouted to Christine, who was also frozen to the spot.

Poppy ran toward the front door, flinging her arms around Christine's neck and trying to drag her outside.

'Let's get out of here,' she cried, but Christine remained rooted.

Without taking her eyes off Gilchrist and Annie for a second, as though her gaze could keep Annie safe, Christine said, 'Get out of here, Poppy – now. Run out onto the street, and look for a short woman with grey hair. Her name is Mavis. She'll help you. She's a nurse, a good one. We work together. And tell her the police will be here very soon.'

'They're almost here, and I've already arrived.' Mavis's voice came from just outside the front door.

Christine felt an enormous sense of relief.

'My colleague is right, Poppy,' said Mavis to the frightened, and obviously confused young woman, 'the best place for you is out here – come away with you now, and let me see if you've been hurt. Christine,' Mavis added firmly, 'the police are coming, they'll be here any moment, I can hear the sirens.'

'You bitches,' hissed Gary. 'I don't know who you are, but you won't get away with this. This one stays with me until I'm out of here safe,' he added stonily, twisting Annie's neck in the crook of his arm.

Natasha Moon appeared behind Gary and Annie at the top of the stairs; she looked panic-stricken. 'What's going on Gary?' she wailed. 'Oh my God, Gary, you're not going to hurt her, are you? She's been so nice to us,' she said in disbelief.

Gary shouted at her over his shoulder, 'Shut your face, you stupid little slapper. This is nothing to do with you – I'm gettin' out of here now. You can stay or go as you please, just keep out of my way.' Then to Annie he growled, 'Move,' and he began to push her down the stairs.

Annie held her ground, grabbing onto the banister even tighter.

'Move, or else I'll cut yer. Don't think I won't – I've done it before and I can do it again.' He pushed the point of the knife into Annie's neck. Christine could see blood starting to trickle toward her friend's chest. It was a terrifying sight.

Christine was absolutely agog when Annie dared to say, 'You cut that poor Rob Brown, didn't you, Gary?'

At this comment, Poppy, who'd been focusing on Mavis on the front doorstep and the half a dozen police cars converging on the house, turned to face the tableau at the top of the stairs.

'Rob?' she shouted. 'What's happened to Rob? Is Rob hurt? You said he was alright. Did you lie to me?'

Christine shook her head. She couldn't believe that Annie was still talking. Her gurgling voice echoed in the eerie stillness that had befallen the group, 'Luckily for you Poppy, and for Rob, your brother survived alright, and he was able to tell the police everything. Rob knows your face, Gary, and now so does Poppy, and so do I, and so does my colleague Christine. Christine is Jacintha Wraysbury's cousin, you know, Gary.'

Gary seemed puzzled. 'Them two are cousins?' He looked from Poppy to Christine.

Poppy replied, 'I'm not this woman's cousin. But there again I'm not Jacintha Wraysbury. I'm Poppy Brown. I work for Jacintha.'

Annie continued, 'We know you thought you had Lady Jacintha held here for ransom, but what you've got is this poor kid, Poppy Brown, instead. Lady Jacintha's assistant. So, whichever way you look at it, you're stuffed. You almost killed a perfectly innocent man – this girl's brother – and you sent a ransom note to Lord Wraysbury threatening his daughter's life. I expect you'll pay the price.'

'What do you know about it?' shouted Gary, sounding just a little panicked, but blustering nonetheless. 'You don't know nothin', you don't, you silly cow. You're just like all the rest of 'em ain't yer? Think yer knows ev'rythin', when you knows nothin', innit? Well, I'll show you. I can always put a woman in 'er place – even my stupid old mum thought she could boss me around. Well I showed her who was boss right enough, when I cut 'er throat. And I can show you lot too.'

'What do you mean, you cut your mother's throat? You told me your mum died and left you this house,' shouted Natasha.

'Well there ya go, Tash,' snarled Gary, 'I always said you'd believe any old rubbish I told yer. Thick as two short ones, ain't yer?'

Natasha's chin started to quiver. 'You and me is over, Gary Gilchrist, you hear. And I won't let you go hurtin' no one else.' Natasha grabbed at Gary's lank, greasy hair, pulling him backwards, twisting his neck, and began to hit him with her little fists. She screamed like a child.

Gary used the hand with which he was gripping the knife to try release his hair from Natasha's grip, slashing wildly behind him, but he also tightened his lock around Annie's neck, tossing her about at the top of the stairs.

Annie roared, and started to squirm, punching Gary in the belly.

Gary let go of Annie and spun around, slashing out with the knife toward Natasha's throat. She wasn't expecting the attack, so curled into a ball, trying to protect herself with her arms.

'Shut up, Tash, you silly bitch,' Gary shouted. The knife bit into the flesh of Natasha's arms, then he found his mark. Natasha stopped screaming. She slid to the floor, her hands at her throat, her eyes wide.

Annie managed to regain her balance enough to be able to take her chance; even as the unfortunate Natasha was falling to the ground, she grabbed Gary's knife-wielding arm and pulled on it as hard as she could, twisting it with both her hands, and with all her might. The knife sliced into her shoulder as he reeled. He lost his balance as he tried to fend her off, teetered for a second with a surprised look on his face, then tumbled backwards down the stairs, rolling, and thumping down the steep flight one tread at a time.

Annie grabbed the banister to support herself, but she, too, was about to topple – her hands cut and bleeding, she began to slip.

Christine felt Poppy push past her, saw her leap over Gary's body, which lay crumpled at the foot of the staircase, and sprint up toward Annie, two stairs at a time.

The police constable who was first through the front door had never seen anything quite like it – a staircase strewn with bodies, walls covered in blood and a young woman screaming at him to fetch a doctor. Luckily, a level-headed superior was right behind him, so he didn't have to decide what to do next.

Christine was pacing along the hospital corridor. She had been for hours. What were they doing in that operating room?

'Come and sit down,' whispered Mavis, but Christine felt that moving about was the only way to make everything alright for Annie.

Carol was wedged into an ugly plastic bucket-chair next to Lady Agatha, who was holding onto her daughter's hand as though she'd never let go of it again. Jacintha's other hand was being grasped tightly by Poppy Brown.

A nurse bustled into the waiting area.

'What's happening – will she be alright?' asked Christine. All faces turned toward the harried nurse.

'Doctor will be out in a minute,' she answered, then rushed off through a set of swinging double doors.

The 'minute' seemed like an age to the little group that had been waiting, tense and tired, for news about Annie's injuries. The paramedics had done what they could for her on the scene, but it had been clear Annie had lost a lot of blood, and no one had told them anything since she'd been whisked into an operating room upon arrival at the mercifully close-at-hand St Martha's Hospital.

Poppy had been cleaned up and pronounced fit to leave whenever she wanted; the police had interviewed Christine, Mavis and Carol, as well as Lady Agatha and Poppy herself. Poppy had spent some time with Rob, who was in another wing of the same hospital, and now all they could do was wait. And wait.

Finally a doctor arrived. He looked as tired as they all were. It was close to midnight.

Christine felt as though a cold hand was gripping her heart; she felt the responsibility of Annie's condition very personally.

They dreaded what the doctor might say, but they all needed to know.

'Miss Parker is in a stable condition . . .'

'Does that mean she's going to be alright?' was Christine's panicked query.

'With time, and a good deal of rest, she'll make a full recovery. Though she'll have some significant scars from the attack. We might need to do some follow-up cosmetic work, but that can wait for now.'

The doctor couldn't have been more succinct, nor his words more comforting to all those present.

Christine, Carol, and Mavis all looked at each other with wide grins and teary eyes. Mavis stood and reached forward to shake the doctor by the hand. Carol promptly burst into floods of tears and hugged Lady Agatha, who hugged back. Poppy pumped the air with a bandaged fist and Christine finally sat herself down and held her face in her hands, not crying, but laughing.

'When will we be able to see the patient,' asked the outwardly calm Mavis.

'Well, if you don't stay too long, you could see her in a few moments; they're just taking her up to the private room that Lady Wraysbury has arranged for. Ward A – Room 1; the best suite in the house,' he smiled, and winked at Mavis as he walked away.

'Come along then,' said Mavis, gathering the group together in her most efficient manner, 'if we're going to see her let's do it and get it over with so she can get some sleep – then the rest of us can get to our beds and do the same.'

Annie looked very small in the large room; she was propped up on pillows, her hands, neck and shoulder area heavily bandaged, her closely-cropped hair covered by a green paper cap, and with tubes coming out of her 'good' arm. Her eyes were open, and she was smiling.

'Oh Annie,' cried Christine as she pushed into the room, 'it's so good to see you looking so . . .'

'Crappy?' offered Annie.

'Well, you have looked better,' conceded Christine.

'It's alright Chrissy, doll',' replied Annie with a feeble wink, 'I haven't got to worry about what I look like in here, and they wouldn't give me a mirror anyway. Besides, they tell me all the scars will be under my clothes – when I'm wearing them, anyway.'

Christine, very uncharacteristically, burst into tears. Her aunt comforted her. Mavis picked up the chart that hung on the wall beside Annie's bed and cast an experienced eye across it.

'You've been a lucky girl,' she pronounced, re-hanging the chart and smiling, 'and I don't think we've got long before you're fast asleep in that bed there, young lady. They've given you some nice sedatives that should keep you resting for a while, whether you want to or not.'

'Oh Mave – I want to – believe me, I want to,' replied Annie. 'I ain't half tired, you know.' Then she added, looking at Carol, 'And you don't look none too bonnie, neither. What time is it? Does your David know where you are, Car? It must be very late, doll.'

'Yes,' replied Carol, smiling wanly. 'I phoned him hours ago, before I left the office to come here. He sends his love, Annie, and said he'll come with me to visit as soon as he can.'

'Ta,' replied Annie, 'and send my love back to him. Say I'm sorry I kept you out so late, but tell him to be grateful that at least I'm sending you home sober this time.'

The tension was easing in the room. Everyone could see that their Annie was still their Annie – all be it a sliced-up and stitched-back-together version.

'By the way,' added Christine, 'let me introduce you to my cousin's valued assistant, Poppy Brown; Poppy, meet Annie.'

'Thanks for coming to rescue me,' said Poppy, meekly.

'They told me in the ambulance it was you who stopped me from falling down the stairs – so thanks for that. I'll come and watch you making up bouquets one day, maybe.'

'That would be great,' replied Poppy, 'but I think I'll be bringing you a few, to brighten this room while you're here.'

'With our compliments,' added Jacintha.

A chuckle rippled around the room. It stopped abruptly when Annie asked, 'How's that little Tash – is she alright?'

Mavis answered; no one else seemed to be able to. 'Both Natasha Moon and Gary Gilchrist are dead, I'm afraid, dear.'

'Did I . . . did I kill him?' asked Annie, looking horrified. Everyone could see she was shaken by the idea.

Christine moved toward her and put her hand on Annie's. 'What could you do, but what you did, darling?' asked Christine quietly. 'It was self-defense. I mean, look at what he did to you. And that poor girl – he just slit her throat wide open. Oh Annie – she was dead when she hit the floor.'

'Trying to save me,' added Annie bleakly. 'Oh Gawd, this is terrible.'

Poppy stepped forward. 'The man was an animal. Lord knows what he'd have done to me, or indeed, to his girlfriend, given time. The police are already searching the house for his mother's remains; he'd told the neighbors he'd put her in a home, but now they're pretty sure he killed her so he could get the house. Miss Parker, the man was a lunatic. And you came to save me. Whoever he thought I was, I'm pretty sure he meant me no good, look at what he did to my poor brother, Rob. He really meant to kill him, you know.' She stopped and drew breath. 'This was never going to end well for everyone.'

The room fell silent.

'I have some news,' said Carol quietly, and she shoved a little plastic stick toward Annie. Annie peered at it, looking confused.

Carol waggled the stick at Annie. 'I did it while I was waiting to phone the police this afternoon – to make the time go faster. I did three of them, and they're all the same. I'm preggers.' She was beaming. 'No wonder I felt so bad – I've caught.'

'Oh, doll,' said Annie tiredly, 'there's me all banged up and you up the spout – what's to become of the WISE Enquiries Agency now then, girls?'

'Don't go worrying your head about that, young lady,' admonished Mavis. 'I'll put money on it that a few months from now we'll all be back at it, somehow.'

'And, until then,' interrupted Lady Agatha, 'you can rest assured there'll be a large lump sum in your company bank account by the weekend. My brother – Christine's father – will be continuing his support of you by providing your offices free of charge, and Annie's private room and medical bills will all be taken care of by my husband. The Wraysbury family will do everything in its power to ensure that the WISE Enquiries Agency does more than survive this. Indeed, we'll do our level best to ensure that, when you are able, it will thrive because of it. You answered mine and my dear daughter's call, in our time of need, and for that I shall be ever in your debt. I have many influential, and wealthy, friends. They also have friends. And I'll wager many of them have need of people who can do what – collectively – you women do. Be assured, I shall be your loudest and most supportive advocate.'

'So I suppose we're going to have to get used to dealing with the Hoity Toity set, then . . .' said Annie as she began to drift to sleep with a wry grin on her face.

'To the Hoity Toities,' said Christine, by way of a mock-toast, but Annie was fast asleep, Carol was already planning the nursery, and Mavis was wondering whether she could catch the doctor before she left – just to check on a few of the medical details for Annie's recuperation. Christine smiled at her aunt and her cousin, and her cousin's aide Poppy.

All family – in so many different ways.

# SUMMER

## OUT AND ABOUT IN A BOAT

### A standalone thriller

'It'll be boring, Dad,' whined Zack; Dave couldn't recall everything sounding boring to him when he was fifteen.

'Can we have a campfire, Dad?' gushed Becky; at thirteen she possessed more confidence and maturity than her brother, but could still delight Dave with her childish enthusiasm.

'That depends on the weather, and what level of fire alert is posted around the lake,' replied Dave, keen that his ex-wife should see he was taking the camping trip seriously.

'And you're sure this cabin's okay?' Debbie sounded doubtful; she and Dave had been separated for two years, but she was still painfully aware of his ability to screw up almost anything.

'Mike at work has had the cabin for years,' replied Dave. He did his best to not snap at Debbie in front of the kids; they'd promised each other they would try to never do that, and it usually worked. Dave was eager to enjoy a weekend with his children in the wilderness, far away from PlayStations and iPhones.

'Mike takes his kids there all the time,' he added enthusiastically. 'He's going to run us up there in his boat, and there's a little rowboat for us to muck about in when we're there.' He saw Debbie open her mouth to protest, so added quickly, 'We'll all wear life vests, at all times.'

Debbie still looked uncertain. Dave pushed on.

'There aren't many weekends we can do this: Zack's got hockey from September until May; Becky's skating doesn't wind up until June, and this is the only weekend in July we can have it to ourselves – come August, Mike and his family will be there every weekend. School's just out – let's have a little R&R? A little time just for me and the kids?'

Dave could tell Debbie was biting her tongue. He hoped she'd see the excitement on the kids' faces and agree with Dave that a weekend away from everything they seemed to constantly plug themselves into might not be a bad idea.

Trying to defuse Debbie's obvious misgivings, Dave said, 'It's BC's second-largest lake, and it's tidal too – so it's really a fjord lake.' He'd only just found that out so thought he'd mention it. 'And it's really lovely, so we all know that means it's one of Canada's most stunning lakes, because it is "Beautiful British Columbia" after all, eh?'

Dave didn't get so much as a smile from anyone for that little quip, so he just kept going. 'And it's just up the road, for heaven's sake, right on our doorstep – it's not like I'd be taking them to the other side of the world. We'll be in the cabin within an hour of leaving the house, then Mike will come back to pick us up the next day. We'll be out of here at eight a.m. on Saturday, and we can all four of us have dinner together on Sunday, and tell Mom all about it. Come on, kids – it'll be fun.' Dave wasn't going to beg, but he'd get as close as he could.

'Why can't I take my PlayStation?' asked Zack, still whining.

'Because we'll be too busy hiking and fishing and bird watching and cooking up a storm for you to want it,' replied Dave, trying to make the alternative forms of entertainment he'd planned sound just as exciting as some multi-level war between androids and aliens . . . and probably zombies.

Zack didn't look convinced.

'I could make S'mores,' said Becky sweetly to Zack. 'You like S'mores.'

Zack grunted, which Dave took to mean he was going to go along with the plan.

'I'll organize the food and drink,' volunteered Debbie.

'But we'll be fishing,' was Dave's bright reply.

'Well, best to be prepared – just in case you don't catch anything,' said Debbie with a sigh.

Dave was delighted; he didn't want to bother with all that kind of boring, practical stuff – he was thinking about fishing lines, trail maps, and compasses. He'd bring along his old guitar, and they could play the board games Mike had told him were stored at the cabin. Dave could picture it clearly – just him and the children, the magnificence of nature all around them, freshly caught fish grilling on an open fire. Wonderful. Idyllic.

'I'll be here at seven thirty on Saturday morning,' said Dave to Debbie as he walked away from the family house in Pitt Meadows to return to his apartment in Coquitlam.

'Don't be late. Don't let them down, Dave,' called Debbie. She looked worried.

'I don't know why you say that. You're always saying that,' snapped Dave, sure the children were out of earshot. 'I can manage to look after my own children for one night, you know.' He hated that Debbie had no confidence in him. 'I'll be here on time, and we'll have great fun.' He spoke with conviction, hoisting himself into his aged, gas-guzzling pickup.

He pulled at the screeching, ill-fitting door. 'They'll have a weekend they'll never forget,' he shouted cheerily as he pulled away.


It was seven fifty-three a.m. on Saturday morning when Dave's truck ground to a halt outside the family house. Debbie was peering through the window, and she, Zack and Becky were out of the front door before he could even unbuckle his seatbelt.

'I knew you'd be late,' hissed Debbie accusingly as she loaded cooler boxes into the back of the pickup. 'They thought you'd forgotten. Becky was almost in tears. Why the hell didn't you phone?' Debbie was seething, battling to keep her voice down.

Dave was angry with himself; he thought he'd got up in time to get everything done – but he'd run out of the apartment without his phone so he'd had to go back for it, then he'd realized he hadn't charged it overnight so he couldn't call Debbie because he had to charge it in the truck where he wasn't able to talk hands-free, and then the traffic was snarled. He'd had to stop for gas on the way because he was totally out; it had been one thing on top of another – all conspiring to make him late.

As Dave apologized to the children, Debbie kept loading boxes. And more boxes. And backpacks.

'You know we're only going for one night, right?' was Dave's exasperated observation when the back of the pickup was half full.

'Which means you'll need bedding, a couple of changes of clothes, swimsuits, sandals, blankets, towels, food, water, and a full medical kit. I guess you hadn't thought of any of that, had you?' Debbie was still hissing at Dave.

'I'll just spit on a bit of old tee-shirt and they'll clean up fine, right kids?' responded Dave, mugging for the kids' sakes.

'Don't even joke about it!' snapped Debbie.

Dave hadn't been joking.

She continued, 'I've packed sunscreen, antihistamine spray and antibiotic spray, bug spray, bandages, and a sling. There's all sorts in there – everything you could possibly need. Okay?'

'Sure,' answered Dave, sighing.

'I've checked the batteries in the flashlights – all three of them, and I've put in spare batteries. Got it?'

'Sure.'

'The toilet paper is in with the bedding.'

Toilet paper hadn't even occurred to Dave.

'I've put Zack's blue sandals with his blue shorts, and his brown sandals with his brown shorts.'

'Why does he need two pairs of sandals?' asked Dave, mystified.

'Because he's like his dad used to be – fussy about his clothes.'

'I was never fussy about my clothes,' he said with certainty.

'This from the man who took longer to pick out his Grad tux than I did my Grad dress,' said Debbie, rolling her eyes.

Dave could remember no such thing, but admitted to himself that Debbie was much better than him at remembering things – especially when they were arguing.

'And listen,' Debbie pulled Dave close, 'Becky has packed a small stuffed dog in with her bedding. It's George, her favorite. If you see it, don't mention it. It doesn't exist – right?'

'Sure,' said Dave sighing again. He added a tired, 'Whatever,' which he knew immediately was a big mistake.

'Don't "whatever" me!' Debbie was whispering as loudly as possible. 'Listen Dave, you're responsible for these children for a whole two days, and I know how difficult it is for you to act responsibly when it's just you looking after just you . . .'

Oh God, thought Dave, here we go again . . .

'. . . so buck up and be a father, Dave, not just a big kid. You're the adult – act like one.'

Dave waved with relief as they finally pulled out of the drive. It was ten past eight, and they were supposed to meet Mike in five minutes. Once they got around the corner, out of Debbie's sight, Dave floored it, which Zack loved. Becky tutted. They finally arrived at the boat launch at the south end of Pitt Lake ten minutes late.

Not bad, thought Dave, congratulating himself on a super-quick trip.

'Sorry, Mike,' said Dave smiling, as he jumped out of the truck. 'Debbie wasn't quite ready, and then we had to pack this lot.' Dave rolled his eyes toward the back of the truck.

'They're all the same,' replied Mike. His work colleague was smiling, but Dave wasn't convinced he'd bought his excuse.

It took thirty minutes to pack everything and everyone into the boat and get going.

As they cut through the rippling water, Zack chatted happily to Mike at the wheel. Dave hadn't seen him so animated in months; if Zack managed a five-word sentence in Dave's company it was usually because he was complaining about something. Becky, on the other hand, who hardly ever stopped talking, was silently gripping the sides of her seat with both hands. It took about twenty minutes of bumpy motoring across the vastness of Pitt Lake to reach its farthest extremities, then about twenty more minutes of slow meandering through shallow waters to finally reach the cabin, which was situated at the end of a narrow finger of water almost completely cut off from the rest of the lake by a large sandbank.

Mike tied the boat to the end of the wooden pier which he proudly announced he and his boys had constructed during previous summers, while Dave walked with Becky to dry land. She didn't offer to help unload the boat, but went away to sit quietly on the rocky shoreline while the boys did the work. Dave thought she looked pale, but she didn't complain, or throw up – for which Dave was grateful.

'I'm fine, Dad,' she said weakly when he asked how she was feeling. Dave ruffled her hair and left her to sit for a moment.

Mike opened up the cabin with a flourish; Dave was somewhat dismayed – he'd expected something truly 'cabin-like', but the place was more like a shack. A newish-looking green metal roof sat awkwardly atop a rickety cedar plank structure, which had weathered to silver-grey with the passing years. The heavily padlocked door opened onto a large room, which was obviously the only living space. One small window allowed a little light to filter in; the freshly disturbed dust glittered in a shaft of sun. A collection of mismatched dining chairs sat around an old kitchen table, a badly deteriorated tan 'pleather' sofa almost hid a number of cots stacked against the wall.

Mike pulled a small, rusty grill from a corner of the room, and set it up outside with the new bottle of propane he'd brought, well away from the cabin beside a log-built picnic table and benches.

'Where's the bathroom?' asked Becky. Dave was worried his daughter was feeling sick to her stomach, but she told him not to fuss; at least her color had returned to normal.

'Round the back,' replied Mike, 'I'll show you.' He walked them all to the outhouse; Dave could tell by his daughter's face that the realization of what 'roughing it' really meant was beginning to dawn upon her, and she wasn't impressed.

Zack laughed at his sister's face-pulling; Becky pointed out that Zack had to use the outhouse too and that it smelled, but that he probably wouldn't notice because he was so stinky himself.

Dave tried to keep the peace, at least until Mike had gone.

The two men returned to the boat to check they'd unloaded everything.

'The trail map showing the route to the tree house is on the pinboard in the cabin,' Mike reminded Dave, 'and don't forget this,' he added, as he handed a long, slim, metal box to Dave. 'Here's the key.'

'A gun case?' Dave was surprised.

'Of course,' said Mike. 'There are cougars and bears up here, and they're not used to humans being on their patch. You never know, you might need it. You know how to use a gun, right?'

'Of course,' lied Dave, taking the surprisingly heavy box from his work colleague. He'd never held a gun case before, let alone a gun.

'Good. I guess you don't have a permit, though?' Dave shook his head. Mike shrugged. 'Unlikely anyone will check. I'd be happier knowing it's here with you, rather than with me in Maple Ridge; you're more likely to need it than me. The rowboat's inside the cabin, behind the door – don't forget to tie it up properly, right?' said Mike.

'Sure.'

'And the fire alert is orange, so you can have a small campfire, but make sure you douse any embers, right?'

'Sure.' Dave thought Mike was beginning to sound a lot like Debbie.

'And don't forget – the kids don't leave that cabin alone after dark unless you go with them, right?'

'Sure,' replied Dave wearily, wondering why they couldn't go to the outhouse without him.

'They won't know what a bear in the bush sounds like, you will – won't you?' asked Mike, as if replying to Dave's inner question.

'Sure.' Dave had no idea what a bear would sound like either in or out of the bush, he'd only ever seen one at a distance. Thank goodness. 'You go on back now, Mike – we'll be fine, honest.' Dave tried to sound convincing.

Good grief, they were only going to be there for a day – what could possibly happen in just a day? Dave waved goodbye to Mike and turned to face the cabin.

'Da-ad – Zack pushed me over and I've cut my leg,' cried Becky sitting on the hard, dry ground surrounding the cabin; she was covered in dust, and sobbing.

'No I didn't,' retorted Zack.

'Yes you did – you did it on purpose,' whined Becky.

'Well you started it, calling me "stinky",' responded Zack, kicking dust at his sister.

'Stop it you two,' shouted Dave as he carried the gun case along the little wooden pier. 'I don't care who started it, or what "it" is. Becky – wash that cut in the lake, and I'll find the medical box.'

Dave was beginning to suspect that a day might turn out to be a lot longer than he'd thought.


It took the three of them some time to sort out the cabin; they tended to Becky's leg, then unpacked, cleaned the dead spiders off the cots and set them up with the bedding, and finally agreed it was time to all change into their swimsuits.

Dave and Zack waited outside the cabin so Becky could have some privacy, then she waited outside the cabin while the boys changed.

Dave reckoned it would take them about thirty seconds, but he hadn't factored in the time it took Zack to pull his bizarrely long board-shorts down onto his theoretical hips, then up again, then down again, making almost imperceptible adjustments until the shorts were at what was, apparently, exactly the right level. Dave pointed out several times that it was just him and his sister who'd see Zack, but Zack replied that it didn't matter – they had to be in the right spot.

'Da-ad,' Becky shouted through the half-open door, 'I know it's July and it'll get hot today, but that water felt super cold when I washed my leg; I don't think I want to go swimming.'

'It'll be fine,' replied Dave, pulling on his faded swimming shorts in an instant and emerging from the cabin triumphant. 'Come help me with the boat.'

'Okay,' said Becky, brightening.

'Can I jump off the pier, Dad?' shouted Zack as he ran along the creaking wooden structure.

'No – you don't know how deep it is there,' his father replied sharply.

'Yes I do; it's four meters at the end of the pier – Mike's boat has a depth-finder and a fish-finder, and it showed four meters there.'

Dave was amazed at his son's powers of observation – not something he'd noticed before.

'Go on then – but be careful.' Dave had barely finished speaking when he heard a tremendous splash and a joyful whoop; he suspected that the carefully positioned board-shorts wouldn't remain in 'the right spot' for long.

He and Becky dragged the boat to the shore; it was a funny little thing – bright yellow fiberglass and shaped like a frog's body, with leg-like extensions that Mike had confidently announced gave it great stability. Dave wasn't familiar with the style of boat, but – truth be told – he hadn't been in a rowboat since his teens, when he and his dad had gone fishing together a handful of times. But he knew how to row, that was the important thing.

'Life vests?' asked Becky, her little arms folded just like her mother's as she stood over the frog-like boat that still sat safely on the rocky shoreline.

'Of course,' replied Dave, pointedly, 'you can fetch them from the cabin, and bring one for Zack too.'

Zack had swum to shore and was shaking himself off. 'Dad, when are we gonna eat?' he asked, plaintively.

'Didn't your mother give you breakfast?' asked Dave, surprised.

'Yeah – but that was hours ago,' replied Zack sulkily. 'I'm starving.'

Dave looked at his watch – it was only ten thirty a.m.

'We'll eat in a couple of hours,' he said.

'Here, Mom packed these for you,' shouted Becky as she threw a bunch of trail-mix bars at Zack.

Zack ripped one open and ate greedily. Dave wondered when Zack's appetite had kicked in; when he'd moved out of the family home it was all you could do to get the boy to eat anything, he'd been so picky about his food. But that was a couple of years ago, Dave reminded himself, and boys could change a lot between thirteen and fifteen. Tough times.

'Will that hold you?' asked Dave, as Zack handed him the empty wrappers.

Zack grunted.

Dave added, 'And what do you expect me to do with these?' He was referring to the wrappers Zack had handed him.

'I dunno,' replied Zack, clearly not caring.

'Put them in the cabin, then let's go for a row about,' said Dave.

Zack grunted again, took the wrappers from his father's hand as though they were covered in acid, and made his way toward the cabin.

'Will it be okay to leave it all open like that?' asked Becky, nodding at the cabin. 'I've got important personal items in there, you know.'

Dave smiled at his teenage daughter, thinking how she was like her mother. Dave and Debbie had known each other since fifth grade; sometimes the way Becky moved, or flicked her shoulder-length brown hair, reminded him of Debbie at that age. But that Debbie was gone – she'd been replaced by a nagging, list-making, penny-pinching woman who always put the kids first and never seemed to have time for Dave . . . at least, not since the kids had been born.

Dave missed the old Debbie; she'd been his best friend. Now she was like his own mom; for years before their separation Debbie had treated him as though he were her third child, and he didn't need another mother – he wanted a wife.

'It'll be fine,' was Dave's far-away reply to his daughter's question. 'No one comes up here – it's like a little secret cove. You saw how careful Mike had to be to get here, all that twisting and winding around the little islands and that big sandbank? And you can only get here by boat, so we'd see anyone coming. Your stuff will be just fine in the cabin.' He winked at her, and she smiled back.

'Da-ad?' Zack called.

'Yes, Zack.'

'Shall I bring some water?'

'Yes, Zack.'

'Okay.'

Zack returned with three bottles of water.

'Let's get going,' said Dave, impatient to get out onto the glassy lake. He settled the children into one end of the boat, with strict instructions that there was to be no messing about, and pushed it out into the surprisingly icy waters.

A few fumbles with the oars and he was rowing; maybe he wasn't all that efficient, but they were moving away from the shore quite satisfactorily. About five minutes later they'd left the shade of the tree-covered hillside that climbed behind the cabin, and were out in the hot sun of the late morning.

'I should have worn sunscreen,' said Becky in a concerned voice. 'And so should you, Zack. You know how you burn.'

Dave could have kicked himself; Zack only had to see the sun to burn, he knew that. Why hadn't he thought of sunscreen for his boy?

'We won't be out in it for long, don't worry, it'll be fine,' said Dave, hoping it would be. 'Look, isn't it beautiful?'

He nodded his head toward the shore they'd just left, and the surrounding mountains; the cabin stood behind a small, rocky beach, set into a low-lying area of brush. Above it soared magnificent cedar-cloaked mountains; there were trees as far as the eye could see, in every direction.

'There's nothing here,' said Zack.

Ahead of him, Dave could see the buoy Mike had told him about; apparently it marked a safe place to swim.

'We'll tie up in a minute and you can both jump in,' said Dave, trying to be cheerful.

'It's too cold,' said Becky, dangling her hand in the water.

'Can I take this off?' asked Zack, pulling at his life vest.

'No, keep it on out here,' said Dave, keen to fulfil his fatherly duties.

'Oh Da-ad,' whined his son.

'No arguments, Zack. I know you're a good swimmer, but you can't be too careful.'

'But I can't dive with this on.'

'Zack!'

Zack grunted.

'Look, Dad, there's a hat in the water,' said Becky, pointing to a ball cap that was floating close to the buoy.

'I bet there's a head in it,' said Zack, mocking his little sister.

'Shut up,' snapped Becky.

'Shut up yourself,' said Zack, splashing Becky with the chilly water.

'Stop it you two,' shouted Dave, trying his best to tie the boat to the bobbing buoy.

'Get the hat, Dad, see if there's a head in it,' shouted Zack joyfully.

'You can't do that – you don't know where it's been,' replied Becky, chiding her brother.

'It's been in the lake, stupid,' retorted Zack.

'I've told you two already – stop it, or it's straight back to the cabin, right now,' said Dave, already exasperated. 'And leave that cap where it is, Zack, your sister's right; you don't know where it's been.'

Vindicated, Becky poked out her tongue at her brother, who'd already lost interest in the cap and was pointing to something else floating nearby.

'Look, Dad, there's that too,' said Zack, pointing at what seemed to be a white rubber glove.

Dave peered at it, and wondered where it could have come from. As it floated closer he got a better look at it. He felt his stomach tighten; he could see fingernails.

Gloves didn't have fingernails; hands had fingernails.

Dave was still grappling with that thought when Zack shouted, 'Get the glove, Dad – maybe there's a hand in it!' He waggled his own wet hand in his sister's face, making her squirm and squeal.

'Right, that's it,' snapped Dave, loosening the rope, 'we're going back to the cabin now, and we're not coming back out in this boat again.'

He started to row away from what he was now quite convinced was a floating, dismembered hand as quickly as he could. He was pretty sure the kids hadn't seen the fingernails, and he was working hard to convince himself he hadn't seen them either. It couldn't possibly be a real hand; he'd get them all back to the shore, and everything would be just fine.

They reached the little beach safely, then Becky busied herself helping prepare an early lunch, while Zack complained about his dad not letting him jump off the pier anymore. Dave couldn't tell him it was because he was afraid there was a human hand floating around out there, so he said it was because the water was too cold.

The food shut Zack up, eventually, then they all cleared everything away, which Becky assured them would deter bears.

Slathering the children with sunscreen to protect them from the searing July sun now directly overhead, Dave proudly announced they were going to have a beachcombing challenge; he'd typed up a list of things they had to find and bring to him in buckets he'd also provided – the winner would get a candy bar. He felt proud that he'd remembered to print out two lists, and pack the buckets and candy. Dave watched as Becky carefully read the list, then began to scurry about. Zack trudged away, kicking stones and muttering.

'Don't go off the beach into the brush – stay where I can see you,' called Dave to Zack as he wandered off.

'So how am I going to find a pinecone on the beach?' asked Zack, as if his father were a complete idiot.

'I've found one,' was Becky's smug reply; she held a massive pinecone aloft.

'There'll be lots of them, Zack,' replied Dave. 'Use your eyes – don't just wander along kicking the stones.'

'This is so boring,' muttered Zack, loudly enough so that Dave could hear him.

'Well your sister's doing better than you, so if you want that candy bar you'd better start paying attention,' was Dave's tart response. Clearly bribery was the only thing that was going to work with his son.

The day wasn't going quite as Dave had hoped it would – but at least he'd managed to convince himself that the 'hand' he'd seen was a leftover from one of the movies or TV shows they filmed in the area. It was probably just part of a dummy they'd left lying around, like those fake 'Jaws' sharks they'd lost out at sea when they were making that movie; he'd learned about that when they'd all visited Universal Studios a few years back.

And it was such a lovely day – the kids would enjoy all the fresh air. He planned an expedition to the tree house after the beachcombing challenge; he'd brought binoculars so they could climb up and watch the bald eagles soar above them. They'd like that.

Then he heard it.

It was the most dreadful sound Dave had heard in his life.

It was the sound of his usually grunting, constantly bored, fifteen-year-old son screaming in abject terror.

Even Becky instinctively seemed to know that her brother wasn't messing about, and her little face showed her own silent fright as she turned to her dad.

'Stay there, don't move,' was all Dave could manage to say to Becky as he ran toward his son, who was, in turn, running toward his father; Zack's stick-thin arms and legs were flailing, his treasure-bucket and his beachcombing list went flying behind him.

'Zack – Zack, what is it?'

Zack looked as terrified as he sounded. 'Dad – there's a dead body.'

Dave didn't have to ask if his son was kidding around. He reached out and hugged him as though he were an infant, and Zack let him.

'It's okay,' he whispered into his son's ear, rocking him gently, 'I'll go look. You go see if your little sister's alright.' He looked into his son's frightened eyes; the poor boy was shaking. 'Go on now – it'll be fine.' He watched as the siblings ran toward each other.

Dave walked over to where Zack had been when he'd screamed. Behind a boulder was the gruesome sight Zack had seen; it was what was left of a man – the face had gone, and a bloody mess was all that remained. There were no hands, nor feet. He was naked. It was truly horrific.

Dave felt his gut cramp. Poor Zack; he shouldn't have to see something like that – not at his age. Never.

Horrific though the sight before him was, Dave couldn't seem to take his eyes off it. For a moment he thought that this, like the hand, might be some sort of dummy left over from a movie shoot. But, as the flies that had been disturbed by his arrival began to settle again on the remains, Dave knew in his heart it was real.

This had once been a person.

Poor Zack.

Dave finally managed to make his body listen to his brain, and he turned to look at his children; they were standing together, their arms around each other. Becky looked tiny beside her tall, weedy brother, but she seemed to be the one doing the comforting. Dave had to do something himself – he knew that, but he didn't know what.

He'd been planning a bonding weekend in the stunning wilderness; now his son would probably be psychologically scarred for life. He wondered what Debbie would say, then realized that, somehow, this would turn out to be his fault. What if she never let him see the kids again?

'Dad, is it really a dead body?' called Becky, obviously not sure if her brother was just making it all up – or maybe hoping he was.

'Yes, it's a dead body,' replied Dave, deciding it was best to tell the truth. He took one last look at the thing, and walked toward his children. 'I think we should just leave it where it is, and try to forget about it; we'll sort it all out when Mike comes back tomorrow. It'll be fine, kids, honest.'

'Well, it won't be fine for the person who's dead,' replied Becky, in a very grown-up tone. 'Do you think he was murdered?'

Dave was stunned.

Zack snapped, 'Of course he was murdered – I told you – they've blown his face away and cut off his hands and feet. You can't do that to yourself.' Dave was amazed that Zack seemed to have overcome his initial horror; Dave hadn't.

'So whoever did it has tried to hide his identity,' replied Becky, quite calmly.

Dave was beginning to wonder if he'd slipped into a different dimension; why were his kids so calm? Why were they acting as though it was the most natural thing in the world to find a dead body – and a mutilated one at that – when you were camping in the wilderness?

'You both seem to be taking this very . . . well,' muttered Dave, not sure what else to say. Of course he was glad they'd managed to pull themselves together, but this reaction was puzzling – worrying even.

Both Becky and Zack looked surprised.

'Dad, we're not little kids, you know,' replied Becky. 'I helped cut up a frog in science last year, and Zack's seen a dead body before – haven't you?' For once, Becky seemed quite impressed with her brother.

'Yeah,' said Zack, with a swagger, 'Pete at school – his gran died, and I got to touch her face and her hand at the wake at his house. She smelled a bit funny, but it was okay.'

Were these really his children? Dave found it hard to believe.

'So you're both okay – you're not . . . upset?' said Dave quietly, now by their side; he was the adult – he had to be sure.

'Yeah.' They answered him as if he'd been mad to ask. Becky even 'tutted' at him, as though he were the one to be pitied.

'Good. I mean . . . I'm glad you're okay.' Dave was relieved, but still concerned about their attitude.

'Dad, you know that glove in the lake, and the ball-cap?' asked Becky.

'Yes,' replied Dave, worrying about what might come next.

'Well, they might belong to him.' Becky pointed toward the hidden body.

'They might,' conceded Dave.

'So they could be evidence; I think we should collect them. They could float away and never be found, and that might compromise the investigation into this man's death.'

Dave was now totally convinced that his daughter had been spirited away and replaced by an alien.

'Where on earth did you learn to speak – and think – like that?' asked Dave, blown away by his daughter's calm maturity.

'She's always watching cop shows with Mom,' replied Zack on behalf of his sister. 'I think they're pretty crappy – but some of them have good dead bodies in them. I like the ones with lots of autopsies when the corpses are all wide open. They're the best.'

Dave watched some TV, but not as much as he'd once done; nowadays he preferred a cold one after work with his buddies, and by the time he got home he'd usually hit the sack right away, because getting up at five a.m. to get a ride to his construction job took it out of him. But, even so, he couldn't imagine that just watching TV could change his daughter so much.

'Come on, Dad – it might be important,' said Becky, sounding excited. 'This could be my big chance; Miss Gilmore at school says I'm good at science. I could make a career of it. This could get me noticed.'

Dave was nonplussed; he'd been worried that his kids would be traumatized for life by finding a dead body, and all his little girl could think of was a career plan.

'I don't think we should go messing around with any of it, and that's that,' said Dave, with all the authority he could muster.

'She's right, Dad,' piped up Zack, 'the hat and the glove could be important.'

'You can tell whoever killed him wanted to hide his identity,' announced Becky. 'Zack said the body had no hands or feet and the face was gone – that way there'd be no fingerprints or dental remnants, so the police might never know who he is. Maybe there's a clue in the hat, or the glove. Hey, Dad, what if there was a hand inside the glove? Then there'd be fingerprints – it could break the case wide open.' Becky's face lit up as she thought of this grisly possibility.

Dave wondered about telling them the 'glove' had fingernails, but then reckoned he'd have to go out and retrieve the blessed thing, and he wasn't doing that. No way.

'Listen, kids, I think we need to forget about the body,' said Dave in his most fatherly voice. Both of his children looked at him as though he were the dumbest person on the face of the planet.

'What do you mean, forget about it? It's right there,' shouted Zack, pointing to where the body lay.

'Yes, Dad,' added Becky, 'that's just not possible. We can stay away from it, sure, if that makes you feel better, but we should look around for clues to help the cops when they get here. You are going to call them, aren't you?'

Dave was astonished he hadn't thought of that himself.

'Of course I'm going to call them,' was his somewhat terse reply. 'In fact, I'm going to do that right now.'

'You can't,' said Zack sounding cocky.

'Why not?' snapped Dave.

'Because there's no signal out here, I already tried,' replied Zack.

'You've tried calling the cops already?' Dave was annoyed with his son.

'No,' Zack sounded as if he was answering a buffoon, 'I tried calling a couple of the guys from school, and there's no signal here.'

'Why would you want to call anyone from school?' Dave was mystified.

'Because I just found a dead body with no face. It's so cool. I wanted to tell them, and I'd like to take some photos. I bet they'd wish they were here.'

Dave shook his head in disbelief, not at the possible lack of a signal – he'd already considered that – but at how Zack could be so cold-blooded about the whole matter. It seemed as though all he wanted to do was show off, while his little sister wanted to act like someone on a TV crime show. Dave supposed he should be grateful they weren't both crying and screaming about the grisly discovery, but he was still concerned that the horror of the circumstances had yet to dawn on them.

He checked his phone – but his son was right, there was no signal. Dave wandered around a bit, hoping the little bars would appear on the phone's screen, but to no avail.

'There might be a chance of a signal out on the lake,' suggested Becky. 'You'd be further away from the mountains out there. Shall we try?'

Dave thought his daughter made a good point, but then they'd be closer to the floating hand. He didn't like that idea.

She pressed, 'We've both got lots of sunscreen on us now, Dad, so we won't burn, and we could pick up that hat and glove – just to keep them safe.'

Dave thought about how much of her mom's persistence Becky displayed, but, unfortunately, he couldn't think of a good reason to not try to get a signal out on the lake.

'We'll all go together, wearing life vests, with no diving, and we'll try to grab the "clues" – if we spot them.' Dave knew he sounded hesitant; he reckoned his kids picked up on it right away and didn't want him to have time to change his mind, because Becky ran to get the little fishing net they'd spotted inside the cabin – to help retrieve the 'evidence' – and Zack enthusiastically pulled the boat to the edge of the water, ready for the off.

'Can you bring something to eat, Becky?' called Zack to his sister.

'Sure,' his sister called back, as though it would be a terrible chore.

Finally, Dave once again pushed away from the beach, pointing the little frog-boat toward the widest part of the finger of water immediately ahead. He rowed carefully, trying to not splash too much.

'Dad, look, there's the hat,' shouted Becky gleefully as she reached out with the net and successfully captured the floating ball-cap. 'Now everyone look out for the glove,' she instructed her father and brother, in her mother's voice.

'You keep checking for a signal on all three of those phones,' said Dave to Zack, who was peering from beneath his own ball-cap in the hot afternoon sun.

'Nothing. Not even one bar on any of them,' said Zack, glumly. 'Why don't we try a bit farther out?'

Dave didn't want to venture too far from the cabin, but he saw the sense of trying to get a signal. 'Let's go as far as those rocks,' he suggested, nodding toward a knobbly little island poking out of the deeper waters of the lake not far ahead of them; it wasn't more than twenty feet long, and was home to a couple of cedars and some moss-covered outcrops.

The kids seemed to be excited by the prospect of getting to the island, so Dave rowed on, sweating in the heat of the early afternoon. He fancied a beer – but hadn't dared bring any adult beverages on the trip, in case Debbie had spotted them.

Finally, panting like a steam train and with his tee shirt completely soaked with sweat, Dave felt the boat bump against the rocks; he pulled in the oars. Looking around, it was clear there was nowhere to tie up, so he grabbed onto a fern that seemed to be growing directly out of a boulder.

'Still no signal,' announced Zack in an 'I told you so' taunt directed toward his sister.

'Well at least we tried,' retorted Becky, rolling her eyes at her brother. 'If you've tried your best, you can't blame yourself if you don't succeed,' she pointed out, quoting their mom.

'Okay, you two,' snapped Dave, exhausted and wishing he didn't have to row all the way back to the cabin again, 'just keep quiet and enjoy the scenery.'

Becky seemed to be taking in the sights around her, while Zack fiddled with his ball-cap and life vest, grumbling under his breath that there was nothing to look at that was interesting, and that he was hungry. Dave felt exasperated; when had Zack become such a pain in the butt? He used to be a great kid – always running and playing and jumping and full of energy; now he just seemed to want to sit, eat, and moan about everything, even out there in the stunning wilderness.

'I can see the glove, Dad,' shouted Becky, excitedly. 'See – it's just there, between us and the buoy. Come on Dad, let's get it.'

Dave had to say something; he had to explain about the glove. 'Becky, I think we should just leave it to float around – it's not going anywhere.'

Dave didn't sound convincing, and Becky wasn't taken in.

'It could be evidence,' she said petulantly.

'Is it a hand, Dad, not a glove?' asked Zack.

Dave was surprised at his son's insight, and decided to come clean. 'I think I saw fingernails on it, so, yes, I think it might be a hand. I think we should leave it alone; I don't want you two having nightmares about floating hands.'

'Oh Da-ad,' Becky wailed at him, 'now we'll have to get it, because what you just said is what could give us nightmares, because it's the unknown. If we collect the actual hand it won't be half as bad as our imaginations could make it, so we won't have nightmares about it. It's basic psychology.'

Once again, Dave wondered what had happened to his little girl. He gave in, let go of the fern and pushed away from the islet, rowing with as little effort as he could manage; he'd splashed himself with the cool lake water, but he was still unpleasantly sweaty.

Becky once again completed a successful retrieval, and hauled in what was, indeed, a human hand. Dave was horrified that his children paid such close attention to it, noting the way the flesh had started to fall from the cut around the wrist area, and commenting calmly on how the fish had started to nibble at it. All he could do was look away, while steering generally toward the cabin.

'We'll put it into a Ziploc box and store it in one of the coolers when we get back,' announced Becky, 'it should keep fresh that way.' Her brother, for once, agreed with her. Dave was shaking his head as he rowed.

God, his kids were weird.

Back at the cabin, Becky secured the ball-cap and hand in a manner she felt appropriate, while Zack planned the next meal. Dave had given up on the idea of them being able to reach anyone by telephone, and resigned himself to spending a night in a rickety old shack with his children, in close proximity to a dead body, and with a decomposing human hand in a cooler box beside his cot. Not quite what he'd imagined.

But the children didn't seem to have missed a beat; Becky had taken over sorting through supplies to work out what they could eat – the idea of fishing now not appealing to Dave at all, considering what any fish they might catch may have been nibbling at – and Zack was trying to work out the directions to the tree house, from the map on the wall.

'Dad, it's real hot here in the cabin – can we go into the forest and find the tree house? It would be shady there, wouldn't it?' asked Zack, applying some surprising common sense.

Dave couldn't think of a good reason to not go; at least it would get them away from all the dead stuff. So they set off into the woods; Zack had the map and led the way, Becky had a small backpack with some snacks and water, and Dave brought up the rear with the compass, though he wasn't really sure why he'd brought it because Zack seemed to be doing just fine without any direction from him.

It turned out the tree house wasn't as far up the hill and into the trees as the map seemed to suggest, but it was a magnificent structure nonetheless. Zack was first to climb the ladder that stood against the tree itself, then Becky followed, and finally Dave hoisted himself up. It wasn't really a tree house, more of a tree-platform, with a brown tarp tented over part of it. Dave knocked a lot of detritus off the tarp, and Becky kicked bits of twigs, needles, cones and leaves off the platform itself.

Then they all took the time to take in the view; they were up inside the trees, with a view toward the lake – due south, Dave's compass told him. They'd climbed a good way up the hillside, and then they'd climbed the ladder, so now they were a couple of hundred feet above the lake itself; the view was spectacular.

Dave loved it, and he sensed the children did too – even Zack grunted what Dave took to be his appreciation. Becky 'wowed' a lot, and Dave was just grateful for the moment, and the distance between him and the dead body.

'Look at the bald eagles,' whispered Becky, pointing in wonder to half a dozen birds wheeling above the forest which scrambled up the hillside beyond the lake.

'They can't hear you, stupid, why are you whispering?' mocked Zack.

'Zack!' warned Dave. 'Let's enjoy this moment – they're beautiful, aren't they?'

Zack grunted.

'I like bald eagles, Dad,' said Becky, still speaking quietly. 'Can we go to Squamish in the New Year? There's an art gallery in Brackendale where all the bald eagle counters gather – I saw it on TV. In 1994 they counted a record of nearly 4000, but the recent counts have been way down. Maybe we could volunteer to help them?' Becky sounded proud that she knew so much, and Dave was suitably impressed. Dave smiled warmly at his daughter; he loved it when she suggested they should do something together.

'Sure,' he replied, 'so how do you count eagles?'

'Well, I don't know, but I'm sure we could help. I know they're easier to count the worse the weather is, 'cos they stay closer to the ground and the rivers then.' Becky still sounded upbeat, but Dave was beginning to have some misgivings about the whole thing.

*Great*, thought Dave, *I get to sit around in freezing rain while my daughter counts eagles.* 'Sure,' he said.

'Who d'ya think he was, Dad?' asked Zack, out of the blue.

'Who was who?' asked Dave, still thinking about bald eagles.

'The dead guy,' replied Zack, as though his father were a complete idiot.

Dave sighed. Of course, the dead guy.

'I have no idea,' replied Dave, 'and there's no point even thinking about it, because there's no way of us knowing. Come on kids, let's try and enjoy all this –' he waved his arm toward the vista – 'rather than that.'

'But it's a mystery,' said Zack, stating the obvious.

'We could examine the body,' suggested Becky, 'and see if there are any clues.'

'I told you he was naked,' said Zack, 'there won't be any clues.'

'There might be – he might have birthmarks, or tattoos,' said Becky, sharply.

'I don't care what he might or might not have,' interrupted Dave, 'you're not "examining the body" and that's that. Forget it, you two. We'll leave him where he is and call the cops when we get back tomorrow.'

Dave could feel himself scowl; the mood was broken for him, and he started to wonder how to entertain the kids for the rest of the day. Obviously they were going to go on and on about the body. He knew he shouldn't have been surprised, but he'd so hoped they could just get back to the way he'd wanted things to be.

'When are we going to cook on the grill?' asked Zack.

Dave was grateful that at least he'd changed the subject. 'We could make our way back to the cabin now and do it right away, if you like,' he said more happily.

Both kids agreed, and they clambered down the ladder and followed the trail back to the shore. Half an hour later, Dave felt they were back on track because they were finally feasting on grilled wieners; some looking a bit like charcoal, some were not more than warm, but they were all perfectly edible, he reckoned. Then they had cookies, all washed down with cans of soda.

Zack went for a swim – Dave deeming it acceptable since the floating hand was now safely out of the water and stored inside the cabin. Becky pulled Dave's old guitar out of the cabin and encouraged him to play, which Dave was delighted to do, but he found it difficult to make his fingers form the shapes he'd learned in his youth, so he just strummed tunelessly for a while, before Becky lost interest and started asking if he could play some 'real songs'. Dave did his best, but he'd never been very good at tuning the instrument, so even he had to admit he wasn't as good as he'd hoped.

Zack toweled off after his swim, changed into dry clothes, and they all gathered together some wood to make a proper camp fire.

Although the sun was still in the sky, it had dipped below the mountains and the cabin was in the shade. Dave could tell it was going to be a clear night, and he suspected they might feel chilled. He and Becky set up the wood ready for a warming fire, and they all pulled on some extra clothes and dragged some blankets out to sit where Becky had laid out the supplies needed to make S'mores.

Dave's watch told him it was seven p.m., and he imagined the firelight dancing in the gloaming later on, his children's faces happy and tired; it would be magic.

Then, before they could even light the fire, Dave heard something in the distance – it was a boat engine.

*Why's Mike coming back early?* he wondered. Despite the dead body, he'd wanted this night alone with his kids. Why wouldn't anything go right?

'It must be Mike,' said Dave, without enthusiasm.

'No, it's a different engine. That boat's much more powerful than Mike's,' replied Zack with authority.

'How do you know?' asked Dave, before he realized he'd just shown himself up in front of his son.

'Mike's has a different tone – can't you hear it?' Zack wasn't even trying to be patient with his imbecile father.

'Yeah, right,' said Dave, as though he could spot the difference.

'It sounds like they're coming this way,' said Becky.

Though it was clear the boat was still some way off, Dave could at least tell from the engine's tone that the speed of the craft had slowed; the boat was probably beginning to work its way through the shallow channels they themselves had negotiated earlier in the day.

Then Dave heard a sound that made his heart miss a beat. He didn't know how he knew what it was, because he'd never heard the sound before, but he was certain it was a gunshot. Then there was another, then another. Then a loud 'Woo-hoo'.

Dave had no idea what happened to him next; it was as though something had taken over his whole being . . . like a switch had flipped in his head. He stood and kicked all the wood they'd gathered for their campfire away.

'Dad! What are you doing?' squealed Becky, leaping to her feet in disgust; she'd spent quite some time making the neat pile and clearly wasn't impressed by her father's actions.

Dave snapped, 'Becky, Zack, I need you to listen to me very carefully and do exactly as I say, right?' Dave's tone ensured they took notice. 'Becky – quick as you can, go to the cabin, get our backpacks and put some portable food and water into them. Put some warm clothes on, then come back here and pack away these blankets into the backpacks too – we might need them. Zack – help me put the boat and the grill back into the cabin, then go get some warm clothes on. Becky – we'll need flashlights and the medical kit as well. Let's move, now!'

Neither child asked a question. Neither moaned, nor kicked up a fuss; they both did exactly as they were told. Finally certain that everything had been cleared away, and that they had sufficient supplies, Dave locked the cabin and put a protective arm around each child.

'We're going to the tree house. Zack, you have the map, right?' Zack nodded. 'We know where we're going and we'll stay there as long as we need to. I'm going to be honest with you, kids, I don't know who's on that boat, but I don't want to find out. Got it?' Both children nodded. Dave knew neither was so stupid that they didn't understand he was deadly serious.

He felt that, maybe, the people in the boat had something to do with the dead body, and he could tell from his children's faces they were thinking along the same lines.

Zack led the way, with Dave following behind Becky. This time, the trip to the tree house took longer; it was dark beneath the trees, their flashlights didn't illuminate much, and they were all carrying heavy backpacks. Dave had also brought along the gun case; though he didn't know how to use the damned thing, what he did know was he couldn't leave it where it might be found by the people in the approaching boat.

As they trudged up the mountainside, Becky stumbled a couple of times, and Dave picked her up, brushed her down, and looked into her eyes to check she was okay; she was obviously apprehensive, but was keeping it together quite well. Meanwhile, Zack was grinding up the hill ahead of them – he was acting like a Sherpa, and doing a great job of it. Dave was proud of his children.

Finally they reached the ladder to the tree house. They were all out of breath and glowing with sweat. Zack went up first, and Dave passed the backpacks up to him, one at a time. Then he made sure Becky got up the ladder safely.

'Stay there – I'll be right back,' whispered Dave as loudly as he dared to Becky and Zack who were peering over the edge of the platform. 'I just want to throw a few branches across the trail – two minutes.'

He was as good as his word, then clambered up the ladder himself.

'Give me a hand, Zack,' he whispered, and he and his son hoisted the ladder up onto the platform, out of sight from the trail. 'Now, both of you, start pulling as many branches around the edge of the tarp as you can,' he said quietly, and soon they had made themselves almost invisible. Finally, Dave felt they were as safe as they could be.

'Good job!' he whispered, as he hugged his children to him. He took stock; Becky and Zack had laid out the blankets while he'd been masking the trail. Their backpacks could act as pillows, and they could roll themselves up in the blankets if it got cold, but, in the meantime, they were fine. They had water, snack bars and cookies, medical supplies and – if they needed it – a gun. Looking at the metal box, Dave lost some of the confidence he'd felt earlier; if he needed to use it, he'd work out how to do that, he told himself.

In the meantime he tried to convince himself there was no real reason to suspect that whoever was on the boat meant them any harm; he was being overcautious. The people on the boat were probably just a bunch of guys letting off some summer steam.

That was what he told the kids.

That was what he told himself.

'I think we should bed down here, kids; we don't want to draw any attention to ourselves, let's just try to get some sleep, right?'

'But it's still light, Dad,' was Zack's accurate observation; the tree house had been built in such a way that it offered a great view of the lake below, but that meant it was also catching the sun.

'You're right,' replied Dave, 'but the main thing is – even if we can't get to sleep yet – we must keep still and quiet. Frankly, kids, I don't want those guys guessing we're here; they shouldn't notice anything amiss at the cabin, not unless they break into it, and I'm pretty sure they won't know about this tree house or the trail, but there's no point giving away our location, right?'

Both children nodded.

'We should have brought the hand with us, Dad,' said Becky quietly. 'What if they find it?'

'Let's not worry about that now, eh? There's nothing we can do about it. Let's just try to make ourselves comfortable; we could be here for some time.' Dave tried not to sound tired, but he was. The strain was beginning to get to him.

Dave noticed that Becky was edging toward him, so he reached out to her, and pulled her into his arms. He could see she was holding onto something; he suspected it was her stuffed dog, but he didn't mention it.

'Dad, they won't . . . hurt us, will they,' she asked, looking up at her father with fearful eyes. She might have been born thirteen years earlier, but she could have been a four-year-old at that moment. Dave's heart skipped a beat.

'Everything will be fine,' he whispered, and Becky relaxed a little, but Zack still looked anxious; he, too, had become a little boy again.

'Dad, do you think these are the people who killed the guy we found?' asked Zack. It was the question on all their minds, and Dave supposed someone had had to say the words out loud.

'I don't know, son. I hope not, because I'm sure that whoever could bring themselves to do that to another human being isn't going to be a very nice person. But I think we've done the right thing, clearing out of the way of whoever is on that boat.'

'Yeah,' said Zack sounding nervous. 'It sounded like they had guns. We've got a gun, haven't we, Dad?'

'We have, Zack – but don't worry, everything will be fine. I won't have to use it,' said Dave, hoping he wouldn't.

Below them, down at the shore, they could hear the boat's engines had stopped; Dave could imagine the boat being tied up at the pier. It was clear to him there were at least three men; they weren't exactly shouting to each other, but the peace of the area was so profound that their voices rang out clear and loud. He strained to hear every word.

'Keep your ears open for names and anything that might tell us who they are,' instructed Becky, suddenly becoming a teenaged sleuth again.

'And keep your voices down,' added Dave.

Both children settled into more comfortable positions, and Dave let his daughter pull free from him; she seemed to be rallying. It was difficult to catch the entire conversation between the three men; Dave thought he heard the name Steve, but it could have been one of them talking about Stave Lake – another local beauty spot – for all he knew. The voices floated about on the cooling night air. One thing was certain – there were so many references to 'him' there was no longer any doubt in Dave's mind that these men had come to either retrieve, or bury, the dead body; he reckoned these had to be the guys who'd killed the man, shot his face away, and cut off his hands and feet.

'It sounds like they're going to bury him,' said Becky, astutely.

'I wonder why they didn't do that in the first place,' said Zack, quite conversationally – which was, in itself, unusual for Zack.

'Maybe they didn't have shovels with them when they killed him,' replied Dave, immediately regretting his words. Luckily all he got was a pair of, 'Yeah's', rather than two horrified children.

'I reckon up there's best,' said a man's light tenor voice. It sounded so close that it made Dave freeze; Becky reached out for her father's hand, and squeezed it.

'Nah, it's too dark. Jeez, you'll kill yourself – it's a hell of a hill, eh?'

'But it's too rocky to dig down here,' came the first voice again.

'Stop arguing!' It was the third man's voice – deeper than the other two, more assertive. Dave reckoned this guy was in charge. 'We've got to get him away from the shore, so he don't float out into the lake. And we've gotta get him away from this cabin. Let's find a place along the shore and up into the trees – but not under the big trees, 'cos there'll be roots in the way.'

Dave agreed with his logic.

'Look, there's a kinda clearing here,' came the first voice again.

'That's not a clearing, it's a trail. Jeez, can't you tell the difference?' said the second voice, mocking the first speaker.

This man's accent wasn't local. It sounded to Dave like a Maritimes accent; he worked with some guys from there, and that was how they talked.

'You're right,' said the 'Boss', his deep voice booming in the darkness below them.

He's definitely French Canadian, thought Dave.

As Dave looked out from the platform, with his ears straining for every word, a part of him noticed the sunset staining the sky with smudges of yellow, gold and red – the night sky darkening above it, with tiny points of light beginning to peep through the deepening blues.

'Beautiful sunset,' he whispered to his children who looked up at the black silhouettes of the cedars against the painted sky; they both, surprisingly, nodded and smiled appreciatively. He hoped they would remember the beauty of this trip, not the horror and fear of it.

But he was apprehensive; what if the men decided to follow the trail to dig the grave for their victim? What if they happened upon the tree house? Dave told himself there was no point worrying; he had to save all his energy for dealing with what was actually happening, not 'what-if's'.

'I'm a bit cold now, Dad,' said Becky quietly, 'I'm going to pull the blanket around me. Do you want to share?' she asked her brother, uncharacteristically.

'Yeah,' replied Zack, equally out of character.

Dave smiled inwardly; it took something like this to get them to huddle together in a blanket. Amazing.

'Come on, let's try up here!' came a loud voice. It was the Boss, and it sounded as though he was pushing through the brush directly toward the tree house. Dave, Becky and Zack all held their breath.

The crashing and cracking of branches, and the cursing as one man or another fell over a root or a branch, seemed to be getting extremely close, but Dave couldn't see the gleam of a flashlight anywhere, so he didn't have a real fix on the men. The noises seemed to get nearer and nearer, then, after what seemed like an age, the voices grew more muffled and, as far as Dave could make out, they'd gone away to their right.

Zack started pointing silently in the same direction, and Dave nodded. There was no doubt about it, they seemed to have picked a spot to stop; then Dave recognized the sound of shovels being pushed into the soil.

Dave was embarrassed that his kids could hear the disgusting jokes the men were telling each other as they dug, and he could have killed them for the language they were using. But he knew his kids would survive all that; in fact, he suspected they probably heard much the same at their school every day, kids being what kids had always been.

By the time the men stopped digging, the darkness was total. There was a slice of moon hanging low in the black sky, but it cast very little light.

'Let's get back down for a few cold ones,' the Boss said; the other two men agreed with him.

As Dave and the children stared into the darkness where they thought the men had been digging, they finally caught sight of a light, wobbling about at ground level. The men crashed their way back toward the shore. Dave wondered how they expected to get the body all the way back to where they'd been digging – he didn't think he could have found a spot in the dark that way. But he told himself that wasn't his problem; his problem was keeping his children safe, and, now – as the night chilled off – warm, and in some sort of comfort. He was hoping the actual burial wouldn't take too long, but, when the men got back to the shore it was clear they were in no hurry to even begin that task.

Dave peered at his watch; the luminous hands told him the men had been drinking beer for at least half an hour. He wondered if they'd ever get on with their gruesome job.

'Can I get some cookies?' was Zack's quiet request.

'Can you reach the bag with the food?' asked Dave of Becky.

'Sure,' she whispered, and pulled one of the three bags toward them. It fell open, and the cookies in their airtight plastic box rolled out and bounced across the platform sounding like a drum in the night. Becky stopped, dead. The three of them held their breath, expecting the men at the shore to have heard the noise.

Somewhere close by a bird flew up into the black sky and cried aloud. Then there was a shot from below them. Becky grabbed her dad's arm. She looked terrified.

'Stop messing about!' shouted the Boss' voice.

One of the other men whooped and shouted, then it became clear they were, indeed, finally setting about their task of burying the body.

Dave worked out from their conversation that the three men had brought a tarp upon which they had placed the body; it seemed the Boss was leading the way, with the two other men dragging the tarp behind them. The noise was tremendous as they hauled their charge through the undergrowth; once again there were stumbles and curses along the way, but, somehow, they seemed to find their way back to the spot where they'd been digging.

'Toss the bastard in,' shouted the Boss; there was a sickening thud.

Becky's eyes were wide with fear when she looked up at her dad. He winked at her, and she smiled, weakly. They were all getting used to the dark by now, and the light from the rising moon, even though it was just a slim silver hook in the sky, was bright enough for them to at least see each other.

As Dave looked across the platform at his children he could see two worried little faces poking out of a large, heavy blanket. They looked so small, huddled together, swathed like that; so scared. And he had brought them to this. He wondered if they'd ever forgive him; he could live with not forgiving himself, but if they blamed him for this, what would that mean for their relationship? It had been tough enough to get them to come with him in the first place; now there was . . . all this. Dave's stomach churned; what if they never wanted to go anywhere with him, ever again?

He was back to pondering 'What-if's', and he told himself not to worry, but he did. He didn't think things would ever be 'fine' again. Not really.

They listened as more shoveling took place, then the Boss finally agreed that a good enough job had been done to deter the wild animals from digging up the corpse. Once again the men blundered their way back toward the shore.

*Maybe now they'll leave*, hoped Dave. But he was wrong.

It seemed that more beer needed to be consumed to celebrate a 'job well done' as the Boss put it, and the men sat around talking and laughing for ages. Dave wondered at their callousness, then told himself he shouldn't be surprised, not after what they'd done to their victim in the first place.

Dave's watch told him it was just gone eleven o'clock when the murderous trio finally started up the boat once again. The relief of their departure washed over him when he heard the boat finally pick up speed to head off into the main part of Pitt Lake, having cleared the extensive shallows.

Dave and his children shared a group hug and all cheered – but still at the whispering level. It had been the longest four hours of Dave's life.

Daring a slightly louder whisper Dave said to his children, 'Look, I know they've gone, but I still think we should stay here.'

'But Da-ad, it's real uncomfortable up here,' whined Zack, 'and I'm starving.' Dave was delighted that his son seemed to be back to his usual self.

'Have a few of these,' said Becky, offering her brother a handful of trail-mix bars.

'I've had loads of those today – I'll have the most painful crap of my life when they all come out,' said Zack glumly.

'Hey – enough of that sort of talk,' chided Dave. 'I know we've been treated to some pretty bad language tonight guys, but I don't expect that type of thing from you.'

Zack grunted.

'I won't tell Mom about the language,' said Becky, meaning to be helpful, but reminding Dave that, somehow, he'd have to explain all this to Debbie when they got home.

'Good girl,' replied Dave, grateful for at least that small mercy.

'Why can't we go back to the cabin, Dad?' asked Zack.

'Because it's pitch dark down there and I covered the trail with branches; it's too dangerous to risk it in the dark. It's better if we stay here till it's light, then we can safely get back to the cabin.'

'Da-ad,' said Becky hesitantly, whispering close to her father's ear, 'I've got to go. Now. I've been holding it for ages, but I can't wait any longer. Can I just go down the ladder and go pee in the bushes?'

Dave could have kicked himself; of course, they'd probably all have to pee before settling down to sleep. Indeed, now that Becky had mentioned it, he realized his own need. He'd better do something about it.

'Okay – we'll put the ladder in place, and we won't stray very far. Zack – you stay up here while I go down with your sister, then, when we come back, you and I can go together while Becky holds the fort up on the platform, eh?'

Two 'Okays' met this suggestion, and they carried out their plan.

When Zack and his dad returned to the bottom of the ladder, their own missions accomplished, Dave heard a noise in the brush. He was beginning to hate the wilderness – it seemed to be full of things designed to ambush his spirits, just as they were rising. There was no question about it: something was crashing through the trees lower down the hill, and heading straight for them – he was sure of it. Zack's face was a picture of terror.

'Up the ladder, quick, Zack,' said Dave in his normal voice, which sounded loud in the stillness of the night, and Zack leaped onto the ladder. His foot slipped and he fell, with a crunch. He let out a yelp, which was followed by a growl from the darkness. Zack was immediately on his feet and up the ladder in a matter of seconds. Dave followed him, and, together, they pulled up the ladder behind them.

Becky was shaking again; Zack was as white as the moon. Dave could see blood oozing through Zack's sock. There seemed to be a lot of it. Dave sucked in a deep breath, and took control.

'Becky, break out the medical kit. Zack, sit down and let me get your sandal and sock off. Stop wriggling.'

'I'll be fine, Dad,' said Zack, in a voice that told Dave he'd be anything but.

'Here it is,' said Becky, putting the little medical bag next to Dave, and shining a flashlight onto her brother's leg so Dave could see what he was doing.

'Oh dear,' was all Dave could manage.

'That's nasty!' exclaimed Becky, looking at the four inch shard of wood sticking out of Zack's flesh, just above his ankle.

'Open up the kit – let's see what your Mom packed for us, Becky,' instructed Dave. He searched for something with which he could grip the splintered shard, uncertain that pulling it out of his son's leg was the right thing to do, but knowing that Zack couldn't sit on a platform halfway up a tree all night with it the way it was.

'Does it hurt much, son?' he asked Zack.

'Not really,' was Zack's pained reply. Dave suspected pride was stopping him from crying like a baby, but that might not last for long.

Beneath them they heard a long, low growl. Dave hoped it wasn't a cougar; if it was, well, he suspected they were pretty good at climbing trees – being cats – but he had a more immediate problem to deal with.

'Son,' he said directly, 'it's going to hurt like hell, but I have to pull out the wood. Then we can clean up the wound and put a bandage on it. Tomorrow we'll get you to the hospital and they can check for slivers – eh?'

Zack didn't reply, but nodded; his mouth was set in a thin, determined line.

'Use the blanket to pull it out, Dad,' suggested Becky, 'you don't want to get a sliver yourself.' Dave knew she was right, and protected his hand with the blanket.

'Ready?' he asked his brave son.

Once again Zack nodded. The growling was now directly beneath them. Dave pulled the wood out of his son's leg. Zack didn't make a sound, but Dave could see a tear trickle down his grubby face.

'Well done, son,' said Dave, and hugged Zack, allowing the boy to wipe his tears on his dad's shoulder, without his sister ever seeing them.

'You're real brave, Bro,' said Becky, smiling at her brother, but looking worried. 'Dad – the growling thing, it's right on our tree, down there,' she said, looking almost as pale as her brother.

'Give me the flashlight,' said Dave in a commanding voice. Becky handed the flashlight to her dad with a trembling hand.

Dave shone the light over the platform and saw a pair of eyes looking up at him. It was a bear. A big one, by the looks of it. And it was starting to climb the tree. The eyes blinked in the bright light.

'Make a noise, kids – as much as you can,' shouted Dave, and, with no further encouragement needed they both let rip, screaming, shouting, and banging on the platform; Dave suspected they were enjoying the release of all their tensions as much as he was.

The bear didn't look afraid, but after a couple of minutes of sustained clamor it ambled off into the bush.

Dave turned his attention to his son once again, shining the flashlight onto his injured leg. The cut was deep, no question, but the bleeding was slowing. Dave suspected Zack had been lucky. He sprayed the cut with the antibacterial Debbie had packed, and mentally thanked her for her foresight. After several minutes, when the bleeding had pretty much stopped, he carefully placed a gauze pad on the cut, and wound a long bandage around Zack's leg, securing it with some of the surgical tape from the pack. He didn't think there was much more he could do. But he wasn't happy. They couldn't go down to the cabin, that was obvious, but it was clear that his son was in for a painful and uncomfortable night.

There were still several hours ahead of them before the sun would be up, and he felt completely helpless. Once again his mind went to the place where his kids would never forgive him for putting them in harm's way – and where his ex-wife would probably forbid him from ever seeing them again.

He tried to snuggle Zack into the blankets, and Becky along with him, but it was difficult because Zack had to keep his leg straight out – it hurt less that way. If Dave had thought that the last four hours had taken their own sweet time to pass they were nothing compared with the next four. He didn't sleep; he was exhausted, yet wide awake. He had to protect his children – from murderers, from bears, and from whatever else might smell blood on the air and decide to check it out.

Dave had never felt so alone, so small, or so pathetically useless in his whole life. He wished Debbie was with them; nothing ever went wrong when Debbie was around – she made everything alright. He missed her. Now more than ever, but he admitted to himself that night, high above the trees, with the moon crossing the sky and the nocturnal creatures stirring all around him, that he missed her every day, in every way. She'd never have let them get into this mess; she'd have made it right. Somehow.

With the first light, Dave felt some relief. The kids had slept, even if he hadn't. Becky was curled into a ball, cuddling her dog and looking just like she had done when she was three years old, while Zack lay flat on his back, snoring fitfully. The dawn chorus was almost deafening, and it woke Zack, who claimed not to have slept a wink. He pulled himself up to a seated position, and assured his dad that his leg was fine, but Dave could tell he wasn't right – he was quiet and withdrawn, but not in the usual way.

When Becky woke it was almost fully daylight; she yawned and stretched, and even asked after her brother.

'Any more bears, Dad?' she asked, smiling nervously.

'No, but I think we should give it a little longer before we venture down,' said Dave, remembering from somewhere that bears don't go to sleep until later in the day, but not sure if it were true or not.

'I need to pee, Dad,' said Becky, quietly.

'Can you wait?' asked Dave, hoping she could. 'Maybe half an hour?'

'I don't know that I can,' she replied.

'Me neither,' said Zack.

'Okay, but I don't think you're ready for going up and down the ladder a lot, Zack, so I'll go down with Becky, like last night, then when you come down, we'll make our way back to the cabin. We'll take our time, so your leg will be okay. Right?'

Both children nodded and they all set about gathering everything and packing it away. Dave finally let down the ladder and, when he was on the ground, Becky followed him. She scampered off into the bush, this time a little further than the night before. She returned and Zack made his way, carefully, down the ladder. Becky held her breath as she watched her brother descend.

'We should check your dressing before we leave,' she said, sounding like Debbie.

'Yeah – okay, but let me pee first,' said Zack impatiently, then he hobbled off to relieve himself.

As Becky stood waiting for her brother, she looked up at the tree trunk and pointed to the scars made by the bear's claws the night before. Dave shuddered; the bear had gotten a long way up the tree, or maybe it was just that big – the marks were way above Becky's head.

'Where are you, Zack?' called Dave, wondering what on earth had happened to his son.

'I'm over here,' shouted Zack, from some way off in the bush. 'I've done my business, now I'm going to mark where they buried the body.'

Dave shouted, 'Get back here now, Zack. That leg of yours isn't right, and I don't want you getting lost. Come back – right now!'

'Okay,' shouted Zack, obviously not happy that his father wouldn't let him be more adventurous.

They headed back to the cabin, with their kit; it might only have been a shack, but it would seem like a palace after the night they'd had. The hike back took longer than it had done the day before, due to Zack's leg. But, finally, they got to the cabin; it was a wonderful sight – they'd all had quite enough of the forest.

Dave checked his watch; it was eight thirty a.m., not too long before Mike's scheduled arrival.

Dave opened up the cabin; whoever those guys had been last night, they hadn't been interested in it. Dave was glad they'd cleared up so well the evening before, but now he encouraged Becky to collect together all the sticks he'd kicked about – he thought a campfire and something hot for breakfast would lift all their spirits.

While Becky gathered the wood and built a pyramid for the fire, he examined Zack's leg, despite Zack's protests. He could see the wound was pretty clean – at least, it looked that way to Dave – but, nonetheless, he applied more antibacterial spray and re-dressed the wound with fresh gauze. Then he gave Becky a hand, and, within the hour, they were sitting around a fire, toasting the last of the wieners and singing songs Dave knew he had no ability to play on his guitar, but he gave it a go anyway.

They were all tired and grubby, and might never be quite the same again, but it was a happy threesome who greeted Mike when he tied up the boat just before one o'clock.

Dave was so pleased to see his work colleague that he cantered along the pier to give him a hug. Mike tried to push him off, and hurriedly offered to help load the kit – then he spotted the bandage on Zack's leg.

'What happened there?' he asked, concerned.

Zack beamed. 'I got a huge piece of wood stuck in there when I fell off the tree-house ladder last night, in the dark,' he said, sounding quite proud.

'What were you doing on the tree-house ladder after dark? You weren't out there alone, were you?' Mike gave Dave a strange look.

'A bear was coming for us – we had to climb up real fast,' replied Zack, excitedly. 'We'd all gone down for a quick pee after the killers left, but then we had to spend the night up there 'cos of the bear.' Zack seemed quite content with his explanation.

Mike was anything but. 'The killers? What are you talking about?' he snapped.

'The guys who killed the dead guy we found on the shore; they cut off his hands and feet, but we found one of his hands, and his ball-cap,' shouted Becky.

Mike looked aghast. 'You found a body? A dead body? Dave, what are they talking about?'

'Yeah,' Dave tried to sound casual. 'We found a corpse, collected what evidence we could, but we had to get out of here when the murderers came back to bury the body last night. I thought it best we spent the night in the tree house, then we came down to the cabin this morning for breakfast.'

Dave thoroughly enjoyed the look on Mike's face. This story could work out quite well for him at the construction site, after all. With him as the hero, of course.

Mike scratched his head in disbelief, but let the subject drop as they filled his boat with everything that needed to be shipped back to Pitt Meadows. Content that everything was secured, Mike looked back at the cabin suspiciously.

'Got everything?' he checked.

'Don't forget the hand, Dad,' called Becky as she ran along the pier to fetch the last cooler box. Dave helped her into the boat.

'The hand?' scoffed Mike.

'Yeah, the hand,' replied Dave, opening the cooler box for Mike to see.

'Jesus H Christ! That really is a hand. Where the hell did you find that?' Mike looked horrified.

'I picked it up with the fishing net, when we were out in the frog-boat,' said Becky, quite calmly.

Dave nodded in silent reply to Mike's enquiring looks; he was so proud of his kids.

'We'd better get it to the cops, as soon as we get back,' said Mike, trying to take charge.

Becky said, 'We tried to call them, but we couldn't get a signal.'

Mike nodded. 'Yeah, there isn't one up here – but we'll be able to call them when we get down the lake-aways,' he said, still looking shaky. 'We'd better get going,' he added, and they all agreed.

Mike steered the boat away from the pier, and Dave looked back at the cabin, the shore and the trees on the mountainside with memories he could never have imagined would be his; he wasn't sorry to be heading back to civilization – but he was trying to work out what to tell Debbie. Even so, he managed to pay some attention to their surroundings.

'Look, eagles,' shouted Becky above the engine's noise – they were taking it slow through the shallows, but the engine was thumping loudly.

'We'll see a lot more when we go up to Squamish to help with the count,' replied Dave, hugging his daughter. She was quite happily standing up in the boat, not sitting and clinging to the seat the way she had the day before.

What a difference a day makes, thought Dave, relieved that at least his daughter seemed pleased at the idea of spending time with him again . . . one day.

'I wonder who that is,' shouted Mike, nodding toward an approaching boat. It was just slowing to begin to negotiate the shallows that led from the main body of the lake. 'They're supposed to give way to us,' shouted Mike, 'but it looks like they're coming ahead. Idiots.'

He gesticulated toward the other boat, signaling that they should stop where they were and let him get out of the narrow channel.

'Dad,' Zack called to his father, 'that's the same sort of boat that was here last night.'

Dave's stomach flipped. He didn't even bother asking Zack if he was sure – he knew his son was right. It might not be the same guys, but if his son said it was the same type of boat, then it was the same type of boat.

'Mike,' called Dave, 'get us out of here as fast as you can – now.'

Mike looked at his work colleague in surprise. 'I can't go any faster. It's too dangerous just here,' he replied sharply.

Dave moved closer to Mike, instructed the children to sit down and hold on tight, then shouted into Mike's ear.

'That's the type of boat that brought the guys here last night who buried the body we found. This is serious Mike – they might be the killers, coming back for some reason. After all, who else would be coming up to this part of the lake? You're the only one with a cabin there. My gut's telling me it's them. Maybe they left something behind – something that could tie them to the murder, or the burial – I don't know, but I have no intention of finding out. Just get us out of here – they're dangerous, Mike.'

Mike shook his head, his brow furrowed. 'I've got to take it easy here, Dave,' he replied, sounding worried, 'but if we can get past them before they get to this really narrow part, they won't be able to turn for quite a distance, and we can get into the lake and get going. After that – well, my boat hasn't got the speed theirs has, but I'll do my best.'

'Thanks, Mike,' said Dave quietly, and patted his colleague on the back.

'You been up to the cabin there?' called a voice from the approaching boat. It was the passenger calling out, over the high-pitched rhythms of the engines.

'Just looking around,' shouted Mike, waving. Dave was glad he'd thought through the implications of his words.

'Nice cabin, eh?'

'Bit small if you ask me,' replied Mike.

The boats were drawing closer together; they were no more than twenty meters apart. Dave could see two men on the boat. There'd definitely been three the night before – maybe these were just two completely different guys out for a jaunt. That's what he told himself. He looked toward the rear of Mike's boat at his children – they were both as rigid as boards, looking terrified.

'You guys just out for a wander about?' asked Dave, waving cheerily.

'Yeah, that's right, just wandering,' replied the guy controlling the other boat. Dave was in no doubt he'd heard that voice before; it was the 'Boss' from the previous night. He felt his insides tighten.

'Lots of eagles about,' Dave called, still trying to sound cheery, and pointing to the sky. The passenger in the other boat looked up.

'Yeah, for sure, eh?' he said. Maritimes accent. No doubt it was them.

The boats were almost level.

'You come through,' called Mike.

'Your right of way, surely,' shouted the Boss.

'Hey – I'm not the cops,' replied Mike, nervously, 'it's easier if you come forward, then I'll push around you; it's wider here than there.'

The Boss was tall, with long blonde hair tied back beneath a bandana, wore sunglasses and a red tee shirt; Dave could see that his arms and neck were entirely covered in tattoos. His passenger was also standing; he was shorter, bald, but also covered in tattoos.

Dave could see that Becky stared hard at them, and Zack showed more than a passing interest, turning his head to look at them as they were mere feet away.

'Looks like the little guy's taken a knock,' said the Boss as they passed right by Mike's boat. He was looking at Zack's leg.

'Stupid kid fell out of a tree being chased by a bear last night,' replied Dave, laughing.

'I thought you'd just been up here for a look-see,' said the Boss, a different tone coloring his voice.

*Why did I mention bears? Stupid! So stupid!* thought Dave to himself.

The boats were moving further apart, but Dave had caught the inflection in the Boss's voice. He had to do something.

'Yeah, just a look-see,' he added. 'He can't lay around at home all day just 'cos he's got a little cut on his leg. I don't want him to think he can't get out and about with any little old injury. And we do get bears in Pitt Meadows, you know.' Dave thought that should take care of it.

The Boss had cut his speed to almost a standstill, and had turned around to study Mike's boat. He seemed to be deep in thought.

'You're right,' he replied, 'get all sorts there, you do.'

'We're off, hang onto something,' shouted Mike, and Dave did as he was told, which was just as well, because Mike's boat shot forward, the front gradually rising out of the water. Dave staggered back and sat down with a thump.

'You okay, kids?' he shouted above the roar of the engines. They were both staring back toward the other boat.

'They're watching us, Dad,' screamed Becky.

'I can see that, baby, but we'll be fine – Mike's a great boatman, and they'll have to go all the way to the far end of the shallows before they can turn around, and even then they'll have to come back slowly, like we did. So don't worry, it'll all be alright – we'll get to the shore long before they do.'

He smiled and winked at his daughter, and she smiled weakly back at him. He wondered when it would all end; they couldn't take much more of this tension. He certainly couldn't take much more of it himself.

'Shall I watch the phones for a signal?' asked Zack. Dave was impressed by his son's cool head.

'You do that – pass one to me and I'll look too,' shouted Dave.

Zack managed to pass a telephone to his father without dropping it, despite the ferocious bobbing of the boat. Both he and his father watched for a signal.

'Dad, I've got bars on my phone,' shouted Zack after about five minutes.

'Pass it to me, son,' shouted Dave, and Zack did so. Dave knew exactly what to do. He called the RCMP, then he called Debbie.

'Hello, Zack – is everything okay?' Debbie's voice sounded worried.

'It's me, Debbie, I'm using Zack's phone – he's fine – listen to me, I need you to do something,' shouted Dave.

'Where are you? What's that noise?' asked Debbie, sounding concerned.

'We're on Mike's boat, heading for the boat launch at the south end of Pitt Lake – don't ask questions, just meet us there. I'm not going to lie to you, Debs, the kids need to see you and have you with them. We've been through a bit of an ordeal overnight.'

'Oh my God, Dave – what's happened?' Dave was beginning to think that maybe talking to Debbie this way wasn't such a good idea after all, but he'd wanted Debbie there when the kids got to shore, for their sakes.

'Debbie – calm down. We're all fine, and we're all safe. Now just hang up the phone and come meet us.' He punched the 'end call' button. He knew she'd act, and swiftly.

'Dad – Dad! They're coming!' screamed Becky.

As Dave turned around he could just about see the boat driven by the Boss exiting the shallows and beginning to enter the deeper waters of the lake. He could see the shore ahead of them, but they were still a fair distance from safety. Even when they reached the shore he wondered what sort of real safety it would offer without a police presence. After all, he reasoned, they couldn't just leap out of the boat and jump into their truck and drive away; they'd have to get off, tie it up, do all sorts of things. Or what if those guys caught up with them on the water, before they even reached the shore? What if they could overtake them? What if they had guns with them? They had done the night before.

Dave decided he didn't like 'What-if's' at all, but also decided to pull Mike's gun case toward himself with his foot, just to be on the safe side.

'They're just about getting up to full speed, Mike – do you think we can stay ahead of them?' shouted Dave.

Mike didn't look around, he called back over his shoulder, 'This is as fast as she goes, and I'm not sure how fast their top speed is, but I'll keep her flat out till I have to pull up – I'll do my best, Dave.'

'Okay, I'm going to get the gun out, just in case we need it,' Dave shouted back, sounding much more confident than he felt.

'What the hell will you need the gun for, Dave? It's for cougars and bears. You can't go shooting at people!' Mike sounded panicked.

'Mike, they killed someone up at that cabin, and they wouldn't be chasing us if they didn't think we knew something about it. They had guns last night, we could hear them shooting; if they've got a gun today, I'm gonna be ready for them.'

Mike screamed, 'I cannot believe the mess you've got us into. Those guys in that boat – they've seen my boat's name, they know I've seen their faces. I'm in this up to my neck, now, too. They look tough, and rough, those guys; we're in trouble, and they're chasing me. Cheers, Dave.'

Dave fiddled with the gun case – it wasn't easy getting the key into the lock, let alone anything else. 'Can you manage?' shouted Mike.

'I can't unlock this damned case.'

Mike motioned for Dave to join him at the wheel. 'Here – just keep her straight and flat out – there's not much to it; just hang on tight. Give me the case and I'll open it – I'm more familiar with the lock.'

Dave gratefully accepted Mike's offer, and they carefully swapped places. Dave felt immediately at home at the helm, and Mike managed to open the lock in an instant. He pulled out the gun, much to Zack's glee and Becky's horror, and loaded the weapon. He wedged himself into the seat and made sure the gun wasn't pointing anywhere dangerous – which only left one direction, straight up.

Behind them, the other boat was gaining; it was touch and go if they'd make it to shore before the Boss caught them. As Mike peered back he could see that the blonde guy was still at the helm, but that the passenger, the bald one, was standing at his side, also with a long-gun pointing into the air.

Dave's stomach churned and he called to Mike, 'We're getting close to shore – I don't know what to do – you'll have to take over again.'

The men changed places; Dave remained standing, the gun on his hip, his eyes not leaving the boat that was getting ever closer. He knew they'd have to slow, to get into the pier. He glanced toward the designated landing area; he could see Debbie's vehicle, then Debbie, but he couldn't see the RCMP, nor anyone resembling a figure of authority.

Where the hell were the cops? If Debbie had made it there in the minivan, surely they could have got a response vehicle there just as quickly?

It suddenly dawned on Dave that if he could see Debbie, then she could see them. He wondered what she'd make of the sight of her husband holding a gun, her two children hanging onto their seats for dear life, and another boat in hot pursuit of her family, with a man holding a gun in that one too.

His relief at the sight of a cloud of dust signaling the arrival of two RCMP vehicles wiped his worries away; suddenly Dave felt more confident that it would all work out alright – then he spotted the effect that his weapon was having upon the officers, who were already out of their vehicle and peering at the scene on the lake through binoculars.

Dave could see Debbie run toward one of the uniformed men. She was waving her arms in the air. Dave guessed she was explaining that her children were being pursued by armed men, and were being watched over by their father.

At the sight of the RCMP vehicles, the boat being driven by the Boss slowed and turned, then the engines roared and the vessel began to speed across the lake's shimmering surface away from the boat launch area. Mike's boat came to a halt, Dave handed him the gun – which Mike unloaded – then, finally, Dave was able to get to his children. The boat was still bobbing on the water as he held them to his chest. They were safe. At last.

'We're fine,' he said quietly, 'just fine. Your mom's here – see? You guys'll be glad to let her get you home safe, eh?'

He studied his children; Becky had her color back and was smiling up at him, Zack's leg wasn't bleeding at all and he was glowing.

'Da-ad,' said Zack, pushing his father away, 'I'm fine. Look, there's Andy from school with his mom and dad, wait till I tell him what's happened.'

'Hey, you'll talk to the cops before you talk to anyone else, Zack, and even then you'll only tell people what the cops say you can tell them. And we've got to get that leg checked out before you can go talking to any of your mates anyway. This isn't over, Zack; those guys are heading back up the lake – they could get off that boat anywhere and literally get away with murder. We have a civic duty to perform, son.'

'I guess,' said Zack. 'You'll come to the hospital with me, won't you?'

'Sure,' said Dave, and gave his son another hug.

'You'll tell them how I said we should collect the evidence, won't you, Dad?' asked Becky, eagerly.

Dave smiled proudly at his daughter, 'No, I won't do that – you can tell them yourself. You were grown-up enough to think of it and do it, so you should be the one to tell them that.'

'Thanks, Dad,' said Becky, beaming.

Debbie hovered on the shoreline; Dave could see the anxiety on her face. Finally they were all off the boat, and his ex-wife was able to hold her children. Dave explained all that had happened to the most senior officer there, who, in turn, relayed all the information to someone on the radio.

'My daughter has something for you,' said Dave proudly, as Becky handed the cooler box to the officer. He looked inside.

'You're a very brave girl,' said the officer, 'very intelligent too; if the corpse had no face, hands or feet, we might never have identified it, even if we can find it and dig it up. This hand might have fingerprints, so if he's anywhere in the system, we can at least identify him.'

'The Boss had a tattoo of a flaming torch on his neck,' said Zack, not wanting to miss out on the limelight, 'and the bald guy had one too.' Dave couldn't smile any wider. 'I reckon they're in a gang and that's their insignia,' Zack added, with an air of authority. 'And I marked the place where they buried the dead guy – I put my red hockey-team cap there.' He sounded pleased with himself.

'I wondered why you weren't wearing a hat,' said Debbie, glaring at Dave, 'though I guess that's the least of my worries, having heard what you guys and your father just said.' She turned to the officer. 'Can I get my son away to be checked at the hospital now?' she asked.

The officer took all their contact details and the cooler box, then allowed them to leave. Debbie said the cops could keep the cooler box when they were done with it, thank you very much.

Dave thanked Mike for his role in their escape. Profusely. And apologized for having dragged him into such a mess. Profusely.

The officer said he thought the suspects would likely dump their boat somewhere further up the shore and flee the area, aware they could be described by everyone in Mike's boat.

Mike told anyone who'd listen that he and his wife were going to take a couple of nights away at a local hotel – maybe they'd even stay away until he knew the cops had picked up the bad guys, because they now knew the name of his boat and he thought they might be able to locate his home that way.

Dave could understand why Mike was scared; he didn't like the idea that the killers had seen him and the kids – he was just grateful there was no way they could know who they were, or where to find them.

It was over. Well, it was nearly over; they'd take Zack to the emergency room at Ridge Meadows Hospital, and Dave was sure they'd say he was just fine – then they could all go home, knowing that tomorrow the RCMP would take their formal statements and they could get back to their normal lives. He'd call the foreman at work to tell him he'd need to take at least Monday off.

But first they had to head to the hospital; Dave followed the minivan carrying Debbie and the kids in his old truck, and they got to see a doctor within the hour. A clean bill of health for Zack, with some precautionary antibiotics and a tetanus shot, meant he could spend his time on the trip home in his dad's pickup calling friends on his cell phone, telling them about his 'great adventure'.

Debbie said Dave could stay for dinner, and the kids were bubbling over with their gruesome story right through their meal. Dave agreed with Debbie when she said she suspected it would be tough to settle the children for the night, and she wasn't wrong; once she'd managed to drag them both away from phoning and texting people, the kids made sure she had to listen to the details of their night up a tree, for the tenth time.

Dave was pleased Debbie had given into the kids' request to let their dad stay for the night; with Zack and Becky upstairs safe in their rooms, and with him fairly comfy on the sofa bed in the den on the main floor, he eventually turned out the bedside light after what had become a very long weekend indeed.

Dave hadn't thought he'd get off to sleep, but he must have done, because the next thing he knew, he was waking up. Something had disturbed him. For a moment, he didn't know what was happening; he pushed himself off the sagging bed and peeped through the curtains. What he saw on the street terrified him.

He grabbed his phone and ran into the master bedroom. 'Get the kids into the basement Debbie. The Boss is outside in a Hummer and I think he's got a gun.'

Debbie look confused.

'Don't turn on any lights!' he added. 'I'm on the phone to the cops right now.'

Debbie grabbed a robe and rushed into Becky's room. Her daughter was as fast asleep as she herself had been just moments earlier, and Dave could hear Debbie was having a tough time rousing their daughter.

'Becky – wake up, darling. We have to get down to the basement – here, put this on, and let me find your slippers. Don't panic – everything will be fine – I'm just going to wake Zack. Come on now, get up!' Debbie was trying to sound calm, but Dave knew she wasn't.

Finally, Debbie managed to get both children down the stairs and into the basement; the family house sat on a ravine, so it looked like a single-level house from the street. However, the back had an extra floor which allowed for access to the bank of a wide gully that ran right along the street. Dave hoped it might prove to be a possible escape route that might save them from whatever the Boss had planned.

Dave ran down the back stairs to join his family. Debbie looked up at him, searching his face for an explanation. She was holding the children tight.

'Listen,' said Dave, knowing he needed to take charge until the cops arrived, 'I know we're all frightened, but we have to act quickly. The cops are on their way, but, somehow, the Boss has found out where we live; he's outside the house, waving a gun around, and threatening us.'

Becky started to cry. 'How did he find us? Why won't he leave us alone? I'm tired of this, Dad. I want it all to stop now. Can't you make him go away?'

Dave's heart broke a little. 'I don't know how he found us, darling, and I don't think I can make him go away, but I can get us away from him. If he tries to come into the house he'll set off the alarm. I think we'll be safe here, because there's no other way to the back of the house from the street. So let's just wait for the cops to arrive and they can sort him out, eh?'

'I don't get it, Dad – how could he find us?' was Zack's plaintive question.

'I don't know that either, son, but he's here and we have to deal with it, right?'

Zack nodded.

Dave was delighted that, for once, Debbie didn't take the chance to have a go at him. When she spoke she sounded as though she wanted to do some damage to someone, but Dave could tell that person wasn't him.

She hissed, 'Given what that creep has already done, there's no doubt he's dangerous. Everything inside makes me want to go outside and rip his head off; how dare he threaten my children? But your father's right; the man outside has a gun, and isn't afraid to use it. We have to somehow keep ourselves safe until help arrives.'

A loud crash made all four of them jump.

'Was that glass?' asked Becky, terrified.

'I think it was the window beside the front door,' replied Dave.

Another crash and a popping noise came next. Becky buried her face in her mother's bosom, crying aloud. Debbie looked as pale as the moonlight streaming through the basement window. Dave hugged his son, his ex-wife, and his daughter.

He looked Debbie straight in the eyes and spoke quietly. 'If that alarm starts to ring, then he's opened the door through the side window. He's already shooting at the house. I'm not going to let him hurt any of us. The instant that alarm starts, we're out the back door and we're going to make our way along the bank of the ravine toward the top end of the road, heading toward the Lougheed Highway. Right?'

Debbie nodded. Dave didn't want to have to drag his family along a dangerous riverbank at night, in their slippers, but he knew that if the Boss got into the house, they'd have to get out of it.

'Why are the police taking so long?' asked Debbie, her eyes pleading with Dave for everything to be alright.

'I don't know, darling, but they'll be here soon, I'm sure of that.' Dave's quiet, assured reply was overwhelmed by the noise of their alarm. It screamed out into the night. They all froze.

'Right – let's go,' ordered Dave.

He pulled open the back door, and ushered his family out into the night air. They scurried over the narrow deck and stumbled down the bank. Across the ravine he could see lights being turned on in bedroom windows. Soon everyone on the entire street behind the ravine, and their own, would be awake, roused by their wailing alarm. But that wouldn't help them. They had to fend for themselves until the police arrived, and that meant getting away from the house.

'Watch your step,' Dave said to Zack who was still not too steady on his injured leg. 'We can't use flashlights; if he gets finds the back door I don't want him knowing which way we've gone. Let's get up to the Wilson place, then we can hide under their deck, okay?' Everyone nodded.

The Wilsons lived five doors up and had a large deck that extended out over the ravine. It would be dark and, Dave hoped, safe under there. But they had to get there first.

It was slow going. All around them lights were glowing, blinds were being opened and dogs were barking.

A shot rang out. Dave could tell by her expression that Debbie, who'd never heard a gun before, knew what it was; it chilled him despite the warm, summer-night air. Just a little further – a few more steps and they'd be able to hide under the Wilsons' deck.

At last they were 'safe'. Debbie was near to tears, but, Becky seemed to have regained control of her emotions. They were all grubby, their nightclothes wet with dew, and their knees green with the stains of vegetation they'd crushed as they'd made their way along the steep bank of the ravine.

'Everyone okay?' asked Dave – breathless and sweating.

Three nodding heads were all he got.

'Right, now let's just sit it out. Keep your ears open, we might be able to make out if anyone's following us.'

Debbie tensed even more; Becky held her brother's hand, and Zack was clearly holding back tears. Then Dave heard a sound he'd never thought he could love so much – the sirens of police cars.

'Dad?' said Zack, pulling at his father's arm.

'Yes, son, what is it?' asked Dave, not feeling at all secure despite the approaching sirens.

'I'm sorry, Dad – it's all my fault.' Zack was finally crying. It hurt Dave's heart.

'It's not your fault, Zack. None of this is our fault; it's all down to the creeps who killed that poor guy in the first place. It wasn't your fault that we found the body. Zack, never think that.' Dave's voice was full of compassion for his son, who looked much the same as he had done on his first day of Grade One.

'It's my fault they found us,' replied Zack, sobbing.

'What do you mean?' asked Dave, still trying to hear if there was anyone crashing along the riverbank toward them, but not wanting his son to be ignored in his time of need.

'I left my hat where they buried the body – to mark the place. My hat's got my name in it.'

'What?' Dave snapped more than he had meant to.

'I'm sorry, Dad. Mom wrote my name in my hat because the whole hockey team has them. The killers must have gone back to the grave and found it there. We're an easy family to find – we're the only Golightlys in the phone book around here. My hat says "Zack Golightly" on it. That's how he found us.'

Dave's heart sank. The Boss knew who they were; anyone connected with the killing knew who they were, and where to find them. What if the Boss was a gang member? He'd certainly looked like one. Though Dave had to admit to himself he didn't really know much about gangs, he knew there were a lot of them around; they were always being mentioned on the news – not a weekend seemed to pass without 'a targeted killing' being mentioned somewhere close by.

Maybe the Boss belonged to a big gang. If so, there'd be loads of them coming after his family. It might never stop. The whole scenario played out in Dave's head in two seconds flat; if the police got the Boss they'd all have to testify to what they'd seen in court; they'd be open to all sorts of intimidation, threats, and real danger. Dave wondered if Canada had a witness protection program like he'd seen in the movies – or was that only in the States? Would his family ever be safe again?

As he looked across at his cowering children, and at Debbie's face, he wondered if she was thinking the same as him. Her eyes were wide with terror.

'Oh, Zack,' Dave said, gently, stroking his son's thatch of sandy hair, 'it's not your fault. We've got caught up in something that's much bigger than anything we could have imagined. But, we'll be fine, just fine. Because we have each other. We'll do the right thing; we'll follow through with this, and we'll make sure the authorities do right by us. Now don't worry about it, let's just keep our ears open and try to work out what's going on up there. Listen – it's gone quiet.'

The police sirens had stopped, their house alarm had stopped, and even the dogs had stopped barking. The silence was eerie. Somewhere close by a slight rustling made all four of the Golightlys draw closer together, but it was just a cat, disturbed by unexpected guests.

Gunshots rang out.

It all sounded so far away that Dave could hardly believe their house was involved. There were a lot more shots, then everything went quiet again. Dave poked his head out from under the deck. He couldn't see anything out of the ordinary – not that he knew what was 'ordinary', under the circumstances.

'You all stay here – I'm going up onto the street to see what's happening.' Dave's voice was quiet and calm.

'No, stay here with us, Dave,' said Debbie, sharply. 'I don't want you getting hurt, Dave – I need you to be safe. Your family needs you.'

Dave raised himself to his full height, and reached around his children, circling them with his arms. Then he reached forward and kissed Debbie – not a peck on the cheek, but a proper kiss, on the lips, the way they'd kissed when they were young and in love. And Debbie kissed him back.

'Eew!' said Zack.

Becky cleared her throat and looked away, containing a giggle.

'Stop "eew-ing" like that,' said Dave to his son as he smiled at his wife, his heart alive with an emotion he hadn't felt in years. Debbie looked so young, so fresh. Maybe it was the dirt on her face, maybe it was her tousled hair and glowing cheeks, Dave didn't know why, but she looked much as she had done when she was a teenager – a pretty girl with dark hair, dark eyes, and a cute little button nose.

'I've got to find out if it's safe for us to go home,' said Dave, sensibly, 'so I'll work my way up the side of the Wilsons' house and see what I can see, right? No one will even know I'm there. Just you guys stay here, where you're safe.'

Dave carefully made his way up the steep bank that led to the street, hoping he would find something that would make him feel normality was returning, but the sight that met his eyes was anything but normal. Four police cars – all with their doors wide open – were standing abandoned close to their house at their end of the close. Their flashing lights illuminated a chaotic scene; flak-jacketed officers, their weapons held high, were darting about and, in the distance, Dave could hear more sirens wailing.

As he ventured from the darkness at the side of the Wilsons' house he could see what he thought were like two bodies on the ground. One officer was kicking something away from the body that lay on the sidewalk. Dave dared to creep closer.

'Stop – show me your hands, then down on the ground,' called a voice behind Dave.

Dave's arms shot up into the air, and he turned to face an officer who was pointing a weapon at him.

'That's my house,' said Dave, 'I was the one who called you – they were after me and my family.'

The officer looked him up and down. Once he was certain Dave wasn't a threat, the officer motioned for him to drop his arms.

'Are we safe? Are they dead?' asked Dave.

'Is there anyone inside the house? Where's your family?' asked the officer.

'We all got out. We hid under our neighbor's deck. Can I fetch my wife and kids now? Is it safe?' asked Dave.

'Let me check that we've cleared the area,' said the officer; he spoke into the radio attached to his body armor.

'There's an ambulance on the way – any of you guys hurt?' he asked.

'No, we're fine,' said Dave, 'but I'd like to get my family safely out from under that deck – do you have a flashlight? Can you help?'

Dave and the officer descended the bank of the gully, then helped Debbie, Zack and Becky up to the street. People were beginning to dare to open their front doors. As the Golightlys emerged onto the street, Steve Wilson, under whose deck they'd taken refuge, came out of his house.

'Dave – is everything alright?' he asked. His face showed he knew very well it wasn't.

'We've had a spot of trouble, Steve, but the Mounties seem to have it all under control.'

'Was that gunfire I heard?' asked Steve, who looked genuinely surprised by Dave's presence, and the fact the entire Golightly family was emerging from his back yard.

'Yeah; there were a couple of guys gunning for us, but the cops have taken them down. We're going to be fine now – but we sure were grateful for your deck out there. I hope you don't mind – we hid under it for a while.' Dave was hugging his daughter to him as he spoke.

'No worries,' replied Steve, looking completely bewildered by what was going on in their quiet little street in the middle of the night. 'But what do you mean there were some guys gunning for you – what's going on, Dave?'

Dave sighed. 'It's a long story, Steve, and we're all too tired for it just now. I just want to get my kids home to get some clothes together, then I'm going to drive them all over to Debbie's mom's house to spend the night. I'll come back and see to boarding up whatever needs boarding up – so the house will be secure, but maybe you could just keep an eye on things while I drive them up to Maple Ridge – I'll only be gone about half an hour.'

Steve Wilson agreed. 'Sure – give me a shout when you're ready to go,' he replied, still looking confused.

'What's going on, Steve?' It was Cherie Wilson, peering around her husband, whose large body almost filled the front door. 'Debbie!' she exclaimed, seeing her neighbor in the middle of the street. 'What the hell's going on? Are you guys okay?' She sounded concerned, then she spotted Dave. 'Oh, hello, Dave.' Cherie Wilson's voice took on an acid edge. 'I guess this is all something to do with you, eh?'

'None of this is Dave's fault, Cherie, really it's not,' snapped Debbie. 'All he wanted to do was give the kids some time on their own with their dad, enjoying all that nature has to offer. It wasn't his fault that some moron had killed a guy and left his mutilated body for them to stumble upon up at Pitt Lake; it wasn't his fault that the killers came back to the place where they'd left the corpse; or that they tracked us down to our home. This wasn't down to Dave. His actions saved us all from God knows what tonight. I'm so proud of the way he looked after us all.'

Zack and Becky beamed; Cherie Wilson looked taken aback. Dave was glowing with pride as Debbie smiled at him, with real warmth.

'So would you all like to come inside our house and continue this "love fest" in warmth and safety, until you can get back into yours?' asked Cherie, still sounding acerbic.

'You guys go on in – I'm going to talk to the cops and find out what's happening; I'll see if they'll let me grab some clothes for you all,' said Dave. He kissed Debbie on the cheek, then she and the children made their way into the Wilson house.

'You'll be okay on your own, Dave?' asked Steve Wilson.

'I'll be fine,' replied Dave, and he made his way toward the end of the close. He was passed by an ambulance, which screeched to a halt almost at his front door. There, surrounded by glass and blood, was the body of the Boss.

'Do you know who he is?' Dave asked the officer he'd seen earlier.

'Yep, we know him pretty well; one Cy Marchand, from Quebec originally. Moved here a couple of years ago and tried to get something going with the local Hells Angels, but they never took to him – too untrustworthy even for them, it seems. We've been looking at him for arms trafficking, but couldn't come up with anything that would stick. He's got two known associates – one of them is over there –' the officer motioned to a body bag being hoisted into the ambulance – 'and the other one is being taken into custody right now.'

'If these guys were after us, should we be worried about anyone else taking up where they've left off?' Dave asked, terrified about what the answer to his question might be.

'Why do you think they were "after you", sir?' asked the officer, sounding confused, and curious. Dave briefly recounted the past couple of days. The officer nodded slowly as he listened.

'You've had a heck of a weekend, sir,' was his pithy comment.

'You're not kidding,' replied Dave. 'And I guess what I'm trying to work out is – is it over? Are these three guys the only ones we should be worried about, or are there more associates of this Marchand likely to crawl out from under a rock, somewhere?'

Dave knew the future safety of his family depended upon the officer's answer.

'I think you'll be okay. Marchand wasn't known to mix with any other groups. In fact, the locals will be glad to see him gone. I can't imagine who the dead guy you're referring to was, but if he turns out to be connected to some local outfit, then the story you've just told me, which clearly marks Marchand and his cronies as the murderers, will probably have you cast as the hero in all of this. There could be some very interesting people wanting to shake you by the hand. But I'd decline those offers, if I were you, sir.'

Dave smiled wryly. He was beginning to feel as though – maybe – it really would all be over, very soon.

'Any idea when I might be able to get into my house?' Dave was beginning to feel a bit more settled – though he wondered why he'd referred to it as 'his' house; he'd been told – in no uncertain terms – to leave it by Debbie two years ago. Now all he did was pay the mortgage.

'It's gonna be a while yet. Is there anywhere you can stay?'

'I thought I'd take my wife and children to my mother-in-law's for the night; she's just up in Maple Ridge. I could take them there, get them settled, and then come back. If you're all going to be here, I don't mind the house being open. But maybe I could just collect some clothes for them all?'

The officer shook his head. 'Can't let you in at the moment, sir. I'll tell my boss you'll be away from the scene for a while. Do you need to get keys for your vehicle? I could go get them if you tell me where they are.' Dave thanked the officer, who introduced himself as Corporal Carr, Ridge Meadows detachment. Then Dave met his boss, then his boss's boss, and finally got the keys for the minivan, because he couldn't recall where he'd put his pickup keys.

Bundling Debbie and the kids into the van, he waved his thanks to the Wilsons and they drove off, leaving the flashing lights and the emergency vehicles behind them.

He knew Debbie's mom was expecting them, and he wasn't expecting a warm welcome at her house, but Debbie said it would be okay – she'd explained everything to her, and how none of it was Dave's fault.

'So is it really over, Dad? Really, really over?' asked Becky as they drove through the delightfully normal suburban streets, past quiet, darkened houses, and trucks parked on driveways beside pretty-by-moonlight gardens.

'Yes, it's over,' said Dave, with conviction. 'The Boss didn't have any known associates but the two guys with him; one of them is dead, and the other is in custody. No one will ever come after us because of this weekend; no one will try to harm us because of it.'

'So we won't have to move house, or school, or change our names, or have plastic surgery?' asked Becky, sounding almost disappointed.

'No, we won't have to do any of those things,' said Dave.

'Good, 'cos, I'm gonna move up to the top line next season,' said Zack, as though hockey was all that mattered in his life, 'and I'm not starting with another team all over again.'

Debbie laughed out loud. 'Darling, darling Zack – you and Becky are going to be just fine. We'll have a couple of days with Gran while Dad gets the house fixed up, then we can all go home. Together. Right?'

'You mean Dad too?' asked Becky, her face happy.

'Well, I think it would be a good idea if Dad stayed for a few days, just to be sure we're all sleeping well, you know? If that's okay with you guys?'

'Sure is,' said both children.

'Just one thing, Mom,' added Zack.

'Yes?' replied Debbie. Dave wondered what his son might say.

'Do you think Gran will give us something to eat when we get to her house – I'm starving.'

'No more wilderness trips for us for a while, eh?' said Dave.

'It was actually quite exhilarating,' said Zack, surprising everyone in the minivan.

'That's a very grown-up thing for you to say,' observed Becky.

Zack grunted at his sister, realizing he'd crossed a line. 'Yeah, well, I guess it wasn't too boring,' he muttered.

# AUTUMN

## THE FALL

### A DI Evan Glover Case

Detective Inspector Evan Glover burrowed his fingers through his hair as the phone rang for what felt like the millionth time that day. His heart sank; the extension number display showed it was his boss's boss, Detective Superintendent Lewis. Again. It wasn't quite three o'clock on Monday afternoon and already Glover was feeling the strain of DCI Ted Jenkins being on holiday for a couple of weeks; all the DCIs and DIs had been told they'd need to pick up some of the slack while Jenkins was away. Glover was convinced he was the only one getting lumbered. He missed the usual buffer between himself and the superintendent.

'Yes, sir, how can I help?' was his measured reply; he was known for his ability to keep a cool head under pressure.

'Glover, we've got a dead body,' said his superior bluntly, 'and I'm giving this one to you for a first look. Doc Souza just phoned it in from Three Cliffs Bay and I want you to get there pronto.'

'Suspicious death?' asked Evan, his spirits rising as he sensed a possible escape from his desk.

'Man's body found on the rocks about noon today. Surfers spotted it and phoned the coastguard. They called it in, and Souza took it herself. She called it in to me, requesting you.' The super's manner was odd; Evan suspected he was holding something back. And not something good.

'Why me?' asked Evan; no point beating about the bush.

'You'll understand when you get there,' was the super's terse and irritatingly cryptic reply.

Evan weighed his next response carefully; known as an insightful detective, rather than a slave to procedure, he nevertheless recognized that the hierarchical structure within the West Glamorgan Police Service required he was polite to Lewis, despite his belief the man had long ago lost touch with what investigating officers faced on the ground on a daily basis.

'So we don't know yet, then, sir,' was Glover's somewhat sarcastic response. He knew Lewis would never pick up on his tone.

'Early days, Glover. See Souza about that. I promised her I'd get you down there as soon as possible. Off you go now. Take Stanley.'

Evan replaced the receiver, silently cursing at Lewis's patronizing tone. However, he reckoned at least this new case might offer some respite from the spate of break-ins he'd been working on for the past week. To little effect.

'Stanley,' he shouted into the corridor, knowing that her bat-like hearing would kick in.

As Evan sorted out his jacket, peppermints, communications devices and keys, Detective Sergeant Liz Stanley stuck her head into his office.

'Sir?'

Evan looked up and smiled. He liked Liz Stanley. She was a good, steady sort. He could never get over how young she looked; despite being in her thirties, her curly blonde hair and generally girlish looks meant she could have been taken for much younger. He also always had to stop himself from laughing at Stanley's accent; her Bristolian burr made it sound as though the word 'sir' was spelled 'srrrrrrr'. Evan had to admit he liked it; it was a pleasant rarity in Swansea.

'Stanley, we've got to head out to Three Cliffs Bay; body found on the rocks there, and the super, in his wisdom, has given it to us for a look-see. Bring a car around, and I'll meet you downstairs in five, alright?'

'Right, sir,' was Stanley's reply as she shot out of Glover's office.

When they were finally on their way, Evan allowed himself to relax into the passenger seat.

'Right-o, put your foot down, Stanley.' He fiddled with the seatbelt as Stanley pulled away from the kerb outside the High Street entrance of the red-brick, early-Victorian structure that rather inadequately housed Swansea's twenty-first-century police force. 'Blues and twos for this trip – the super said we're to get there "pronto", so I think we can make some noise.'

Stanley smiled. 'You love this stuff, don't you sir?' she ventured.

'Damn right, Stanley,' was Glover's satisfied response. 'There are few perks to this job – but screaming through the traffic, lights flashing and sirens blaring, is one of them. Off you go.' Evan beamed as they made their way noisily through the vehicles snarling Swansea's busy, if now rather rundown, city center.

His mind wandered as they wailed through the traffic; you couldn't really talk when the sirens were blaring, nor make phone calls easily, but he knew he'd have to call Betty as soon as he could to warn her he might be home late.

It was a relief to Evan when Stanley reverted to flashing lights only, once they had cleared the main roads and began to wind along the hedge-bounded country lanes characteristic of the Gower Peninsular – the picturesque area where Three Cliffs Bay was located. He had to admit it wasn't a bad place to visit on what was a surprisingly warm, sunny day for the last week of September. They were due some good weather; he'd all but grown webbed feet during what had been the second wettest August in history.

Evan prodded his password into his mobile phone; this might be his only chance to call home. He could picture the telephone ringing out in his neat little house.

'Hello?' A breathless voice; he'd obviously caught Betty busying herself with something.

'It's me, love,' he announced, smiling.

'Hello, *cariad*. Everything alright, is it?' Betty's voice always sounded worried when she asked him that question, which she invariably did.

'Fine, ta, but I might be a bit late tonight. Stanley and I are on our way out to Three Cliffs; a body's been found, and we're off to check it out.'

'Ah, that's a shame, *cariad* . . . I mean the body, and you being late.' Betty's voice was comforting. 'It's that special veg soup tonight, so I'll keep it hot, don't worry.'

Evan inwardly grimaced. He knew Betty was only feeding him the stuff for his own good; he needed to drop a few pounds before they went on their long-overdue holiday, but the soup was disgusting. He reasoned that a week from Saturday they'd be off to Scotland, where he'd be able to happily over-indulge. After all, who in their right mind wouldn't when visiting a region where deep-fried haggis was served with chips, preferably followed by a deep-fried Mars bar, and where dozens of whiskies would be begging to be tasted.

In the meantime, there was the misery of the soup to contend with. Evan liked his food; sometimes he never knew when he'd get his next proper meal, so when he had one he wanted it to be just that – a proper meal, not some excuse for one, with no fat and just ten calories a serving. But there was no denying he'd filled out a bit over the summer; his shirts were pulling at their buttons just a bit, and his trousers could have been a little looser.

The days when he could eat whatever he wanted because he'd be running it off at rugby practice, or playing it off on the rugby field at the weekend, were long gone, and his small frame – ideal for his beloved position of fly half – was now beginning to feel the strain of carrying what was, probably, about an extra stone. He sighed, and resigned himself to vile, watery, vegetable soup for a couple of weeks; it was a small price to pay, he supposed.

'Just under two weeks now,' Betty added brightly. Evan knew she was referring to their holiday; he was crossing off the days on the kitchen calendar.

'I know, not long. And I might not be too late tonight. Might be a jumper, might not. Might be an accident – we'll see.'

'Thanks for phoning, and say "Hello" to Liz? Tell her to look after you for me? And don't go too close to the edge – you know what you're like with heights.'

Evan signed off, sighing, but smiling. Betty was right, of course, he wasn't good with heights, and he hoped this investigation didn't mean he'd have to go peering over the cliffs at all.

'Betty says "Hello",' said Evan, pocketing his phone.

'And did she tell me to look after you, too, sir?' asked Stanley, risking a wry smile at her superior's expense.

'As per usual,' conceded Glover.

Three Cliffs Bay was still about ten minutes away, so, with no information about the case to discuss, Stanley made a personal observation.

'I expect she'll be looking forward to your holiday, sir?'

Glover and Stanley didn't often have 'personal' conversations. They kept their off-the-job socializing to a minimum, too; Evan didn't think it was fair to impose himself on Stanley in her spare time. He knew he'd never liked it when his superiors insisted upon inviting him to their homes or social gatherings, so why should he make Stanley suffer?

'She certainly is,' he replied, then decided to deflect the conversation a little, 'but you're off before us, aren't you? Scout Leaders' Camp, next week, isn't it?'

Stanley nodded. 'Yes. It's nice that, when all the kids go back to school, we scout leaders get to go to our own camp, and compare notes. And I suppose you could say we let off a bit of steam. I'm only an assistant leader in Swansea; I was a leader in Bristol, but I still get to attend.'

'So where exactly does this week of canvas-covered debauchery take place?' asked Glover, smiling.

'We're off to a place in North Devon; it's got an excellent camp lodge. The bloke who runs it is a good sort, and there are at least four pubs within walking distance, so we never get on any one landlord's nerves too much. But the best thing about it is––'

'Don't tell me, it's the toilets, right? It's actually got some?' Glover laughed.

'How did you guess, sir?' asked Stanley, quite taken aback.

'Third Swansea, 1973 to 1976, Wolf Patrol,' answered Glover, giving the scouts' three-fingered salute to his subordinate. 'I remember digging "lat pits" at camp. Filthy job. And it always seemed to be me who got to do it.'

'Same here,' replied Stanley wryly. 'But this place has a really good personal hygiene block – all white tiles, hot running water, closed shower cubicles – the lot.'

'Ah, the joys of roughing it,' smiled Glover.

'The joys of not roughing it quite as much as usual,' replied Stanley, laughing.

Evan realized they'd become a little distracted. 'Next left, Stanley,' he announced. 'It's just before Penmaen Church, a tiny turning . . . there.'

The car swung awkwardly into the narrow turning. Stanley managed to successfully avoid the hedges threatening the pool-car's paint job. They pushed along the lane as far as possible, then their way was barred by a straggling group of other official vehicles.

'Try and squeeze it into that corner there,' said Evan indicating a slight widening in the lane, and he leaped from the still-moving car.

'Sir,' was Stanley's formal reply.

All thoughts of personal conversations were now gone.

'Anybody here seen Rakel Souza?' cried Evan as he approached an ambulance and a police car at the end of the lane.

'She's just coming up now, sir,' came the reply from a suddenly erect uniformed constable who, until that moment, had been leaning nonchalantly against his car, laughing at the two uniformed men who were struggling to maneuver a heavily-laden stretcher along the narrow, winding path that led up, almost vertically, from the beach below.

Glover could see Souza was much closer, and decided to wait where he was for her. He assumed any recovery team personnel had already left; they'd have been needed to retrieve a body from the cliff face, or base.

By the time Dr Rakel Souza reached Glover she was smiling warmly. Despite the dark hue of her skin, Evan could see her cheeks were rosy; she almost seemed to be having a good time – she might have been on a carefree seaside hike for all he could gather from her expression.

Evan enjoyed an excellent working relationship with Souza – they were friends as well as colleagues. It was true that, professionally speaking, DI Evan Glover and Dr Rakel Souza had shared many a post-mortem, but Evan and Betty also enjoyed spending time together as a foursome with Rakel and her husband Gareth. They'd shared plenty of dinners at each other's homes – neither couple having children – and even the odd weekend away from Swansea together, though it had been some years since they'd had the chance to do that.

Evan liked Rakel; she'd been brought up a strict Roman Catholic by her immigrant Goan parents, had attended Swansea's St Joseph's Catholic school, and had excelled academically, then in her chosen career. She was exceptionally bright, diligent and hard-working; he couldn't have hoped for a better colleague – and friend. It only helped that her maths teacher husband, Gareth Williams, had once been a fellow rugby player of Evan's.

'Lovely day for it!' was Souza's first observation, followed rapidly by, 'unless you're this poor chap, of course.'

Glover took in their surroundings. But for the emergency response vehicles, and the sad reason for their being there, it was, as Souza had noted, a lovely day; the sun was still some way above the horizon, the sky was a pale, fresh blue, and the sea glinted invitingly below them, surrounded by the craggy forms of the Three Cliffs themselves and the vivid green of the grass on the hilltops. It was stunning.

Then Glover looked at the stretcher. To business.

'Do we know what happened?' he asked.

'I suppose you mean can I tell you "did he fall, or was he pushed"?'
Dr Rakel Souza, Director of Forensic Pathology for West Glamorgan,
and HM's Coroner for the region, seemed pleased with herself at being
able to use the well-worn phrase.

Evan admired Rakel for her enthusiasm for everything she did, and
the incredible knowledge upon which her enthusiasm rested. 'Can you
say?' he asked, hopefully. Maybe there'd be some resolution to his
superior's earlier caginess.

'Not yet, Evan,' was Souza's quiet response. 'If he wasn't dead or
dying when he went over, the fall would most likely have killed him.
His injuries are extensive, especially around the head and neck. I
suspect spinal shock – a broken neck to the layman – but I'll have to
have a better look at him back at the "ranch". I can tell you I can't see
any immediately obvious signs of attack – but, to be frank, even that's
pushing it, given the state of the body.'

'Bad?' Evan suspected he could guess the answer.

'Bad,' replied Souza, sounding grim. 'He's bounced down a couple of
hundred feet of jagged cliff face. Not pretty.'

'Any chance of an ID?' was Evan's next, obvious question.

'Yes, I'm afraid so, Evan. And you're not going to like it. The reason I
mentioned your name to DSI Lewis, was because of this.'

She handed Evan a wallet enclosed in a plastic evidence bag. He
manipulated the wallet inside its protective cover until he managed to
get it open.

He caught his breath. No. It couldn't be.

Peering out from a blurred driver's license photograph, was the
unmistakable face of The Great One, the one and only GGR Davies
himself – the best fly half who ever earned a Welsh Rugby Cap, and
Evan's sporting hero of thirty years' standing.

He couldn't believe it.

'This is GGR's body?' His eyes begged Souza to deny it.

'I'm so sorry, Evan,' said Souza softly. She reached out and touched
him gently on the arm. 'I know what GGR meant to you – and I have to
admit I can't be a hundred percent sure it's him because of the damage
to the face. But all the other observable physical attributes are
consistent with it being the case. I fear The Great One is no more. It's a
sad day for you, I know, and a sad day indeed for Welsh rugby. Just
wait until I tell Gareth. To say he'll be gutted would be an
understatement of epic proportions. If I had any sense I'd go out now
and buy shares in the Fire Dragon Brewery; the amount of beer that
will be drunk when news of GGR's death breaks will be staggering.'

Glover couldn't have agreed more. The huge party thrown by the Fire Dragon Brewery – from which GGR had retired as a 'super salesman' just a week ago – had been headline news across the whole of Wales. He could imagine the next set of headlines: 'GGR Dead!' or 'The Great One – Gone!' Not many people in the world could be recognized by merely their initials, but GGR Davies was one of them.

Immediately, the 'did he fall, or was he pushed?' question took on a whole new meaning for Glover. He knew that, if the body was confirmed as being GGR's, he wouldn't have a moment's peace until the manner of the man's death had been fully explained; no peace in his own mind, and no peace from the press, or his superiors. He cursed DCI Jenkins's holiday once again.

On a personal level, he was still trying to come to terms with the loss of the sporting hero he'd watched through the glory days of Welsh rugby – when GGR had stuffed it to the English, and anyone else who'd dared allow the man to get his hands on the ball. Four Triple Crowns in a row, three Grand Slams; those were the days. And GGR had been there every time Wales had chalked up another record; he'd been magic. He was more famous than all the other players of his generation put together. He'd inspired a thousand Welsh schoolboys to get out onto the field and run toward the try line like a train. Including Evan himself.

Could it really be his remains on that stretcher being hauled up from the cliffs? Surely GGR Davies was immortal?

'When will you know for sure?' was Glover's miserable question to Souza.

Souza gave it some thought. 'Well, it's going to be an unpleasant identification for any family member, so I'll start with dental records.'

Glover pulled himself together. *Focus on the job, focus on the job.*

'Right-o, Rakel, not a word about this possibly being GGR to anyone, until we know for sure. Get him back to your place and put a rush on identification, quick as you can – right? I'll co-ordinate with Lewis.'

Souza nodded. 'I'll handle the PM myself; I won't hand it off to anyone else,' she confirmed.

'I'll hang onto this –' Glover nodded at the wallet – 'and we'll do some digging around about GGR's supposed whereabouts. This might not be him. He might be going about his business completely unaware that someone has his wallet in their pocket.'

Glover suspected he was clutching at straws. He continued, 'Before you go, Rakel, can you point out to me where the body was found? Maybe we can work out where he might have . . .' He hesitated. '. . . fallen from.'

'Absolutely,' replied Souza, 'I'll walk you over now – we found him pretty much directly below where the RSPCA lot found the dog.'

'RSPCA? Dog?' asked Evan.

'Wheaten Scottish terrier, found dragging a shooting stick tied to its lead, over on the cliff top there. The RSPCA have taken the dog; your Forensic Investigation Team have the stick. I noted the telephone number printed on the dog's collar. Dog's named Arthur, by the way. Here's the phone number.'

Souza handed Evan a scrap of paper with a mobile phone number scribbled on it.

'Damn!' said Evan, his sunny disposition now completely clouded. 'GGR had a dog named Arthur – I saw them together in the photos on the front page of the Evening Post last week. Oh Rakel, I'd give anything for it to not be him.'

Rakel Souza patted him on the shoulder. Her small, bird-like frame meant she had to reach up to do so, even though Glover wasn't tall.

'Thanks for the sympathy,' said Evan, 'the phone number's a start – let's give it a go.' Pulling out his mobile phone, he dialed the number Souza had handed him. He heard the ring tone on his own phone, and quickly realized he could also hear a musical tune coming from the approaching stretcher. He pushed the button to disconnect. The music stopped. He redialed. Once again the unmistakable strains of 'Bread of Heaven' could be heard coming from the stretcher that was now just a foot or two away. He let it ring, then the music stopped and Glover heard a familiar voice; a voice that had given triumphant post-game interviews through the 1970s; a voice that had given opinions about rugby internationals throughout the decades that followed; a voice that unmistakably belonged to GGR Davies.

'Sorry I missed you. Leave a message and I'll ring you back. *Diolch.*'

Evan felt as though he'd been kicked in the belly; it wasn't a formal identification, but he reckoned it was pretty close. 'Looks like we've got several strong reasons to believe it's him then.'

Souza sadly nodded her agreement. 'Gareth will be beside himself. Worshipped GGR, he did.'

Evan squared his shoulders. 'I'd better take a look at him, I suppose, and I'd better get that phone too; it could help us out. Amazing it still works.'

Souza took charge. The injuries to the man's head and face, were, as she had warned, significant. It was difficult to recognize any features, as few remained.

Evan found himself struggling to be objective; given the number of dead bodies he'd seen over the years, it never ceased to amaze him that each one felt like the first. He had no idea how Rakel did what she did. He couldn't have stomached it, he knew that.

The facial injuries aside, Glover quickly assessed the body and noted the lightweight red jacket – from the inside pocket of which Souza extracted the telephone, placing it into a suitable protective bag – the plaid shirt, and khaki trousers, all torn by the sharp rocks and soaked by the sea. They clung to the body, wrinkled and gaping, revealing jagged puncture wounds.

It was a sorry sight.

Souza signaled that the remains should be taken to the waiting vehicle.

'Let me show you where I think he might have gone over,' said Souza, as Evan motioned to Stanley to follow, 'then I'll get back as quick as I can and get going with a formal identification.'

Evan was lost in thought as the threesome walked across the headland, their eyes narrowing against the descending sun and stiff breeze. 'We'd better proceed as though it is GGR, so let's see what we can find here,' he said.

'Here' turned out to be a grassy dell below the highest point of the cliff top, shielded from the wind by high rocks on all sides except that facing out to sea. The grass was badly trampled about and Evan could see quite clearly where the pointed end of a shooting stick had been stuck deep into the ground, then dragged out by a no doubt distressed little dog, probably wondering what had happened to its master.

'No obvious sign of a suicide note, or any other items lying about, were there?' Evan knew the Forensic Investigation Team would have done a thorough job – a large area was cordoned off.

Souza shook her head. 'Nothing.'

'If the dog's been running around, doubtless chased about by some pretty heavy-footed RSPCA types, there might not be anything here that's of much use for us. But I'm sure I'll get the FIT report in due course. We'll hold off on the door-to-door around the farms and what-not in the area until we know more, and until we know if it's GGR, or not. Let's sort out next of kin, Stanley.'

Stanley nodded her understanding, and headed toward the two uniformed officers who were still kicking their heels beside their car.

'Anything for us down there?' asked Evan, peering toward the edge of the cliff, but remaining at least ten feet back from the precipitous edge.

'To be honest, it would be hard to say,' replied Rakel Souza. 'When the surfers initially spotted him, down there close to the base of the cliffs, he was, apparently, upside down, lodged between two outcrops. It was the red of his jacket that caught their attention. By the time HM Coastguard arrived by sea, the tide was coming in, and they couldn't get close enough to effect a retrieval; their craft would have been pushed into the rocks. In any case, it was clear to them – from the injuries they could see – that he was dead. I was in my office when the call came in and, frankly, I thought a run to the seaside might be more pleasant than ploughing through my coroner's paperwork. As you know, I like a bit of scampering up and down cliffs – in my spare time, usually – but this wasn't a job for me. The recovery team brought him up. By the time they got to him, the sea was already washing over the body. Now the sea's at least ten feet above where they found him – so I suspect anything that might have been down there would have been washed away. I've had a good look down at the cliff face with my binoculars, but I couldn't see any evidence of exactly where he might have struck as he fell.'

Evan grimaced. How could Souza be so objective?

'Sorry Evan,' added Rakel, obviously noticing the effect her words were having on him, 'I suppose I see it all a bit more scientifically than you; I've watched my fair share of rugby over the years, as you know, but when GGR was at the height of his fame as a player I had my nose stuck in a book, doing my best to pass all my exams at school.'

Glover nodded. 'I understand. Not much chance of anything useful down there,' he nodded toward the bottom of the cliff, 'and we're not likely to find much that's undisturbed up here, either. So it's over to you for a formal ID. But you know what I really need, Rakel?'

'Let me guess,' was Souza's sarcastic reply. 'Was the fall the actual cause of death? Any clues as to the manner of death – natural, accidental, suicidal, or homicidal? Bluntly put, is there any reason to expect foul play?'

'Exactly. Pronto.'

'Right-o, I'm off then,' said Souza as she slapped Glover gently on the back. 'I'm sorry for you, and for my poor husband, that it's probably GGR,' she said quietly. 'It'll be big news this, I know – and I also know DCI Jenkins is away. Do you think Lewis will put you in charge of this one?'

Evan smirked. 'I shouldn't think so. He wouldn't want a mere DI running a case as high profile as this one. He'll find a DCI to take it on, but maybe I'll be allowed to join the team. And there's bound to be a team, even if it's not a murder team, as of now, because we can't be sure how this happened. But it's GGR, after all. Probably.'

'Yes, probably. Well, if Lewis has any sense he'll get you to act up for the case. You're just the man for the job, Evan. I know how much you idolized GGR, and I know you'd deal with this case with intelligence, insight, and respect for the dead. You'd better talk to Lewis soon, though – I know he was keen to hear from you; I'd told him about the wallet, see? No doubt he'll want to prepare for the media onslaught. Tell him I should have something formal by morning, if not before, but I'll get out of your hair for now and let you get on with your side of things. Bye, Evan.'

'Bye, Rakel, and keep me posted?' Evan called toward his departing colleague.

He turned his face toward the last rays of the sun, and breathed deep; such beauty marred by such a tragedy. No matter what the reason for GGR's demise, it was a sad day for anyone who loved rugby, and the seagulls cried above him as if mourning the passing of an extraordinary man, which GGR had certainly been.

Evan snapped his eyes open, and turned purposefully toward his car. Better get going.


It was still only four p.m., according to Glover's watch. He thought it strange that it had taken such a short time for his world to have shifted so much.

Maybe just one missed step had ended the life of an always-nimble man who had made pride swell in a nation's heart for a decade or more. Or maybe there was an altogether more complicated, darker, reason for The Great One's demise. It was up to him to at least begin the process to find out. And he knew exactly where his first port of call would be – the Davies house, up on the South Gower Road.

Everyone knew GGR owned a small-holding from where his locally well-known wife, Gwladys, took their fruits, vegetables and eggs to the seasonal stall she had operated under the great glass roof of Swansea Market for at least the last thirty years.

The Glovers themselves had often benefitted from GGR's wife's green thumb, and he knew many people shopped at her stall just to be able to say 'These are from GGR's place, you know' when they presented their family with an evening meal, or visitors with a hearty Sunday lunch. The cachet was not to be ignored, even after all these years.

Just minutes away by road, Glover's car soon crunched to a halt on the graveled hard-standing in front of the Davies' white-painted, stone, Gower house, topped with its dark slate roof and trimmed with glossy black woodwork – the norm for the area. The place looked spic and span, but deserted; all closed up, and just a little melancholy. Knocking at the door brought no response.

'Probably still at the market, if that's where she is today,' commented Glover to Stanley, weighing whether they should set off for the city center to try to catch Gwladys Davies before she left her stall for the day, but uncertain they'd make it in time.

As if voicing Glover's own doubts, Stanley asked, 'Do we know if she's even at the market at all at this time of year?'

'I think with it being apple, blackberry and cauliflower season, she's likely to be,' replied Glover, listing some of his favorite foods. 'They're the sort of things they grow here. You phone the market and find out, while I call in to the super.'

The pair moved apart to allow for privacy, and made their respective calls. Concluding their business almost simultaneously Stanley spoke first.

'Mrs Davies has been at Swansea Market since she set up her stall at about nine this morning, sir. Left about forty minutes ago; she'd sold out of everything so she left early, they said. In fact, if she was coming straight home, she should be here soon,' concluded Stanley, looking at her watch.

Glover nodded. 'The super wants me to follow up with her as a first priority. Sounds like he's already pulling out his few remaining hairs with worry that, somehow, the presumptive identity will leak; he wants us to break the news to the likely widow before anyone else can. So we'd better hang about here. Not much else we can do right now.'

Glover felt like a wound spring; he wasn't desperate to be the bearer of such devastating information to the woman he'd always known as a jolly, rotund person, smiling at customers across a well-stocked veg stall, but he really wanted to get going with the investigation.

The trouble was, of course, he didn't really know what he was investigating. He'd have to wait until Rakel could give him some insight into how, and maybe even why, the man had ended up at the bottom of the cliffs.

There was always the chance he had jumped, but Evan thought the presence of the man's dog made that unlikely; why would a person take their dog to the spot where they planned to throw themselves off a cliff? Even Glover, not a dog owner himself, felt that would be an unkind thing to do, causing unnecessary distress to a – presumably – beloved creature. And that wouldn't be like GGR at all – not the man known for his support of youth rugby, and seen almost weekly in the local newspapers surrounded by beaming boys.

No, it didn't feel like a suicide. No note – though, of course, there might have been one tucked away inside the man's clothing.

Glover found it hard to believe GGR would choose to end his own life; at sixty-five he was comparatively young, and still adored and respected by everyone who'd ever heard of him. Saving a possible diagnosis of some dreadful disease, Evan couldn't come up with any reason why GGR wouldn't have been looking forward to a long and active retirement.

'There's a car coming, sir. This might be her now.' Stanley's comment pulled Glover back from his reverie.

Sure enough, a small red hatchback with luminous yellow capitalized lettering announcing 'DAVIES FRUIT & VEG' pulled up in front of the cottage. A moment later, a short, slightly greying woman of significant girth pushed herself out from behind the steering wheel. Glover recognized GGR's wife.

'Can I help you?' she asked cheerily enough, her bright blue eyes – which matched Glover's own in their intensity – shining happily at the pair. She glanced at their unmarked car, then returned her gaze to their faces.

She froze. 'You're the police.' It was like an accusation.

'Yes, Mrs Davies, we are,' replied Glover, as comfortingly as possible. They both showed her their IDs.

Gwladys Davies's face was stony. 'It's Geraint, isn't it? Something's happened to Geraint. What's the silly bugger been up to now?'

Glover judged her response as being more angry than concerned.

'Maybe we can talk inside,' was Glover's hopeful response.

But Mrs Davies wasn't budging. 'You can tell me right here, right now, thank you very much.'

Definitely anger, thought Glover.

'Drinking and driving again, is it?' she sounded disgusted. 'I'll give him what for, you see if I don't. You lot keep letting him off, and he keeps doing it. Where is he this time? Got him locked up somewhere safe till he sobers up, I hope. I suppose I'll have to come and get him again. Well, I'm emptying this lot out first – he can bloody well wait until I'm good and ready.'

Mrs Gwladys Davies opened the hatchback of the car and started to pull out empty crates and boxes, tossing them across the little courtyard with strength and fury.

Glover could hear her muttering, 'Bloody man' under her breath, and felt terribly sorry for her; this was probably the last time she'd ever be angry with her husband. It was hard to be angry with someone who was dead. She was happily cursing the man she'd soon be mourning, and Glover hardly had the heart to stop her.

He grappled with how to break the news; it was never easy, but this time it would be truly as hard for him to tell her, as it would be for this woman to hear his words. He knew the couple had no children; he wondered about other relatives.

'Family liaison's on the way,' whispered Stanley into his ear, almost telepathically. 'Coming in an unmarked car, of course. We don't want any tongues wagging yet, though they will soon enough, I suspect. Should be here in about fifteen minutes.'

Glover smiled, and winked his thanks.

Turning his attention to the red-faced woman in front of him, Glover knew he couldn't put it off any longer. He swallowed hard, and set about changing her life forever.

'Mrs Davies,' he raised his voice to get her attention, and succeeded. 'You're right, Mrs Davies, it is about your husband, but it's not what you think. I really do feel it would be better if we could speak to you indoors. Maybe there's a friend or a neighbor you'd like my colleague to fetch.'

The woman tutted at Glover. 'Why on earth would I want anyone with me? What are you going to tell me? That he's dead or something, is it?'

Gwladys Davies smiled at her own silly suggestion for a split second, then her face fell. She stopped in her tracks, a wooden slatted crate in one hand, a flattened cardboard box in the other.

'Oh my God – he's not, is he?' Her eyes were wide with disbelief. Her mouth hanging open.

'A man's body was found at the base of Three Cliffs today, Mrs Davies, and we have good reason to believe it is that of your husband, Mr Geraint Gareth Richard Davies.' It seemed strange, and almost heretical, to Glover to be speaking the man's full name like that. 'We found Mr Davies's wallet and mobile phone on the body, and I believe you have a little dog . . .'

'Arthur. Where's Arthur?' she cried, looking around in a panic.

'Arthur's fine – he's been taken away by the RSPCA,' Glover reassured her.

'I want Arthur!' shouted the woman. 'Tell them to bring him back to me. He doesn't like other dogs. He needs to be home with me. Tell them to bring him home now.'

Glover was somewhat taken aback by the woman's fixation on her dog. He nodded to Stanley, and knew she would understand that he meant her to get hold of the RSPCA and arrange for the dog to be returned to its owner. But he also knew he had to continue with his difficult task. It was far from over.

'Maybe if we could step inside?' he tried again.

Gwladys Davies waggled a bunch of keys toward Glover. 'It's the little gold one,' she whispered. She seemed to have shrunk, to have somehow deflated. She looked completely bewildered.

Glover handed the keys to Stanley and moved to support the woman, who had dropped the boxes she had been holding with a clatter, and was hanging onto her open car door in an effort to support herself.

'Let's get you inside and organize a cup of tea, is it?' said Glover, gently, as he steered the woman, whose legs weren't working at all well.

'I can't believe it. I don't believe it,' she whispered, as Glover sat her down, carefully, on a wheel-backed wooden chair beside her large, well-scrubbed, pine kitchen table. She looked up at Glover with dry eyes, silently beseeching him to tell her it was all a lie.

But he couldn't.

'Mrs Davies,' he began, keen to spare the woman the ugly details of her husband's condition, 'our people are working on a formal identification as we speak, but we're in little doubt about it being your husband. However, do you happen to know what he was wearing when he went out with Arthur this morning?'

Maybe the clothes would clinch it.

'I know exactly what he was wearing; I lay out his clothes for him every morning,' was the woman's proud and confident reply. 'He had on his nice new beige trousers that I got him for his retirement do; they're that good old-fashioned twill material, they'll last for years, they will. And he wore his yellow-and-green checked shirt. He probably wore that horrible red windcheater thing they gave him from the brewery, knowing him, though why he will insist upon wearing it when he's got so many other nice jackets, I'll never know. That waxed cotton coat I got for him? Never wears that, does he?'

Maybe it was possible to be angry with the dead, after all, thought Glover; or maybe Gwladys Davies was in denial. But her description clinched it for him; there was no doubt in his mind it had been GGR's body on that stretcher.

'I know this must be very difficult for you, Mrs Davies, a sudden death is very upsetting. So is there someone you'd like my sergeant to get hold of for you? Maybe even your family doctor?' Evan was almost begging her to say yes. The presence of a friend or a relative, and the use of some heavy sedatives, usually meant the burden of comforting a bereaved one could reasonably be passed along to family liaison – and he could get on with his job.

Gwladys Davies thought for a moment, then said sharply, 'Get Ann from the farm across the road. Geraint's sister lives in Cardiff now – she's gone very posh has Janice – and she'll take forever to get here. Drives like a snail, she does. I suppose I'd better ring her to tell her. But what do I tell her? What happened exactly? Are you sure it's him?'

Glover knew how long it had taken him to face the facts, so wasn't surprised the man's wife was unable to accept the news. He explained again about the dog, mentioned the wallet and the phone, then added the confirmation of the clothing. The woman was ashen as she took a cup of hot tea off Stanley; her hands shook.

'Did Mr Davies seem quite his usual self when you left him this morning?' ventured Glover. The possibility of suicide had to be explored, however unlikely it might seem.

Gwladys Davies was quick to respond. 'If you mean was he grumbling about anything and everything, shouting at me for no reason, and badly hungover, then yes, he was. Didn't get home till gone midnight. A taxi brought him. So of course he didn't feel like getting out of bed at six this morning – not like some of us have to.'

She was still angry with the man; Glover wondered just how much resentment had simmered, and maybe boiled, between the two of them when he was still alive.

Her mouth pursed, then she added, 'Supposed to be walking Arthur, then sorting out picking up the car this morning, he was.'

'So there was nothing out of the ordinary?' pressed Glover. 'Nothing preying on his mind – worrying him?'

Gwladys Davies put down her mug and narrowed her now steely-blue eyes at Glover.

'You mean do I think he flung himself off the cliffs, don't you?' Her mouth was pressed into a narrow, white line. The jolly woman Glover remembered from the fruit and veg stall in Swansea Market seemed to have evaporated – maybe she was just a concoction for the customers, and this was the real person GGR had lived with. The wrinkles seemed to sit very comfortably around her angry little mouth, indeed, they seemed to have been formed as the result of many years of wearing a habitually judgmental expression.

'Yes, that's what I mean, Mrs Davies.' Glover didn't mean to be unkind, but he felt her direct approach should be met with a matching response.

'Don't be so bloody ridiculous! Geraint was many things, but he wasn't a man who would hurt himself. He'd no more jump off Three Cliffs than I would. Besides, he'd never do anything to mess up that face of his. I suppose he is a mess? They always are when they go off the cliffs.'

Glover found her remarks curious, given the circumstances.

'I'm afraid that, yes – as you have clearly deduced – your husband's remains bear the marks of a significant fall. But I appreciate your insights, Mrs Davies. So you don't think it likely that your husband took his own life. Do you know of anyone who might have wanted to do him harm?'

'So, if he didn't jump, then he must have been pushed?' was her disdainful retort.

Glover was beginning to hate that phrase.

'We have to explore every possibility, Mrs Davies – I'm sure you wouldn't want us to leave any stone unturned.' Glover was using his 'pacifying' voice. It wasn't working.

'Inspector –' the woman made Glover's title sound like an insult – 'there's no way Geraint would have jumped, and no, there's no one I know of who hated him enough to push him off. If you don't know how he ended up at the bottom of the cliff – and it's quite clear you don't – then might I suggest you go away and find out.'

Her tone was mocking Glover, and he didn't like it. One bit.

She continued, 'The chances are he was still half-drunk from last night so slipped and fell. Always boasting about how he was still so nimble on his feet, he was. Well maybe he wasn't quite so nimble this morning.'

Glover was disappointed with the way the interview was going; he was somewhat shocked to hear about GGR's drinking habits, and even more surprised to find that his wife wasn't the cheery woman he'd expected, but a bitter and angry woman, who, even now, wouldn't stop making spiteful comments about his hero.

'Excuse me, Mrs Davies,' Stanley seemed unhappy about interrupting, 'do you think it would be better for me to walk across the road to your friend's farm, or is there a telephone number where I could reach her?'

'She's number three on the quick-dial thingy,' replied Gwladys in a businesslike manner, 'the phone's in the hall out there – just ring star, three, star and you'll get her. Ann Edwards. But don't tell her what's happened – I'll tell her when she gets here. Ta.' She looked at her watch. 'She should be there; probably getting tea ready, I should think.'

It appeared that the thought of her friend preparing an evening meal overwhelmed Gwladys, and it set her off into floods of tears. Glover suspected she was beginning to accept that her husband was, in fact, dead; that she'd never again prepare a meal for him. He could do nothing but wait as she wailed and snuffled.

When her sobbing gradually subsided, Glover couldn't help but feel relieved; relieved that she'd shown some sort of emotion other than anger, and relieved that she'd finally stopped.

Stanley re-entered the large farmhouse kitchen and announced, 'Your friend will be right over, Mrs Davies.'

'Thank you, dear,' she managed to reply, her tone now much softer than before. 'Maybe you had better get Dr Morris for me, if you can – he's number four on the thingy. Thank you.'

A knock at the front door drew Stanley's attention. 'I'll get that, and phone your doctor.' Moments later Stanley returned with a female officer in tow, who busied herself around Mrs Davies; she offered more tea, enquired about the location of biscuits, and asked if the poor woman fancied anything else to eat, offering to cook something.

While Gwladys Davies was fending off the attentiveness of the family liaison officer, Glover whispered to Stanley, 'Let's get the friend in, tell the liaison to make sure the woman's taken care of by her doctor for the night, and we'll get out of here. Until we know a cause of death I don't know if this woman's just a widow to be pitied, or a suspect. Either way, we'd better make sure one of our lot is with her at all times – right?'

Another knock at the front door was again answered by Stanley; the neighbor had arrived.

Glover was only too well aware that most murders were committed by spouses. He didn't know if they were even dealing with a murder yet, but – if it turned out that they were – he might already have witnessed something that would prove useful for the investigation. All that anger from the widow? It was quite something.

As he was leaving, Glover turned once more toward the still-snuffling Gwladys and said, as comfortingly as he could, 'Be assured, Mrs Davies, that I'll be in touch if we get any more news, and this officer can be here with you all night, if you'd like that. We can't have you feeling lonely, now, can we? But could you maybe just tell me the exact time you left your husband this morning? Was he due to meet with anyone up at Three Cliffs?'

Glover was taken aback by the torrent which broke forth from Gwladys Davies.

'Ten to eight, I left,' she snapped, 'same as usual. Well, usual since he retired, anyway. I know it had only been a week, but he didn't know what to do with himself already. Couldn't help but get under my feet, he couldn't, and he held me up something rotten. "Helping" he said he was; but he wasn't helpful at all. Usually out by eight for all those years, you see, both him and me; him off to see his customers, me to the stall in the market.'

Glover was glad when she drew breath.

The she was off again. 'But now? Well, he'll have to find something to do with his time; I can't cope with his sort of help. And plans? No, no plans that I know of, other than getting the car back. That was his problem, see? Never had any plans. I've been telling him and telling him to find something to do.'

Gwladys managed a wistful smile. 'He'll enjoy playing more golf, I suppose – loves it he does. But you can't do that every day, can you? Well, I suppose he could, but he doesn't like the rain, see? Makes his arthritis play up, doesn't it? Those knees of his. Never give him any peace, they don't. He was just going out to walk Arthur when I left him this morning. Oh . . . poor Arthur. You must get him home to me, you must.'

Glover found it all extremely interesting.

As Evan Glover was brushing his teeth, his mobile phone started to ring in the pocket of the jacket hanging on the banister downstairs. It was six forty-five a.m. It had to be DSI Lewis.

'Shall I get it?' asked Betty, calling from the kitchen.

'Yes please, love,' was Evan's gurgled reply.

'Detective Inspector Evan Glover's telephone,' said Betty.

'That you, Mrs Glover?' asked Superintendent Lewis.

'Hello Michael, how are you?' Betty made a point of addressing all Evan's superiors as equals – they weren't her bosses, after all.

'Who is it?' called Evan.

Betty called, 'It's Michael.'

Evan hurried to take the call – he knew about Lewis's dislike of dealing with spouses; twice-divorced himself, Lewis seemed to have a unhealthy disrespect for officer's partners.

When Evan finally grabbed his phone from Betty, who gave him a wicked grin as she passed it to him, he listened patiently while his superior explained how deeply concerned he was that Glover's immediate superior was on holiday, and how he very much wished DCI Ted Jenkins was around.

'I intend being very "hands-on" with this case, Glover,' said Lewis.

'I should imagine so, sir,' replied Glover, warily.

'It's not a case I would ordinarily place under the control of a DI.'

'No, sir.'

'Not good optics, for a case like this.'

'No, sir.'

'But we're stretched, so I am appointing you to act up to DCI for the duration. You'll report directly to me. Big responsibility for you, Glover. But I think you're up to it.'

Evan's gut rolled. 'Thank you, sir. I won't let you down, sir.'

'No, you bloody well won't,' snapped Lewis. 'Full update on my desk, in an hour.'

Evan looked at his phone when Lewis had gone, and organized his thoughts.

'I'm acting up. In charge,' he said to Betty, who was hovering at his elbow.

His wife beamed. 'Of course you are. You'll be brilliant, *cariad*. I've put coffee in a thermal mug for you, and I've shoved a couple of those granola bars into a bag – in case you need a snack.'

Evan grinned. 'It's not my first day at school, love.'

Betty kissed his cheek. 'No, it's much more important than that. I'm so proud of you. Now go – you'll be great, I know it.'

Evan kissed her, grabbed the coffee, and shouted, 'I'm off to see Rakel; I hope she's got something. As you can imagine, I might be late tonight.'

'Don't worry, I'll keep the soup going,' came Betty's less than welcome reply.

Glover pulled the front door closed behind him and jumped into his car. It was just before seven a.m. He wondered what Rakel had found. As he negotiated the blessedly light traffic, he slurped at his coffee – it was good and hot, and actually tasted of coffee, which was a blessing.

Rakel Souza welcomed Evan to her office while she munched a fast-food breakfast sandwich.

'DSI Lewis is taking a very "hand's on" approach with this one.' She rolled her eyes and added, 'His phrase – so he wants everything, and I mean everything, to go through him. He's been phoning me almost every hour, on the hour, through the night. The man's driven me nearly insane. Frankly, I don't know how I've kept my cool. By the way, he just phoned me to tell me you're acting up as DCI for this case. Congratulations . . . I think.'

'Thanks. It's going to be a challenge dealing with him, and this case. So, let's get to it. What did you find? I know we're all grateful that you've been at it all night, but Lewis – for all his involvement in the details – didn't tell me a thing. What have you told him?'

'As much as I can, but I told him I needed you to come here to see something; I didn't want to just tell you about it on the phone, or see it in photos. Come with me to the dirty rooms.'

Glover knew that 'dirty' signified the presence of corpses; the public were never allowed into 'dirty' areas – they only got to see the remains of their loved ones from a 'clean' room. None of this rolling out of corpses from chilled drawers to be pawed over by anyone and everyone, like they always seemed to be doing on those American TV shows. The West Glamorgan NHS Trust's Health and Safety Regulations wouldn't allow for that sort of thing; they got enough stick about not keeping the wards clean, without letting members of the public come into contact with all sorts of who-knew-what in the mortuary.

Glover hated the mortuary, not because of what happened there, but because of the smell; 'sweet' certainly wasn't the word for it. Of course, it depended on what Rakel and her team had on the go at any given time, but not even the chilly conditions, nor the use of various chemicals, could mask the unpleasant realities of the place. He hoped he wouldn't have to be there for too long, and tried to prepare himself for the task of viewing the corpse, this time possibly completely splayed open.

As Glover pulled on the required gloves and paper coverall, and donned the ridiculous little hat that completed the outfit, Souza brought him up to date.

'It's definitely him, Evan. I got the man's medical and dental records last night, and there's no question about it.'

Glover was disappointed; somewhere inside him there'd been a slim thread of hope that the body had somehow been set up to appear to be GGR.

'He's had a huge amount of dentistry done over the years,' continued Souza, watching with a smile as Glover fiddled with the paper cap, 'some of it involving a good deal of metalwork. However, I think what's most amazing is that throughout all those years of rugby, he never broke a single bone, except his nose. His records tell me he broke that eight times, necessitating some septorhinoplastic surgery because of the damage to his septum. Had an ACL rupture, a couple of concussions, and lost several teeth as I said, but nothing terribly serious, considering.'

'Despite the fact he played well into his thirties, very few people could catch him on the field,' was Glover's glum reply.

'True. However, although he looked not too bad on the outside – except for the terrible injuries from the fall, of course – his innards told another story,' added Souza, sounding grim.

'Definitely the observable early stages of hypertropic cirrhosis,' she continued, 'he probably thought he was suffering from constant indigestion, but it was an enlarged liver that was doing it. There are some faint signs of jaundice, but he might not have noticed that, given his generally ruddy complexion. He also had a touch of liver palm, but if he helped out on the small-holding I dare say he could have put the characteristic reddening at the ball of his thumbs down to general wear and tear of the hands. I suppose working for a brewery for forty-odd years has its damaging side-effects, after all,' she concluded.

'Alcohol induced then?' asked Glover.

'Most likely; booze is by far the most common cause of cirrhosis. He's drunk a lot of it, for a good number of years, I'd say. But I'm getting some other tests done too – liver, kidneys, heart, body and blood chemistry of course, toxicology reports and so on. I can't say too much right now, but there are a few other physical issues I'm concerned about.'

Glover looked quizzical.

'Don't ask, Evan, because you know I won't guess. What do I know? His arteries don't suggest he was overly familiar with the words "low fat"; he had surprisingly good muscle tone for a man of sixty-five who was obviously otherwise generally unfit, and he has very small testicles. He might have had a few years left in him, but only with a significant change in lifestyle, I'd have said.' Souza looked serious as she pushed open the swing doors that led from the 'clean' offices to the mortuary itself.

Glover was still grappling with her comment about the man's testicles; he felt compelled to speak. 'Now, you know me, Rakel, a man who likes plain language when it comes to your area – so why the comment about the testicles? What does that mean?'

Souza continued to walk slowly toward the rooms where the post-mortems were conducted. 'Nothing, necessarily, by itself, and that's why I hesitate to make any assumptions.' She was obviously being cautious. 'What I can tell you is that the testicular atrophy, the relatively lean muscle mass for his age, the liver and kidney condition – all taken together – plus the number of hypodermic wounds in the man's thighs, lead me to suspect that GGR Davies was a long-term user of anabolic steroids.'

Evan took a moment to consider Rakel's comments. He was stunned.

GGR on steroids? It made no sense.

'But he hasn't played rugby in nearly thirty years, Rakel, why on earth would he be taking steroids?' asked Glover, somewhat confused.

'Calm down, Evan. I'm telling you what I've found, and how I interpret those findings, without the benefit of any conclusive test results – so please bear that in mind?' Glover nodded his agreement.

'So,' continued Souza, 'what we have here is the possibility of a man who might have become a steroid user at an early point in his career and continued to use them thereafter.'

The thought horrified Glover; what would all those records, caps and cups mean if GGR had achieved it all because of steroid use?

'Or,' added Souza, noting her friend's horrified expression, 'we have a man who began to use steroids as he aged, feeling the effects of having taken knock after knock on the field. Steroids aren't able to actually build muscle, you see, Evan, they're used to allow for a quicker recovery time after exercise and to increase tolerance to pain, which allows the user to push their body further and faster so they can build more muscle and stamina. Maybe GGR used them to allow him to manage his aches and pains and to allow him to play round after round of golf, which I understand he did.'

Glover preferred that idea; if his hero was using steroids, and if he hadn't used them during his career, and if they were for medicinal reasons only, well . . . that might be acceptable. Betty's cousin had just had a steroid injection in her hip – not all uses of steroids were bad, he reasoned.

'Is there any way to tell how long he'd been using them?' Glover dared to ask. *Do I really want to know?* was what he was asking himself.

'No, other than for years,' replied Souza. 'He's obviously been what you might call a "responsible user", but there are some suggestions of cumulative liver and kidney damage, which would be normal, and some effect on the heart. Pretty frequently observed side effects of long-term usage – meaning years, not months. But as for whether he was using them when he was playing – which I'm sure is what you mean, Evan – there's no way of knowing. Of course, you have to bear in mind that anabolic steroids weren't banned substances in sports when he was playing. They're Schedule Four drugs now, as I'm sure you know, and banned throughout sport. GGR wasn't involved in the sport anymore, so no one would be testing him.'

She shook her head. 'You'd think they'd be tricky to get hold of, but they are more prevalent than you'd think in Welsh rugby, at all levels, it seems. As I'm sure you know, many people have uninterrupted access to them for decades. Looks like GGR was one of them. But the steroids, if they are confirmed, aren't what killed him. At least – I don't have any test results yet that suggest they did. No, this is what I wanted you to see.' Souza shouted to be heard above the fans that droned constantly inside the, ironically, spotlessly clean, 'dirty' white-tiled room.

She moved purposefully toward the cadaver on the bench. Glover was thankful that GGR's body had been stitched closed; giant 'scarecrow' stitches marked a large 'Y' shape across the whole torso. He was struck, once again, by the amount of damage sustained by the man in his fall.

'Let's have it then,' said Glover, somewhat abruptly, wanting to get out of the place as soon as possible.

'Can you see this?' asked Souza, lifting the head to show the back of the man's skull.

'I can see lots of things,' answered Glover bleakly; it was difficult to work out which injuries had been sustained in GGR's descent versus those which had been inflicted when Souza had removed the top of the skull as part of her investigations.

'Here,' said Souza. She pointed to a depression just at the base of the pitifully battered skull.

Glover drew nearer to the pathetic figure on the slab – he didn't want to, but he had to. 'How do you know that wasn't something that happened to him as he fell?'

'I knew you'd ask that,' smiled Souza, and flicked a switch on a light box suspended on the wall beside them. 'Because of this,' she exclaimed triumphantly, pointing to the illuminated, yet still somewhat indistinct, image in front of them.

Glover had to squint to make out the detail. How was anyone supposed to make any sense of X-rays? He assumed they were of the once-wonderful GGR. As Souza had mentioned, the man had a lot of metal implanted into his teeth and jaws; indeed, it looked as though most of his teeth were actually screwed in.

'Okay, Rakel, what am I supposed to be looking at? All those screws?' Glover was puzzled and a little frustrated. Souza, on the other hand, seemed quite excited.

'See this here?' she pointed to a series of lines at the base of the skull area on the screen. 'That wasn't made by craggy rocks – but by a blunt instrument.' Souza sounded as delighted as she might have done if she'd just discovered the usefulness of the Rosetta Stone. 'It was definitely the fall that killed him – massive head and neck trauma as we saw, and the spinal shock he suffered as a result killed him almost instantaneously. However, this initial injury was what might have caused him to fall in the first place, or it might have made it easy for someone to steer him toward, or even over, the cliff edge. This bash on the head would have made him woozy at least, possibly semi-conscious.'

Glover took a moment. He was trying to make sense of what Souza had said. It sounded a lot like manslaughter, or possibly murder.

'So, let me get this straight,' he said, keen to understand the full implications of what Souza was telling him, 'GGR was hit on the back of the head just before he went over the cliff? These marks are not an old injury. The bash on the head and the fall are definitely related?'

'Yes. My findings are that the trauma to the back of the head immediately preceded the fall – by a matter of moments.'

'And do we have anything other than "blunt instrument" at this point?'

'Ah ha!' was Rakel Souza's delighted response. 'I knew you'd ask me that too – and I am pleased to be able to oblige. Come with me, Evan. I've spent hours on just that question – and I'm pretty much one hundred percent sure of my information.' Rakel Souza directed him toward a computer screen where she pushed a couple of keys; a photograph of a golf club appeared.

She waved at the screen. 'Meet Massive Martha III – the largest driver there is. Only been available for about six months. And it's the only face-pattern and size that fits what I have observed on GGR's head. And, even more than that, I can tell you he was struck by a left-handed club.' She glowed.

'They have left-handed golf clubs?' Glover was a keen non-golfer; he hated private golf clubs and all they stood for, and that had poisoned his mind against the game itself. It didn't surprise him at all that it might have been a golfer who'd done for The Great One. Putting his enmity toward golfers to one side, he listened to Rakel Souza's patient explanation.

'Yes, Evan, they have left-handed golf clubs, for left-handed players, like me. But, no, it wasn't me. By the way, I suppose I am officially confirming that, unless anyone can come up with a way for a man to bash in the bottom of his own skull with a golf club, then we're looking at a murderous assault. Whether he fell or was pushed after the blow to the head, it was the blow that was the root of it. So you can tell Lewis it's official; it's a suspicious death, with murder or at least manslaughter in play. In a way I'm sure that will cheer you up no end, because now you'll get all the people and resources you need for the investigation.'

'Well, you're not wrong about the resources, Rakel. But I still wish it wasn't him.'

Rakel sighed. 'I know, Evan; even if he might not have been quite the man you thought he was, it's still GGR.'

Glover looked thoughtful. 'Tell, me, Rakel, would the blow have taken great strength?'

'On balance, and considering the physics involved, not really. Also, the angle of the injury doesn't help us in terms of the height of the person who delivered that blow. The ground where I suspect GGR was struck, in other words, where the dog had been tied up in that little dell we saw, was quite uneven, as you know. Thus – relative to GGR – a short person could have been standing on higher ground, or a taller person on lower ground to deliver the observed angle of the strike.'

Glover realized Souza's comments allowed for just about anyone at all to have been the assailant, but decided to continue with his confirmation of the details. 'So, a tall or short, strong or weak, man or woman could have inflicted the blow, right?'

'Correct.'

'And, to broaden the field further, should I assume that they would not necessarily have to be a left-handed person to be able to swing a left-handed golf club?' Glover wasn't feeling happy.

Rakel Souza smiled. 'It's a correct general assumption, but I'd bet that if they were right-handed, we'd see the other part of the club presenting on the skull.'

Souza drew back from Glover and adopted a teeing-off stance. 'You see, if you're right-handed, you'll automatically swing through with the right arm directing from the back,' she demonstrated, and encouraged Glover to work through the motions with her.

He did his best.

Rakel continued, 'A right-handed person's dominant arm is their right arm and they'll need it to control the club through the swing. But if you're left-handed, you'd swing through with the left arm.' Again, they both tried the motion. 'I would suggest it would be extremely awkward for a right-handed person to swing a left-handed club and achieve sufficient force at impact to produce what we see at the base of GGR's skull, which clearly indicates the striking face – not the back-side – of the club came into contact with his body. It would be a highly unnatural set of movements for a right-handed person, though not impossible.'

'Good work, Rakel,' said Glover. 'Now all I have to do is find a left-handed golfer who wanted to kill GGR.'

'Hmm, a left-handed golfer who's serious enough about their game to want to spend a few hundred pounds on just one club, let alone the rest of the stuff in their bag. But don't forget that the person wielding the club at GGR's head might not have actually owned the club, or might not even have been a golfer at all. Frankly, these drivers are designed to be pretty foolproof, so anyone making even a first attempt at a swing could have connected in the way the evidence suggests. Sorry.' Souza seemed to be apologizing for the fact she wasn't making Glover's life any easier.

He forced a smile. 'Well, I can always start with every golfer in the area, and go from there; there can only be . . . well, I don't know how many there'd be of them. But, that aside, this has been a great help, Rakel. Really. And I'll make sure Lewis knows it.'

'Ah yes, DSI Lewis,' replied Souza. 'I suppose I should warn you that he's a bit of golfer himself – plays off a seven handicap at his club, I hear.'

'That fits,' tutted Glover, rolling his eyes. 'Maybe it was him, out there at Three Cliffs on Monday morning taking a swing at GGR. Too much to hope for?' He smiled at Souza. 'Anything else I should know right now?' he asked, keen to get away.

'Not until I have those results back, Evan. I can put in the hours, as can my team, but you can't rush science, and that's that. As soon as I know anything, I'll phone you. Well, I'll phone Lewis, then I'll phone you, because that's how we're playing this time – Lewis is "hands-on".'

'You, me, and Lewis, all three of us with our hands all over it. Thanks Rakel, talk soon,' called Glover as he left Souza's insufficiently deodorized surroundings.

Tearing off his protective paper clothing with delight, Glover checked his watch – almost eight a.m. He'd get to the office to connect with Stanley, phoning Lewis on the way; he'd left a list of things for Stanley to take care of that morning, and had no doubt she'd be well on the way to completing her tasks. Now he had a few other things he needed her to organize.

Glover knew Stanley was good, but suspected it would take her longer to find the answers to all Glover's questions than it would take Glover to drive from West Glam General Hospital to HQ, so he took a few minutes to sit in the car park and get the facts straight in his mind. He sent a comprehensive text message to Stanley, then phoned his superior – who warned him the word was out about GGR, and the newshounds were already sniffing around.

As Glover finally eased out of the car park to join the rush hour traffic, he was glad it was moving slowly enough to give him time to think; that day the whole of Wales would begin to mourn its hero. GGR was gone; The Great One was dead. A national tragedy.

How had he died? That would be the first question on everyone's lips, of course.

Murder? It was a scandal. A national scandal.

Who did it? Without an immediate answer to that question, the next comment would doubtless be that the police were useless.

The importance of the task at hand began to weigh even more heavily on Glover. He knew it wouldn't be easy; even with the extra workforce a murder investigation allowed for, he and Stanley were going to feel the strain. Glover remembered he'd be losing Stanley in a few days. He cursed aloud. Here he was, working on a case that might well splatter his name all over the local papers (which he always hated), a case that involved a man he'd idolized for as long as he could remember, and he'd be stuck without Stanley. Wonderful.

Glover entered HQ at the rear of the building to avoid the mass of media vehicles clogging the High Street, then clattered up the echoing stone staircase toward his office.

'Stanley,' he called as he marched along the corridor.

'Sir,' came Stanley's reply from inside Glover's own office.

When Glover entered what he often referred to as his 'cell', it was clear why Stanley was there – she was 'entertaining' Detective Superintendent Michael Lewis, who wasn't exactly smiling.

'What the hell are we going to tell them all, Glover? The chief's all over me,' were the first words out of the super's mouth. Glover stopped in his tracks. It was clear from Stanley's face that panic was beginning to get the better of her; the super could be a bit of a bear when he wanted. But he was right; what were they going to tell the media? How much – or how little?

'Well, sir,' Glover began cautiously, thinking on his feet, 'this is a very high profile case, sir. National importance, not just local or regional. But we really can't say much right now – so how about you work with the public relations people at Regional HQ and get a statement prepared confirming identity, expressing regret, promising investigation of all possibilities and so forth. You could just read the statement, put out an appeal for anyone who saw GGR out at Three Cliffs yesterday morning, and apologize for not being able to take questions because of the ongoing investigation. It would keep it short and sweet, sir, and they're a bit less frantic if you throw them a bit of something every so often, aren't they? Even announcing you're going to tell them something at a certain time seems to shut them up for a while.'

Lewis seemed somewhat mollified, and wandered out of Glover's office muttering something about getting the top brass at Region involved with doing some actual work.

Glover assumed he was in the clear to get on with his job, at least for a little while. He was relieved. Time was pressing, and he didn't want anyone to think he was dawdling. He had a team to get together, get briefed, and get working.

But first, Stanley needed to be filled in. It transpired she was much better versed in golfing than Glover might have expected.

'We have golfing weekends with the scouts, sir,' was Stanley's explanation for understanding all about golf clubs. Glover was beginning to wonder what other aspects of Stanley's scouting involvement might come in useful. He had no idea scouts even played golf.

'So, it's going to be a murder investigation, then, is it, sir?' she continued. 'I saw the team was getting set up first thing this morning.'

Glover noted she was finally beginning to adopt the Welsh habit of asking non-questions. Glover smiled. He liked this young woman.

Stanley continued, 'And, if it was a golf club that inflicted GGR's original injury, then I'm sure it's going to interest you to know he spent the whole of Sunday at a golf and rugby tournament.'

'A golf tournament? Dozens of golfers? Hundreds of golf clubs? Marvelous. Where?'

'He was at the Brynfield Golf and Rugby Club, sir. Annual tournament, it seems. The two clubs which share the facility play golf against each other in the morning, then have a sevens rugby match in the afternoon. GGR was there to present the awards at the end of the day – guest of honor, sir.'

'So,' said Glover, starting to burrow his fingers through his hair in what he knew to be a habit that displayed distressed concentration, 'maybe something happened that set someone off, and they took it out on GGR the next morning on Three Cliffs?' It didn't sound probable to Glover.

'Could be, sir,' was Stanley's guarded reply.

'Do we know anything about how GGR was logistically involved in the event?' Glover asked.

'Yes, sir. In fact, you can talk to Jerry about it. Do you know DS Hill, Jerry Hill, sir? We share an office. He was at the tournament itself, sir, and I've asked him to hang about until I knew if you wanted to talk to him.'

Glover's face brightened a little. 'Excellent. Let's have him in right away.' As Stanley left her boss to fetch her office-mate, Glover leaned back in his chair, and popped a peppermint into his mouth. He was crunching into it with vigor when Stanley reappeared.

'DS Hill, sir,' announced Stanley as a tall, thin, dark-haired young man, with a pallid complexion and deep-set brown eyes, walked apprehensively into Glover's office. Glover had spotted him about the place, of course, and had seen him in action when they pulled large teams together, but he'd never formed much of a real opinion about the chap. Not as a person. Not as an officer, or a detective. Now was the time.

'So, Hill, Stanley tells me you were at the Brynfield Club on Sunday when GGR was there?'

'Yes, sir. I was, sir.' Polite, at least.

'And what can you tell me about the man, and the day, that might help with our investigations?'

DS Hill looked puzzled. 'Well, nothing, sir, I don't think, sir.' He half-looked around at Stanley, awkwardly squirming in his chair. 'I mean, if GGR died at Three Cliffs yesterday, I don't see how . . .'

Clearly the internal gossip mill hadn't got hold of the key facts. Glover was relieved; he was anxious that the details about GGR's manner of death didn't leak out, yet.

'Don't worry about how it might help me, just tell me,' said Glover firmly. Hill almost jumped. Glover was beginning to wonder if the man was sound – he certainly didn't seem to have much backbone.

'Well – it's an annual match, sir. I belong to the Brynfield Golf Club, and we share a clubhouse with the Brynfield Rugby Club, as I'm sure you know. Every year we have a tournament – club against club, one dozen men per club play golf in six fours, then a dozen from each club play a game of sevens rugby – allowing for five substitutes. Usually the golf club wins the golf, and the rugby club wins the rugby, but the big deal is to try to get the double – that's when you win the Howells' Cup, sir.'

'And GGR's role in all of this?' pressed Glover.

'He gave the after-dinner speech and the prizes this year. Did a very good job of both, too – highly entertaining.'

Glover wondered if Hill was this poor at answering questions when his own DI asked them.

'I need details, Hill. Specifics. Did GGR arrive before dinner? After dinner? What? Tell me everything about GGR and the tournament.' Glover knew he sounded terse. Maybe that would work.

Hill looked cowed. His tone suggested he was sulking. 'Well, I was out following the golfers all morning, supporting the team and all that. GGR wasn't there, though I heard he played a round that morning. We came in for lunch, and I did see GGR at the bar just as we were off to the rugby. Next . . . I saw him having drinks with a group of the rugby lot before dinner, then he sat at the top table for the dinner itself. Afterwards he made a speech, and handed out all the prizes, including the Howells' Cup – which we won, sir. First time ever.' Hill seemed pleased with himself.

Glover snapped, 'Anything untoward?'

Hill looked uncomfortable. 'I saw GGR arguing with one of the rugby lot just as we were all off out after lunch. It didn't seem like much – just a couple of raised voices and some finger wagging, in my opinion.'

'Any bad blood between the teams? Anything on or off the field of competition?' asked Glover sharply.

'Well, you know, sir, boys will be boys, but it's mainly good-humored rivalry. Usually. But on Sunday night, well, there was the usual banter between tables over dinner, as I'm sure you can imagine, and afterwards GGR did his speech, which was very entertaining as I said – something about knocking over a sheep on a country lane and shouting "mint sauce" as he drove off.'

Hill half-smiled as he remembered the tale, looked up, saw Glover's stern look and hurriedly added, 'Well, it was funny at the time, sir, and then, after all that, and the presentations and so forth, someone mentioned cockles and whores and it all seemed to go off for no reason.'

'Cockles? Whores?' Glover queried. 'What do you mean, "go off"? Explain yourself, man.' He was quickly losing patience with this young officer.

'Yes, cockles sir, and I believe whores, sir. I have no idea what happened next, honestly I don't, but within seconds it seemed like there were bodies all over the place.'

'Anyone hurt?' asked Glover.

'Not so you'd notice,' was Hill's response.

'What about GGR?' Glover shot back. 'Was he involved at all?'

Hill looked thoughtful. 'Well, he did go down at one point – he was beside the bar at the time, I recall, and just, well, disappeared. He, literally, went down. Then I saw someone picking him up and sort of dusting him off. But it was difficult to tell exactly what was going on. The whole thing only lasted a few minutes, sir, and then it was all over and done with. Brought a bit of an abrupt end to the evening's events, too. Which was a shame really. Though it being a Sunday, a lot of us – especially the rugby club people – had work the next morning, so I suppose there was that, too.'

'So I'm assuming it was you who stepped in to restore the peace?' asked Glover pointedly.

'Well...' DS Hill scratched his forehead in place of an answer.

'You're a police officer, Hill – you're bound to uphold the law and maintain the peace. So what did you do?' Glover stood and leaned over his desk toward the young man.

Hill looked apprehensive. When he finally replied, he did so in a voice that suggested he wasn't sure what to say.

'Like I said, sir, it seemed to me that initially it was all pretty much par for the course, as far as the chatter and name calling was concerned, then one of our lot mentioned cockles, someone took the bait – and before I really knew what was happening, one of the front-row players from the rugby club, huge bloke, sir, and I mean really huge, was sort of over the table and at someone else's throat.'

'And?' pressed Glover.

Hill nodded. 'And . . . there was pushing and shoving, and chairs being punted around the place. A couple of tables went over, so there was glass and beer everywhere, then some of the older ones started pulling people apart, and it all seemed to calm down. I mean, within just a few minutes, it had started from nothing, blown up and calmed down. Mind you, like I said, it was then that most people decided it was time to make their way home. I didn't really have time to get involved, sir, and once it stopped, it wasn't going to erupt again because people were leaving.'

'And all this was because someone mentioned cockles and whores, eh?'

'Well, it seemed so, sir, or could it have been "cockle wars"?'

That made more sense to Glover; the Cockle Wars went back to the 1980s, just after GGR had retired, he recalled. At the time, the women who hand-gathered the tiny little shellfish – a local delicacy – from the sands of the Burry Estuary used donkeys and carts; nowadays men drove Land Rovers to do the job. There'd been a few particularly bad years back then; cockle harvests were down, and the families with the licenses to gather them began in-fighting – which was a horribly complicated business, because most of them were related, somehow.

Often, one family member was set against another, sometimes severing marriages, or pitting children against their parents. There'd been a spate of nasty pub fights in the Penclawdd area right throughout one summer, Glover remembered, and the problems had simmered on for years. But he'd thought it had all finally been settled in the mid-nineties, when a co-operative had been formed between all the license-holders, and they'd invested in a jointly-owned modern processing facility for the lucrative, and by now, internationally famous cockle crop.

If the Cockle Wars were still causing fist fights, might they have had something to do with GGR's death? Glover had some vague recollection that GGR's wife had at one time sold cockles on her stall at Swansea Market. Could she be connected to the Penclawdd cockle business somehow? You were only allowed to sell what you gathered, he knew that much. At least, that's how it had been once upon a time. He'd get Stanley to check into the minutiae of the Swansea cockles business – it would be a learning opportunity for her that might produce a valuable lead.

He looked at the young man in front of him; there was no comparison between him and Stanley, he thought. He'd trade five Hills for one Stanley any day. 'Right-o – get out of here and get this all down on paper, Hill,' he barked, annoyed at the man's lack of insight and action, 'and fill in every detail – names, times, actions, who said what, who did what, and so on. Everything you can remember. And get it onto Stanley's desk before you even think about leaving the station.'

'I won't be much good with names, sir,' replied Hill sheepishly. 'I don't know a lot of the people who were there . . .' He looked terrified, then he brightened. 'But I know who would, sir; Kevin Waters, the Brynfield Club's general manager, he'd have lists of names and everything. I've got his phone number in my office.'

Glover looked up at Stanley. Stanley nodded. 'I have Mr Waters' number here, sir,' she replied efficiently; Glover reckoned even she was getting fed up with Hill. 'Shall I bring the car around, sir?' she asked, almost reading Glover's mind.

'Give me five, and I'll meet you in the courtyard,' replied Glover to Stanley, then he looked disdainfully at Hill and barked, 'And what are you waiting for?'

It was finally clear to Hill that he was dismissed.

Glover grabbed his peppermints, jacket and keys, and walked with Stanley toward the stairs. 'I just want to say hello to the team, though I expect they'll still be getting themselves sorted out, then I'll be with you. Phone the Brynfield Club and tell them we're on our way; I need to see this Waters bloke and anyone else who can help. I'll want names of attendees, and so forth – you know the drill. I also want to see that bar where GGR "disappeared from sight".'

Soon he'd escape from HQ, and any chance of being accosted by the media, and would be on the road to the Brynfield Golf and Rugby Club, which Glover expected to be populated by annoying little men with huge egos, wearing plaid trousers and unbecoming sweaters.

As they made their way through the Swansea's early-morning traffic, Glover asked Stanley to bring him up to date with her investigations. Stanley obliged as she drove steadily toward their destination.

Mrs Gwladys Davies had spent a fitful night, according to the officer who'd stayed with her; having been attended to by her doctor in the evening, she was now still heavily sedated. It was unlikely she'd be fit for more questions before noon, the doctor had estimated. Upon Stanley's second set of enquiries, the family liaison officer assigned to GGR Davies's widow had confirmed the presence of a set of golf clubs at the Davies house. She had told Stanley it was clear GGR had been a keen amateur player, and it appeared he belonged to several golf clubs in the Gower, Swansea, and Swansea Valley areas – something the liaison officer had deduced from a pile of membership cards and parking passes she'd found heaped on GGR's desk. Stanley passed this information on to Glover.

'I expect that simply being The Great One was enough to get him through the doors of most places, without a membership card,' was Glover's observation, but he noted – and complimented – the liaison officer's endeavors in any case.

The enterprising officer had also discovered, upon being encouraged to 'check' rather than 'search' the house by Stanley, that, other than the usual array of home medicines, GGR had no unusual phials of any sort, anywhere. She had, however, spotted a small, padlocked fridge in the cellar. She thought this strange.

So did Glover. He wanted that fridge opened – if GGR had any steroids in his house they'd need to be kept cool at least; a locked refrigerator sounded ideal. He asked Stanley to arrange for the appropriate paperwork. Stanley replied it was already in hand, and that DC Hughes was following that up at the office.

Glover further gleaned from Stanley that, so far, the team hadn't been able to discover whether GGR had any enemies, though they could say with some confidence that he seemed to have no financial problems. That being said, when Stanley told Glover the Davies's bank balance, he was shocked, especially when he considered how well-rewarded the young international rugby players were in an age of endorsements and sponsorships. He and Stanley chatted about how GGR would, no doubt, have been a multi-millionaire if he'd been playing in the twenty-first century, as they sat in the traffic jam that was the Mumbles Road.

It seemed that most of the Davies's income came from the small-holding, though Stanley and Glover agreed GGR probably had quite a good source of undeclared income – the Brynfield tournament being one example of how local organizations would probably hire him to exploit his fame, and reputation. Stanley had managed to discover from DS Hill that GGR had been paid five hundred pounds by the club to be their 'guest of honor', a fee that was the norm for one of his appearances, it seemed.

It was clear to Glover that if GGR could manage just one such payment a week, he would have a nice little income that he and Stanley suspected the taxman wouldn't know about; many organizations would be happy to cover his payment under some sort of 'miscellaneous' heading in their event's expenses.

Even so, it was clear that GGR and his wife weren't living the high life; he'd stayed on at his job with the Fire Dragon Brewery until his sixty-fifth birthday, where he'd earned a fair salary for what didn't sound like an onerous job. Indeed, Stanley told Glover she'd got the impression from GGR's boss at the brewery that he hadn't been so much a 'salesman' proper, but, rather, more of a 'relationship builder' – popping in to visit valued customers on a regular basis, and – likely as not – hanging around for a couple of pints of Fire Dragon Dark, his favorite tipple, so that the pub, restaurant, or club in question could boast to its clientele that GGR was a 'regular'.

It saddened Glover that this pattern of behavior fitted with GGR's wife's assertion that her husband was known to drink and drive.

On that specific topic Stanley was brimming with information.

GGR had no police record – not for drinking and driving, nor even a parking ticket. However, Glover had been pleased, but not surprised to gather, that Stanley had chosen to dig deeper than the official record. She'd carried out her own informal investigation across several local police stations throughout the Gower, Swansea City itself, and up into the Swansea Valley, and had discovered that GGR was pretty well known to a lot of the local uniforms. Stanley recounted how GGR had spent more than a few afternoons, evenings and even nights at several local stations, having been stopped for erratic driving.

'What were we to do?' Was the usual comment or question from the policemen Stanley had spoken to. 'It was GGR, after all. We weren't going to do him for drinking and driving.' It seemed either the officers in question couldn't bring themselves to do it, or else they'd never have been forgiven for it by their brother, father, uncle, or even mother, if they had.

They claimed GGR was usually pretty much in control of his faculties, apparently, and none of them had even bothered to breathalyze him. Gwladys tended to collect him after a few hours, and, when he came back to the area the next day to collect his car, he'd sign autographs and pose for photographs and so forth.

Glover saw a pattern emerging, but didn't want to believe it; it looked as though GGR's job led him to drink, and that the West Glamorgan Police Service couldn't overcome its admiration of the man to the point where they'd take him off the roads for good.

Glover wondered what he'd have done if he'd seen his idol endangering others by driving what was, after all, a lethal weapon when he'd been drinking. He hoped he'd have done the right thing, but had to admit to himself that he wasn't one hundred percent sure. Maybe even he would have given The Great One just one more chance? And what then? Another? And another?

Stanley called Glover from his unhappy thoughts as she announced, 'Almost there, sir,' and added, 'any particular way you want to play this?'

Glover replied sullenly, 'Follow my lead, as per, Stanley.' He stepped from the car almost before it had stopped moving.

It was a beautiful morning – the sun was shining, the air was clear, and the clouds were bubbling on the horizon as Glover looked out across the sparkling sea.

The Brynfield Golf and Rugby Club was one of the most prestigious in Swansea, and made no bones about being one of the most picturesque in all of South Wales; it sat atop a hill that rolled down to the seashore. The rugby pitch was on level ground at the club's highest elevation and was surrounded on three sides by small stands, the fourth side being open to the sea.

The golf course was largely 'below' the rugby field – an undulating links course where the weather, and wind, coming in from the sea meant conditions could change from minute to minute, let alone from day to day.

Below the course was the stunning Brynfield Beach itself, from which the club took its name. The promenade was almost an anachronism, sporting, as it did, a row of dozens of identical wood-built Victorian beach huts, each with its own brightly-painted front door, and an appealingly raked and elaborately decorated roof.

Each was the rental property of a fortunate and much-envied family; whenever someone new moved to the area they did their best to get their hands on one of the huts, but were always beaten back by the archaic rental agreements with the local authority, and the ever-lengthening waiting list.

There were local jokes aplenty about who you'd have to kill to get your hands on a Brynfield Beach Hut. To Glover's knowledge, no one had tried the murder route.

Turning his attention from the sea and the shore, Glover was struck by two features of the clubhouse complex itself – the three smugly-gleaming Jaguars parked in the car park, and the ugliness of the modern redbrick-built extension that had been stuck onto what had once been a pleasantly proportioned, and delightfully symmetrical, Edwardian yellow-stone original building.

Glover wondered how on earth they'd ever managed to get planning permission for the eyesore, then reminded himself there were probably more than a couple of club members on the local authority planning committee, and maybe they'd been able to influence their peers . . . or something along those lines. Exactly the sort of 'golden inner-circle' stuff that annoyed him.

Glover was not only a man who had little time for politicians, he was also a man who cared not at all for institutions he judged to be rife with either politics or social climbing. Golf clubs came squarely under both headings in his mind.

True, he'd belonged to a few rugby clubs in his time, but only when he was actually playing; he hadn't hung onto them as the center of his social life once his knees had given out and his playing days were over – he saw them as organizationally necessary to allow a team game to take place, and often a good facility for team members and their friends to socialize beyond the boundaries of the game itself. But as for the 'golf club' and the 'rugby club' network – the committees, the titles, the vice-this and the immediately past-that – he couldn't bear it.

Glover told himself to put his negative opinions to one side as he strode toward the main entrance of the clubhouse, but, for all his good intentions, it only took a matter of moments before he was quite happily considering throttling a short, balding man, who accosted him and demanded to see his membership card while he was still in the car park.

Glover held up his police ID with great satisfaction, and formally introduced himself and Stanley. The pompous little man then insisted he would personally accompany Glover to meet the golf club captain and the club's general manager. They located the two men in the bar-restaurant, nursing coffee mugs as they examined a large selection of photographs spread on the table before them.

'Good morning, gentlemen.' Glover moved past the small, scampering man and showed his credentials once again. 'I am Detective Inspector Glover and this is Detective Sergeant Stanley. Following our enquiries surrounding the death of GGR Davies, we have discovered he spent the majority of Sunday here, at the Brynfield Club. We have some routine questions we'd like to ask. I take it all three of you gentlemen were here for the tournament?'

Although clearly taken aback by Glover's appearance, it was the Brynfield Golf Club captain who pulled himself together first, and spoke with an over-jovial tone, which perfectly matched his over-jovial attire. Personally, Glover couldn't imagine how a man in his sixties, and measuring somewhere in the fifty-inch range around his middle, could possibly think that a canary-yellow, V-necked sweater would be becoming under any circumstances, except if the clothing were designed to serve as a safety garment, allowing the wearer to be spotted at a great distance, presumably when in peril. Glover was saddened that people so often managed to live down to his expectations.

'Ah, Detective Inspector – yes, what a tragedy,' the club captain cooed unctuously. 'The Great One, indeed, graced us with his presence on Sunday. I believe I am correct in saying it was his last public appearance. Indeed, the local television people have already been in touch with me about any photographs of him we might be able to make available to them, something our wonderful general manager is helping me to discern at this very moment.'

Glover controlled the gag reaction pricking at the back of his throat. *More likely you couldn't get onto the phone quick enough when you heard the news*, was running through his mind, as he eyed up all three of the men now clustered around the circular table.

'And you are?' was what he said aloud to the obsequious man in yellow.

'This is our golf club captain, Mark Edwards,' piped up the annoying little man who'd 'greeted' Glover at the front entrance, as though the man in yellow couldn't possibly be expected to account for himself – it would clearly be too much trouble.

'And you?' barked Glover at the little man.

'Why, I'm the assistant captain, Frank Cuthbert.' He seemed taken aback that Glover wouldn't know. 'And this,' he continued, clearly intending to do a complete job, 'is our general manager, Kevin Waters.'

Stanley wrote down the names while Glover labelled the men in his mind; the Canary Captain, the Argyle Assistant, and – for the man named Waters who sported a network of mottled veins on his enlarged nose – Very Little Water.

With the Canary Captain leading, supported by the Argyle Assistant, and with Very Little Water nodding in silent agreement, Glover asked questions which allowed him to piece together what GGR had done for most of the day in question.

It appeared he'd arrived at about ten a.m., had eaten a hearty cooked breakfast in the restaurant, then had played a 'courtesy round' of golf behind the tournament competitors; GGR had paired with the captain of the rugby team, and the Canary Captain had been joined by the club's resident medic, Dr Bill Griffiths to complete the foursome. They'd been last in from the course for lunch, by which time some people were beginning to drift out to get good seats for the rugby match. GGR had partaken of a bar meal, then had a few drinks while chatting to various members, and had, the threesome believed, finally taken himself off to watch the game, though none of them had actually seen him there.

None of the trio could recall seeing GGR again until the pre-dinner drinks at six p.m. After mingling at the bar, GGR had provided entertaining company at the top table. The Great One had delivered a well-received after-dinner speech, presented the awards and, finally, the much prized Howells' Cup. He'd then enjoyed a few more drinks before being taken home in a taxi around midnight. It seemed that GGR had been thoroughly entertaining, and the life and soul of the party. The word 'tragedy' was repeated until it almost lost all meaning for Glover, and he was glad when the Canary Captain finally shut up.

No mention was made of the after-dinner fracas Glover had been told about. He wasn't surprised; in fact, he rather looked forward to winkling the information out of the men.

'So, you had a pretty unremarkable tournament, gentlemen?' was Glover's sardonic question, at which all three heads nodded rapidly – and a little too violently.

'Everything pretty much as you'd expected?' Again there was nodding. Glover pounced. 'So, just a bit of polite banter over the rubber chicken, and no fisticuffs at all, eh?'

All three men seemed suddenly very interested in their shoes, and Glover knew he had them. He suspected the Argyle Assistant would break the silence first; he did, and gushingly at that.

'Oh, Detective Inspector, it was dreadful – honestly, we had no idea it would end up the way it did. We've had a few harsh words over the years, and even a bit of pushing and shoving, but this year – oh my word, it was quite frightening.'

'So there was a fight?' asked Glover, almost innocently.

The Canary Captain glared at his Argyle Assistant, but recovered quickly and tried to take control of the interview, employing his most obsequious tones.

'You have to understand, Inspector, that our members abide by the normal rules of public, and of course golfing, etiquette when they are on the premises. Unfortunately, some of the rugby club members are clearly used to a different set of guiding principles – and things rather got out of hand. Luckily, some of our more responsible members were able to restore peace.' The man had no idea that blaming the fight on the rugby members was likely to rub Glover up the wrong way.

Glover waged a brief internal war with himself – and the publicly acceptable persona won. 'I'm sure it was all surprising and unexpected, gentlemen, and I also understand – from one of our off-duty officers who was present – the situation was quickly contained. Now, while I ask my sergeant here to take a look through those photographs you were studying, and ask you to make sure she gets a complete record of all those who were here on Sunday, I'm going to take a look around, if you don't mind.'

It wasn't a question, and everyone in the room knew it.

'I could show you around, if you like,' offered the previously un-forthcoming Very Little Water. Glover judged the man was keen to leave the others, and wondered if he had information to share he couldn't speak about in the presence of two people who probably oversaw the payment of his salary.

'Thanks,' replied Glover, 'that would be most kind of you.'

Before they left, they were joined by a small man with thinning fair hair, wearing a worried expression. He walked quickly toward the group; Glover noted the man was smiling, but that his mouth twitched nervously.

'Ah, a new member for us? And his good lady-wife?' was the man's initial question. Glover felt himself cringe.

Waters looked at Glover and smiled almost wickedly, then returned his gaze to the worried looking man. 'A potential member? No, Bill. This is Detective Inspector Glover, and this is Detective Sergeant Stanley. They're looking into GGR's whereabouts on Sunday. This is Dr Bill Griffiths, Inspector, our resident sports injury specialist. Both he and I live here, at the club, don't we, Bill? We are "residents" in the true sense of the word.'

'Ah, yes, GGR. Terrible news. Heard it on the radio this morning,' said the little man in a quiet voice. 'Such a strapping chap. And such a hero. A terrible tragedy, indeed.'

Glover got the impression he was simply saying what everyone would expect; there didn't appear to be any real emotion in the man's voice at all.

'I understand from Mr Waters here that you played golf with GGR on Sunday, Dr Griffiths. Is that correct?' Glover always thought it best to check 'facts'; they often turned out to be nothing of the kind.

'Please, call me Bill, everyone does,' responded the nervous man in his quiet voice. 'GGR arrived early – we weren't expecting him until lunchtime, but he was here by ten, and we chatted over breakfast, you know the sort of thing. I hadn't actually met the man before, so it was a great opportunity for me. Luckily I wasn't called upon to perform any medical examinations on Sunday, which meant I was able to agree to make up a four with The Great One himself. I was honored to play with him.'

Glover found the doctor's manner odd; the words were all right, but his delivery was . . . stilted. He couldn't help but think of a poorly-acted amateur dramatic production.

As Glover strained to catch every almost-whispered word, the physician continued, 'They can always reach me from the clubhouse on my mobile phone if there's a problem, but there wasn't, so we enjoyed a good few hours; just him and me, and the two club captains, of course. It was lovely weather; clear, a little light breeze off the sea, but nothing too chilly. The course is almost like a nature trail – so much to see as you play.'

Put like that, golf sounded almost civilized, thought Glover. 'What sort of things did you and GGR talk about?' he asked.

'Well, to be perfectly honest nothing in particular, that I can remember.'

The Canary Captain butted in. 'I overheard you two talking about people you had in common in Clydach.'

'Possibly. Yes, I think you might be right,' responded the doctor. 'And I recall now that we talked about beer too; I used to live not far from the Fire Dragon Brewery in Clydach, you see. We discussed the smell of yeast and malt on the morning air, and how it can affect your entire digestive system. Of course, GGR was the most famous man at the brewery and he often attended local functions, so we both knew some of the same people.'

'And did you spend time with GGR after you'd finished the golf?' asked Stanley.

'Let me think . . .' was Bill Griffiths' response, and he did, while everyone waited. After about thirty seconds of silence he said, 'I saw him around and about throughout the lunch period, but then I was on the sidelines by two p.m., which is where they need me for rugby matches, for obvious reasons. After that, I wasn't involved in the drinks or dinner at all; being an employee of the club I was merely required to come out after dinner so that I could be thanked by the club captains. I hung around at the back of the function area until they called my name; I got a round of applause, then I went back to my office. I'm not one much for speeches myself. I saw GGR at the head table at that time, but that was it.'

'Well, thank you, Dr Griffiths. Just one more thing – were you here all day Monday?' asked Glover.

'I was working from two p.m. until nine p.m., then had an early night. Before that it was my morning off; I drove into Swansea for a few bits and pieces, and was back here by eleven. I played a few holes before I had lunch, then took my first appointment,' replied Griffiths almost cheerily. 'It was another lovely day.'

'As you say,' said Glover. He was pretty sure he'd got all he was likely to out of the man. 'Mr Waters was just about to show me around, so, if you'll excuse me, I'll let DS Stanley here take a note of times and places of where you all were on Monday, and I'll be back shortly.'

Glover was still hoping Waters wanted to have a private word with him, so he allowed the man to lead him toward the new extension of the building, away from the little group and the costumed golfers who seemed to be wandering about all over the place.

Once they were out of earshot of anyone else, Glover took his chance. 'Am I right in thinking there's something you'd like to tell me, privately, Mr Waters?' Glover thought it best to be direct.

Waters looked around and said quietly, 'It's Kevin, and yes, I do. Let's go outside – I'll feel more comfortable there.'

The men pushed open the double-doors and stepped out into the bright, and surprisingly warm, sunshine. They walked away from the clubhouse. Waters led Glover to a path leading down toward the beach below them, skirting the golf course. The man was obviously considering how to say what he wanted to say.

He looked around before he spoke, and dropped his voice. 'I admired GGR a great deal, Inspector, and I want you to remember that when I say what I do. I also don't like to speak ill of the dead, but I have grappled with all this since Sunday, and feel I should tell you. You see, my whole life I've been involved in rugby; I've watched it, I've played it, I've loved it – I was even the steward at two rugby clubs before I took this job here. And GGR was the greatest, bar none. But the truth is ... well, I saw some things I didn't like at all on Sunday. And I think you should know about them. But ... well, frankly I don't want you to think badly of me, Inspector. I'm not a nosey man, and I don't want you to think I was snooping. It's just that I sometimes see things other people don't. These functions? They all have a drink or two, and I don't touch the stuff. I had a few problems a few years back, so I don't drink at all now.'

That explains the nose, thought Glover. 'I won't think badly of you, Kevin. Just tell me what you saw; you'll be glad you got it off your chest.' Glover was used to this – someone seeing something they shouldn't have seen, or wishing they hadn't seen, then not wanting to reveal it because of what it might suggest about their character. He was just glad this man was coming forward so quickly; often people held information back for quite a while, and that could really hinder an investigation.

'Well, the truth is that I've seen my fair share of GGR having one too many over the years, in various establishments, Inspector, and he was a pretty miserable drunk. Indeed, I think he was getting worse. He didn't come here often – maybe once a month or so – and, of course, he's always been the Fire Dragon rep for the club, so he was usually here on "business". But how downing five pints, then insisting upon driving away from here can be called "business", I don't know. I don't like that sort of thing; even when I was drinking I'd never have driven after a pint or two myself. If he'd been a member I'd have taken his keys off him and put him into a taxi; but he was GGR, you see, so they wouldn't let me say a dicky bird to him.'

It was a pattern that was beginning to annoy Glover.

'Anyway, recently, his temper seemed to get shorter with each pint he drank. On Sunday night, long before I knew he was dead, I'd been thinking about how many pints he'd tucked away through the day. I reckon he must have had about fifteen – and that's just what I saw.'

Glover nodded sadly. 'Well, I'm glad he went home in a taxi that night, at least,' was his sighing response.

Waters nodded. 'Mind you, even then I had to dress it up like it was a treat for him because he was the guest of honor; it was the only way he'd let me get away with it. But that's not the main problem.'

Waters hesitated and looked around again. He continued in a low voice. 'I'd noticed how much GGR was drinking, and I'd also noticed that he got fired up pretty quickly when the argy-bargy went off . . . he was in there swinging as quick as he could be, and someone decked him pretty quick too – and though I don't know who did it, or why, I do have my suspicions. You see . . . oh dear, it's all a terrible mess . . . How do I begin?' He paused for a moment, then said, 'I knew we were going to be busy here on Sunday, so I asked the daughter of one of the golfers to come in to give us a hand with serving the food during lunch, and for the dinner. She's only sixteen, a sweet girl. Anyway, she came to find me at about four o'clock in tears, saying that GGR had touched her. Inappropriately.'

Glover's heart sank.

Waters added, 'I couldn't believe it, but she said she'd gone to one of our locker rooms with him so he could sign a rugby club shirt for her grandmother, and he'd put his arms around her and tried to kiss her. Very upset she was. So I told her to go home. You see, I think it was her father who hit GGR in the bar after dinner when all that bother happened later on. I have to admit I couldn't really see who did it, but I do know that Dave – that's the girl's father – was standing right beside GGR over at the bar when the fight broke out, and that they'd been having words.'

Glover took the information on board; he didn't like this picture of GGR – not one bit. It also opened up another avenue of enquiry; the girl's father might have been angry enough to have another go at GGR – maybe on a clifftop, with a golf club – the next day.

'Thank you. I'll need the father's name, and the family's address if you have it, please.'

Waters nodded.

'Anything else?' asked Glover.

'Well, yes, there was . . .' Waters hesitated; Glover wondered how much worse it could get. 'You know I said GGR was drinking a lot?' Glover nodded. 'Well, he was also going to the toilet a lot.' Waters half-smiled. 'Now I realize that the two are usually inextricably linked, but what struck me as odd was how long he was gone every time. I began to wonder if there was something wrong with the man, so I thought I'd better check up and see. So I followed him in . . .'

Glover could tell that Kevin Waters was struggling with his embarrassment. Finally the man said, 'When I got in there, well, he wasn't at a urinal, he'd gone into a stall, which is fair enough, you know . . . but one of the rugby lads was in the stall next to him, and I saw GGR pass him something under the stall partition.'

Glover could imagine the scene; Waters following GGR into the toilets, not seeing him at a urinal, bending down to check if he was in a stall and, if so, which one. But Glover thought it unlikely that Waters would admit as much.

'Did you happen to see what it was that was being passed?' asked Glover – hoping for something that might be useful.

'I'm pretty sure I do know what it was, and that's the problem. A few years back I was steward at the Glan-y-Mor club, and there was a big hoo-ha about a couple of the players who were on steroids; they'd been storing them in their lockers at the club, so I saw a lot of the stuff then. And I'm pretty sure that's what GGR was passing to the bloke in the next stall – three glass bottles. Steroids. As I said, I don't like to speak ill of the dead – but it's what I saw, and I thought you should know. I'm sure it's got nothing to do with him dying, but . . . well . . . what do you think?'

Glover knew exactly what he thought; it sounded like his hero hadn't just been injecting the stuff into himself, but that he was supplying it too. Glover could have cried. A doper, a drunk, a groper, and now a dealer. What else would he find out about his beloved GGR before the day was over? He felt sick. He steeled himself.

'Thanks, Mr Waters. Kevin. I appreciate your openness. Do you know who it was he was passing the drugs to?'

'Yes, one of our front row; funnily enough, the one who seemed to kick off the fight that night. I've been thinking "Roid Rage" ever since I saw it. And I've been having a think about a few other things too.'

Glover held up his hand to warn Waters that they were being approached by some golfers. Waters nodded and bowed his head, kicking at the sandy soil with his toe. He looked as deflated as Glover felt. Both men were seeing their hero in a different light; Glover was beginning to think that, quite soon, the rest of the world might see him that way too.

When the golfers had passed, Glover again drew close to Waters and said, 'Yes, Kevin – you said you'd been thinking about some other things?' He dreaded what the man might say next.

'Yes. You know how GGR would come here on behalf of the Fire Dragon Brewery?' Glover nodded. 'Well, he used to come to Glan-y-Mor when I was there, and my other club too. And I know he goes to loads of rugby clubs all around the area. And I began to worry that maybe . . . well, you know . . .' Waters started to bob his head about like a character in a Monty Python sketch. 'You know. . .' he said again, twitching.

'Spit it out, man,' was Glover's exasperated response.

'What if he was supplying other players with the same stuff, as he went around all the clubs for the brewery?' The thought hung in the warm air, and it made Glover feel sick.

Dear God, why hadn't he thought of it? Anyone else, and he'd have been right onto that. He could have kicked himself. He was annoyed he wasn't seeing this case as clearly as he should.

Could GGR really have been using his brewery job to cover him taking supplies of anabolic steroids to dozens of rugby clubs in the area? Maybe for many years? Glover kept himself in check, and hoped none of his thoughts had shown on his face.

'It's something we'll look into, of course, Kevin – but I wouldn't trouble yourself about it for now,' was about all he could muster. Luckily the sound of his mobile phone rescued him from having to say anything else. He checked the number – it was the super. For once, he wanted to take the call.

'I really should take this, it's my boss – is there anything else?'

'That's enough, isn't it?' asked Kevin Waters with feeling.

'It's enough if it's all there is,' replied Glover carefully.

'That's all, Inspector,' was the man's reply and he waved as he took his leave of Glover.

'Sir?' was Glover's somewhat terse reply to the superintendent's call.

'How's it going there, Glover? Come up with anything yet?'

Glover considered his reply. 'There are some interesting lines opening up for enquiry, sir, and I'll be getting the team to pursue some possible leads just as soon as I can phone them, sir.' He hoped the super would take the hint. He didn't.

'Anything you feel you can talk about right now?' The man was obviously desperate to know what was going on.

'All due respect sir, I don't think I should go into any details until I'm sure of my facts. But, as I said, we do have some areas that need some pretty detailed enquiries made. So if I might, I'll hang up now, so I can speak to my team . . .'

Lewis seemed taken aback and acceded, which was what Glover had counted on. He walked back to the clubhouse as fast as he could, pushed open the swing doors and called for Stanley. Heads turned as his voice rang out in the relative quiet of the club, and within moments Stanley appeared at the front entrance. She had a thumb drive and a large envelope in her hands.

'I've told them they can't release any photos until we say so, sir. I've got all the names and addresses you were after, and I've got this.' She held up the thumb drive with pride.

'And that is?' asked Glover, curious.

'They recorded GGR's speeches and presentations. This is the recording. I thought it might be useful.'

'Good job, Stanley.' Glover was pleased. 'Bring it with you – we're going back to the team, I'll fill you in as we go.'

'Get anything, sir?' was Stanley's enquiry as they made their way back to the car, and Glover gave her the bare facts.

Stanley's face was a picture. 'That's quite a lot of options, sir. Possibly an angry father, maybe some very angry drug users, and the general chance of someone he might have annoyed when he was several sheets to the wind.'

'Very politely put, Stanley,' replied Glover as they pulled out of the car park. 'You drive – I'm on the phone,' he added redundantly, as Stanley was already behind the wheel and Glover was already dialing.

Glover had phoned in his requirements to the team back at HQ and had been informed that a thick sea mist on the Monday morning had completely obscured the entire Three Cliffs area, so no one would have been able to see anything useful until about eleven a.m., even if they'd been staring through a pair of binoculars right at the spot where GGR was attacked.

This fact also raised the possibility that GGR might not have seen his assailant until whomever it was had been very close to him.

A call to Souza told Glover the test results were back; Souza confirmed the man's use of anabolic steroids, that at the time of death he'd had a blood alcohol level above the legal driving limit, that his stomach contents showed whiskey, bacon, eggs and banana, but there was nothing else out of the ordinary – if those results could be called ordinary.

By the time Glover got off the phone they were five minutes away from HQ.

'What should I know about what you found out, Stanley – anything?'

Stanley answered succinctly, 'There are about forty Brynfield Club members who are left-handed, and only about half a dozen of them have the golf club in question; the golf pro was pretty helpful with that, sir – he knows the players and their clubs. I have their details. Oddly enough, the captain, assistant captain, Waters and the doctor are all lefties, as was GGR. Only the captain and GGR owned a Massive Martha III club, sir.'

'Good to know,' was all Glover managed before they peeled into the courtyard at the back of HQ, and he leaped from the vehicle, leaving Stanley to park the car.

Facing his team in the squad room, moments later, Glover had their undivided attention. 'Right – waggle a limb as I call out, and give us an update,' he shouted. 'Door to door?' A hand shot up at the back of the room.

'DS West, sir. Just one thing of note, sir. The couple who found the little dog and called it in to the RSPCA – they're on holiday from the north of England and confirmed they first saw the dog, abandoned and running with its lead attached to the shooting stick, at about ten thirty a.m. They'd gone for a walk, hoping the mists would clear, which didn't happen until about eleven a.m., and they encountered the dog on the top path, above Three Cliffs. They tried to catch it but it kept slipping away; it then disappeared into the mists on the top of the cliffs. Not knowing the area they didn't follow, but called the RSPCA. Might help with the time he went over, sir?'

'Good point, West, thank you. Anything else?'

'Nothing more, sir – the mist problem. No one saw GGR himself that morning at all, sir.'

'Public tips?' Glover scanned the room.

'Here, sir, DC Bidder, sir – not a thing, sir. Lines have been very quiet – except for the crackpots.'

'Who's on the Cockle Wars, Stanley?'

'Hughes, sir,' she replied.

'Hughes?' barked Glover.

'Yes, sir. Here, sir. I pulled all the files, and there are a lot of them. I discovered GGR's wife was a Davies even before she married him; belonged to one of three families in Penclawdd with the Davies name, each of whom had one of the original cockle-gathering licenses. Gwladys Davies's mother was a gatherer, and Gwladys herself was granted the stall in Swansea Market mainly because of the cockle license. She sold her family's cockles there until the co-operative was formed in the 1990s, but thereafter, what with all the new health and safety requirements for selling foodstuffs, she decided not to move to a stall with chilling equipment. Her family gave their cockles to the co-op and she kept going with just the fruit, veg, and eggs. Her father got into a bit of trouble in the 1970s and 1980s, but mainly pub brawls and public peace issues, all related to the cockles. No mention of GGR in any of the files, sir. Updates in the files suggest that everything's quiet on the cockle front, but that – if ever it does kick off – it always seems to involve two particular families; the Dewi Davies family – which isn't connected to GGR or his wife at all – and the Huw Price family. It seems that the Dewi Davies family lost their license and the Price family got it instead, sir. No love lost there, it seems.'

Glover suspected the cockle war issue might be a dead end, but he'd follow it for a while yet. 'Stanley – what was name of the rugby player who started the fight at the Brynfield Club on Sunday night?'

Stanley looked through his notes. 'It was a Bob Price, front row player for the Brynfield Rugby Club.'

Glover gave it some thought.

'Hughes – liaise with Stanley and try to find out if the Price in the fight is related to the Penclawdd Prices, right? And, whether he is or not, I want him in here this afternoon for questioning.'

Two voices shouted 'Sir!', and Glover continued. 'Steroid abuse? Who's on steroid abuse? Any facts for me?'

'Evans, here, sir. The Welsh Rugby Union has what it calls a "rigorous anti-doping stance". But there are about 98,000 registered WRU players, and they only carried out 304 tests last year. Word on the street is it's rife throughout all club levels – amateur and semi-professional. Dopers are risking that they won't get tested. Nothing in any of the files about GGR being involved at all.'

Glover was horrified by the figures quoted, but couldn't help but be unsurprised by that last fact.

Evans continued, 'I've printed up all the stats for you including a list of names of all players currently suspended, and those whose suspensions have ended. There are two in particular I've highlighted, the two most recently suspended.'

'Thank you, Evans; get hold of those two, and get them in here to see me this afternoon. Right-o, GGR's client list for the brewery – who's on brewery duty?'

'Me, sir – I've got the list: twenty-two rugby clubs, thirty-five pubs, ten restaurants, five golf clubs. Seems he went to each rugby club about once a month, then bi-monthly for the rest.'

'Stanley – movement on the Davies property front?'

'Yes, sir; the fridge in the cellar revealed three hundred phials of anabolic steroids, all on their way in now; the FIT people also confirmed that GGR's own golf clubs are a left-handed set, but there's no Massive Martha III. They've taken the rest of them anyway. The missus is still out of it – family liaison still on the scene. The sister's due to arrive from Cardiff this afternoon, and plans on staying over. No luck finding any hidden bank accounts etcetera so far, sir.'

'Thank you for all your work, people – now back to it; I know I've just given you a lot more you can be getting on with.'

Glover turned to leave the room.

'Sir?' It was the DC handling the incoming public calls.

'Yes, Bidder, what is it?'

'I know I said there was nothing much on the tip-line, sir, but there was a call from a Mr Everett of Llangennith – said he needed to speak to you urgently. He said he'd punched GGR on Sunday, and needed to explain it to you. He seemed a bit distressed, sir.'

'And what did you tell this distressed Mr Everett, Bidder?'

'I thought you'd like to see him, sir, so I asked if it would be convenient for him to come in to talk to you. He got here about ten minutes ago. He's in Interview Room One.'

Glover beamed. 'Your quick thinking has just saved me a drive out to Llangennith, and I thank you for it.' Bidder glowed, and stood more erect. Glover was known to be generous in his praise for a job well done.

'Go and tell the man I'll be with him in five, Bidder.' The DC nodded and left. 'Come with me for a second, Stanley.'

The pair left the team room and stood in the corridor. 'Stanley, what do you think of the mood in the room?'

'Grim, sir,' was Stanley's considered opinion.

'I agree, Stanley – I know they all want to find out what's happened, but there's a pall hanging over everyone; it's as though they've all lost a family member. I'm sure they'll work hard, but I need them firing on all cylinders. I tell you what – get a large screen set up in the squad room so we can all watch the recording of GGR's speech from Sunday night together, after I've seen this Everett chap. It'll give me a more appropriate chance to focus them on the nature of our job. So sort that, then meet me downstairs; I want you to come with me to interview Everett – he's the father of the girl Waters told me about. Watch him like a hawk, Stanley. Right? And I need you to be the one pushing his buttons about his daughter's possible promiscuity, right?'

Stanley nodded, unhappily, and muttered, 'Sir,' glumly, then phoned a DC with Glover's instructions about setting up equipment in the team room. A few words sufficed.

Just as they reached the interview room, Glover said, 'Looks as though GGR planned to continue with his supply system, even if he'd retired from the brewery; I don't suppose anyone would bat an eyelid if GGR showed up at their rugby club for a few pints once a month, in fact they'd probably let him have it on the house. And it seems we have more proof of his love of booze in terms of his stomach contents – whiskey that early in the day, and considering he would have been off to collect his car from the golf club if he hadn't died? Not good. The car's being checked too, right?'

'Yes, sir,' was what Dave Everett would have heard the younger police officer say as the older one opened the door.

'Detective Inspector Glover, Detective Sergeant Stanley,' said Glover by way of introduction. 'And you are?'

'Dave Everett, Inspector, thank you for seeing me.' The man was tall, slim and red-headed. Glover wondered if that indicated a temper. It didn't look as though he'd slept much – a naturally pale-skinned man, there were blue marks beneath his watery, grey-green eyes.

'Thank you for coming in, Mr Everett I understand you have something you want to tell me?' Straight to the point. Always the best way.

'I struck GGR Davies a hefty blow on the chin at a golf and rugby tournament at the Brynfield Club on Sunday evening. The man had acted inappropriately toward my daughter and I hit him. He fell to the floor with the force of my blow. I am not apologizing, he deserved it. But I thought you should know.'

Glover suspected the man had been rehearsing that little speech for some time. It sounded theatrical.

'What do you mean by "inappropriately", Mr Everett?' asked Stanley.

Everett looked at Glover in query, and Glover nodded. Everett nodded back and looked at Stanley. He'd been given permission to answer.

'My daughter had never met GGR before – though, of course, she knew all about him. My wife's mother has always been a big GGR fan, so Heather – that's my daughter, she's only sixteen – asked GGR if he would sign a Brynfield rugby club shirt for her grandmother. Heather was going to be paid twenty pounds for helping out with serving the food at the club on Sunday, and the shirt was nineteen pounds and ninety-five pence, so she bought it with the money she'd have been paid. That's the sort of girl she is. Thoughtful. Selfless.'

He looked at Glover pointedly, then continued. 'GGR asked her to bring the rugby shirt to the women's locker room so he could sign it – the men's locker room was inundated with those who'd been playing in the rugby competition. She took the shirt along at the time he'd said. four p.m.' Glover could see the man was shaking. 'When she got there, he said she'd have to pay him with a kiss, so she pecked him on the cheek – but he grabbed her . . . bottom and her –' he swallowed hard – 'he grabbed my little girl's breasts, the bastard. It was an assault, that's what it is. He sexually assaulted my baby girl.' It was clear that Everett was overwhelmed.

'Try to stay calm, Mr Everett,' cooed Glover.

'Do you think your daughter led him on?' asked Stanley.

Everett looked horrified. 'Why would you say that? She's shy. She's not like that. You don't know her!' He was shouting.

There was the temper Glover had been wondering about.

'We often find that parents don't really know their children at all. She might be a very outgoing girl in reality,' added Stanley, using an unpleasant tone.

'I take offence at that.' Everett was on his feet. 'Can't you tell her to stop?' he shouted at Glover.

Was Glover seeing the reaction of a man who'd gone and bashed his daughter's groper over the head with a golf club? Or of a man torn apart by anger that a national hero, essentially untouchable, had stepped across a line any father – any decent man – would draw?

He said, 'No need to get upset, Mr Everett – I'm sure my colleague means that, sometimes, parents think of their children as just that, children; even when they start to grow up and change, parents just don't see it.'

Glover paused, for effect; the effect was that Everett chewed his lip.

Glover pressed on, 'But, sometimes, others see something else; they see a beautiful young woman, where a father still sees a child. Maybe GGR misunderstood her childish enthusiasm for a bit of a come-on. He wasn't a father himself, you see, so he might have misinterpreted.'

Everett resumed his seat, but glared angrily at Glover. 'Don't make excuses for the man. Heather is tiny, I mean she's not . . . well-developed at all, if you know what I mean. She is still a child. Anyone groping her must have had some sort of a problem. She's a kid. Look.'

Everett handed Glover a photograph of what appeared to be a twelve-year-old, in a school uniform. Glover passed it to Stanley. The girl was pretty, in a fresh-faced way; she wore her hair short, in a boyish cut, and had a smile that was still toothy and unaffected.

'When was this taken, sir?' asked Glover, politely.

'Two months ago. That's what I mean – she looks like a kid still, doesn't she?'

'Oh, I don't know – a bit of make-up, lipstick, and her hair played around with, and she could look quite different, I'd have thought,' said Stanley.

'Shut her up,' shouted Everett at Glover. 'Heather never wears make-up. I was there on Sunday – and I know she wasn't wearing any then; and don't go thinking she was dressed like a tart – she was wearing a golf shirt and tracksuit bottoms, like all the bar and serving staff. Not dressed up at all.'

'So what happened exactly, Mr Everett?' asked Glover patiently; they weren't going to get any further with that line of questions.

'You mean, about me hitting him?' replied Everett.

Glover nodded.

'Well, Heather didn't come to me about it at all; she'd gone to Kevin Waters. He's our GM, and the one who asked her to work on Sunday. He sent her home. I was at the rugby match, see, and I hadn't got back to the clubhouse when it happened. I don't suppose she knew where to find me. Fine father I turned out to be.'

Glover had suspected guilt – and there it was at last; the man hadn't been there when his daughter had needed him.

Everett looked deflated as he continued, 'Anyway – I didn't even notice she wasn't around until about halfway through dinner. I hadn't seen her serving, so I asked Kevin about it; he took me to one side and, eventually, told me what she'd said. I couldn't believe it.'

Glover spotted the incredulity in the man's voice; it was to be expected.

He pressed on, speaking more quietly. 'I phoned her at home, right then. She was in tears – she hadn't talked to her mother about it, it seemed, but it all came out when I asked her. And I had no reason to doubt her; she's a good girl, is Heather.'

Glover suspected Everett believed this to be the truth, even if it proved not to be the case. He'd have to meet the girl himself and decide. But that was for later.

'I am assuming you were angry, Mr Everett?' Stanley asked.

Everett glared at her. 'Of course I was bloody angry. Any father would be.' He spoke to Stanley as though she were an idiot.

'So how did it come about that you punched GGR?' asked Glover.

'After phoning home I went up to the bar for a drink – a big one – and GGR was in that part of the room too. He'd finished all his speeches and all that – I'd missed it all when I was on the phone to Heather. Now, I don't know what happened – I wasn't really taking any notice – but all of a sudden a fight broke out; people were taking swings all over the place and . . . well, something just snapped inside my head and I lashed out at GGR. I don't think anyone saw me, and I'm pretty sure not even he knew it was me who hit him. I just whacked him one on the chin, and down he went. It was a sucker punch; cowardly, and not my sort of thing at all. When I'd hit him I felt normal again, and I just walked away. I don't know what happened afterwards. I went to the Gents and washed my face. By the time I went back into the bar area everything was back to normal – people patting each other on the back, and many making for the door with lots of farewells – someone was handing GGR a pint. It was as though none of it had ever happened. But it did. And, now that he's dead, I thought I'd better tell you.' Everett seemed drained.

'So you didn't speak to GGR again that evening?' asked Stanley abrasively.

'I didn't stay long after that, I couldn't face it. I got in a taxi and went home to see Heather. I never saw him after that at all.'

'Where were you on Monday morning, Mr Everett – between eight a.m. and noon?' Stanley's tone was abrupt.

'At work – you can check with my office. So, no, I wasn't pushing GGR off a cliff in the Gower,' was Everett's equally sharp reply.

'If you could give us your work details we could check that quite easily, Mr Everett,' said Glover in his most reasonable voice. 'Maybe you'd like a coffee while we follow up on that? You could tell Stanley here how you like your coffee and she could bring it for you.'

The man looked delighted that the spiteful minion would be relegated to being his fetcher and carrier, which was just what Glover wanted. He instructed Stanley to follow up on the office alibi – which he suspected would hold. Glover thanked the man for coming and told him that, if everything checked out at his office, there'd be no need to bring his daughter in, at that time.

As Stanley attended to Everett's coffee, Glover dragged himself back upstairs and looked at his watch. One o'clock. He was making progress, but it was slow. And his main emotion was of hopelessness – he was utterly dismayed at his findings so far about GGR.

He decided he deserved a break; he'd call Betty, and hear a sane voice just for a few minutes. But not right now – now he wanted to see that recording of GGR's speech, and he needed to do something to rally the troops a bit. He was pretty sure he'd have to face the super soon, too, though he congratulated himself on having managed to avoid him for so long. Glover kicked himself for even thinking of the man, as he heard his superior's voice behind him in the corridor.

Inwardly, Glover rolled his eyes, but to his super's face he said brightly, 'Sir – just the person. I was about to call you in to join the team; we're going to watch a recording of the speeches GGR made at the Brynfield Club on Sunday night, and I thought you'd be interested in seeing it.' Glover was a pretty good liar, all in all, and he knew Lewis wouldn't pick up on the sarcasm in his tone.

Whatever Lewis had been about to say, it was clear the thought of actually seeing GGR's last speech before he died put it quite out of his mind, and the man beamed. 'Thank you, Glover – I think it will be an important event to witness.' His serious tone almost made Glover smile.

By this time the two men had reached the team room, where they were joined by Stanley, who whispered to Glover, 'Everett's alibi checks out – I've sent him home, but asked him to remain available.'

'Good job,' replied Glover. One door had closed then, thought Glover to himself, as he asked everyone to take a seat so they could see the TV monitor that had been set up in the corner of the room. Of course Lewis got the best seat in the house.

Glover stood at the front of the room and told the team what they were about to see – adding that it would be a chance for them to note if anything had been said, or had happened, during the speeches that might have a bearing on what had happened to GGR the following morning.

The mood in the room was one of apprehension; people seemed uneasy at the thought of watching GGR just hours before his death. Glover and Stanley took their positions at the rear, perched beside each other on the edge of a desk.

DC Hughes was in charge of making the screen and the recording work, and, after a few hiccups, a rather dark and somewhat grainy picture appeared. It was clear the microphone was nearer the camera than the top table, so the voices of the main speakers echoed, whereas whispers at the back of the room could be heard more clearly. Still, thought Glover, it was better than nothing. Maybe there'd be something . . .

The golf and rugby captains made a few comments, then there was a vote of thanks for Dr Bill Griffiths, who couldn't be seen in the shot, as well as one for Kevin Waters and all the staff who'd helped make the day a success. Then GGR was introduced, with all the usual references to his stellar career, and a few comments about how he'd been a regular at the Brynfield Club for so many years.

Glover watched with mixed emotions; had he seen this tape before his day had begun he'd have been watching it as an avid fan – a chance to gain an insight into a more intimate side of his boyhood hero. As it was, he was looking at the face of a man he was beginning to hate; a man who'd had it all, but had decided to abuse the trust put in him by young players, at least one young girl and, frankly, the entire community.

The applause on the recording finally subsided, allowing GGR to speak. Glover heard, once again, that familiar voice; gravelly and jovial, warm and comforting. Not slurred at all, which made him wonder about how very often GGR must have drunk large quantities of beer, given that, by all accounts, he'd probably have sunk the best part of two gallons of beer by that point in the proceedings.

Glover felt the mood in the squad room become more intense as GGR began to speak – all ears and eyes were focused on The Great One.

GGR opened with the expected acknowledgements of the club's officers and staff; he expressed surprise that the day had gone so well, given that both golfers and rugby players were involved, which earned him a good laugh, then he began his speech in earnest.

'I've thought long and hard about what to talk to you about tonight, gentlemen, trying to work out what it is that golfers and rugger buggers have in common – and then the answer came to me – of course, it's beer!'

A round of applause and laughter followed.

'About which, given my years with the brewery, I know quite a bit. Indeed, you could say I know beer inside and out.'

He shouted 'Cheers!' and raised his glass to the crowd, then he drank down a full pint in a matter of seconds. The roar in the Brynfield Club showed his audience's appreciation of this feat. In the police team room there was a ripple of chuckles.

GGR continued, 'I suppose I've had a blessed life. The perfect life some might say – playing rugby for Wales and working for a brewery. The only thing missing is being the lead tenor in a male voice choir . . .'

Laughter.

'The sad truth is, I can't carry a tune. But there – the rugby and the beer make up for it, I suppose.'

The man knew his audience, there was no doubt about it. Glover wondered how many of the officers he was looking at suspected just how well GGR really did know beer, from the drinker's perspective; he guessed that, even if they'd known, they wouldn't have cared.

GGR continued, 'So, beer. It is what I think the writers of "Bread of Heaven" had in mind when they wrote that hymn; I know there's been many a time it's been a meal in a glass for me. All that goodness in there gentlemen – hops, barley, water – it's almost a health food. But not all beers are created equal; it takes years and years to invent a good new beer. I'm sure many of you are aware that Fire Dragon Dark has been my tipple of choice for as long as I can remember, but I wonder if you knew that I was involved in the development of a beer that they actually wanted to name after me?'

Clearly no one knew.

'However, I said I could think of a better name than mine – so they called it Fire Dragon Fireworks.'

A ripple of understanding ran through the team room, while on the tape a series of 'Ahs' and 'Ohs' flew about, and a round of applause broke out.

Glover wasn't much of a a frequenter of pubs, except when work required it, but even he knew about Fire Dragon Fireworks; the brewery sold it for only two months each year, and it was powerful stuff.

GGR seemed pleased at the reception he was getting, and carried on with enthusiasm. 'Believe me, gentlemen, there was a lot of tasting that had to be done to get that one right.'

Laughter.

'It took about a year, all in all. Then, to launch it, we had a big party up at the brewery. All top secret it was before that night. Maybe some of you remember it – hiding the packaging, not letting anyone see the end result – then the grand unveiling, in every bar where it was served. At the brewery itself they allowed me to have the first pint pulled . . . and the second, and the third . . . well, it's good stuff, isn't it?'

A cheer went up in the Brynfield Club.

'Just as well they only sell it for two months. Fireworks is right, eh chaps?'

Glover could hear comments close to the microphone about how strong the beer was, and how the hangover the next day was equally powerful.

GGR drank from the fresh pint that had been placed in front of him. 'I'm not too sure about this seasonal beer thing myself, but if you're going to have one at all, it should be a good one. Not too keen on the Christmas ales, me – all messed around with, and too fruity for my liking, but I have to admit I thought a beer to celebrate Guy Fawkes Night was a good idea; all that standing around in chilly fields waiting for the dud Catherine Wheels to turn, you need a good beer to keep you warm. And speaking about Catherine Wheels, the launch party at the brewery had some of those girls there who wander around with free beer, and I bet you can guess where their Catherine Wheels were. No duds there, gentlemen!'

Sniggering close to the microphone.

'Yes, it was a delight to be able to develop a beer that people like as much as they do that one – it'll be here in the bar at the beginning of November – the fifth year for the brewery to put it out, and I hope you all lap it up; I know I will. Oh, but that launch party, boys. I have to say – and, remember, I don't work for them anymore – the Fire Dragon Brewery does a bloody good job with its beers, and its parties. I had to leave before the fireworks display they were having that night – the little woman had plans for the evening, and I didn't want to be late – or there'd have been fireworks of a whole different sort!'

Big laugh for that one, on the tape and in the squad room.

'No, no, seriously gentlemen, I don't want to speak ill of the wife – I'm sure many of you know my Gwladys . . .'

Spontaneous, if polite applause on the tape.

'. . . she's put up with me nearly forty years now . . .'

More applause.

'. . . and she's happy that I've finally retired. I think. But, back to the launch of Fire Dragon Fireworks; like I said, good party, good beer, and strict instructions from the wife to not be late home. So there I am, wending my way through the lovely lanes of Clydach. It's pitch dark out there – I don't think they can afford street lights out that way . . .'

He paused to allow for laughter, and drew some.

'. . . and I have to admit I was putting my foot down a bit, when all of sudden what's in front of me but a bloody big sheep. Huge it was, and on the side of a narrow bit of road. Well, gentlemen, there was no way I was going to miss it.'

There were a few groans.

'Luckily I drive one of those Swedish cars they say are safe because they do a moose test; if the car can cope with hitting a moose, it's safe. Well, in this part of the world I can now confirm we have developed the sheep test, and I can tell you I hardly felt a thing. I was tempted to stop and stuff the sheep in the boot and take it home for a stew, but as it was, I just wound down the window and shouted "mint sauce" at it and got off home.'

There were laughs and calls of 'mint sauce, mint sauce' around the room on the tape.

In the team room the joke didn't seem to go down as well as at the dinner, but there were a few chuckles. On the recording, GGR was enjoying himself as much as his audience was – Glover could tell he was a man who knew it wasn't just what you said to a crowd like that, but how you said it, and GGR was hamming it up a treat.

'Now, now, don't get me wrong,' GGR continued, 'I'm not one for "hunting and gathering" my own food, that's what the wife's for, and who knows, maybe that poor sheep was somebody's darling . . .'

Laughter broke out.

'. . . see, now – there's a chap who knows what his wellies are for,' cracked GGR pointing at someone in the crowd.

Hoots of laughter at that one.

'. . . but when I got home and the wife saw the mess on the front of the car, she laid into me good and proper, so I did get to see the fireworks after all!'

Hoots of laughter and applause followed.

GGR quietened the crowd. 'But enough about beer – I am well aware you'd rather be drinking it than hearing me talking about it, so I'd better get on with these presentations and let you all get to the bar.'

For the next ten minutes GGR read out names, handed out plates and handfuls of cash, and finally the Howells' Cup – which was accepted, to the accompaniment of much cheering, by the golf club captain and the twelve members who'd played in the tournament. GGR thanked everyone again, encouraged them all to visit the bar one last time, and not to forget the arrival of Fire Dragon Fireworks in about five weeks' time, then the recording shut off.

There was, disappointingly, no sign of the fight that had ensued what must have been just a few minutes later.

Everyone in the squad room was quiet. Glover rose and addressed the room.

'Well, there we have it – GGR's last public appearance. Any questions? Observations?'

Before anyone had a chance to comment, Detective Superintendent Michael Lewis rose to his feet and turned to face the room. 'Wonderful man – quite wonderful. Talented, entertaining, and a real supporter of youth rugby. He'll be sorely missed. And it's we who have to find out exactly how he met his demise. He might not have been playing any more, but he was a man in his prime, with a full and busy retirement ahead of him. Whoever caused his death has robbed him of that – so come on, let's have some action. I want results. Glover – my office for an update, now.' And he was gone.

He'd said all the things Glover hadn't wanted him to say; the team had been on a little up-slope, now Lewis had sent them off into a downward spiral again. They needed a pep talk; they knew what their responsibilities were – they didn't need reminding of that. Glover could have happily strangled the man.

'I'll be ten minutes, sir – have to make a couple of really important calls,' called Glover toward the super's back.

'Quick as you can, Glover,' was what he heard in reply, but was halfway to choosing to ignore.

'Stanley, did you get anything from it?'

'Well, sir, I do have a question.'

Glover noted her hesitation. 'And that is?'

'So the Welsh really don't mind the sheep jokes, then?' She seemed genuinely puzzled.

'Well, I wouldn't go around making jokes about it yourself, Stanley – it's the sort of thing we take pretty well from one of our own, but from an Englishwoman? Let an old rugby player get a few cheap laughs with it, but I'd steer clear of the whole thing, if I were you.'

'Good advice, I'm sure, sir.'

Stanley seemed to consider the matter closed, as did Glover, who headed off to his office, and a chance to call Betty. Now, maybe even more than earlier, he wanted to hear the voice of his wife; not 'her indoors', not 'the little woman' nor any of the other phrases which annoyed the hell out of him – but his wife. His love, his comfort, and his anchor. He didn't like it when people made fun of their wives just to get a cheap laugh – something else that rankled about GGR.

'Is that you?' asked Betty as she answered the phone.

'Yes, love, it is. How are you?'

'How are you is more like it?' replied Betty, sounding concerned. 'I just saw the lunchtime news – God, it's a mess, Evan.'

Glover was suddenly aware that he'd managed to not only miss the media people who might have been trying to talk to him, but was also completely unaware of what the public was being fed in terms of what he had no doubt was misinformation. He thought he'd better find out what the rest of the world thought was going on.

'So what's the news then?'

'Well, first of all, I had to go down to town this morning – we're almost out of cabbage and I needed to make you some fresh soup for tonight.'

Glover swallowed hard – how he hated that stuff.

Betty continued, unaware of – or else choosing to ignore – her husband's silence on the matter of the soup. 'So I popped into Swansea Market, and you should see Gwladys Davies's stall; her name is draped in black velvet, and where the fruit and veg should be there are dozens of photographs of GGR, all with their own little funereal attachments, surrounded by flowers and candles, and piles of cards, and little notes. It's like a shrine. They've even set up a book of remembrance for people to sign; the queue was right around the middle of the market. And I tell you what, Evan – the mood all around town was like a funeral itself; we Welsh are good at this sort of thing. Lots of conversations in hushed tones – even the market itself sounded like a church.'

Glover wasn't surprised; Betty had hit the nail on the head – the Welsh had a talent for enjoying misery. He could also imagine all the stories about 'I was there when GGR . . .' did this, or that, being swapped. He wondered if pub landlords would go so far as to drape black swags on the framed GGR rugby shirts on their walls. He suspected many would.

Mind you, with the history the nation had, it was hardly a surprising response; marginalize a people, take all their land off them, try to wipe out their culture and tell them they aren't allowed to speak their own language and see what you get. And that was one of the real reasons why GGR had been such a hero – he'd always managed to stuff the rugby ball right down England's throat. It was a small compensation, but his nation had taken it, and had loved him for it.

Evan's momentary lapse of concentration had clearly been noted by Betty, who had stopped speaking; even on the phone it seemed she could tell when Evan was distracted.

'Sorry,' said Evan quickly, 'I was just thinking about what you'd said – and you're right, we're good at that sort of thing.'

'So it seems,' said Betty. 'And if you believe the news on TV today it seems there's a fight breaking out about where and when his memorial should take place. They interviewed his sister in Cardiff and she was all for the WRU dedicating the next Wales versus England international to his memory at the Principality Stadium; but then there's a group saying there should be a special service at the Cardiff Arms Park, because he never actually played at the new stadium. Swansea's Lord Mayor was on next, saying it should be held at St Helen's – where he played for the All Whites, whereas some people think it should be at the Liberty Stadium, where the Ospreys play. Wherever it ends up being there's going to be a lot of singing – it looks like every male voice choir in existence will be there; they had Bryn Terfel on the telephone from Milan saying he'd drop everything and fly in from wherever he was in the world, and they had Max Boyce on camera saying he'd write something especially for it. They expect the biggest-ever gathering of international players from the 1970s to the present day there, too. Wherever "there" turns out to be. It'll be quite the event.'

'Sounds lovely,' was all Evan could manage. The words felt like dust in his mouth; all that celebration for a man who was . . . well, not what people thought he was in any case.

'But enough about my day – how's it going with you, *cariad*? Need to talk?'

'Oh Betty, love, you have no idea how much I need to talk. Have you got five minutes? I can't let the team see how I'm feeling – but I've got to let it out somehow.'

'Always got five minutes for my husband,' replied Betty, warmly. Evan Glover could imagine her settling into the kitchen chair to listen, so he talked, and talked. Betty was quiet, except for the odd exclamation of disbelief. In just a few minutes she, too, was made aware that the man being lauded by everyone who'd ever worn a daffodil or eaten a leek on St David's Day was not what they had all thought.

'Did you say there was a Dr Bill Griffiths at the Brynfield Club?' she asked when Evan had finished.

'That's right. Know him?'

'Short man, fair hair – worried expression?' she asked.

Glover was always proud of his wife's perspicacity. 'That's right – used to live in Clydach.'

'It sounds like him – very sad. When I was grief counselling for that couple of years I spent a lot of time with him and his wife, Linda. In fact – they were a big part of the reason I gave it up.'

Glover was glad to talk about something other than GGR. 'Why so?' He knew Betty had gone through a tough time during that period of counselling – and that she'd been glad to shift back to her more generalized practice of psychotherapy – but she'd never been very forthcoming about the details. He wondered what it had to do with Dr Griffiths.

She sounded thoughtful as she spoke. 'Their little boy was killed, and they came to me because they wanted some help outside the NHS. Bill was the GP up there in Clydach, and he didn't want to work with anyone he knew. So I got them; they came into Swansea for sessions for about six months. But, obviously, I couldn't help them – or else I didn't help them enough, because she committed suicide, and he had a complete breakdown. Like I said, it was all terribly tragic – and that's why I lost confidence in my suitability for that specific role. In myself, to be honest. When I found out she was dead, I didn't feel I could do it anymore. Not the grief work. Not after that.'

Evan could feel his wife's sadness. 'I'm sorry, love,' he said gently. 'What happened to their son?' He felt he should have remembered, but he was ashamed to admit he didn't.

'It was bad; a hit-and-run in the lane right outside their house. He was only four, and she thought she'd strapped him securely into the child seat in the back of the car, then she'd gone back to make sure their dog was safely inside the house, and to lock the front door. She couldn't find the dog and thought it might have gone out onto the road. As she went to check, she was passed by a car, and then she saw the car hit the dog. The car just kept going. Of course she ran to the poor dog, terribly upset, only to discover that her little boy had also been struck. She couldn't be sure what had happened – but it seemed the dog had run out onto the road, and the little boy, Josh – Joshua Griffiths, that was his name – had somehow got himself out of his seat, and the car, and he ran after the dog.'

Glover was beginning to remember something about it; it hadn't been a case he'd worked on, but there'd been a lot of work-hours thrown into it, he seemed to recall.

Betty continued, 'See, the car had hit them both. The dog was dead, and by the time the ambulance came, so was the little boy. They never got the driver, and she just couldn't come to terms with the guilt. Her husband, Bill, had been at work at the time; he'd rushed home, of course, but he was too late to help his boy. Their sessions with me were always fraught; she couldn't forgive herself, he couldn't forgive himself. He thought that if he could have got there sooner he might have been able to help the boy, you see. She used to go on and on about the driver, how fast the car had been going, how it almost knocked her down too, and how the man – she was sure it was a man, a man in a silver car – was shouting and laughing as he ran into the dog. She always wondered if the man had done it on purpose. She often said that if only he'd hit her he might have missed her boy. She was a mess. I was always pretty sure their marriage wasn't going to survive it in the long run – often that's the case – but I didn't see her overdose coming. Looking back, I suspect the signs were there, but I'd missed them – completely. I suppose his breakdown was the only way his psyche could cope with it all; complete shutdown. So it's good to know that he's back on his feet. I'd never met him before the tragedy, but I suspected he'd have been a nice chap; probably always lived on his nerves, but a nice, steady sort.'

Evan Glover's mind was racing – though his thoughts weren't wandering; he'd heard every word, and it got him thinking.

'Betty, love, what sort of dog did they have?'

'Why on earth do you want to know that?'

'Humor me,' was Evan Glover's gentle answer.

'Oddly, I happen to know it was a white standard poodle, because Linda Griffiths would show it at the Clydach fair every year; won some sort of prize up in London at some point.'

Glover was silent for a moment, then he asked, 'And do you know when the boy was killed?'

'I know exactly when it was; it was November fifth, five years ago this coming November – it was Guy Fawkes Night and they were off to a fireworks display. That's why she wanted the dog inside the house; it would have been frightened by all the fireworks going off that night. I don't know where the display was to be held, though.'

'I think I do,' answered Evan Glover, cryptically. 'Listen, I have to go. I'll phone later, but I think it might be a late one tonight.'

'I love you.'

'And I love you too, Betty. I don't think I tell you enough, but I hope you know it.'

'I do. Be safe.' Betty blew a kiss into the receiver.

Glover put down the telephone and was out of his chair in one movement. Sticking his head into the corridor he shouted, 'Stanley!' as loud as he could.

Stanley was there in seconds.

'Stanley – get me everything we've got on a hit-and-run: November fifth, five years ago; a boy named Joshua Griffiths; Clydach area. And make it fast.'

'Sir?' Stanley was puzzled.

'New line of enquiry – just get it done, and back to me pronto. Go.'

As she was leaving, Glover called her back. 'Stanley, where was Dr Bill Griffiths on Monday morning?'

'I'll have to check my notes, but I'm pretty sure he said it was his morning off and that he went to town.'

'That's how I remember it too,' replied Glover. Then he looked up and shouted, 'Go on, scarper,' and Stanley scarpered. Again.

Glover paced around his little office. If it wasn't the Cockle Wars, and if it wasn't something to do with steroids, and if it wasn't the distressed father of a groped girl, maybe this was it. He pulled open his office door and marched back to the team room.

'Let me see that video again,' he said to DC Hughes, who quickly got the equipment working for Glover. Glover turned down the volume so the team wasn't distracted, sat close to the set and listened again to GGR's speech.

That must be it.

'Sir,' Stanley was back. 'We don't have anything here on the Joshua Griffiths case, because all the paperwork is up at Valley HQ. But I know who led the case, sir: DCI Treharne.'

'Right-o, Stanley,' replied Glover, and he reeled off a list of questions to which he wanted Stanley to discover the answers. 'When you know all that, come into my office – if I'm on the phone, wait with me.'

'Sir,' was Stanley's efficient reply.

Glover made his way back to his office; he was mindful of the fact the super was waiting for him, but, if he was right, then it was much more important for him to talk to DCI Treharne at Valley than to bring the super up to date. He suspected the super wouldn't see it that way, but he reckoned that was the super's tough luck.

Glover put down the telephone; DCI Treharne at Valley HQ had pretty much confirmed Betty's version of the Joshua Griffiths story, in all its tragic details. A family destroyed by a reckless driver. They'd never had anything much to go on; the wife had only been able to tell them it was a silver car – no description beyond that. It had been dark and misty. She'd been distracted. They'd monitored car repair shops for six months with no luck, and there was no forensic evidence, no glass or paint transfer, for them to work with. There hadn't even been any skid marks – the driver hadn't so much as slowed down or braked at all, it seemed. Glover believed Treharne when he said they'd done the best they could; Treharne lived in the area, and Dr Griffiths was his own GP.

Glover crunched into a peppermint; where the hell was Stanley? No point calling her – if she wasn't in Glover's office then she didn't have all the answers Glover needed, so he'd just be interrupting her needlessly, and – given the way the super'd been all over him the last couple of days – he knew only too well how unproductive that could be.

Think – that was what he had to do. He needed to consider all the facts, yes, but then he had to work out the truth; Glover knew only too well there could be a world of difference between the two.

'Sir?' It was Stanley.

'Sit – and speak,' was Glover's reply. Stanley did both.

'Sir, you wanted to know what Waters, Griffiths and the golf captain did after we left them this afternoon. They have all left the club, sir.'

'Times?' asked Glover, crunching a fresh peppermint.

'Waters almost immediately after we left; the captain decided against playing today and left shortly after we did, and Griffiths left about half an hour ago.'

'Thanks.'

'You asked me to check what type of golf clubs GGR used. Well, he did use a left-handed Massive Martha III, as we know. I checked that fact once again with the pro at the Brynfield Club, and it's definitely not one of the golf clubs in his bag at his home, and no one has reported finding a "spare" lying about at the Brynfield Club. GGR's wife, who is now quite with-it by the way, has confirmed that he would often take "a bloody big golf club" with him when he walked the dog – to "play about with his swing" she said. I have to say she's in no better a mood today than yesterday – and she rather flew off the handle with me about us "allowing Geraint's sister to give all those TV interviews". I did try to explain that we have no control over that sort of thing, but I think that one might come back to you, sir.'

'Thanks for the warning,' was Glover's eye-rolling reply.

'Next – the car. GGR's car was still at Brynfield, as we knew. There's no reason to think it couldn't easily be identified as his; it had Fire Dragon Brewery and Welsh Rugby Union Youth stickers on the back window, and all sorts of items with his name on them strewn about inside it. It's a six-year-old silver Volvo. Otherwise, no distinguishing marks or features. No accidents reported for the VIN number.'

'So his car is silver, then,' said Glover sadly, shaking his head. The pair exchanged a significant glance. Glover sighed. 'Oh God. Right. Next.'

'The Brynfield rugby club captain, who was playing with GGR on Sunday, confirms they had a lengthy conversation about how GGR liked to walk on Three Cliffs; he portrayed it as his "morning ritual", though the captain did comment that, since GGR had only been retired a week, he suspected it was a good intention rather than a ritual. They even talked about the "harvest mist" that comes in at this time of year, and GGR made it clear that he loved it. All four of them talked for some time about how the mist changes sounds and smells. Apparently he was quite taken with mist, sir.'

Glover raised his eyebrows.

'I know, sir,' was Stanley's understanding reply.

'And finally?' asked Glover, as he rose from his seat and looked out of his grubby little window.

'And, finally, the launch date for the Fire Dragon Brewery's Fireworks beer was Guy Fawkes Night five years ago, sir.'

'That nails it,' said Glover gravely. 'So we have motive, means and opportunity, Stanley.'

'It seems so, sir.'

'But a missing suspect.'

'As you say.'

'So what do you suggest, Stanley?'

Stanley looked taken aback. 'Well, we are looking for his car,' she replied, hesitantly.

'Yes.'

'And they know at the club that we want to interview him,' she continued, painfully.

'Yes.'

'I suppose we could consider where he might go?'

'We could Stanley – and where do you think that might be?'

Stanley's eyes grew wilder by the second.

'Think like a scout leader, Stanley; how would you track him? Where might a psychologically wounded assailant go?'

Stanley seemed to buck up a bit. 'Well, sir, a wounded animal often tries to return to its lair, to an area it has scented a good deal, so maybe he'd head for his old stamping ground?'

Glover, his back still turned toward Stanley, nodded his encouragement.

'Or what about where he can visit his loved ones?' Stanley looked impressed with herself.

'Very good,' replied Glover. He wasn't patronizing Stanley, he was pushing her, and was pleased with the results. 'So we could check his old home, wherever his family is buried – anywhere else?'

'Scene of the crime, sir?'

'Less likely, I think – it's probably a zoo down on the South Gower Road today, Stanley. I can only imagine what Traffic Division is having to deal with down there.'

Stanley looked rather less pleased with herself. 'Well, I'm not sure where else to suggest, sir.'

'We could always try downstairs, I suppose.'

'Downstairs, sir?' Stanley looked confused.

Glover smiled. 'Sorry Stanley, I've been leading you on a bit. While you've been talking, I've been looking out of the window – and I've been watching him walk along the road toward the station. He's not having an easy time of it – it's busy with the press and all that lot. And he's doing a sort of crab-like dance; he's not coming straight to us, he's wandering along the other side of the road, going back and forth, not forward.'

Stanley rose and joined her boss at the window. 'I see him. Shall I pop down and unofficially make sure he gets through the front door? Or do you want to do it officially?'

Glover thought for a moment. His quarry finally crossed the road, walking toward the front entrance of the police station. 'Let's get downstairs so he doesn't have time for any second thoughts, Stanley. I'm sure you're quicker than me – off you go.' Stanley shot out of Glover's office, with Glover himself in hot pursuit.

As Glover left his office he heard the unwelcome voice of the super behind him. 'Glover – where the hell have you been? I've been waiting in my office for you. I've promised the chief an update – come with me, now.' The man was almost squeaking he was so angry.

Glover stopped in his tracks, sighed heavily and turned to face his boss. 'Sir,' he began politely enough, 'I cannot talk to you at this precise moment, but I promise you will be the first to know of any developments – which I am expecting imminently. Now, if you'll excuse me,' and Glover was off.

'No, I will not excuse you, Glover. Come back here!'

Glover suspected that, behind him, there was a certain amount of foot-stamping going on, but he didn't look back to see the expression on his superior's face; he could imagine it.

As Glover reached the bottom of the staircase he could see their man talking to Stanley just inside the front door. Glover tried to catch his breath, and pushed open the security door that prevented anyone from barging into the station.

He smiled, and extended his hand. Once their hands met, he tightened his grip and his face grew serious. 'William Griffiths, I am arresting you on suspicion of murdering Mr Geraint Gareth Richard Davies. You do not have to say anything, but it may harm your defense if you fail to mention when questioned something which you later rely on in court. Anything you do say will be given in evidence. Do you understand that you have been cautioned?'

Dr Bill Griffiths looked at Glover with dead eyes. 'I understand. I did it.' He spoke simply; it was the voice of a man who was utterly defeated.

The desk sergeant dropped his pen and his mouth fell open. Glover could sense the uniformed officer's excitement – it was palpable.

'If you mention this to anyone – I'll have your job, and your pension,' Glover said to the sergeant. The desk sergeant's response was quick, and to the point.

'I understand, sir. I'll open up and let you have Interview Room Two, sir. Alright?'

'Thank you.' Glover looked pointedly at the officer and said, 'Not even a phone call home. If I get so much as a sniff . . .'

'You've made yourself abundantly clear, sir,' was the terse reply as the buzzer sounded and the heavy door was released.

'Would you like some coffee, Dr Griffiths?' was Glover's question as they entered the interview room.

The doctor looked dazed; he peered at Glover with bloodshot eyes, then half-smiled. 'That's very kind of you, Inspector, but I don't really feel like a coffee. I wonder – might I have a cup of tea? Out of a proper china pot, and a cup, not a mug, if that's at all possible. I don't want to be a bother – but that would be lovely.'

Glover nodded at the PC who was standing inside the interview room door, then took his seat, indicated that Griffiths should do likewise, and nodded to Stanley to start the recording devices. He stated the facts for the record. He then asked if Griffiths had attacked GGR Davies at Three Cliffs the previous morning.

'Oh yes,' was Griffiths's matter-of-fact reply. 'I don't know that I meant to do it when I went there – but it seemed like the right thing to do when I was face to face with him. An eye for an eye. It seems fair.'

Glover couldn't see any emotion on the face of the man in front of him. Bill Griffiths had shut down. An automaton was speaking for him. The nervous energy he'd noted when he'd met him had evaporated. Glover felt sorry for him; he tried to ease him through the interview.

'Can you tell me exactly what happened, Bill? Was it the speech on Sunday night that set you off on this path? You didn't miss the speeches at all, did you? You heard GGR alright, didn't you?'

Griffiths didn't lift his downcast eyes. He nodded. 'You saw the recording?'

Glover nodded. 'I did.'

'Then you know what he said. He was actually making a funny story out of it. It made me see that Josh's death meant nothing to him. The man was too drunk and too stupid to put two and two together – he didn't even know what I was talking about when I confronted him with it.'

'So, it was when he said that he'd hit a sheep when he was leaving the Fire Dragon Fireworks beer launch that you knew he'd at least seen that he'd knocked down your dog. A large, white, standard poodle, wasn't it?'

'Yes – Milly. She was a lovely girl. Won a prize at Crufts one year, she did. But that wasn't why we loved her; she was such a gentle old girl. Linda and I had her before Josh came along; we couldn't get pregnant, and for four years she was our only baby. Then Josh was born, and we had the complete family. He was such a happy little boy; he and Milly would play together, she looked after him like he was her own – she was still taller than him when they both died that night.' Griffiths sobbed, dry-eyed.

'And when GGR joked about leaving the launch party with a fair few pints in him, I suppose your next move was to hunt down his car in the car park.'

'Oh no, I'd been with him earlier in the day when he was rooting around in the boot trying to find something. I already knew he had a silver car. A lot of people do; trust me, I've noticed every single one of them for the past five years, and have wondered if each one was the one that killed my boy. But, until he told the story, the fact I knew he had one meant nothing. But I didn't sleep at all Sunday night – I just went through it all in my head, and worked it out.'

'I see,' said Glover gently. 'So why did you go to Three Cliffs yesterday morning, Bill? What was your intention?'

'I hadn't even bothered going to bed, so I was out early – I just wanted to . . . get away. But you can't, can you? You can't get away from what's in your own head, and somehow I intended to confront him with it. I wanted to see something in him that showed he understood what he'd done. When we were golfing he'd talked about his own little dog, which he didn't seem to care for a great deal, I must say, but he'd spoken of where he liked to walk with it, so I knew where he'd be.'

'As it turned out,' the doctor added thoughtfully, 'I was there long before him.'

Glover noticed a wry smile on Griffiths's lips.

He sighed. 'I sat in the little dell at the top of the cliffs for what seemed like hours before he arrived. It was quite wonderful. Everything was grey and shifting; I was completely enveloped in thick mist. Although the sea was far below me, it sounded as though I could reach out my hand and touch it. I can't tell you how much I enjoyed that time there. I don't know how long it lasted, but I wanted it to go on forever. I felt very close to Linda and Josh there – as though I could hear them calling me. I felt safe. I could actually feel them there. I was at peace with the world. And I haven't felt that way for a long time.'

Glover nodded sympathetically.

Griffiths sighed heavily. 'Then he came blundering along. Just like he'd taken them from me before, he did it again. I couldn't feel them anymore. He was singing loudly and totally out of tune, puffing on a horrible cigar, and he had his giant golf club with him; I don't like those things – they're so unnecessarily large. If it hadn't been for the harvest mist he'd have seen me from some way off, and might even have avoided me. But, as it was, he was almost right next to me before he saw me at all.'

He paused seeming to recall the moment, 'Anyway, he was surprised to find me there, but greeted me jovially enough. He reeked of alcohol, and was even swaying a little on his feet. Loud. Drunk. Insensitive. I didn't see GGR the way I'd thought of him for years. All I could see was a murderer. He asked me why I was there and I told him. "Because you killed my son." He told me not to be so stupid, so I told him about Josh, and how he and Milly were knocked down in the lane outside my house in Clydach, not far from the brewery, on the night he'd been at the beer launch. I described Milly, and told him what my wife had seen. And do you know what he said, Inspector?'

Glover had to admit he keenly wanted to know.

'GGR Davies laughed. Laughed, and said I was talking rubbish. Then he said that, even if it was true, there would be no way to prove it. Besides, he was GGR and no one would believe it of him.'

Unfortunately, Glover could imagine the GGR he'd just begun to know saying exactly that; he'd had a glimpse of the level of entitlement the man had felt . . . had been led to expect, in a society where he was all but a God.

Glover sighed.

'I'm sorry to hear that, Bill,' he whispered.

And he was. In every way.

The doctor continued, 'And then – I don't really know what happened. Honestly . . . I'm not trying to cover anything up – I just don't know what happened next. I know he'd tied up his dog and laid the golf club against the rock face, and I seem to remember picking it up. I think he turned away and I just swung at him with his club. But then, it's all a blank. I don't even know what I did with the golf club – did I throw it over the cliff? Did you find it?'

Glover didn't react.

Griffiths didn't look up. 'I don't remember getting back to my car and I don't remember driving. But I must have done, because I remember getting cash out of the wall at the bank – in fact, that's the next thing I do remember, and I don't even know why I did it. As I put the cash in my wallet I could see I already had money in there. Then I realized what had happened, but I still didn't know the whole story. I went back to work on Monday afternoon and I just sort of got on with things. As normal.'

The man shrugged, 'I didn't feel right, but no one said anything to me, and I got out of there as soon as I could. But I still couldn't settle. I didn't sleep much Monday night – I woke in the chair at one point, all sweaty and aching, so I went out for a walk on the front, along the beach. Then I got ready for another day, and I wondered if I'd actually gone to Three Cliffs and seen GGR or not; I was beginning to think I'd dreamed it all. Then I heard the news on the radio, and I knew I hadn't. Then you came to the club, and I had to face you, and lie. But I knew I couldn't keep on doing it . . . I couldn't keep on lying about it. It's always been difficult without Josh and Linda, and I knew that I just couldn't do it anymore. Besides, with their killer gone, there's no need for me to carry on. It's over now.'

Glover looked at Stanley – who pushed the tea the PC had brought toward Griffiths; he hadn't touched it so far. Griffiths lifted the cup from the saucer and drank it down.

He looked up and smiled at Glover and Stanley. 'That was the best cup of tea I've ever tasted,' he said. It was the first emotion he'd displayed. 'Strong, sweet, just the right amount of milk.' His words slurred a little, but he looked happy.

Glover smiled back at the man. Then he stopped smiling.

Something was wrong. Griffiths's eyes weren't focusing; his pupils were dilated. He'd kept his eyes firmly fixed on the desk during his confession, but now Glover could see something was amiss.

He turned to the constable at the door. 'Call for paramedics now, and fetch the duty medic as quick as you can.'

He leaped out of his seat and rounded the table.

'Bill – what have you done, Bill?' Glover shouted at Griffiths, who was beginning to slump.

Stanley was on her feet in a second. They caught Griffiths before he slid out of his chair.

'Overdose of some sort?' asked Stanley of Glover.

'I suspect so,' was Glover's response.

'Have you taken something, Bill?' shouted Glover again.

'Nothing you can do. All over now,' replied Bill Griffiths dreamily.

'We've got to try to keep him moving, sir,' was Stanley's unusually assertive comment, and Glover nodded. He patted Griffiths's cheeks and tried to keep him conscious.

A doctor was with them in a matter of moments, the paramedics ten minutes later. Glover and Stanley paced about outside the interview room as every revival technique was attempted.

'He probably walked about on the street outside until he began to feel the effects,' was Glover's observation, 'then he came into us to tell us what he'd done before he went.'

Stanley nodded. 'Do you think he might have got away with it, sir? I mean he's had one nervous breakdown already – and it sounded to me like he snapped; another break with reality. They might not have locked him up at all; it might have just been treatment.'

'I think you might be right, Stanley, but there was nothing for him to "get away" with; he was living in his own hell already.'

'So you think his account was accurate, sir?'

'We'll never know for sure – but GGR's recorded version of events that Guy Fawkes Night and the Josh Griffiths case do rather line up. And GGR was probably right – we wouldn't have been able to prove anything, not after five years. Frankly, from what I've seen in the last twenty-four hours, you could have had photos of him actually doing it, and people wouldn't have believed it of him.'

Glover was angry. Angry and sad. The fact that Griffiths was finally pronounced dead didn't help.

Back in his office, Glover raked his hands through his hair, crunched a peppermint and slurped cold coffee – three devices he used to try to calm himself; none of them worked.

Rakel Souza was on her way from West Glamorgan General; a death in custody was a nightmare, and he needed the best person available on the case.

Interview Room Two had been sealed off, and Glover suspected Lewis would be after his blood.

Word had got out about the fact that Griffiths was a suspect in the GGR case but, Glover thanked God, it hadn't left the station or reached the media yet – though they, of course, had been beside themselves with glee when an ambulance came screaming up to HQ and paramedics had started running about. The clamor to know what was happening was clearly audible through Glover's window.

'Right, Stanley – I'm off to see the super. He needs all the facts – and I intend to give them to him.'

'Any requests for a last meal, sir?' was Stanley's wan reply.

Glover managed a smile. 'I'll just take my peppermints, that should do it,' and he went off to face his fate.

Glover called Stanley into his office within ten minutes. 'Shut the door, Stanley, there's a good sergeant.'

Stanley settled herself across the desk from her boss.

'I've told the super everything,' began Glover, 'about Joshua, Linda and Bill Griffiths. I've filled him in about GGR taking steroids, and our suspicion that he was supplying them around his Fire Dragon client list. I explained about him groping that girl at the Brynfield Club, and I've given him chapter and verse about GGR's drinking and driving – and how our lot have been letting him get away with it for years. And do you know what he said?'

Glover's tone made it clear that his question didn't require a reply.

He pressed on, 'He said that we'd never be able to prove anything about GGR killing Josh Griffiths; that his own steroid use was his own business, and the dealing was something we'd never be able to get anyone to testify to; that no breath tests meant we'd never known, as a police service, that he'd ever actually been drinking and driving. He said the man's reputation had to be protected, and we should proceed as though Griffiths's statement was one made by a man in extremis, but which couldn't be used to damn GGR after his own death. He wants a cover up, Stanley. The bloody man wants a cover up. So that there can be a national outpouring of grief for a murdering, drug-taking drunk, who was enabled by everyone around him.'

Stanley remained quiet.

Glover stood up and started to pace.

'It's not right, Stanley. The truth should come out about that man. Lewis says we can't undermine him – that it's important he remains a dead hero. That the memory of him as an inspiration is important. More important than the truth.'

Glover raked his hands through his hair. 'I know he's got a point, Stanley. What good would it do to smear The Great One in death? We can clean up after him as far as the steroids are concerned; no one we know of except the Griffiths boy, and his mother and now his father, were directly affected by his drinking and driving, and he did – and still does – inspire a great deal of good. But let me tell you this, Stanley – I feel sick to my stomach about it.'

Glover resumed his seat.

Finally Stanley spoke. 'So?' Her question hung in the air.

'So . . . we'll do as our superior officer instructs,' replied Glover bleakly. 'Griffiths's confession to the killing of GGR will be made public, but not the reasons for it. Of course they'll come out at the inquest, but I have a feeling that someone – and I can tell you right now it won't be me – will be there to undermine the "suggestions" that Griffiths made in his statement. No mention will be made of the drinking, the groping, or the steroids, because they are not "pertinent to the case", as Lewis put it. And that's that. There's no one left to jump up and down on Bill Griffiths's behalf, or on behalf of his family, so it'll be GGR who wins and Bill Griffiths' name will always be mentioned with GGR's; he'll be known forever as the man who went mad, and killed a hero. It's disgusting. Why the hell do we do this job, Stanley?'

Stanley remained silent.

Glover was boiling. 'Why do we do it? Why do we not stop to eat, or sleep, or see our loved ones while we pursue the case, gather the facts, interview the endless suspects? Why? To bring the bad buggers to justice, that's why. To allow people to sleep soundly in their beds knowing they are safe. Bill Griffiths was a healer – a medical practitioner who apparently worked hard to ensure good health in his local community. GGR Davies habitually sat behind the wheel of a car, drunk; he was the epitome of a dirty old man, groping a sixteen-year-old; he endangered the long-term health of maybe hundreds of people with those steroids, and that's without considering the cheating at rugby aspect. And he killed a little boy. He killed him. I'm as certain of that as Bill Griffiths was. I cannot believe we're going to have to live with this, Stanley.'

Glover squeezed his eyes shut and rubbed them hard. Then he looked at his watch. It was six thirty p.m. It had been less than thirty hours since he'd taken the call about a body being found at Three Cliffs from Superintendent Lewis. In thirty hours his life had changed forever.

He resigned himself to a long night at the station; a death in custody entailed a huge amount of paperwork. He and Stanley would have to be interviewed; there'd be no veg soup for him that evening.

'Stanley – I'll be out in five – go and tell the team the super's version, and let them go. They've had a long day.'

'Sir,' was Stanley's only remark as she left the room.

Glover picked up the phone and dialed Betty. She answered in her sing-song tones, which always lifted his spirits.

'I'll be late, sorry, love, no dinner for me – you go ahead.'

'You alright?'

'Fine.'

'Get someone?' asked Betty.

'Yes. Bill Griffiths. The doctor. A full confession. Then he died in front of me, poor bugger. Overdose, I think.'

He could hear his wife's voice catch as she said, 'Oh Evan, I'm so sorry, *cariad*. It must have been awful for you.'

Had it been awful to see Bill Griffiths slip away, rather than be paraded about to be vilified by all? Actually, Glover thought it might not have been the worst thing that could have happened to the man. Griffiths had no one left in the world he loved; he felt that he had visited retribution upon the man who had killed his son and, eventually, taken his wife from him. For Bill Griffiths, it was all over.

'I think he was happy, Betty – happy that he'd done the right thing, in his own mind, and happy it was all over. Not that I'm saying people should go around taking justice into their own hands, mind you. But I'll tell you all about it later, when I get home.'

'Alright. I'll be up – whatever time it is. And we can talk as much as you like. Or as little as you like.'

Glover had known she'd understand.

'Just one thing, Evan.'

'Yes?'

'Did you find out – did GGR fall, or did Bill Griffiths actually push him?'

Glover thought about it, and realized he still didn't know.

'I know he didn't jump. As for the other questions, I don't think we'll ever get the answers. But there's one thing I can tell you, Betty, GGR had fallen so far before he even got to the top of Three Cliffs that morning, I don't know how I'm going to stomach all the memorials. Maybe we could postpone our trip to Scotland and fly off somewhere else – somewhere warm, where they don't play rugby at all, and where GGR isn't known, or mourned. Where he doesn't mean anything.'

'I think you're hoping for a bit much there; wherever we go we're still Welsh, there's no hiding it, is there? And Wales means rugby. We're almost defined by rugby, and rugby means GGR. So, unless we change ourselves we'll never escape it. Not until the Welsh stop playing rugby.'

'And that'll never happen,' reflected Glover. 'Like I'll never not be a policeman.'

# ACKNOWLEDGEMENTS

The collection of novellas 'MURDER: Season by Season' was published in 2008. Ten years has passed since then, and I have been fortunate enough to have had a dozen novels published between 2012 and 2018. I'm glad I've taken the chance to rewrite these tales, and re-publish them, with the benefit of a great deal more writing experience under my belt.

In the case of the first, third and fourth novellas in this collection, these are true 'second editions' of the originals. In the case of the second novella, the story about the WISE Enquiries Agency, that older tale just didn't hold up to the passing of time – too much had become anachronistic within it – so here's a 'more changes than a second edition' version of that one.

I hope you enjoy them all. They 'take place' between the short stories and novellas you'll find in my collection *Murder Knows No Calendar* and *The Corpse with the Silver Tongue* (the first Cait Morgan Mystery), *The Case of the Dotty Dowager* (the first WISE Enquiries Agency Mystery) and *The Wrong Boy* (a novel featuring DI Evan Glover).

My thanks – as always – to my wonderful husband for his patience and support. My editor Anna Harrisson has been most helpful, as has my copy editor Sue Vincent.

Many thanks to all the bloggers, reviewers, booksellers and librarians who have played a part in you finding this book. And my thanks to you for choosing to read it. If you enjoy/ed it, please consider leaving a review for it on one of the many platforms where algorithms mean such reviews are a great way to help authors get the word out about their work.

Thank you,
Cathy Ace
www.cathyace.com

CPSIA information can be obtained
at www.ICGtesting.com
Printed in the USA
LVHW031437220219
608471LV00001B/179/P